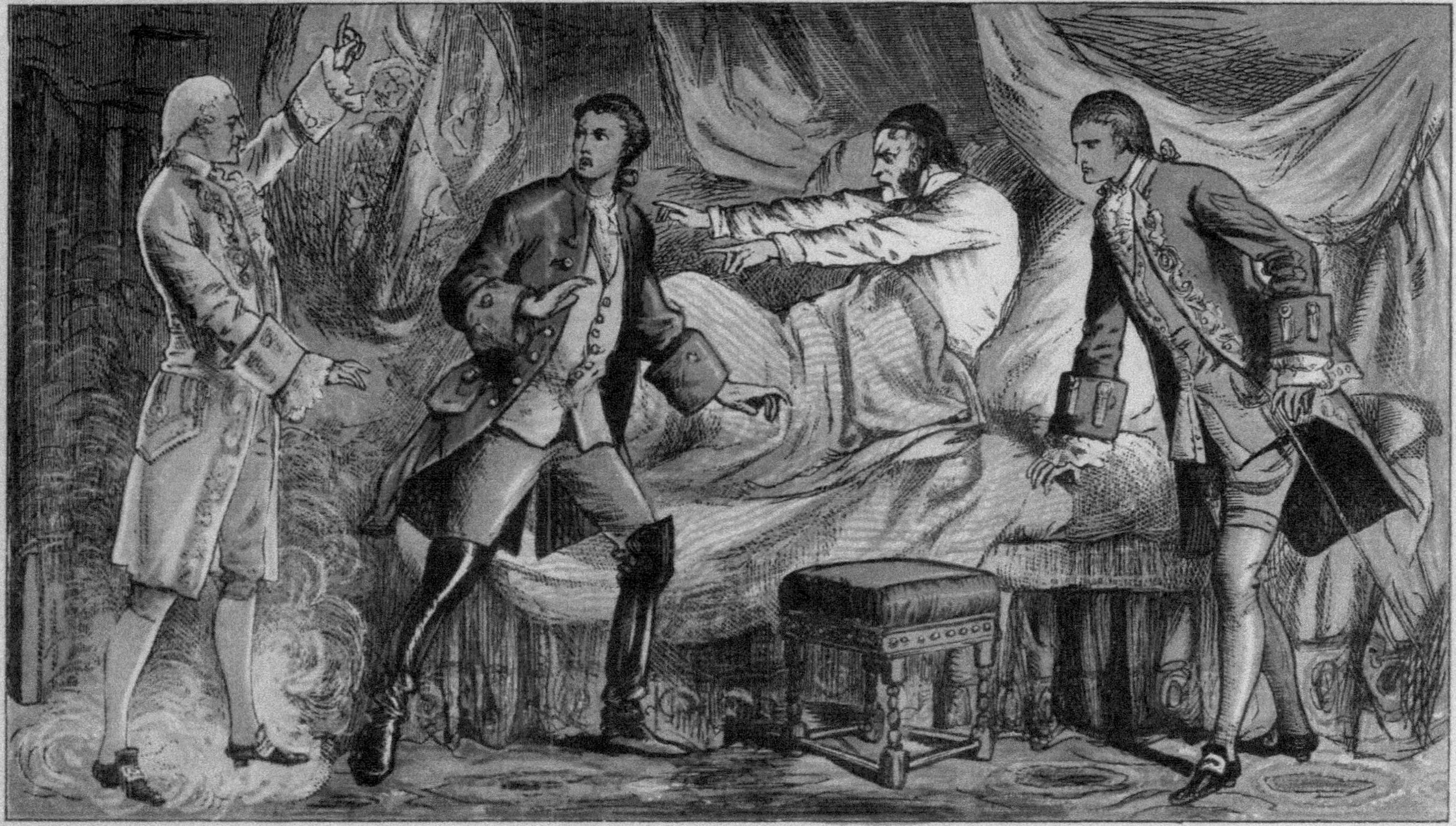

"'SEE, OSCAR,' CRIED THE DYING MAN, 'THE MESSENGER OF DEATH FOLLOWS HIM.'"

See an early Number.

RUPERT DREADNOUGHT;

OR,

The Secrets of the Iron Chest.

No. 1.

BOOK I.

LAYING THE TRAIN:

CHAPTER I.

SILENT DEATH—THE OLD HOUSE NEAR THE TOWER—THE REVEL OF THE POISONERS—THE MIDNIGHT HOUR—THE EXPECTED GUEST.

DEATH flapped its raven wings over the City of London, yet revelry was at its height everywhere.

It was New Year's Eve, in the year 17——.

London, in spite of the intense cold, was then under the influence of an epidemic—slow, sure, inevitable.

What it was no one knew.

Some called it the Plague, and imagined that the great decimation of fifty years before was about to be repeated.

But it had not the peculiarities which were characteristic of that hideous affliction.

The patients did not turn black, neither did they die swiftly.

They lost their natural colour truly, but it was a deadly pallor which succeeded to it.

The patient, moreover, died away by slow degrees, lingering generally a month and suffering no pain whatever.

There was another strange phenomenon, moreover, connected with it.

Though an epidemic to all outward appearance it seemed not to be catching.

Nurses never died of it.

Patients had been nursed through all stages of the disorder by persons of every variety of temperament.

But these persons never suffered.

The rich, moreover, appeared to be the most liable to the torments of the fell disorder.

Some few poor persons had been attacked and died, it is true.

But these, when their cases were investigated, always turned out to be heirs in the second or third degree to some large and disputed property.

As the whole of London suffered under the same calamity, a numerous band of doctors were engaged in endeavouring to stem the fatal tide.

But not one had been successful.

Not a single patient attacked by the pestilence had been known to recover!

Then the dread suspicion came suddenly into men's minds.

Was it poison?

Could there be a conspiracy of wretches, so large, so carefully organised, as to spit forth their venom upon a whole capital?

And if so, what was the poison used, that it defied all efforts at cure and discovery?

Again and again were the bodies of patients opened and carefully dissected.

But in vain.

The symptoms in all cases were the same, but no trace whatever of any poison could be discovered.

It was on this New Year's Eve, when thousands were dying everywhere, that the song and the dance resounded merrily in every quarter of the city.

People seemed to have taken up the motto of the desperate reprobate—

"Eat, drink, and be merry, for to-morrow you die!"

No one knew when they would be seized—in the dance—at the supper-table—in the silent night.

So, as I have said, there was everywhere singing and dancing, and merry music; and nowhere seemed it merrier and more enthusiastic than at a large house, whose high, frowning walls sheltered it on one side from the curious gaze of walkers near the old Tower of London, and whose large windows on the other side shed forth a blaze of light over the river Thames.

It was built, in fact, so close to the river, that the waters lapped its walls, and at high water its vaults were considerably beneath the level of the river.

In the huge drawing-room of this house was collected a motley assemblage of men and women.

Both were dressed in the extreme of fashion, and seemed on excellent terms.

But all were masked.

The gentlemen wore masks, which completely concealed their features; but the ladies allowed some glimpses of their pretty mouths to be seen, and their bright eyes flashed through the eye-holes of the black velvet.

Every kind of dress was to be seen in that gay gathering, from Turks to nuns, from ancient priests to gay cavaliers.

All seemed full of jollity.

Yet, in the midst of all this merriment, many an anxious look was cast at the clock, which now pointed towards the hour of twelve.

As the hands of the time-keeper approached nearer and nearer, the music stopped, the dancers gathered into groups, and while earnest conversation was carried on in low tones, all seemed to be listening for some one.

There were two persons in particular who seemed most anxious for whatever event it was they expected to happen.

The one was a woman apparently of about twenty years of age, dressed in an Italian dress with short petticoats and low boddice, displaying a pair of exquisitely formed limbs, and a pair of gleaming shoulders, rich with youth and health.

Her companion was also young, but about five years older, and dressed in a huntsman's dress, which showed off a figure replete with manly beauty.

His mask nearly concealed his features, but you could see that he had a heavy moustache, and a pair of eyes which vied in brightness with those of his fair companion.

"This delay makes me nervous, Alford," whispered the girl. "Can it be that anything has gone wrong, and that, for the first time, a victim has escaped?"

"No, no; fear not," replied Alford. "You are a nervous creature, Lesbia. Who that heard you talk in such a manner would believe that you were one of the band which has spread such terror throughout London?"

A slight shudder passed through the frame of the young girl.

"I tremble to think of that sometimes, Alford," replied Lesbia. "I have strange dreams of a night, and phantom forms hover threateningly over me. They are but phantasms of a disordered brain I know, but what then? The deeds we commit are no phantoms, and——"

"Stay!" cried Alford, quickly; "say no more. The clock strikes twelve."

The first stroke of the clock sounded.

Then, in an instant, every voice was hushed.

Men and women both stood motionless; voiceless as statues.

These men and women, young, handsome, gay, knew that another year had come for them—ANOTHER YEAR OF NAMELESS HORROR!

The past year could open up hundreds of graves.

Graves of old and young, rich and poor, hurried to their doom by remorseless villany.

And all this glitter and tinsel of joy, derived its being from the treasures of the murdered.

As soon as the last chime of the clock had sounded, the statues sprang once more into life.

Strong arms encircled slender waists; lips met lips in loving kisses; the music burst forth again, and away the revellers rushed once more in the mazes of the giddy dance.

It was a scene of mad jollity—a revel of demons.

They cast off all thoughts now but those of eager enjoyment, and in the excitement of the moment thought only of pleasure, the evil pleasure of being possessed of other's wealth, of being with the ones loved, yet unknown.

Even this did not last long.

Another hour passed.

Again the clock sounded.

The first hour of the new year had gone!

Then there came a hush over all.

For a solemn voice had spoken above the din and confusion of the music—

"HE COMES AT LENGTH!"

Who was it who came thus?

That he was expected by all was evident.

The dancers stayed their movements, as they had done at the striking of the twelfth hour, and eagerly glanced at the door.

Presently it opened, and a young man entered.

A tall, fine-looking young man, with a handsome countenance withal.

He had no sooner entered than a man detached himself from the crowd of merry-makers—a man dressed in the costume of a Turk—and hurried forward to meet him.

He was habited so as to appear old, but in spite of this it was easy to see that it was but pretence.

"Well," he said, "is it all over?"

"Yes," replied the new-comer, "he is dead. Give me wine, for I faint and shiver with dread."

The old man led him away at once into an inner room, the dancers making a line for them to pass.

But before we follow them and explain this mystery, we must ask our readers to accompany us to the bedside of two dying men.

CHAPTER II.

THE DYING EARL—THE LETTER—THE JOURNEY—THE SURPRISE—THE ATTACK IN THE STREET—THE MYSTERIOUS FRIEND—STEALTHY STEPS—THE MASKED INTRUDER—THE QUARREL—THE HIDDEN ASSASSIN—THE ESCAPE—THE VOW OF REVENGE.

IN a large bedchamber, in a house near the Tower of London, lay an old man at the point of death.

The surroundings of the room showed plainly that Poverty was an unknown visitant.

The curtains that shaded the high windows were thick and embroidered with gold; the carpet soft and noiseless to the tread; the bed draped with all elegance; the furniture and the pictures massive and grand; the escutcheons of the Dreadnoughts over the high hearth, speaking of the grand old deeds of the family.

But yet all had an air of chilly discomfort. The glare of the white drapery, and the silence and the steady flame of the low-turned lamp, seemed to tell of the snowy shroud, the voiceless tomb, the Life passing away!

Near the bedside sat a young man about eighteen years of age.

He was a well-made youth, with regular features, which all would have denominated handsome; but there was on them a strange look—a wild look of sorrow, which augured ill for his peace of mind.

Ever and anon his eyes were cast sorrowfully upon the pale, ghastly face of the sleeper, as if with the passage of that life would pass also the whole hope and purpose of his existence.

In the midst of his watching the door gently opened, and a servant entered, glidingly, bearing in his hand a letter, which the youth took eagerly.

It was addressed to Master Rupert Dreadnought.

"It is from Helen," he murmured, as by a wave of the hand he motioned the domestic to remain, "well I know her dear handwriting; what can it mean? Ah! what is this? in danger?"

The letter ran thus:—

"DEAREST RUPERT,—Come to me at once. I am at the house of Lady Beaumaurice. I have fled from the home which your dear father gave me, and even though he is dying I dare not come to him. I will not delay you; but it is urgent—it is absolutely necessary both for you and for him that I should see you for a moment.

"HELEN."

Rupert re-read the letter, and then leaning over his father, glanced earnestly into his face.

"He sleeps," he said. "Edward, you see to him. An hour only shall I be away. Should he wake, tell him that Mistress Helen Penraven has sent for me on urgent business."

Without further delay, Rupert passed out of the room, and having placed on his hat and sword issued forth into the night.

He had not far to go, not more than half a mile,

and the distance seemed even less to him as he walked along thinking of the strange summons which had called him from his father's death-bed when he had imagined the fair one who had written to him to be safe away from her enemies in the country house of the Dreadnoughts.

He arrived almost ere he had imagined himself to have arrived half way at the stately mansion of the Beaumaurices, and rang a loud peal on the clanging bell.

A servant lazily answered the summons.

"Is Lady Beaumaurice at home?" demanded Rupert Dreadnought, impatiently.

The man stared at him.

"You have not, then, heard the news, Master Dreadnought?" he said.

"What news?"

"Her ladyship died this morning of the mysterious plague."

"Gracious heavens! And Mistress Penraven, is she not here?"

"No, Master Rupert; we have not seen her bright face for more than a month."

"Heavens! what can this mean?" he cried. "I have but just received a letter from Mistress Penraven saying she was here and awaiting me. Ah! I see it all now; it is a ruse—a vile piece of treachery to take me from the bed of my dying father! I must hasten back at once!"

Then, without further parley, he quitted the house and prepared to return.

He knew well that that night was a crisis in his fate; he knew that his father had strange secrets to reveal, and he knew well also that there were those who eagerly desired to prevent the transmission of these secrets.

He felt, therefore, the necessity for prudence.

The way he had to go was not long, but it was very dark and full of intricate courts and alleys, where assassins might lurk in the shadows to pounce upon the unsuspecting wayfarer.

By keeping to the open streets he might have avoided these dangerous ways, but there was no time to lose; his father was on his death-bed; this forged letter was intended to separate them; who, then, could tell what hideous crime might not be perpetrated in his absence?

Loosening his sword in its scabbard, so as to be ready for action, he took one glance round him and plunged away into the darkness.

He had not proceeded many paces before he fancied he heard footsteps near him.

He stopped and glanced round.

But again all was still.

With a fervent hope at his heart that he would be able to reach his father's bedside in safety, he once more advanced, but, just as he reached a dark corner of a street, there was a rush of feet, and a loud voice cried—

"Halt, there! Whither so fast, young sir?"

At any other time Rupert would have looked upon the three masked and ruffianly strangers who now sprung out from the gloom, as some of those night prowlers who, at that period, infested the City of London; but he now saw in their appearance part of a preconcerted plan.

Drawing his sword, he at once planted his back against the wall, and prepared to do battle with his enemies.

He knew well there was no probable chance of aid.

The place was dark as pitch; there was an air of murder around—a silence like that of the grave.

The spot was well chosen for an assassination.

"What want ye with me he cried?" as the ruffians approached him, sword in hand.

There was no reply; only a vigorous attack from all three together.

Their deadly animosity, evident in their savage thrusts, showed they were no cut-purses, but personal foes, or men set on by personal foes to destroy him.

But if they had suspected an easy conquest they were mistaken.

Rupert Dreadnought, young as he was, had a wrist of steel, and it was not long before one of his assailants had to hang back, wounded in his arm.

"Come on, Gilbert," shouted he who was bravest of the three; "this young gallant will soon be tired. We know you well, Rupert Dreadnought," he added, "and 'twould be best to yield."

"Yield!" laughed Rupert, "I know not the word!"

"Then you will die ere you leave this spot. We have sworn it. We know well your father to be dying; we know he has secrets to impart. Mark me, Rupert Dreadnought, those secrets shall never be yours, for, if you enter your father's chamber again to-night, it will be as a corpse to be placed by his side in death!"

"Boast not," cried Rupert; "there is no time for words, and but little for action. Clear the way for me. I cannot waste such precious moments with braggarts and assassins!"

As he spoke, he made a desperate lunge, which separated his two enemies, and would have left him free passage, had not the third man, who had been wounded, come up on the instant.

It was now that something strange and mysterious occurred.

Before this nothing was to be seen but the four combatants, whose bright swords wreathed round and round like serpents; nothing was to be heard but the clash of steel, and the hard breathing of the three men, as they strove against the one, and their blood ran in curdling streams over the pavement.

But now one of the shadows seemed to detach itself from the rest, and a mysterious figure (man, or boy, or woman, it could not be seen, so dark was the spot and so sudden the appearance) dashed in among the three men, and, rushing between the legs of one, hurled him in the air so that he fell with a crash, stunned and bleeding, on the rough pavement.

Then it disappeared as quickly as it had come!

Rupert's eyes followed the apparition inquiringly until it was lost to view, but little did he think who that strange friend was, or what an important part he would take in the unravelling of the wild secrets of his life!

The tide had now turned.

Startled by the sudden appearance of an unexpected friend, the two assassins lost confidence, and taking advantage of an unguarded moment Rupert made a brilliant lunge and ran one of his adversaries through the body.

"Now," he cried, as the assassin fell with a thud and a groan upon the jagged stones, "now we will see if Rupert Dreadnought will not return home safe and sound to hear his father's dying curse upon his enemies!"

But the battle was virtually over.

The third man made but a feeble resistance, and, presently, making a feint, he stepped back, and turning suddenly, fled away through the darkness.

Rupert made no attempt at pursuit.

His mind was busy with his father's approaching death, and eager to hear his dying instructions; and, keeping his sword still unsheathed, he hurried once more towards home.

The old earl had not been disturbed since his departure, and when the youth entered he dismissed the servant and resumed his place at the bedside.

Presently the sleeper moved, and the aged eyes opened.

"Are you there, Rupert?" he asked.

"Yes," said the youth, turning eagerly, "yes; I will never leave you."

The old man put forth his thin hand, which the youth pressed eagerly.

"Good Rupert; good son," said he. "I am dying fast, but my sleep has refreshed me; and now, while I have strength, I would speak to you. Draw near, and lean over me that I may pour into your ears a tale of terrible sorrow—the foundation of a life-long vengeance. Is the door fast?"

"Aye, father, well fastened."

"And have the servants their orders?"

"Yes. No one shall be admitted; fear not. At my sword's point I will defend the peace of your last bed!"

"Have any of my hungry relations come here and been refused?"

"None as yet. I have been summoned this evening, on a false errand during your sleep, and have been attacked by assassins in the street, but they have not attempted as yet to come here. They have, perhaps, thought it best after all *not* to do so. However, fear not; if they do come——"

The old man started.

"Hark!" he cried. "Stealthy footsteps approach. See—quick!—who comes!"

The youth, with his hand upon his sword, sprang at once to the door, and opening it, listened.

Up the broad, marble staircase, the steps of some one approaching were distinctly audible.

A moment's thought decided Rupert, and, closing the door behind him, he advanced towards a part of the corridor where a lamp shone above, and illumined with its dull light a square landing.

Here he waited.

Not for long.

In a few moments a man's form emerged from the gloom.

Another form, gliding stealthily, followed him, and, unseen by Rupert, concealed itself in the shadow of the staircase.

The new comer was a man wearing a mask, dressed in the garb of a gentleman, but with a kind of flashy gaudiness about him, which proclaimed the parvenu, the man risen from the dregs of society.

RUPERT DREADNOUGHT.

He advanced with a swagger towards Rupert.

"What want you, sir?" demanded the youth, haughtily.

"I come to see Lord Desmond Dreadnought," replied the stranger.

"'Tis too late," replied Rupert, "you cannot see him."

"Is he, then, dead?" said the other, in an anxious tone.

"He is not; but death is hovering over him with eager wings, and he desires, before he passes away, to commit to me a sacred trust. He will see no one."

"Tell him my name; say that a friend of Everard Dalby is without. Go quickly."

"I refuse; I have sworn to guard his death-bed from intruders, and with my good sword here I will keep my trust."

"Insolent boy!" cried the masked intruder, "who are you who thus bar my passage? Stand aside, ere I chastise you!"

"And is it thus you would force yourself to the chamber of death?" cried the youth, who at once suspected his connection with the midnight assassins. "I will tell you who I am. I am Rupert—soon, alas! by the death of a good father, to be Lord Dreadnought. Therefore, I have command here, and, if you value your life, retire at once and intrude not upon time.

"Stand back! I recognise no right to bar me from his presence!" cried the other. "I must and *will* see him! I come with news that he would long to hear. So, while the spark of life still lingers within him, let me see and speak with him."

"I have told you that yonder chamber of death shall on *no* pretence whatever be entered by a living soul save me," replied Rupert Dreadnought, firmly, as he stood still erect and sword in hand. "If you do not quit this house quietly, within five minutes, my servants shall cast you into the street, for I will *not* measure swords with you."

A sneering smile curled upon the lips of the stranger.

"Coward!" he muttered.

For an instant the young man's sword was raised.

But only for an instant.

"No," he said, as he dropped it, pale and angry withal, "I will not be forced into a quarrel. Ho there, John and Leonard!"

Hardly had he uttered these words when the man who had glided so mysteriously after the masked stranger rose from the dark shadow of the staircase, took aim and fired.

In the hurry of the moment, however, the aim was defective, and the ball whizzed by without effect.

Then, ere Rupert could attack the villain, he plunged down the stairs, and disappeared, but not before one glimpse had revealed to him that it was the villain who had attacked and fled from him in the street.

In an instant after a door was flung open, and two men appeared armed with short daggers.

In spite of the modern times, the old Lord Dreadnought invariably kept armed retainers about him.

Why, this was a mystery.

In fact, his whole life had been one which no one could fathom.

The two men glanced in some surprise at the scene before them, and the foremost said—

"What is the matter, Master Rupert, and who fired the shot?"

"My father is dying, as you know. He has a wish to see no one but myself. This man intrudes, and brings with him a hired assassin. Quick, seize him and bear him away, and at the same time see if you can trace the cowardly villain who attacked me. At another time I may meet this man, and demand of him an explanation of the planned murder which so signally failed this night."

The face of the stranger underwent a fearful change as Rupert uttered these words.

His features assumed a ghastly pallor, as if the denial which Rupert had given him had foiled the purpose of a life.

"Curses on you!" he cried, shaking his clenched fist at the young heir. "Curses on you! We *shall* meet again when there are no menial curs to bar my path to you. Farewell, Rupert Dreadnought, and remember."

He dashed down the stairs as he spoke, while the youth returned gently to the sick chamber.

His father was eagerly awaiting his coming.

"Who was that with whom you were having so loud a converse?" said the old man.

"One who calls himself a friend of Everard Dalby," replied Rupert; "he said he came on most important business; but still I took your word and bade him go."

The dying man smiled.

"You did well, my son," he said. "But why that shot? Did he refuse to go?"

"He did, and some hired assassin made a coward's attempt against my life."

"And you forced him hence?"

"I did; yet not by my own sword," replied Rupert. "Its stainless blade shall never drink the blood of braggarts save at the last moment when no chance is left, and the instinct of self-preservation is uppermost, as it is with all. I sent him hence by calling forth our menials, and threatening to cast him forth into the street as we should cast a dog."

"And he went?"

"Aye, in a moment."

"And the assassin?"

"They are even now upon his track," replied Rupert.

A strange smile flitted over the brow of the dying man.

"Well, well," he said, "I rejoice at this. But this is no time for smiles. I have not long to live, and now I must unfold to you the strange history I have so often spoken of. You love me?"

"Yes, by the Heaven above us, yes!"

"I do believe it; but by thy sainted mother—by all thy hopes of happiness in the future—by your wish for my dying blessing—you must swear one thing ere I reveal to you the secret of my heart. Swear this, and there shall be a glorious task before you—a recompense on earth and in Heaven!"

His father glanced eagerly at him as he spoke.

"Tell me, father," replied the youth, kneeling, "and I will swear. I need but to know *your* wishes to accomplish them."

The old man placed his hand upon his son's head.

"Brave, generous youth," he said. "I knew what your answer would be. I have many enemies—men who have made my life most bitter, who have plucked every rose from my path and in its stead planted a thorn, who have made existence a curse instead of a blessing, and robbed me of every pleasure I might have culled—and against these and theirs I exact from you an oath of vengeance!"

"I swear it!" said Rupert, raising his hand to Heaven. "I swear it!"

"A deadly, an unremitting, unceasing vow of vengeance!" said the old man.

"Yes, never ceasing until death, so help me Heaven!" said Rupert Dreadnought, solemnly.

"Then, good and worthy son," resumed the old earl, "while I have yet strength within me to remember my sorrows, I will tell you my story."

CHAPTER III.

EARL DREADNOUGHT'S STORY.

It was a story of a cruel wrong that the old man had to tell—the old, old story of a stern father—a young love—a false friend.

With its details we have nothing now to do.

They will be sufficiently described in other portions of our history.

Suffice it to say that Rupert Dreadnought listened with a beating heart to his father's tale of love—how he had wooed and won his heart's treasure—how his father had forced him abroad—how his beloved Alice had been left in the care of *Robert Penraven, his bosom friend*, who had promised to watch over her, and guard her for him.

Then came the revelation of treachery.

"Fighting against the enemies of my country in foreign lands," said the old earl, with faltering accents, and with tears rolling down his cheeks, "I received a letter from Penraven telling me of Alice's death, entering into all the sad details, and endeavouring to console me."

"I cannot now attempt to describe to you my feelings on receipt of this letter.

"I need only say that I felt mad.

"The whole world appeared a blank, and I cared not how soon a friendly bullet shortened a career that had no longer in it any object.

"I never heard again from Penraven.

"Indeed, I did not trouble to tell him where I was, and the letter he had promised in a day or two never arrived.

"I became soon distinguished in the army; wherever the fight was thickest there was I.

"I was always ready to join the maddest forlorn hopes—always the first to scale a rampart—always ready to head a desperate expedition.

"But Providence seemed to keep a special watch over me.

"I was never even wounded.

"I have seen dear comrades struck down at my side; I have been in the midst of a carnage where a mist of blood seemed to hover in the air, and the very atmosphere smelt thick and faint.

"But never a bullet or a sword-thrust reached me."

"I became sickened at length of fighting, as it were, against a charmed life, and I determined to return to England.

"The lapse of time had something to do with this.

"I had had plenty of time to think, and I saw how impious it was to fight against fate.

"When I *did* return, I found how foully I had been deceived.

Alice was *not* dead—the story had been invented by Robert Penraven to deceive me, and keep me away from England, that he might have the field open to himself.

"Alice Rainford I blamed at first quite as much as I did him.

"But she was not so much to be censured when the truth came to light.

"Her father had fallen into difficulties—she had received *a printed notice of my death*, and had accepted him to save her father and herself from misery.

"The villain had woven a deadly scheme of treachery, and he had succeeded in persuading her to become his wife.

"The ceremony had not yet taken place when I reached England, and discovered the enormity of my friend's villany.

"I at once proceeded on the wings of injured love, towards my old home, resolved to thwart his plans, but the villain heard of my coming, and took plans to baffle me.

"Aided by some gipsies, and a villanous brother (who is the father of Oscar, your enemy), he seized upon me, carried me away to a lonely house, and there for a long time I languished, helpless and alone.

"I will not dwell upon the hideous misery of that time.

"Heaven forgive me for the thoughts that rushed into my mind.

"I was a murderer then, in thought, if in nothing else.

"I resolved to devote my life to vengeance, but that unfortunately I have been unable to fulfil, and I leave that task to you.

"At length I was released.

"I sought my enemy everywhere in vain, and in the search I met with one who soothed my aching heart at last, and recompensed me in some degree for the treachery which had been the ruin and desolation of my youth.

"That one was your mother; Helen, my ward, is my Alice's youngest child."

"Her child!" exclaimed Rupert, in astonishment.

"Yes, indeed. She was sent to me by Alice herself, after she had discovered Robert's treachery, and begun to experience his cruelty.

"I leave her to you as a sacred trust. See to her happiness. If you can love her, marry her.

"That is my first wish. Now for the GREAT WORK OF YOUR LIFE.

"Set out to-morrow, see Helen Penraven, place her in a place of safety, and, as I have said, visit her often; and if you can make it consonant with your feelings make her your wife.

"But *not* before five years.

"During that time you must work out your oath of vengeance. Go, my son, towards yonder pilaster."

The youth obeyed.

"Touch the rose which is on the left hand side."

"It is done, father," said Rupert.

"Now, then," said the earl, "you will see a chest."

"I do."

"Come here, then, and I will place into your hands the key of the mystery."

With much wonder in his heart, the youth obeyed the words of his father, whose failing voice now betokened the swift approach of death.

"See," said the old earl, as he drew something from beneath his pillow, "see, this is the key; but remember you have sworn to do my bidding."

"I have."

"**And I trust you, my son,**" said his father, fondly, "**yes, I trust you. In this iron chest there are five compartments. Each compartment contains a parchment detailing my wishes, and the money wherewith to accomplish them. Each reveals to you a mission of vengeance which you have sworn to carry out. But, remember, until one vow is fulfilled the second must not be investigated. When you have seen that Helen is in safety, then open the iron chest, read carefully the matter contained in the first compartment, but beware of looking at the second. While you are seeing to Helen's safety, bury the key in the back vault of this house under the third stone from the door. It will there be in safety. Come, my son, come nearer; I feel exhausted; but I feel also happy in the thought that you will fulfil my wishes.**"

"Yes, to the last letter, dear father," said the youth, with tears in his eyes.

The old man held his son's hand in his, and remained silent a moment.

Then he said faintly—

"It is come, Rupert; it is come! Farewell. REMEMBER YOUR VOW!"

And, with these words, the spirit of the old earl passed away, and the NEW EARL, pledged to A LIFE OF MYSTERY, sank at the bedside to weep!

AND THE CLOCK STRUCK TWELVE AS HE KNELT!

CHAPTER IV.

THE SECOND DEATH—ANOTHER VOW OF VENGEANCE—THE INSTRUCTIONS OF THE DYING MAN—THE APPARITION!—THE DEATH OF A TRAITOR.

We must now turn to the room where the second man lay dying—the man whose nephew had entered so strangely the mad revel of the Poisoners.

At his bedside sat the youth some two hours before he had passed in among the dancers.

There was a wondrous likeness between uncle and nephew; the same dark-looking features, the same savage, piercing eyes, the same thin-lipped mouth.

He, too, had been listening to a commission of vengeance, though given in a different way.

For it was Robert Penraven—Sir Robert Penraven, who was lying on that bed of death, not half a mile distant from the room where his old enemy, the man he had ruined in happiness for ever, lay dying also!

"Oscar," said the old baronet; "Oscar, you see I am fast dying.

"Yes."

"Repeat your oath, then."

"Yes, yes, I repeat it once more; but why this exaction? I *shall* perform it."

"My adopted child, forgive the petulance of deadly sickness," replied Penraven; "but I wish to speak of Helen, your cousin. You must rescue her, tear her from the hands of my old enemy."

"He is dying."

"Yes; but he leaves a son on whom your vengeance must fall swiftly and surely. He has concealed Helen somewhere; those papers will tell you where. When the breath leaves my body, fly at once to the spot indicated there, and convey her to some place far from London, where none of that evil brood shall see her."

"I will."

"And mark me," said the baronet, "if she loves young Dreadnought, *kill her* rather than allow her to mate with one for whom my hate is unextinguishable even in death. Remember this."

"I do, uncle," replied the youth, looking impatiently at the clock.

What could this look signify?

Was he eager for his uncle's death?

Had he assisted in hastening it?

This at present is a mystery we cannot pretend to penetrate.

But it seemed truly as if he was anxious for the moment to arrive which should see the breath pass from the body.

The old baronet observed his anxious looks.

"Why do you so eagerly gaze at yonder clock?" he asked at length.

The youth started.

He had no idea that in his dying state the baronet would observe him.

"I am thinking of Dreadnought," he said.

Penraven's eyes sparkled with demoniacal glee as he answered,

"You are sure he is dying?"

"Yes, sure. I am reckoning the minutes as they fly."

"And the messenger will come?"

"Yes. I have so arranged it."

The baronet smiled.

"Good boy, good boy," he said. "Give me some more wine. I must not die before I know that my greatest foe is gone."

The youth rose immediately, and approached a table whereon were bottles of sparkling wine.

Pouring out a large quantity in a deep glass, he approached the bed, and his uncle drank eagerly.

The draught appeared to revive him, and he, too, looked at the clock.

"It is approaching midnight," he said. "When did you hear last?"

"About an hour since."

"And he was then dying fast?"

"Yes."

"And so must all his brood!" exclaimed the baronet, to whom the wine had given a renewal of false strength. "So must all his hated brood. Not one of the detested stock must be left. Ha! what is that?"

As he spoke there was a loud knocking at the door.

"He comes!" said the baronet, excitedly.

The next moment the door was flung violently open.

A chill wind invaded the apartment, shaking the curtains, and nearly extinguishing the lamp that stood by the bedside.

Then a man entered.

He was a roughly-dressed fellow, wearing a sword, but evidently of no gentle blood.

But it was not at him, rudely as he entered, that the dying man looked.

It it was not his appearance that made him stare and, half rising in his bed, clutch his son's arm, and, with starting eye-balls, glare upwards.

It was a far stranger and more terrible vision which he beheld with his glaring eyes!

Entering behind the messenger of death, and floating above him, with one hand extended over the man's head, and pointing threateningly, warningly, was the white, misty form of the dead Earl Dreadnought.

His eyes were fixed on those of the man who was so soon to join him, but who seemed truly as if he were roused into new life through very horror.

"See—see, Oscar!" he cried; "the ghostly form that follows him! See, 'tis my old enemy approaches. He glares at me! He points with shadowy hand! Oh! mercy—mercy! save me from this horrid thing!"

"YOU HAVE DONE WELL!" SAID THE CHIEF OF THE POISONERS.

The man who had entered the room of the dying man stood transfixed with wonder and alarm, as the excited speaker pointed over his head at some unreal thing which no one else could see.

"What means this?" asked he.

"I know not," said Oscar; "but is the Earl Dreadnought dead?"

"He is. He died but a few minutes ago, and I have hastened to inform you."

"And was your presence suspected?"

"It was not; but, see, your uncle beckons, and, by the look upon his face, his days are numbered too."

The old man was now of a green and ghastly pallor, as with deadly fear.

The dews of death upon his brow were big and heavy.

The eyes stared wildly—the hands clenched fiercely together, as if in mortal agony.

"Oh, it is terrible!" he muttered, as Oscar bent over him. "He comes to summon me. See how he glares and smiles in triumph on me! Oh, this is death—death! Oscar—REMEMBER!"

Then he fell back with a groan, and the youth, listen as he might, could hear his voice no more!

Over him, too, the shadow of death had fallen, and the two youths, bound to deadly vengeance by a terrible vow, were alone in the world!

Leaving the messenger to keep lonely vigil by the side of the dead, we will follow Oscar now to the Poisoners' Revel, and see how he fared there, and how he fulfilled the first promise he had made to his adopted father.

CHAPTER IV.

THE POISONERS ONCE MORE—ROSALIE ST. AUBYN—THE SUMMONS TO THE SECRET CHAMBER—THE MYSTERIOUS MASK—THE TRAITOR—THE OATH OF RETRIBUTION.

As the young man entered the brilliantly lighted room where the Poisoners were holding their revel, the company, male and female, as I have said, moved aside to allow him to pass, and murmurs of various and mysterious import might have been heard from all sides.

Sir Oscar Penraven, however, took no notice of any one, but walked onwards with firm step towards a part of the room, where sat a man dressed in the dress of a cavalier of the time of Charles I.

This man was seated apart from the rest, and seemed to possess a kind of authority over those around him.

He greeted Oscar Penraven with a haughtiness that evidently foreboded evil, for the brow of the young man became pale as marble.

"He is dead," said Oscar.

"You speak of your uncle?" said the cavalier, in a stern voice.

"I do. He passed away but half an hour since."

"And the property?"

"Is left as you desired it—to me; and is at the disposal of your dread tribunal."

"It is well. And when will the title deeds be given over to me?"

"The day that sees my uncle buried," returned Oscar, "will see the papers also in your hands."

The cavalier mused a moment.

Then he glanced at the clock.

"It is time," he murmured.

Then he beckoned Oscar to him.

"Leave this room," he said, "and pass into my private study. You know well the way. I have a secret of the utmost importance to reveal to you, and I will follow you, therefore, in a moment."

The young baronet moved away sick, and faint at heart.

He felt that some strange event was about to happen.

The manner of the old man had told him this plainly enough.

He had not much time for the indulgence of these thoughts, however.

A fairy vision sprang before him.

It was a young girl dressed in a light, fantastic garb, which showed the whole of her rounded shoulders, and a leg as far up as the knee, well formed and large, while a pair of eyes of bewitching brightness gleamed through the holes of the mask.

"Oscar, or rather, Sir Oscar," she cried, "whither go you so fast?"

Oscar started, and a smile overspread his pale features.

"Whither? To the study of our chief, Dr. Henzollern," he answered; "he has need of me; but wait for me, Rosalie. Even in this terrible hour a smile from you has power to give me joy."

He raised her plump white hand to his lips as he spoke, and kissed it.

A roseate hue overspread the neck and bosom of the young girl, showing how pleased she was at the compliment.

Strange, that in such a scene of terrible revelry, such a frail and modest thing as a blush should have survived!

"Yes, I will wait for you," replied the young girl, tenderly pressing the hand of Oscar Penraven; "but be not long."

"I will not. Wait yonder, near our President's chair. Farewell, for the nonce, dear Rosalie."

So saying, he passed behind a curtain, and disappeared.

The young girl watched him till he was out of sight, and then turned once more towards the dancers, murmuring—

"He will come again. I know it."

"*If he be alive!*" said a voice by her side.

She started sharply round, and saw standing near her a tall man, masked like the rest, and dressed in a fantastic garb, which resembled the costume of the old buccaneers of the West.

"Did you address me?" she said, in a voice of some dread as well as anger.

"I did."

"And why? You cannot know my heart."

"I do; better than you know it yourself," returned the man. "That youth," he added, in a low voice, as he laid one hand upon her shoulder, and with the other pointed towards the door, "that youth whom you are striving to lure into your toils may never return. 'Tis a dangerous place this for traitors, so beware!"

"I am no traitor," returned the girl, quickly starting from his grasp, with neck and bosom crimsoned with anger and alarm; "leave me, or I will pronounce a word that shall consign you to an instant death!"

A low laugh escaped the lips of the mysterious stranger.

"I, too, Rosalie St. Aubyn," he said, "could pronounce that word, and seal your fate also. But remember my words. This is no place for traitors. If they are discovered, *they die!*"

Then before she could make reply he strode away, and passed behind the curtain, beneath which Oscar Penraven had disappeared a moment before.

"This man has cast a dread upon me," said the girl, shudderingly, as she passed towards the fire which played merrily at one end of the apartment. "He knows my name and yet I know him not; neither could I through his mask catch one glimpse of any feature save his red gleaming eyes. I shall advise Oscar of this. And yet what meant he by *his* terrible words of warning?"

Meanwhile, leaving Rosalie St. Aubyn to doubt and wonder, we must follow the young baronet into the study of the President of the Poisoners.

It was a dismal room, hung with black tapestry, and filled with heavy furniture, and strange old books, while on stands and shelves were an infinity of miniature phials with liquids of every imaginable colour.

When Oscar Penraven entered there was no one present, but no sooner had his foot touched a certain plank in the flooring than a bell rung, and two men entered.

One was the man with the red, gleaming eyes, who had so alarmed Rosalie St. Aubyn, the other was a stranger.

These two ranged themselves on either side of another curtain, which evidently concealed a door, and in a moment after the President entered.

Advancing to the table which stood in the centre of the room, he said, in a solemn tone of voice,

"Oscar Penraven, you have hitherto acted honourably and truly towards our Society."

"I trust I have," replied Oscar, firmly, yet respectfully; "my wish has ever been to aid you, as I have proved in the last few hours."

"We know it, and therefore at the dread meeting which took place this day in this room," continued the President, "your name was not set down in the list of traitors. You remember, however, that about a month since you enrolled the name of one Lawrence Gascoigne, for whom you became guarantee?"

"I did."

"You had good reasons for believing him faithful?"

"We have been friends since youth," replied Penraven.

"Good. We were satisfied at the time that you did not hastily or without judgment enrol his name in our catalogue of true men. We therefore acquit you of blame."

"Blame! for what?" exclaimed Oscar, in a tone of genuine astonishment.

"You will know in a few moments. Were you aware of his means of subsistence?"

"I believed him to be independent."

"He was not; he was a spy in the pay of the Government!"

The words fell like a thunder-clap upon the ears of the young reprobate.

"A spy!" he repeated, under his breath, "impossible!"

"It is true," continued the President, "but fortunately for us his thirst for gold was so great that he defeated his own purpose. Listen, and I will tell you the story of his treachery.

"Three nights since, I and another member of our Society were traversing a dark and dismal street, where even now some ruins can be seen, relics of the Fire of London, when we thought that we heard voices engaged in earnest conversation.

"We stopped suddenly beneath the shadow of a wall, and listened, for it is our business to learn the secrets of all.

"'I thought I heard footsteps,' said a voice, which I at once recognised as that of Lawrence Gascoigne.

"'Oh, no, it is your fancy,' replied the other, who was an utter stranger to me. 'You are so infernally nervous that it's ten to one you spoil the whole affair.'

"'No, no, I am not nervous,' replied Gascoigne, 'though well I might be, knowing the terrible vengeance which will fall upon my head if I am discovered. Listen patiently, and I will tell you all quickly.'

"Then I listened, my blood curdling the while, as he told the whole story of our Society—its foundation—its rules—its terrors.

"'Well,' said the officer, when Gascoigne finished, 'you tell me enough to take my breath away. The reward which is offered for the discovery of these villains is enormous. We must share it between us. But there is one whom I must first consult.'

"'Who is he?'

"'Gerard Offley, the cleverest of all the secret agents of the Government.'

"'Is he a true man?' asked Gascoigne, the traitor, in a trembling voice.

"'Yes, yes, we may depend upon him, especially when such a reward is in view. It would be only madness on his part to tell others, and so lessen his own chance of a large share.'

"'True. And when will you bring him?'

"'I will meet you here at ten to-morrow night at this very spot, and we can then make arrangements for descending upon the gang of Poisoners at their next revel.'

"The traitor then departed, and we saw the other spy passing away in another direction.

"'Your doom is sealed,' thought I.

"But I restrained my anger.

"There was every chance that the other man would reveal at once to Gerard Offley the reason of the secret meeting, which had been arranged for the next night, and it was best, therefore, to permit the assemblage of spies to take place at the appointed time.

"Accordingly, I and my companion quitted our hiding-place, and on the following night we repaired to the ruins again with a dozen companions.

"This force I so disposed that there could be no escape for our enemies.

"They knew exactly what to do, for their orders were most precise.

"At length the hour of ten came, and precisely as it struck, your good friend Gascogine made his appearance.

"A few moments after came the two Government agents.

"'This is my friend, Gerard Offley,' said the one I had seen on the night before.

"'Glad to see you,' said Gascoigne; 'you are to your time.'

"'George Beckford never fails,' returned the Bow Street runner, pompously. 'Now, Master Gascoigne, let us hear your story once more.'

"He did so.

"The officers listened intently—eagerly to every word.

"'When will their next revel be?' asked Offley.

"'To-morrow night.'

"'And this friend who introduced you, this Penraven, is to be captured and suffer with the rest.'

"'Yes,' returned Gascoigne, 'yes, he would never forgive me, and might prove a dangerous foe in the future.'

"Impossible!" murmured Oscar Penraven.

"It is true," replied the President of the dread tribunal. "Well, this villain, who was ready to sacrifice his own friend's life in this heartless manner, proceeded then to detail to his hearers the same that he had detailed on the night preceding in regard to the revel of to-night.

"Gerard Offley listened eagerly, and when Gascoigne finished, he exclaimed—

"'We will break in upon them when they think themselves most secure.'

"'As *I* do upon *you*,' I exclaimed, in a loud voice.

"This was the signal agreed upon.

"When my voice was heard they were to fall upon and kill the officers, except Gascoigne, who was to be reserved for a more terrible fate.

"'You have betrayed us, villain!' cried Gerard Offley, as the shadows seemed to take life, and the men surrounded them.

"They gazed at him with murderous eyes.

"But they had no chance of acting, whatever might have been their feelings.

"My friends rushed forward; bright knives flashed in the air, and Offley and Beckford died upon the instant.

"For an instant Gascoigne stood at bay.

"But it was not for long.

"A heavy blow struck him senseless to the earth, and when he again awoke he was in yonder iron room, from which that curtain and a thick door separates us."

"And why is he there?" asked Oscar, trembling, for he guessed the fearful import of the President's words.

"Listen," said the latter, "and, though your oath should tell you, I will explain."

CHAPTER V.

THE VICTIM—THE IRON ROOM—THREE CHOICES OF DEATH—THE TERRIBLE TASK—THE SILENT COMBAT—THE STRUGGLE IN THE DARK—THE TRAP-DOOR—THE REVEL ONCE MORE.

"You remember," continued the President, "the oath that you took when you first entered our Society?"

"I do well."

"If anyone introduces a friend, and this friend becomes a traitor, the person introducing him is bound by oath to kill him. Is it not so?" asked the President, gazing fixedly into the eyes of the young baronet.

A shudder passed through the frame of Oscar Penraven.

Nevertheless he answered firmly—

"Yes, it is so."

The President pointed to the door before which hung the curtain.

"Go, then," he said, "your victim awaits you. See, there on the table are your weapons—a bottle of poison, a knife, and a pistol. It may be that when he sees his doom to be inevitable, he will relieve you of the necessity of shedding his blood by voluntarily taking the fatal draught. But remember, his death must be certain—and by your hand! Go, we await you here."

The youth who had so lately quitted the still chamber of death, shuddered again as he approached the place where his victim was confined.

He knew the task, terrible as it was, was inevitable.

Nothing but his own death could relieve him from it.

So he advanced boldly, in spite of the fact that he fancied he heard the rustling of wings near him, and felt a chill air invade his very veins.

The room where the victim sat communicated, as the President had said, with that in which he had just made his unexpected announcement, and, as soon as the two sentinels had withdrawn the bolts, there was little difficulty in making his way into the iron room.

As soon as he had entered the door was barred again, and he was alone with his victim.

It was a small room, with nothing in it but a small table, a chair, and some heavy hangings in one corner.

All the walls were painted black, and here and there small gratings were placed in the walls to admit the air and also to permit the chiefs of the terrible Society to see and hear all that passed within.

Neither Gascoigne nor Oscar Penraven were aware of this.

The former started from his chair with a smile as Oscar entered.

"Ah, my friend," he said, "they have then permitted you to see me."

"They have," returned Penraven, avoiding the outstretched hand. "You see for the last time the one whom you would have betrayed and destroyed for money."

A fear of something—an indefinite dread crept into the heart of the prisoner as Oscar spoke.

He looked eagerly into his friend's face.

"What do you mean?" he faltered. "I never intended to destroy you——"

"Hold!" cried Oscar Penraven, "hold! I know all; and *you* know the terrible vow which binds us to each other."

"I do."

"You know also that it was I who introduced you to the Society."

"It was."

"I believed you faithful, and I took the oath for you, swearing that you were a good and true man and bidding myself to take your life with my own hands if you turned out a traitor."

"A mere mockery to alarm the weak-minded," said Gascoigne.

"It is no mockery," returned Oscar Penraven, solemnly. "I come to fulfil my vow. See here my weapons; poison—the dagger—the pistol!"

Gascoigne staggered back to the farther corner of the room, and pressed his hand to his brow, upon which now the large beads of perspiration had burst forth.

"You are mad!" he cried; "you cannot mean it; this is murder—cool, deliberate murder."

"And pray what would your act of treachery have resulted in? What, but cool and deliberate murder? Besides, what oaths have you taken yourself? Are we not members of a band of poisoners—sworn Agents of Death, bound to him by terrible vows of slaughter? What is our trade but murder?"

Gascoigne groaned.

"Choose," said Oscar; "here is a poison which will bring to you an instant death, sure but painless. I offer it you now in the name of old friendship. Drink!"

"Truly a friendly offering," said Gascoigne, eying his adversary with eager glances. "I refuse it."

"You refuse?"

"I do. I will fight for my life."

And, with these words, he sprang towards his foe.

But Oscar Penraven was too quick for him, and a sharp stab in the arm warned the spy to be more careful of his foe.

OSCAR PENRAVEN.

It was for him a most fearful position.

He had, with the courage which is so often found in those who assume the administration of the country's laws, resolved to risk his life in order to discover the cause of the hideous calamities which were decimating the metropolis.

It would be wrong to say that in all this the spy had not an idea of gain.

But of this desire we must all of us plead in some degree guilty.

All of us desire money, no matter how wealthy, no matter how old we are, and no matter how useless it will be to us when gained.

Every man, no matter how spendthrift he may be, loves gold, if it is only for the pleasure of handling it and spending it before the admiring crowd!

Now he had lost all his aims!

He gazed at his friend, the one (bad though he might be) whom he had purposed to betray, and waited.

What could he do?

Even if he succeeded in betraying this friend—now his enemy—would it avail him?

Yet how useless to think thus.

The first danger is always the worst, and it was naturally the first impulse to save himself.

He looked, therefore, with savage determination at his enemy, and was just about to make a dash at him, when Penraven fired.

But the ball took no effect.

There was a flash, a report, and the ball spun back from the iron wall.

The poison had been refused, the pistol had missed its aim.

There remained only now *one* weapon, the dagger.

With this he now prepared to attack his foe.

Gascoigne's eyes glittered with terrible meaning.

But Oscar was not dismayed.

Young as he was, he knew that his own life depended upon his acting promptly, and he at length rushed headlong upon his victim.

Gascoigne was an older and a stronger man; but he was unarmed, and was, moreover, weakened by the knowledge that he was surrounded by foes, in the centre of a band of determined murderers, who (if Oscar failed) would in all likelihood rush upon him like a pack of bloodhounds.

The struggle, therefore, hideous and terrible as it was, was not of long duration.

The dagger, short, easy of use, and sharp, was a fearful weapon, used as it was against an unarmed man, and in the course of a few moments the spy lay gasping in horrible agony in one corner of the iron cell.

"Oh! in mercy spare me!" cried the wretched man, "for the sake of old friendship! For the love of God, spare me!"

There was no answer in words.

Oscar Penraven had his work now to perform, and he knew that there was no use in attempting to shirk it.

It was life or death to him.

Either he or the wretched spy must be the victim of that night.

So he nerved his arm for the deed.

The hot breath of the murderer rushed in horrid gusts upon the cheek of the dying man.

The steel lightened the darkness—the voice of the dying gurgled out a curse. Heaven whispered its promise of revenge and justice through the tremulous tones of the passing spirit, and then—

All was over!

During the struggle, the lamp had been extinguished, and the place was therefore buried in utter darkness.

But, even through the gloom, it seemed to Oscar Penraven as if the ghastly white face of the dead man was glaring at him, and telling him of a vengeance to come!

Oscar, strong and full of nerve as he was, trembled as he imagined to himself this horrible vision.

He was old truly in sin.

But yet he was but a youth.

His frame might be tall and powerful; his mind might have been schooled in crime; but, nevertheless, age is something, and he could not be so coolly villanous as those who had served a long apprenticeship in crime.

Resolved, therefore, to escape as quickly as possible from the scene of horror, he stooped to pick up the weapon which had fallen from his hand in the last struggle.

As he searched, his hand came in contact with the face of the murdered man.

He started back, and uttered a wild, piercing cry.

A cry, driven from his bosom as it were by intense horror!

In an instant, as if by magic, the place was illumined by a bright ray of light, which came with a rush through the open door.

The President and the two sentinels were standing there, gazing with evident interest at the scene.

"You have done well," said the Chief of the Poisoners, addressing Oscar Penraven, who was standing leaning upon the table in the centre of the room. "You have done excellently well; the villain is dead!"

"Quite dead!" returned the youth, shudderingly.

"And our secret is safe. Come," added he, addressing the two men by his side, "come, let us bury him, and let the thought of this night's work be buried for ever in oblivion!"

The men advanced with him into the room, and then, closing the door, proceeded to bury the dead.

It was a strange burial!

The flooring of part of the chamber, being touched by a spring, moved away, and disclosed a chasm, dark and mysterious, and emitting a dank and fetid odour, while the rush of waters could plainly be distinguished beneath.

"Whither does this lead?" asked Oscar Penraven, with a shudder.

"Below is the river—the swiftly-flowing river," replied the Chief Poisoner, "and this body, borne away by the rushing tide, will carry with it our secret for ever. Come, is all ready?"

While this brief conversation had been going on, the two attendants had raised the body of Gascoigne, the Government spy, and approached the yawning gulf.

One moment they steadied their awful burden over the abyss.

Then they loosed their hold, and it fell with a dull sound — down among the plashing waters, which sent back an echo like the yell of a warning avenger!

Little did they dream who the AVENGER would be.

Oscar Penraven gazed at them silently.

For the first time in his life his hands had been stained in blood!

It was a commencement of a career of crime, a good schooling in murder, and when the President clapped him on the shoulder, and bade him follow him, he started as from some fantastic dream.

"Is he dead?" he asked.

"Aye, dead and buried, too! It was well done. But come, let us rejoin the dancers, and presently we will drink to the health of the new Baronet of Penraven."

Oscar shuddered.

He had wished for wealth, freedom, and distinction.

What cared he for it now?

There was a mist of terror before his eyes which took from him all memory of the death that had given him his wish.

"I am bloodstained," he said. "My hands are yet hot from crime; I cannot go into a scene of revelry like this."

"Foolish boy!" exclaimed his Terrible Companion, "foolish boy! They will know nothing of this deed. A few glasses of wine, moreover, will revive your spirits, and you will look upon this death scene as some hideous dream. Come."

He said the last word somewhat sternly, and taking Oscar Penraven's arm, led him through the black-tapestried room, beneath the curtain, and into the ball-room, where the Poisoners were still whirling round and round in the giddy mazes of the dance.

They were old in crime.

The hideous doings of the past year, and the awful prospects of the new year, had no effect upon *their* merriment.

Here soft eyes greeted him, a soft arm passed into his, and a soft voice murmured to him—

"You have been long, very long, Oscar, and you look pale and ill. Drink!"

The maddened youth seized eagerly the proffered bumper, then another and another was tossed down his parched throat, and in a few moments, reckless, intoxicated with terror and strong wine, he whirled away with his fair companion among the gay and hideous throng.

CHAPTER VI.

THE IRON CHEST—HELEN PENRAVEN—THE WARNING VOICE AND THE WARNING HAND—IS SHE IN DANGER?—THE PURSUIT—THE BATTLE ON THE DARK HEATH—THE SUDDEN RUSH AND FLIGHT—MURDERERS ON THE TRACK.

WHEN Rupert Dreadnought rose from the spot where he had knelt by the side of his beloved father, now lying in the still majesty of death, he had re-registered the vow which he had taken.

Once, and once only his eyes turned wistfully towards the iron chest which contained the wonderful secrets which were to be his guiding stars in after life.

But his mind was firmly resolved.

His first task was to seek Helen Penraven, the daughter of his father's enemy—the cousin of his own sworn foe—the one upon whom already his youthful heart was set.

He knew well where Helen had been placed by his father.

It was in a house some miles from London; in a lone and sombre spot, yet in itself a garden of beauty.

It was in such a place as this of necessity that she would be most safe, and the young girl herself was quite as eager as they to escape for ever from the hands of her stern and terrible father, and a cousin whom she feared no less.

A few hours' sleep was absolutely necessary to the young lord ere he went upon this journey. His vigils had been long and frequent.

Scarcely for an hour had he allowed his father to be under the care of any but himself.

What terror would have been his had he known that the disease of which his father was dying was an unnatural one—the prevailing epidemic—the Breath of Poison!

Little dreaming, however, of such a horror, he had tended him with eager hope, and now exhausted nature demanded a short repose.

It had been Rupert's resolve, at first, to make his journey at once, but the bright sun of the morning deterred him.

His life was one now of secret vengeance, and if he were to be followed by enemies, the day was the very worst time he could choose.

After mature consideration, therefore, he resolved to put off till the night his journey to Sandmount.

The sun, however, which had promised to be so bright soon changed its mind.

One of the thoroughly English rains began falling about noon.

Plash! plash! plash!

Regular and unceasing, the steady and monotonous shower deluged the streets.

Plash, plash, plash, fell the big drops on the flooded thoroughfare.

Scarcely a single figure, as evening came on, might be seen struggling through the heavy rain, which at times makes the most fashionable avenues in London appear to be deserted, like that city of the dead of which we are told in old legends where nothing of seemliness and shadowy splendour was wanting save the activity and pulsation of actual life.

Plash! plash!

Drearily it plashed against the window-panes of the room where the dead man lay.

But towards night it seemed to clear up suddenly, that is to say, the rain ceased; but as the atmosphere warmed a steam of humid vapour rose from the ground and concealed from the one side of the road the view of the other like a November fog.

"Good," thought Rupert Dreadnought, as he prepared to start upon his journey; "this will effectually baffle all pursuit. No one, however well-sighted, could see me through this mist."

He forgot the consequent danger to himself from the same cause.

A horse was ready saddled at the door, and as eight tolled from the clock of the neighbouring church, he set forth rapidly upon his journey.

From the spot where he started, it was no long journey into the dark, wild roads of Essex, and he soon found himself dashing along on his steaming horse over a lonely and tree-lined road.

The mist was not quite so dense here as it was in the City of London.

But still it was very dark, and on a road where no lamps were it was dangerous travelling to the unwary.

Rupert, therefore, had soon to slacken his pace, and proceed cautiously, for here and there heavy market carts had made deep ruts in the road, and large stones and pieces of timber lay about, which greatly endangered the horse's legs as he stumbled and staggered on.

There was no definite reason for such continuous and rapid exertion.

He had no right to suppose, in fact, that Helen was in danger, except from the fact of the forged letter which had so strangely called him from his father's dying bed.

And this, moreover, hardly gave him sufficient reason.

It might simply have been the idea of the moment, and have no reference to any imminent peril to *her*.

But a warning voice seemed urging him continually forward.

A warning hand seemed to beckon through the heavy mist.

The old earl, grim in the majesty of Death, appeared hovering near, leading him still onward to the point where the first step in his mysterious mission was to be taken.

With such incentives, therefore, it was not wonderful that he urged his steed on to his full speed as long as he was able.

Frequent stumbles, however, as I have said, warned him to be more careful.

He slackened his pace.

As he did so, he fancied that he heard the sound of horse's feet behind him.

It was very faint, and soon died away in the distance, though in what direction it passed it was difficult to say.

He stopped and listened a moment.

But it did not recur again, and he allowed the matter to pass away from his thoughts.

About two miles had now to be travesed, and at a cross-road, where four roads met, he had to leave the highway and ride out over a broad moor.

Just before he reached this cross-road, the fog began to lift, and when he arrived at a point where more than one suicide lay buried beneath the heavy clay, the moon broke through the shimmering haze, and showed to the astonished eyes of Rupert Dreadnought three shadowy horsemen on the other side of the road.

In an instant he reined up, and prepared to defend himself.

But there was no need of fear, at any rate at this moment.

No sooner had the three strangers beheld him than they dispersed in different directions, and the far-off clattering of their hoofs soon told that they had passed away.

Though there was no reason for immediate alarm, however, Rupert felt certain that the mysterious appearance of these men had reference to himself, and he accordingly loosened his sword in its scabbard and ere he advanced another step he examined the priming of his pistols.

Then, with a feeling of renewed confidence, the bold young adventurer went forward on his journey.

He was now out on the lonely moor, but the bright moon had risen and dispelled the mist, and he could, therefore, gallop swiftly and fearlessly forward.

Taking advantage, therefore, of the temporary cessation of the dismal weather, he put spurs to his horse, and dashed away at full speed.

No one interfered with him now, and although distant sounds now and then caused his horse to start and prick up its ears, the animal steadily persued its way.

At length in the distance he could see looming out of the darkness the outlines of the house where he hoped to see Helen Penraven.

There was a portion of the heath just before he reached the house where a mass of trees clustered and formed a miniature wood.

So dense was it that any terrible crime could have lain hidden in its gloomy depths.

Just as Rupert neared this place, he descried once more the shadowy forms of horsemen, and ere he could see more than that they were now four instead of three, his foemen were upon him.

Who they were it was impossible for him to say, for they were all masked and attacked him savagely yet silently.

He was for the moment bewildered.

There was no apparent method of escape, but yet the idea of surrender never crossed his mind.

This, however, was apparently more the object of his adversaries than immediate murder.

They surrounded him but made no effort to slay him.

"What means this mummery?" he shouted, in an angry voice. "Tell me what want you with me, or let me pass in peace."

It was a strange voice that answered him.

"Surrender!" it exclaimed, "we give no explanation."

"Tell me to whom I surrender, at least," replied Rupert, who resolved to endeavour to temporise with his strange enemies. "This is but sorry courtesy, even in warfare, to meet a foeman in a dark spot and demand surrender without word of explanation. Is it money you require?"

A derisive laugh echoed loudly over the dusky heath.

"Money; no, we demand no money," replied the man, who had made himself spokesman, "neither do we desire your blood."

"What then?"

"The surrender of yourself to us. There are weighty reasons why you *must* go with us. If you refuse to do so, wounded and helpless you will be taken. Yield while you are safe."

A rapid train of thought flashed through Rupert's mind.

He glanced round him.

Already, as I have said, he could see the dark outline of the house he sought.

There, without doubt, his beloved awaited his coming.

What could be done?

To surrender was madness.

Much as they affected to desire to save his life, they doubtless only wished to spare him now for future tortures worse than a brave man's death.

In this moment his mind was made up.

He would either cut his way through them and dash away at full speed towards his destination, or he would perish in the attempt.

Suddenly, before they had any idea of his intention, he pulled the bridle sharply, made his horse rear, and then applying the spur, went plunging away along the hard road.

"After him, my men!" exclaimed a voice, which he fancied he recognised, "let him not escape."

Several shots were fired at him as he dashed away along the road.

But none reached him.

Fortune seemed to favour him.

As he dashed away, the moon became obscured, and he was enabled in spite of their pursuit to make his way towards the wished for goal.

The gate was closed as he reached it.

It was a high iron gate, and there was no chance of leaping it.

There was no time to ring, or, indeed, make any summons, and he glanced wildly round for a means of entrance.

Chance gave it to him.

The wind had been violent on the night before, and a wide gap was visible in the high fence, where the woodwork had been blown down.

Rupert at once turned his horse's head, leaped the broad ditch, plunged across the dark grounds and reached the wide-porched door in safety.

The men whom he had left behind him on the road did not for the moment attempt any pursuit.

They remained on the spot where he had left them as if to reconnoitre.

They knew well, of course, his destination, and they were perfectly aware, therefore, where to come up with him, but this apparently was not their wish.

Eagerly they discussed the subject, and at length their leader turned his horse's head in the direction which Rupert had taken.

In the course of a short time they came in sight of the house, and stood where they could see the bright lights in the windows.

"Now, my men," said the latter, "we must enter and secure him, and Helen Penraven also. If he resists, his blood be on his own head."

Then the four men, like hungry wolves eager for their prey, advanced stealthily towards the old house on their mission of murder.

GIVEN AWAY WITH Nos. 3 & 4 OF] [“RUPERT DREADNOUGHT.”

“‘FORWARD, LADS,’ CRIED TOM THE WATERMAN, BEATING DOWN THE SWORD OPPOSED TO HIM.”

See an early Number.

RUPERT DREADNOUGHT.

"NOW," CRIED RUPERT, "LET US CUT OUR WAY THROUGH THEM!"

CHAPTER VII.

THE TREACHEROUS SHOT.

A LOUD ring brought a servant to the door, and our hero leaped almost from his horse into the hall.

The servant glanced in surprise and some alarm as he beheld him.

Rupert shut to the door impatiently behind him before he addressed the wondering domestic.

"See to the door," he cried; "there are enemies about. Tell me at once if they surround the house. Where is Mistress Helen Penraven?"

"I will conduct you to her, Master Dreadnought,' replied the servant, who knew not that he had so lately become an earl. "She is upstairs at this moment, dreading a visit from her cousin."

In a few moment he had passed up the stairs, and was in the presence of her he loved, who, with a start of pleasure, sprang forward, and was locked in his arms.

She was a beautiful creature.

It is almost a temptation to describe her.

Yes I will, for my readers will see her before them I hope for many a long day, and her portrait, therefore, ought to be impressed upon their minds.

Rather below than above the middle height, she was attired in a tight-fitting velvet dress, which displayed to advantage her exquisitely moulded figure.

It was tight round her pretty waist; it fell in voluptuous folds over her finely-moulded limbs, and being cut low according to the fashion of the times, it revealed to the admiring beholder the whole of a soft white bosom, whose outlines might have charmed the eye of any sculptor.

Her arms, bare nearly to her shoulder, were clasped by simple gold bracelets, while over her creamy neck soft, brown ringlets fell in careless profusion.

Her eyes were dark blue, contrasting exquisitely with her hair, while her bright complexion and rosy cheeks rendered her an object of intense admiration.

Rupert's eyes wandered over her exquisite person with the true delight of a lover.

"Dearest Helen," he said, "how glad I am to once more clasp you to my breast, and yet—"

The lovely girl raised her tiny hand and playfully placed it over his lips.

"Nay, say not so," she said; "you have ever that word 'yet' to spoil all."

"Alas! this time, dear Helen," he answered, "it is no jest. My father, the one in whose kindness and goodness we have so long trusted, is dead!"

"Dead!" murmured Helen.

And she shuddered.

It is a terrible word for all.

But more terrible than can be imagined for the young.

Life in its prime and beauty seems so bright, and joyous, and full of hope that death—a sudden cutting off from all human ties and love, is something hideously depressing to a youthful mind.

"Dead!" she murmured.

"Aye, Helen," replied Rupert, "he *is;* gone at length from among us. He has left to me, *the last of our race*, moreover, a strange and terrible mission; a work to be fulfilled which will take years to accomplish. And during these years I am forbidden to claim the guardianship of you, my dearest love, by making you my wife."

It may be deemed by some unmaidenly, but a glance of disappointment beamed from the eyes of She had for a long, long time been taught to believe that ere long she should become the loving worshipped wife of Rupert Dreadnought, and that his strong, encircling arms would shield her from all harm.

Rupert could see by her eyes, and her change of manner, how truly sad she felt at his words.

The look struck to Rupert's heart.

For an instant his resolution faltered.

Here was a young girl, warm with youthful love ready to marry him; ready to yield herself up to him at once, while he had wealth, position, everything achieved for him by his father.

Why not marry her now, and be in a position to claim the right of guardianship?

The thought was only for a moment.

He remembered his vow.

"Grieve not, dear Helen," he said; "my father dying bound me by a vow, and this vow in the sight of Heaven I must keep."

"Yes, Rupert," replied the young girl, sadly; "yes, a vow made by you to your dying father must be kept; and *my* father—what of him?"

Rupert shook his head.

"Alas!" he answered, "my bad news is good news in this instance. Your father also is dead."

"Dead!"

"Yes; the same hour that launched my father into Eternity, saw him, too, pass away, no doubt in hate and ill-will with all. His legacy to his nephew I know not, but, if I am not incorrect in my surmise, there will be a deadly feud on both sides."

"In which, for *my* sake, Rupert, you will risk danger."

And, as the words left the coral lips, the bright eyes beamed up tenderly in his face.

He pressed her tenderly to his breast, and kissed her rosy mouth, as he murmured—

"For *your* sake, dear Helen, I will not imperil myself in vain."

Scarcely had the thrilling kiss been given and returned—scarcely had the words been spoken, when there was a sharp report, and Rupert staggered back with a cry of pain.

CHAPTER VIII.

IN UTTER DARKNESS.

THE shot had sped so suddenly, that for the moment Rupert felt so confused as to be totally unable to tell whence it came, but it was not long before he was enlightened.

Before Helen could run to his aid, there was a rush of feet and the room was filled with masked and armed men, who dashed in between the lovers and separated them.

This was all he saw, for in another moment all was blank—utter, impenetrable darkness and oblivion.

When he awoke from this condition, the surrounding atmosphere was as gloomy as it had been fancifully made by his dream.

All was utter darkness.

The air around, too, was dank and chill.

Where could he be?

Had the vow made to his father come at last to so abrupt an ending?

Was his young life to be crushed thus in its very beginning?

He spread out his hands to their full extent.

They came in contact with nothing—nothing but cold, chill air.

What was to be done?

He could think of no plan of safety.

Then suddenly a hope entered his mind.

The time had passed without his being able to count the hours.

It might, therefore, be night, and the blessed light of day might reveal to him some method of escape.

He was just wondering in his own mind what was the intention of his cowardly captors, when a deep, sonorous voice sounded near him.

"Rupert Dreadnought," it said.

"I am here," said Rupert. "Have you come to triumph over me?"

"I have not," replied the unseen and mysterious speaker. "I am come to let you know your fate."

"Speak on," said Rupert. "I fear you not. But tell me who are you?"

"Your sworn foe," returned the other. "I am Oscar Penraven."

"Helen's cousin!" murmured Rupert. "'Twas so I suspected. Tell me why I am here?"

"On the night when your father died," said Oscar, "you took a solemn oath. Is not that correct?"

"It is."

"I know its nature. I know that I stand first on your list of enemies. You wish the hand of my cousin Helen; you wish to take her away from my protection; you have been commanded to do so, and you have sworn to obey; is it not so?"

"It is," replied Rupert; "but ask me no more. I shall refuse to reply to questions which affect the solemn secrets of others. I refuse this, and shall reply to nothing further on this subject."

"'Tis well. Listen to your fate," returned Oscar, with cruel emphasis. "You love Helen. She shall never be yours!"

"Heaven will shield her."

"Aye, Heaven will help those who help themselves; but I will take care that you see not the light of day before the one great event happens which shall crush your hopes for ever! There is a husband already chosen for Helen; and while you remain thus hidden from the world, you will have the satisfaction of knowing that she is being wedded to one who will take her for ever from even your eyes."

"And who is this husband?"

"Myself. When this marriage is consummated, you will be delivered up to a tribunal of those who were your father's enemies, and whom you have made also your own enemies by accepting the responsibilities which death might have destroyed for ever."

There was silence after this.

With these mysterious words, Oscar Penraven quitted his post of observation, and Rupert was once more alone.

A vague suspicion of poison crossed mind.

But this was speedily dismissed.

There was a more terrible lot in store fo to poison him would be to shorten the which it was intended to doom him.

For the sake, therefore, of preserving hi for future exertions, he partook of a he and soon after fell asleep.

CHAPTER IX.

THE WHITE HAND.

When he awoke from his slumber, he wa by a ray of light which shone full on his f

It was sunlight, but the atmosphere which it had passed had taken from it all i and cheeriness.

It was a sign, however, that he was n excluded from the outer world.

He sprang up, therefore, and examined ture.

It was a small opening in the side of the it showed, at least, that there was some co tion with the outer world.

In his utter wretchedness—imprisone lonely darkness without a voice to cheer stood by the small chink of light and ga the few inches of sky which constituted, a all his world.

As he did so, the bright sun and the bi seemed to warn him against despondency, t of bright days in store, and to bid him work.

As he looked, the light was suddenly s and a white hand was thrust through the o

He could not, of course, recognise t fingers, but a note was thrust into his hand

He opened this eagerly, while the h more disappeared.

It was in a female hand, tremulously an written, and read as follows:—

"Have courage. Though hidden from t you have not lost all your friends. Be at th at ten to-night, and you shall receive ins how to escape."

A bright glow of pleasure invaded the he prisoner.

He was not forgotten then.

Whoever his fair protectress was, he re in the deed the hand of Helen.

It was she, no doubt, who had sent him the warning.

And yet——

Might not treachery be afloat?

He rejected this idea, however, almost as formed, and resolved to await in hope and co the coming of the hour of safety.

Yet how could he tell the hour?

The darkness would fall, and time fly by possibility of reckoning.

As darkness came on, however, he stoo aperture and waited.

The hours went by on leaden wings, as i

Then a voice—a soft female voice—one, however, which he did not know, said,

"Rupert Dreadnought."

"I am here!" he cried, eagerly.

The hand was introduced once more into the aperture; but in the utter darkness, Rupert could not see it.

How gladly would he have pressed it to his lips, but this was rendered impossible by the fact that on *his* side of the wall bars were placed to which the hand could not reach.

"Here is a letter," said the voice, "take it quickly."

"If I do it will be impossible to read it," said Rupert.

"I have not forgotten that," replied the voice; "here is flint and steel and a taper. Quick, take it, for I hear footsteps approaching."

Rupert lost no time in taking the flint and steel through the small opening.

Just in time.

He had hardly succeeded in doing so when there were hurried steps without, and a rushing noise among the bushes, as if his unknown friend was making an attempt to escape and enemies were pursuing her.

Then there was a faint scream, the report of fire-arms, and all was once more still as before.

"Pray Heaven my fair friend has met with no mishap," he murmured. "Strange mystery this. It was *not* Helen."

Though his heart, however, was yearning to discover the mystery, he was still cautious for a time.

As his friend had been watched, and perhaps seen, in her act of kindness, it might be dangerous to strike a light, and he remained, therefore, for some time clutching the letter.

At length, however, some time having passed, and his impatience getting almost the better of him, he struck a light, lit his taper, and opened the letter, which contained a key.

It was from Helen Penraven, and read as follows:—

"MY DEAREST RUPERT,—I write these few lines in haste (and in fear too, for I am watched each moment) to give you the means of escape. The messenger who brings this is trustworthy, and if you receive with this a key, a taper, and flint and steel, you will know you have received all I send. God bless you, Rupert; that is all I can now say of our love. I must give you directions how to escape. The key I send you is a master-key. Now you are in possession of a light, you will find a doorway in the corner of your cell. Open this, and it will admit you to a long and dark corridor, which will lead to another door. This door is also to be opened by this key; and you will then find yourself in the fresh air. Be careful then, for if you plunge forward you will fall into a deep moat, and the splash would arouse those who would destroy you. It is Oscar Penraven himself who has sworn to marry me; therefore, when you escape, make haste to my succour. For three days I shall be in safety; a longer delay will be fatal to all our hopes.

"Yours for ever,

"HELEN."

Again and again Rupert Dreadnought pressed the missive to his lips.

Then placing it in his bosom, he rose up and began to examine the walls of his prison.

They were black, murky, and dripping with moisture.

For a long time it was impossible to see any indication of a door, but at length in one corner he saw the shining of metal, which turned out to be a lock.

He lost no time in inserting the key, and, then, having first put out the taper, he opened the door which was to lead him to liberty.

His heart beat loudly as he passed out into the dark passage and unhesitatingly plunged forward into the gloom.

He met with no obstacle.

As he went on he heard occasionally the loud laughter of men making merry, but there was no light to indicate whence the sounds proceeded, and he did not trouble himself to make discoveries.

The passage was a long one and full of oozy slime, but he soon arrived at the further extremity, and feeling for the lock, inserted the key, and found himself in the open air.

The difficulty now was the moat, but he hesitated not.

Letting himself gently down into the water, he waded across, rose in the neglected garden, and in a very short space of time emerged upon the high road.

He had no horse now, and he would therefore be compelled to walk to London, unless some friendly hostelry should afford him the means of conveyance.

Nothing dismayed, however, he plunged along the road, and was soon making his way across the dusky heath.

CHAPTER X.

IN WHICH ALLAN OF THE GLEN MAKES HIS FIRST APPEARANCE IN LONDON.

ON the edge of the moor where it suddenly ceased, and where three roads branched off from it, there stood an inn which, from its dark and uninviting appearance, seemed scarcely a place for a traveller's entertainment.

Nevertheless, it *did* drive a thriving trade in consequence of being the only house of the kind within a radius of some miles.

Here, accordingly, Rupert Dreadnought stopped, and contrived, after much bargaining, to obtain from the landlord a horse which, although its beauty was a thing of the past, was yet able to carry him at a tolerable speed towards London.

He met no adventures.

His enemies, secure in the idea that he was immured in the underground vault, had no idea of watching for him; and so, until the streets of the metropolis were reached, he scarcely met a soul.

At the first town hostelry he dismounted, and in order to break all clue to his proceedings and his whereabouts, left his horse there in the stable.

Then he advanced on foot, and soon found himself in a long, narrow street, in the oldest part of the city.

He was just turning a corner when a loud outcry was heard; and, as he passed round, a blaze of light revealed a curious scene.

Before a low but brilliantly-lighted house of entertainment were a crowd of men, women, and boys, laughing, shouting, and screaming, and moving about with quick and confused motions.

They were all of the lowest class, and much excited by drink, and their language was of the vilest and most blasphemous description.

It was quite evident from their words and actions that some unfortunate individual was the object of their ridicule and torture.

"Let him have it."

"Kill the Scotch fool!"

"Ha—ha! there he had it."

"Ah! he has drawn his knife—crack his sconce!"

It was evident by their cries that they were all attacking one, and Rupert Dreadnought, ever ready to aid the weak, drew his sword, and forced his way through.

He saw now the object of all this disturbance.

Against the wall, defending himself with his short Scotch sword against the insensate crowd, was a tall, fine-looking youth, with light hair, fair, sun-freckled face, and bright gleaming eyes, whose full highland dress proclaimed him to be a native of Scotland.

His face was red now and convulsed with passion, and one or two of the crowd around him bore evidences of his anger.

"What," cried Rupert, as he dashed in among the drunken crew, and placed himself at the side of the young Scotchman "what, all you upon one! Cowards and savages, come on *now*, and try the metal of my sword!"

There was a hush among the crowd as these words were pronounced.

Then came an ominous whispering and growl of discontent, and one of the ragamuffins sprang away as if on some errand.

"Good luck to you, master," cried the Scotch youth (in his broad dialect, which, during the course of my story, I shall purposely omit), "good luck to you. Do not risk your life for a poor lad like me. I've a strong arm, and it'll be a strange thing if I cannot make good my way through these cowards."

"Oh! I never desert a friend," cried Rupert; "it is *not* in my nature. Stand back there, we desire no delay. Back there, or blood will be spilled."

The crowd moved slightly back at the sight of Rupert's bright sword.

Then after a moment it recovered itself, for there was a rush of feet and two stout, tall fellows sprung into the midst of the combatants, sword in hand.

The new comers were ruffians of the lowest stamp, dressed in faded clothes of elegant cut and material, with here and there large rents, which, as well as their red and bloated faces, spoke of past and recent debauches.

"Hillo, my young brawlers!" cried the taller of the two, "what do you here disturbing our peaceful neighbourhood?"

"Talk no folly," said Rupert, angrily, "but let us pass. I have no time for drunken combats in the street. This inoffensive lad has need of my protection, and he goes with me."

The man who had constituted himself spokesman of the crowd, turned round at this and appealed to them.

"What say you, good people!" he cried, with a sort of mock solemnity, "of what have these fellows been guilty?"

"That Scotch stripling yonder has plundered James Whitethorn's shop," cried one.

"He is a Scotch thief!" cried another.

"The other is a confederate of his."

"Kill them both."

"They have broken the sanctuary of the Golden Acre. Kill them."

These threatening cries were received by the two bullies with evident satisfaction.

Not so by Rupert.

The Scotch youth knew not what the Golden Acre signified; but Dreadnought was well aware of its character.

It was one of the most fearfully criminal parts of London.

A kind of self-elected sanctuary of vagabonds, it harboured thieves, bankrupts, forgers, coiners, even murderers of the deepest die, and being more confined in space than the world-renowned Alsatia, it was very easy to call assistance at a moment's notice.

There was no doubting that their position was one of great danger; but it was also as evident that the slighest show of hesitation or fear would be their destruction.

Rupert turned hastily to his companion.

"You have courage and you have a sword; can you use it?" he asked.

The eye of the young Scotchman brightened valiantly.

"I can," he said. "Let us begin."

They were brave words, and Rupert understood at once that he could trust in the speaker of them.

"Good," he said. "We will cut our way through our enemies, and then we will make for yonder hostelry where the red light illumines the street."

One glance told the Scotch youth what the speaker meant.

Nearly the whole street was involved in utter dark-

HELEN PENRAVEN.

ness for a long distance, but at the further extremity there was a cheerful light, which showed the opening into a wide square.

In an instant, now, the Scotch youth darted forward, and both he and Rupert Dreadnought were at once engaged in a desperate conflict.

The bullies who had been brought forward to fight the battles of the people of Golden Acre were no cowards, and they could fight as well.

This both our heroes soon discovered to their cost, for, far from being able as they had anticipated to make one dash and penetrate the mob, they found the crowd closing in on them, and aiding by a variety of troublesome antics and even blows the half drunken brawlers.

Boys rolled upon the rough pavement and crawled between their legs; women flung mud at them as they sought to disable their adversaries, and it soon became evident to both that unless some assistance came or some change came over the scene they would find a terrible and abrupt termination to their adventure.

But not for a moment did Rupert regret what he had done.

He certainly in this hour of peril, as in other hours of need, thought of Helen's sweet face, and prayed that nothing might happen to separate him from her.

But there was no cowardice in his heart, no desire to evade the contest.

Bravely the swords clashed and rang together.

Yet no progress was made.

A babel of voices sounded round them; women shrieked; men shouted; boys yelled; and all laughed at intervals as the two bullies gained some unexpected advantage in consequence of some stealthy stone or brutal knock from a stick.

Seeing that for a time, at least, they must husband their strength, the two strangely connected companions placed their backs against the wall.

"Ah! ah!" shouted one of the brawlers, "ah! ah! they yield. At him, Franklyn."

"Right, right, my man is safe, Brandon," shouted the other, with a swagger. "Now, now, together."

Neither Rupert nor the Scotch stranger spoke, but a contemptuous laugh escaped their lips, and as a reply, the former suddenly sprang forward, and cut the boaster across the arm.

Just as he leaped backward with a yell of pain, Dreadnought made a second pass, and in an instant his blade had plunged through the villain's heart.

A yell, a shriek of execration arose from the crowd, and one man, who, from his dress and his brawny arms, seemed a smith, leaped forward, seized the sword of the dead man, and attacked Rupert savagely.

But aid was coming from an unexpected quarter.

There was a sudden rush of wheels, a sudden blaze of light, and a carriage, driven at full speed, came dashing round the corner of the street.

The crowd which was now spread across the street at once necessitated the pulling up of the horses, and the coachman reined them in with such suddenness that the animals nearly fell upon their haunches.

As the carriage stopped a head was protruded from the window.

Then a loud voice cried—

"What does this mean? Why do you not drive on?"

One glance, however, proved to the speaker that what he desired was an impossibility, and opening the door he sprang out among the brawlers, followed quickly by a friend.

As they dashed in among the wondering crowds, there was a flash of light, and a sudden cry of recognition.

"Ah, Rupert Dreadnought! well met, and just in time!" cried the foremost.

"Ah, Stanley Sherrington!" exclaimed Rupert "you are just in time. Now for a good rush!"

Once again, and now with renewed vigour, the two friends dashed upon their enemies, and this time with good effect.

The cowardly gang—many of them now wounded—began to give way.

The Scotch youth, who had but an indifferent weapon, but who, on the other hand, was no mean swordsman, had now succeeded in severely wounding his adversary, and the bully, finding himself undoubtedly getting the worst of it, began to give way.

This was the critical moment.

"Quick, to my carriage!" cried the one whom Rupert had spoken of as Stanley Sherrington. 'Now, while the cowards are drawing back! Have no compunction—strike right and left!"

Rupert and his new companion at once obeyed the injunction of their unexpected friend, and, dismayed by the fearful fate of the bully, the yelling mob at once began to retreat.

As they did so the swordsmen quickened their steps, and not noticing in their haste that a second ominous whisper was going the round of the savage conclave, they made their way towards the carriage.

Hardly had they reached it and entered, when a loud shout again arose.

The cowards recovered their speech, now that the gleaming blades could no longer be seen.

"The horses! the horses!"

"Drag them from the carriage!"

"Smash the Scotch rebels!"

This was a new turn of the tide.

A dangerous turn too!

They at once recognised the peril, and prepared to act.

"Now, Rupert," said Sherrington, "put your head out of one window while I do the same out of the other. Here is a pistol. I will give orders to my coachman to drive on while you shoot any man who attempts to stop the horses. I will fire away at the crowd at the same time."

This plan was at once adopted, and as Stanley Sherrington shouted to the coachman, the blacksmith and the remaining bully dashed forward.

"Now!" cried Sherrington.

The coachman whipped his horses; then there were two sharp reports, and with a loud cry the two ruffians fell back among the mob.

The carriage now dashed away, the frightened horses needing no whip nor incitement of any kind to exertion, and it was but a few moments before they had passed the bright, red lamp, and left the Golden Acre and its fierce and bloodthirsty inhabitants far behind them.

CHAPTER XI.

THE ADVENTURE IN THE OLD HOUSE.

It was at the corner of a wide and handsome street that Stanley Sherrington ordered his coachman to pull up.

"Why stop you here?" asked Rupert; "we are not near your home."

Sherrington laughed.

"No, no," he cried; "we are not bound for home. I and my friend, Hubert Redfern, are compelled to meet our free companions at yonder tavern. A glass of something strong and hot, Rupert, would not suit you ill now, I imagine, after our recent battle. Let us enter together."

"And who are your companions, Stanley?" asked Rupert Dreadnought.

"We belong to the Mohocks, a good and brave Society," said Sherrington; "we seek amusement everywhere and in everything. We wage war against drunken citizens and meddlesome watchmen, and we sometimes even exact black mail in the way of kisses from the fair sex. We force the rich sometimes to disgorge at the voice of Poverty, and do good deeds between whiles, in fact, to pay for absolution for the bad. There is our character written out in full."

For an instant Rupert Dreadnought hesitated to join him.

It seemed scarcely right while the body of his grand old father was lying in the stately silence and majesty of Death, yet unburied, in his chamber, to enter a scene of wild and reckless gaiety.

But he was in need of aid.

In need of it at once.

Who more likely, then, to assist him in his perilous and daring enterprise than these reckless spirits?

"Good," he said; "I will accompany you."

"But your strange and ill-clad friend here?" whispered Sherrington.

The Scotch boy caught the words.

"I will go my way," said he, meekly; "or if there is danger threatening the one who saved my life, I will remain all night to shield him from it."

There was such a depth of earnestness and sincerity in the words of the Scotch boy that it touched the hearts of the hearers.

"My young friend," cried Rupert, "are you in need of service?"

"Yes, sir, I am," replied the Scotch boy, eagerly. "And if you have the chance of giving me aught to do, there is no one in the world I would more gladly serve under."

"Have you no friends in London?"

"None, sir."

"Well, well, here is my address," said Rupert. "Come to me to-morrow night at eight, and you shall have your wish. I will find something for you to do."

A wild gleam of pleasure shot from the eyes of the wild-looking Scotch boy.

"May Heaven reward you," he said; "you are the first friend I have met in London."

"Stay, however," added Rupert; "mayhap you are hungry. Have you money?"

"I have not," replied the Scotch youth, with a look of the utmost shame. "I was spending my last coin in purchasing food when I was accused of theft."

"Come, come, Rupert," cried Stanley Sherrington; "the Mohocks are waiting."

He also had listened with some interest to the conversation with the boy, but he became impatient as he saw the evident inclination of Rupert to hear more.

"Fear not; I shall not detain you long," returned Rupert, as he hastily wrote a few words on a scrap of paper, and gave it to the boy, together with some money. "Go with this to my house; show it to the servant who admits you, and ask to be taken to the kitchen. Make yourself at home there, and you shall in the morning tell me your story."

With many thanks, incoherent from their very sincerity, the Scotch boy remained standing some few minutes after the young men departed into the house of entertainment.

Then, with a bewildered feeling of pleasure and gratitude in his heart, he walked away

We shall follow his footsteps at present, and narrate a strange adventure that befell him in Rupert's house.

What happened at the meeting of the Mohocks, and who the Mohocks were, we will describe at a future period.

The appearance of our young Scotch adventurer was, as may be imagined, far from prepossessing at this moment.

His clothes, torn and stained before, were more torn and stained now than ever, while here and there marks of blood showed plainly on his face and his habiliments.

When, therefore, he presented himself at the door of Rupert Dreadnought's dwelling, it was with some difficulty that he could make the domestic believe that his master had sent him.

"We want no beggars here," cried he, in a contemptuous voice. "I will not take your letter. Some begging petition, no doubt."

"Have a care," cried the Scotch youth, reddening with anger, "or as sure as my name is Allan of the Glen, I'll force your insolent words down your throat. I am a friend of your master's—have fought side by side with him, and I demand admittance."

The domestic, who was one of the fat and pompous style, cared not for an encounter with the ragged wayfarer, and seeing Allan's hand gliding naturally to his sword, he thought it best to be civil.

So he took the paper.

The words there contained soon altered his manner.

"This way, young sir," he said. "You must forgive my words. You will confess that appearances——"

"Are against me," laughed the youth; "but lead on, I shall forgive you with a truer heart when I taste some of that good fare which I can smell even now in your kitchen. Bread and a little spring water has been all my fare of late."

The entrance of the strange guest into the room where the servants were indulging in a hearty supper was, as may be imagined, the signal for a general stare of astonishment and a general volley of exclamations.

A whisper, however, from his companion settled matters, and with some amount of ill-grace among the well-fed, well-clothed lacqueys, he was admitted to a place at the hospitable board.

Once installed among them, he lost no time in making friends.

His voracious appetite being appeased, he became talkative, told his adventures, and interspersed his words with snatches of his native melodies.

Instead then of despising and ridiculing him, the servants looked upon him as a valuable acquisition to the circle, and were sorry when the hour came which summoned them to bed.

It was in a chamber not far from that in which the dead earl lay in the majesty of death that Allan of the Glen was placed to sleep.

It was a comfortable room though small, and looked out upon a garden in the rear of the house, pleasant with flowers and greenery of all kinds.

He did not spend much time, however, in admiring the things around him, neither did he trouble to undress.

Two or three times he looked almost suspiciously at the snowy white bed as if scarcely knowing what to do. But he did not enter it.

Its excessive cleanliness seemed to frighten him, and at length, with a sigh, he rolled himself up in the remnant of his plaid, and lying on the hearth-rug, fell off into that sweet, sound sleep, which only comes to tired youth.

Poor lad! The hard floor was a welcome and soft couch to him.

He had slept beneath haystacks, and by the roadside, in the sunshine and the storm; and the soft bed of luxury provided for him would have afforded him no rest.

He was a light sleeper, however, and had scarcely enjoyed an hour's slumber when he was awakened by a slight noise.

All was in complete darkness, for he had extinguished the light; and so, as he rose up on one hand to listen, he was somewhat confused as to where he was.

Quickly the thought came to him, however, that he was in the house of his benefactor, and then was seen a mysterious vision.

Outside the window was a man who was endeavouring to open it.

Again the noise was heard that had awakened the sleeper.

It was the mysterious stranger gradually wrenching away a portion of the woodwork.

A feeling of joy entered at once the heart of Allan of the Glen.

Here truly was danger, but here also was a chance of serving his new master and benefactor.

He raised himself up quietly, and, crawling to the window, hid himself behind the tapestry, drew his sword, and waited.

The night was very dark, and, although everything around was very still, the man was under no fear of being discovered from without.

A heavy pouring rain was descending in a steady deluge, sending the pedestrians from the streets, and turning what had been a scene of gaiety a few hours before into a scene of cold wretchedness.

So the man worked on.

It seemed an age to Allan as he listened anxiously and watched, but it was not, in fact, long before the steel tool of the mysterious workman had forced its way, and ingress was free to him.

By the dull light Allan could see that he was masked, and that, although he wore a sword, he had not drawn it.

In fact he considered himself quite in safety, and when he had glided in, he noiselessly closed the casement after him.

In an instant Allan's views were changed.

Sheathing his sword, he remained still behind the curtain and watched.

The man drew from his pocket a dark lantern, and opened it.

It shot forth a brilliant light, and every object in the room was plainly visible.

The man glanced first at the bed; and saw it was empty.

"Good!" muttered the masked intruder. "I am in luck. There is no one here."

He glided, as he spoke, towards the little door which communicated with the apartment where lay the dead body, and as soon as he had entered, Allan of the Glen followed him.

There was heavy tapestry in the chamber of death, and the man was fully occupied with his own thoughts, so that the Scotch youth found no difficulty in following him, and concealing himself once more.

The man glanced round, and seeing a lamp upon the table, lit it.

Then he gazed intently at the walls, as if studying their configuration.

At last he uttered a low cry of pleasure, and sprang forward.

"I have it now," he cried, as he glided his hand rapidly along the smooth surface of a pilaster, and then touched a knob.

In an instant a door flew open, and discovered a dark closet, while a cold rush of air swept round the room.

Allan of the Glen at once conceived an idea of action.

He would imprison this man in the closet until the return of his master, and the secret of the mysterious visit would then be discovered.

He lost not a moment.

Springing forward impetuously, just as the man peered into the darkness, he seized him, and ere the stranger could turn or offer any resistance, he had pushed him forward with all his strength into the darkness.

What happened next occurred so quickly that Allan had not even the time to slide back the panel!

There was a wild cry, the sound of a heavy body bumping against projections, then a loud splash, and all was as still as death.

"HE IS DEAD!" SAID RUPERT, AS THEY BORE HIM FROM THE SECRET PANEL.

For a moment Allan stood as if petrified with horror at what he had done.

Then he rushed back to the table, seized the lamp, and, returning, raised it above his head, and gazed into the darkness.

All he could see was that he himself was standing on a small ledge, and that below him was a deep, dark well.

He could not see the bottom, but he could guess what was there.

A mangled, ghastly corpse!

What should he do now?

Should he awaken the servants, and tell them what had happened?

Or should he await the return of his benefactor?

The latter, which was, of course, more consonant with his feelings, was, however, only possible if he permitted the man to die (if there were yet a spark of life in him) or left his mangled body there.

He was relieved of his anxiety, however, in a manner he least expected.

There was a quick step along the corridor, and in another moment the door opened, and Rupert Dreadnought entered.

CHAPTER XII.

THE DISCOVERY—RUPERT DREADNOUGHT'S MISGIVINGS—THE DESCENT OF THE WELL—THE DEAD BODY—THE MYSTERIOUS PAPER—THE ROBBERY OF THE RING—THE WARNING.

RUPERT glanced with astonishment at Allan as he entered.

The Scotch youth's face was white with fear and anger with himself, and he was leaning against the table for support.

Rupert's heart sank within him, and his eyes shot fire.

What did the scene mean?

Why was Allan standing there, with the secret panel open, and desecrating by his presence the chamber of death?

Had he already become ungrateful?

Was he giving this return for his benefaction?

"What means this?" he cried. "Why are you here?"

The Scotch youth sank on one knee.

"Oh, forgive me, sir!" he cried; "I am not here for any evil purpose. The story I have to tell you will prove that I have but sought to do you a service, and I fear, have done you an injury."

"Quick, then, to your tale," said Rupert Dreadnought, who, although half convinced by the manner of the lad, was yet unable to understand the meaning of the scene; "be not afraid; if you have done wrong unknowingly I am not the one to blame you."

Briefly then the youth told his tale.

Rupert listened in utter wonderment.

The panel which was now opened he had imagined to be that which concealed the Iron Chest with all its *wondrous secrets*, and now that he looked in there were nothing but dark, murky walls and a deep, and apparently fathomless, pit.

"You have done no wrong," said Rupert; "I commend you for it. If you had *not* been here Heaven knows what mischief this midnight robber might have done. He came here for no good purpose, and his end is his own reaping."

As he spoke he went to the door and called aloud for the domestics.

In a few moments three of the male servants made their appearance, half dressed.

They stared in utter astonishment at the open panel.

"Go, fetch a rope, a long and strong one," said Rupert, quickly; "it is for life or death, so let there be no delay."

A stout rope was soon brought by one of the men, and they proceeded in a body to the panel.

"Below there a man is lying," said Rupert Dreadnought; "he came as a robber and he has doubtless met his fate. Which among you will have courage to descend?"

The Scotch boy almost interrupted him as he spoke these words.

"Stay, sir," he cried, "it is I who did the deed, I alone will descend. Give me yonder dark lantern that the stranger has left upon the table. I will bring him up whether alive or dead."

There was no attempt upon the part of anyone of the domestics present to dispute with him the task.

They were awestruck by the scene which, as it had been but half explained, to them seemed strongly and wildly mysterious.

The Scotch youth smiled in spite of everything, as he adjusted the rope round his waist and fixed it round his left arm.

"This puts me in mind of my Highland home," he said, "when my comrades used to let me down from craggy mountain points to rifle the nests of the wild mountain birds."

The retainers watched him with eager interest, as he approached the dark panel and prepared to descend.

"Before you do this," said Rupert Dreadnought, as the Scotch boy passed himself over the edge, "let me give you a caution. I know nothing of this place. I never, till now, was aware of its existence, and it may be fathomless and filled with deadly vapour for aught I know. Therefore, if you find your strength giving way, at once give a signal and let us raise you quickly again to the surface. Your life is too good to throw away upon a midnight robber—an assassin for aught we know."

"Fear not for me!" cried Allan of the Glen; "you risked your life to save mine. I risk mine now that you may know what danger threatens you."

Then he turned to the servants.

"Now, lads, be quick," he said, "and lower me rapidly."

The brave youth was soon descending at a rapid pace, and both Rupert and his domestics gazed down with interest at the light of the lantern as it grew less and less in the deep distance.

Presently it became so small that they could scarcely see it, and the strain on the rope become so great that it seemed as though it must break.

"'Tis a fearful depth," said Rupert, as he leaned over the dark opening, "no man can be alive after such a terrible fall."

As he spoke the rope grew slack.

He had evidently reached the bottom.

"Throw down another rope," cried Rupert Dreadnought; "with a man, perhaps dead, in his arms, this one is not sufficient to bear him safely to the surface."

At this moment there was a sharp tug at the rope.

Then another, still more impatient.

"Quick," exclaimed Rupert; "in such a place he might suffocate."

The servants, eager always to obey their young master, at once flung down the rope, with increased eagerness, it may be said, because they were themselves anxious to solve the mystery.

The second rope was soon apparently adjusted, and they began slowly to raise the two men.

It was at once easily seen that the midnight intruder was either dead or insensible.

Had he not been so, he would have aided in the ascent, whereas what they were bringing to the surface was a dead weight.

It was not long, however, before the curiosity of all was gratified.

The Scotch youth, white as a ghost, and shivering as with cold through his battle with the dense miasmatic vapour, staggered upon the brink of the black pit, and dropped by the side of the masked man, whom the servants lifted in and placed upon the ground.

"He is dead," cried Rupert, as he felt the heart of the latter.

Then he removed the mask.

The white marble features (stained here and there with blood from the wounds which he had received against the rough edge of the pit) were those of a perfect stranger.

"What can this mean?" murmured Rupert Dreadnought.

"Perhaps, sir——" said one of the domestics.

Then he stopped hesitatingly.

"Speak out," cried his master; "what is it you suspect?"

"Perhaps the story you have heard is not the correct one."

"In what way?"

"Perhaps, after all, this Scotch youth," returned the man, lowering his voice, "may have some knowledge of this man, and, in endeavouring to secrete him, may have killed his friend."

Not for one moment did this suspicion enter the brain of Rupert Dreadnought.

"No, no," he said, "*he* is no traitor. I am certain of it. Let us search this man; perhaps upon his body we shall find documents which explain the mystery of his presence. For *my* part, I believe him to be no common robber."

The search was at once made, but for some time nothing could be found. At length one of the domestics took from his pocket a torn, ragged piece of paper, which he handed to his master.

Rupert Dreadnought at once took it, and read as follows:—

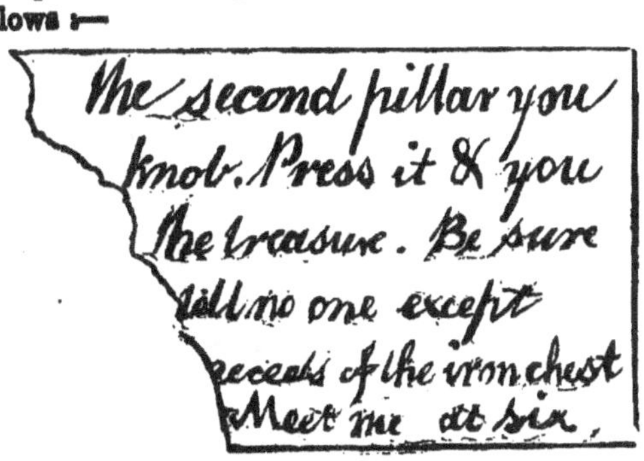
The second pillar you
knob. Press it & you
the treasure. Be sure
tell no one except
secrets of the iron chest
Meet me at six.

"This is a strange thing," said Rupert, "a very strange thing. There is no name here, or anything, in fact, which will afford a clue to the mystery."

The document, torn as it was, proved, however, that the person who had so mysteriously entered the house was no common robber, but an emissary of the enemy.

"Take this carrion out of my father's death chamber," said Rupert, sternly, as he ceased the examination of the stranger's body. "Place him below; then fetch in the watch, and see if his features are known to them."

The Scotch lad, who had now recovered from the effects of the foul air, approached Rupert as the men bore the body away.

"My benefactor," he said, "how can I thank you for your kindness to me, and how excuse my conduct?"

There was real pain and sorrow visible in the youth's features.

Rupert placed his hand kindly upon his shoulder.

"My lad," he said, "in the first place you have acted quite properly in this matter. You had every right to believe that this man was a thief; the paper contained in his pocket proves you were correct. He came here for plunder; he has met his death. To-morrow night I shall be able to let you prove to me the gratitude I believe you truly feel."

The Scotch youth seized his benefactor's hand.

"Oh! I thank you for this," he cried. "Yes, I *do* indeed feel gratitude. I who am fatherless and motherless, and have never yet known a home! how can *I* avoid feeling gratitude to one who has saved my life? I shall wait eagerly for to-morrow night, and then, if needs be, I will lay down my life for you."

"To-morrow, or rather to-day, for morning approaches, I will hear your story," said Rupert. "This day is fixed for the funeral of my beloved father; and in the evening, when darkness closes in, I am about to proceed upon an errand which may prove a perilous one. Now retire to bed, and be assured of my firm friendship."

The Scotch youth then turned away with a murmured blessing, and Rupert Dreadnought proceeded towards the bed whereon his father lay.

Reverentially he uncovered the face of him whom in life he had so greatly loved.

"Now, perhaps," he said to himself, "I can, with respect, take from his finger the large emerald ring which he bade me guard with my heart's blood. No doubt among so many secrets this may point to some other mystery."

He drew down the white satin coverlet, on which, embossed in golden threads, glittered the semblances of an earl's coronet, and raised his father's hand.

The ring was gone! while clenched in the stiffened fingers of the dead was a piece of paper, on which were inscribed these words—

"*Rupert Dreadnought, mysterious enemies surround you! The ring you coveted so much is gone. It is in the hands of those who will use its mysterious agency to your destruction. You are no match for those who have sworn to be your death, and to ruin while you live every plan you desire for our ruin. When we meet—when you are face to face with him who now wears your father's ring, you will tremble, in spite of all your boasted courage, at what I shall reveal to you.*"

"Curses be upon these treacherous hounds!" he cried; "nevertheless I will not swerve from my duty. In spite of all," he added, as he placed his hand upon the cold brow of his father, "I swear to proceed with my task; in spite of the world."

He little knew, when he said these words, the secret which the ring contained, or the power it placed in the hands of his enemies.

CHAPTER XIII.

THE ORPHAN OF THE GLEN ALMOND—THE MYSTERIOUS FLIGHT—THE CHASE OVER THE SCOTCH MOORS—THE BATTLE—TWO TO ONE—THE FALL OF THE LOWLAND TRAITORS—ELSIE OF THE GLEN—THE STRANGE ADOPTION—THE HIDDEN PEOPLE—MARY MACPHERSON—THE DISAPPEARANCE—THE DISPERSION OF THE OUTLAWS—THE FUNERAL OF THE OLD EARL, AND RENEWAL OF THE OATH OF VENGEANCE.

THE story which Allan of the Glen related to Rupert Dreadnought on the following morning, if told in his own words, would enable little of his true history to be known by the reader.

So we will tell the story ourselves.

Early one morning, about fifteen years before our story opens, the inhabitants of the town of Perth were aroused by the furious clattering of horse's feet, and those who succeeded in reaching their windows in time, saw a sight which made them wonder.

Mounted on a powerful but somewhat heavy horse was a man whose features they could not distinctly see, but his general appearance betokened one belonging to the lower class of society.

On one arm he carried a child apparently about three years of age, and with his disengaged hand he clutched a long and heavy sword.

Following close at his heels, and evidently mounted on swifter horses, were two men, who, with loud curses, called upon him to stop.

The only heed he paid to them was to urge his horse to still fiercer exertions and wave his sword now and then defiantly over his head.

This was all that the townspeople of Perth saw.

They went by like a flash of lightning, and until they had reached the open country there was nothing to be seen beyond a simple pursuit.

Shots, certainly, were exchanged, but they fell harmless, and had the stranger with the child been able to hold his own there was every probability that there would have been no bloodshed.

His object seemed rather to escape than rancorously to seek their destruction.

Riding hard as he was, over somewhat dangerous and uneven ground, he, nevertheless, kept looking again and again over his shoulder to see how the distance between him and those who followed diminished or increased.

His horse, strong as it was and able to do an immense amount of work, was no match for their lighter and swifter steeds, and at length, though most unwillingly, he was compelled to draw rein.

"Hold!" he cried, wheeling round his horse and confronting them so suddenly that their rushing steeds fell nearly on their haunches, "hold! What want you with me?"

"The child!" cried the foremost of the horsemen.

"I refuse to yield him," answered the man, defiantly.

"Then you will meet your death," said the other; "there are two of us to one. Our horses have proved more than a match for yours. Yield the child, and we will no further molest you."

The man in the cloak laughed loudly in disdain.

"Whenever did one of *my* name yield to a braggart's menace?" he cried. "No—no, I yield not."

"And yet the child fared better with its wealthy friends."

At these words the eyes of the pursued flashed fire.

"Friends, say you! rather talk of deadly foes," he shouted. "I am his best friend—I, his father. Friends, indeed, who would educate him to despise his kindred—to laugh at his father, whose greatest prize lay in the flashing of his bright sword! No—no," he cried, casting an eager glance round the country, and carefully taking in the details of each vale and mountain, "no, no, rather let his home be among the wild crags, and his only mate the eagle, than hear him lisping amid your Lowland traitors."

"Come, come," cried the foremost horseman, "come, come, time presses. Either yield the boy at once, or prepare to meet thy doom."

"Once more I ask you, what want you with him?" asked the mountaineer, hugging it more closely to his breast.

"We cannot waste time," said the horseman; "we wish to take him to those from whom you wrested him by stealth; we desire to restore him to wealth, and save him from beggary and starvation. Now, no more delay; restore him."

"I will not yield him," answered the man. "No, no; surrender is a cry which with my dying lips I'd laugh to scorn. I will fight you both. I will place the child on yonder grassy mound. Then I will fight you one by one, and if I cannot beat you both, you wretched Lowlanders, then may the noble name I bear be for ever buried in the dust of oblivion and disgrace. Will you consent to this?"

"Upon your honour as a Highland gentleman not to attempt to fly," said the Lowlander, "we will confer together on the point."

"I will not move an inch," said the Highlander.

The Lowlanders neared each other and conferred together for a few moments in a low voice.

Then the one who throughout the affair had been spokesman, advanced.

"We accept your terms," he said. "We will dismount, and I will fight you first."

The Highlander, who, with his wild and chivalric notions of honour, could not for a moment conceive it possible that any treachery was intended, at once proceeded to comply with the request.

He dismounted, and carrying the child to the grassy mound he had indicated, he kissed it, and bade it be quiet no matter what it heard or saw.

Then he advanced, sword in hand, to meet his first opponent, taking no notice of the fact that the other man had dismounted also.

The fight began, but he soon found that the game of his adversary was a treacherous one, and that neither he nor his friend meant open fight.

While the man in the road parried and warded the bold strokes of his foe, the other began gradually, but not unseen by the Highlander, to approach the spot where the child lay.

The ruse was apparent in a moment.

One was to steal the child while the other kept the Scot at bay.

In an instant, just as the Lowlander was close to the child, the Highlander drew a pistol and fired.

The traitor staggered, uttered a loud cry, and then, throwing his arms above his head, fell back upon the ground.

"Ah, ye villains!" cried he, "ye think to cheat me of my child, but a father's arm, when raised in such a cause, is not easily beaten down," and he attacked his foeman furiously.

The Lowlander was no match for him, and after many rapid passes he succeeded in stretching his enemy desperately wounded on the ground.

Then, taking the child once more in his arms, he rode away.

After riding as rapidly as he could for about an hour, he reached a point in the mountains where a path led abruptly from the high road down into a deep glen.

The glen — Glenalmond, as it was called — was well known, and avoided by the Lowlanders whose business called them along that lonely highway.

By some it had the reputation of being haunted, and well it might in those superstitious times, for terrible crimes were said to have been committed there.

Travellers were said to have been inveigled into its shadowy recesses and cruelly murdered.

Certainly peaceful travellers along this route *had* disappeared, but when at length the authorities were roused, and the place was explored, the glen was found not only free of all signs of foul crime, but free of all inhabitants.

Save one, or rather two.

These two were an old hag and a huge wolf-dog.

Both were ugly and forbidding; both were fierce, and disliked by everyone.

But there was no sign in her wretched hovel, perched as it was among the trees on the slope of the glen, of any wrong doing, neither was there a shadow of possibility that she or her dog either could have effected the mischief which had been done.

She spoke civilly to the officers, laughed a hideous laugh of merriment at the idea that the glen was a place of ill-omen and butchery, and finally dismissed them, convinced that she had nothing whatever to do with the matter, and, in fact, knew nothing of it.

They were wrong in two ways.

In the first place there had been no murders committed.

In the second place the old woman *was* cognizant of all that had transpired, and was chief actor in the disappearance of the travellers.

But there was another and a very simple explanation.

All those who had vanished so strangely were well known, not only to be carrying goods of great value, but *to be enemies of the Pretender*, whose firm friends these "Highland bodies" were.

But, as I have said before, they were not murdered.

ROSALIE ST. AUBYN.

Pounced upon suddenly, they were carried to old Elsie's dwelling, and there bound.

At the back of her hut was a door communicating with a second room, and into this without delay the captive was led.

Then one of his captors raised one of the rough stones, and descended about ten steps, which led into a corridor cut in the solid rock, and leading upwards by a rapid ascent.

After about a quarter of an hour's scrambling along the rough-hewn path, the captive would be astounded to find himself on a high table-land, surrounded by trees which served to screen a kind of colony.

It was a hidden hamlet, of which old Elsie's hut was really the gateway!

Here the captives were kept until their disappearance had somewhat blown over, and then they were carried away by night and shipped abroad.

A new method of filling a royal treasury, or, rather, the treasury of an expectant king.

It was near Glenalmond that the stranger and the child halted.

He gave then a long, shrill whistle, and waited patiently.

In a very few moments a black object made its appearance on the summit of a block of sand-stone, and a grey face peered over.

This face was Elsie's.

It disappeared as quickly as it had come, and in a few moments an answering whistle told the anxious stranger that the road was clear.

He at once urged his horse up the narrow, rocky defile, and in a few moments was in the front of Elsie's dwelling.

Here he fastened his horse and entered.

"Here, Elsie," he said, "is my child. I give him into your charge. Let no one have him; rather take his life than cast him again into the clutches of his kindred, who desire only to murder him that they may have his property. Let him dwell among the Hidden People; let him be one of them till I can come to claim him."

As he spoke this hurriedly, giving no further explanation, he drew from his pocket a purse of gold, and placed it in her hand.

"This," he said, "will help to keep the boy till I come again."

"And when will that be?"

The stranger smiled.

"Ah!" he said, "I know not."

Then he thought a moment, looking fondly at the boy the while.

Then he brought his clenched fist fiercely down upon the table.

"Remember, Elsie," he cried, "no cozening with Lowlanders. Let him be brought up in the free Highlands, on the brisk mountain air, as little knowing of their ways as the mountain deer, which will be his companions. I must go now. God bless you, Allan."

He knelt down on the hard ground as he spoke, and embraced the little one fondly.

"Stay," cried Elsie, "stay. What is your name?"

"That must remain a secret," he said, "until *a stain now on its honour* is removed for ever. Call him Allan. If years roll on years, there is something by which I shall know him again."

He then, without furthur comment, quitted the room, and leaping on his horse, dashed away once more on the high road.

A little sand strewn on the rocky path obliterated all traces of his deviation from the high road, and when search was made for the wild and reckless rider, not a trace of his whereabouts could be found.

Allan remembered well the scene on the Moorlands.

It was indelibly impressed on his memory by the pistol shot, and the desperate sword contest so terribly interesting to a child's mind.

But after this all was monotony, until, at length, as he grew up towards manhood, he fell in love, and the sweet companionship of Mary Macpherson lessened the dreariness of his life.

At length the hiding place of the Hidden People was discovered by an astute officer, and the authorities came down upon them with a large number of troops.

"I won't keep you much longer now," said Allan of the Glen, as he sat in Rupert Dreadnought's chamber narrating the story of his life. "The rest is a scene of horror.

"The soldiers made their way through the subterranean passage and found the Hidden People ready armed to receive them.

"A desperate and bloody battle ensued.

"Men, rather than be taken prisoners, were seen to fling themselves from the lofty crags, and secure certain death in the chasms below.

"When I saw most of the leaders taken prisoners, and all hope lost, I leaped across a wide fissure in the rocks, and made my way round to the glen where I hoped to see my Mary.

"In this I was deceived," said the youth, with a trembling voice; "she was gone. I have never seen her again."

"Never seen her!" exclaimed Rupert. "Whither, then, had she gone?"

"I know not—I have never known," replied the youth. "I have sought her everywhere in vain, and at length, disgusted with my own native land, which had robbed me of my father and my bride, I quitted it with scarcely a farthing in my pocket, and came to England.

"*You* met me when I was weary and fatigued, and set upon by bloodthirsty assassins."

"And why were you accused of theft?" asked Rupert Dreadnought.

"I know not. I gave my last piece to the man at the shop near which you found me for a piece of bread, and, thinking I had more, the villanous rabble at once set upon me, calling out 'thief,' to turn the sympathies of all against me. Here my story ends. Your kindness saved me."

"Yours is a strange and eventful history," said Rupert Dreadnought, "and contains a mystery which even yet you may unravel. You have no proof that your father is dead?"

"None whatever, save his prolonged and unaccountable absence."

"Then you may yet find him. While there is a shadow of life there is also the shadow of hope. I will aid you in your search for him. But now the time approaches for the mournful obsequies of my father. After that I must set myself at work to accomplish his last wishes."

We will not pause to describe the funeral of the old man.

Suffice it to say that the obsequies were carried out with great pomp, and that a numerous retinue of weeping friends followed him to the grave.

Among them was Allan of the Glen, transformed by new clothes into a clean-looking, handsome youth, whose features alone betokened his Scotch descent.

The young orphan remained by the grave after the others had departed.

Allan waited near, but did not obtrude his presence on his master's sorrow.

When all had departed from the vaults of the grey old church of St. Andrew's, Rupert Dreadnought knelt, and after invoking his father's blessing on his head, he renewed his vow.

There was no shrinking, no qualification in his oath.

Boldly, and in the sight of Heaven, he renewed it as a vow which he had a right to keep when once registered by his father's death-bed.

After this he himself locked the vault, placed the key in his pocket, and quitted the church with Allan of the Glen.

He shook off his tears and his grief as it were as he passed out once more into the bright and open light of day.

"Now," he said, cheerily, to Allan, as they rode back towards the old house, "now we must commence the work. To-night, Helen Penraven must be saved!"

CHAPTER XIV.

THE BURIAL OF THE KEY—THE DEPARTURE FOR THE HOUSE ON THE MOOR—THE MOHOCKS—THE PURSUIT—THE BATTLE—THE ESCAPE—THE ARRIVAL AT THE HOUSE—A TERRIBLE DISCOVERY.

PURSUANT to his father's earnestly expressed desire, Rupert Dreadnought, when he arrived once more at his home, proceeded at once to bury the key.

The vault he knew well.

It was one in which it had been his father's custom to keep some rare and curious wines, and it was with the excuse of seeking for some of this that he descended, with Allan of the Glen, into the damp cellar.

Allan had never seen such a place, and stared about him like one lost.

But the necessity for work soon roused him, and at this special kind of labour Rupert soon found him an able assistant.

The youth, who had so often raised the heavy flagstone in old Elsie's hut, was not long in raising also the loose stone which lay third from the door.

Underneath the stone was a soft, black soil, emitting an aromatic smell.

"What can this be? Let us search further," said Allan, as he raised a little of the earth with his broad-bladed knife.

Rupert caught his wrist.

"Profane it not," he said; "*there may be a mystery here, but it is not yet time to unravel it.* No, this path of vengeance must be trodden slowly, cautiously, methodically, as my father directed me."

Then he placed the key of the IRON CHEST upon the earth, covered it over, and replaced the stone in its proper position.

Taking up a bottle of curious wine to deceive the domestics as to the object of his descent to the vault, he then passed up-stairs and led Allan into his own private room.

It was a gem of a place.

Just such a place as suited the character of its clear-headed, brave young owner.

Guns, swords, pistols, ancient breastplates, and other pieces of mail were scattered about, or hung against the wall.

To qualify these was a goodly array of books upon every conceivable subject, even Love.

"My lord," said Allan, "this is a place where I could be happy for years."

Rupert stopped him.

"Stay," he said; "there is one thing I must impress upon you."

"What is that, my lord?"

"What you have just repeated. You must no longer call me my lord. I wish for the present to drop the title entirely. While I have work to do and a vow to carry out, I am plain Master Dreadnought, unless, indeed, circumstances compel me to change my mind. Now, then, Allan, since you know this, select your weapons, and we will proceed to the rendezvous where I expect to meet some of my brave friends and companions."

Allan had soon made his selection.

A pair of large horse-pistols, and a short, strong sword, something like that he had wielded among the Hidden People, were his weapons, while Rupert Dreadnought chose the finest and thinnest of all the blades, and two short, light pistols.

"You can ride?" he asked, as they descended the stairs, after drinking up the wine to warm their blood, in preparation for their long journey in the cold.

"Yes, well."

"That is good," said Rupert. "Our horses are fresh and fast, and my friends are not the right sort of men to let the grass grow under their feet."

Within a few moments they were in the saddle, and making their way with all haste towards a spot beyond the Tower of London, where Sherrington and some of his Mohock* friends had promised to await their arrival.

There were no great number of passengers or vehicles in the street, and it was not long, therefore, before they reached the rendezvous, where six shadowy figures on horseback were gathered beneath a high wall, which sent its gloomy shade far across the road.

"Ah! here comes our worthy leader," cried Sherrington, who had been foremost of the party, "we have been long expecting you."

"I am not long behind my time," said Rupert Dreadnought; "we will at once advance."

They accordingly waited [illegible] but immedi-

* "A set of men have lately erected themselves into a nocturnal fraternity under the title of the Mohock Club, a name borrowed, it seems, from a sort of cannibals in India, who subsist by plundering and devouring all the natives about them. The president is styled 'Emperor of the Mohocks,' and his arms are a Turkish crescent, which his Imperial Majesty bears at present in a very extraordinary manner, engraven upon his forehead. Agreeable to their name, the avowed design of their institution is mischief, and upon this foundation all their rules and orders are framed * * * In order to exact their principle in its full strength and perfection, they take care to drink themselves to a pitch that is beyond the possibility of attending to any notions of reason or humanity, then make a general sally, and attack all that are so unfortunate as to walk the streets that they patrol. Some are knocked down, others stabbed, others cut and carbonadoed. To put the watch to a total rout, and mortify some of those inoffensive militia, is reckoned a *coup d'éclat.* The peculiar talents by which these misanthropes are distinguished from one another, consist in the various kinds of barbarities which they execute upon their prisoners. Some are celebrated for a happy dexterity in 'tipping the lion' upon them, which is performed by squeezing the nose flat to the face, and boring out the eyes with their fingers. Others are called 'dancing masters,' and teach their scholars to cut capers by running swords through their legs, a new invention, whether originally French I cannot tell. A third sort are the tumblers, whose office it is to set women on their heads."—*See Spectator, No.* 324, *March* 27, 1711.

[This account and what follows may, of course, be received as somewhat exaggerated, but there is no doubt that the Mohocks in those days were pests and scourges society There were many, however, who, like Stanley Sherrington and his friends, had joined the society under a misapprehension, and who, while joining in their *fun*, endeavoured always to discourage their more mad and violent freaks.—*Author of* "RUPERT DREADNOUGHT."]

nely starting off at a quick trot, were soon in the open country.

Darkness had fallen, but the moon and the stars were brilliantly gleaming, and only occasional clouds intercepted the gentle rays which they cast upon Mother Earth.

I have before described the route from London to the old house where Helen Penraven was immured, and I need only say, therefore, that no interruption occurred until they reached the inn at the cross-road, where Rupert on the night of his escape had borrowed a horse.

On passing this they saw something moving in the distance.

It was difficult at first to say what this something was.

Dense clumps of trees, as will be remembered, grew on the hedges of the road across the heath, and at first it seemed, truly, as if one of these were moving.

But presently, as the moon burst suddenly from behind a cloud and inundated the scene, the truth was evident.

A party of horsemen held the road.

A spy had informed Oscar of Rupert's intended journey, and the enemy were on the alert.

Rupert hesitated not, but only glanced round him at his companions.

The Mohocks whom Sherrington had brought with him were all tall, young, stalwart men; and there was not much fear as to the result of an encounter with those who might be hired assassins.

"Let us dash onwards," cried he; "if they are friendly they will make room for us, seeing we are in haste. If they are foes we will cut our way through."

"Bravely spoken!" cried Sherrington; "let us put spurs to our horses then, and draw our swords."

Keeping their glittering blades as far as possible out of sight, the little squad of brave, determined hearts rushed eagerly along the high road.

It was as Rupert had at first imagined.

The body of men who held the road were foemen.

Masks concealed their faces, and they were all attired in black.

In order to make a pretence of not being the first to commence the quarrel, they jogged their horses leisurely towards Rupert and his friends, and when the latter came up with them there was a perfect shout of feigned astonishment.

"How now, gentlemen," said a strange voice, "what means this conduct on the king's highway?"

There was no answer.

Almost as the words left his lips the horses and men met with a crash and the conflict commenced.

The opposing body, however, were by far the more powerful in the way of numbers, and they had moreover so disposed their horses that it was impossible for any but an overwhelming force to burst through.

Instinctively, as it were, recognising the fact that all parley was now useless, they began the contest at once.

Yet in the contest there was a strange similarity to the former one.

The masked men seemed desirous of barring their foemen's progress.

But nothing more.

They appeared not to fight to kill.

They were soon, however, compelled to change their tactics.

Rupert's friends gave no quarter.

It was a demand and a blow with these wild young spirits.

"Let us pass," was the demand.

Then came a whirling gleam of steel, and men fell back cut to the chine, with scarcely a cry to mark the moment of their death.

Blood flowed freely on every side, streaming down the flanks of the horses and over the roadway.

Horses, riderless, went plunging away through the darkness, over the dark moorland.

Both sides suffered.

But the Mohocks were used to desperate fighting, and, with the exception of a few unimportant wounds, they got off comparatively free.

Suddenly, just as the battle was at its height, there was the report of a gun at a short distance off.

It acted like magic.

In an instant the masked men drew away from their opponents.

There was no more desperate fighting on either side.

As soon as they had retreated far enough, they suddenly broke and dashed away in different directions over the moonlit moor.

"Hurrah! they fly!" shouted the Mohocks.

Rupert restrained their ardour.

"Stay," he cried, "there is treachery afoot! Silence!"

In an instant the little band ceased their outcry.

"The report of the gun, my friends," said Dreadnought, "was a signal. That signal came from the direction of the house where Helen Penraven is immured. You understand me now, no doubt, my friends. While we fight here, treachery is at work with her. So let us lose no time, but hurry on, and let these cowards fly whither they please."

This was scarcely what the Mohocks liked, but they had for the time being submitted themselves to the command of Rupert Dreadnought, and so they cheerfully complied with his request.

On, therefore, they once more pushed, and within a very short space of time, they drew up before the half-ruined wall and ragged hedge which surrounded the house where Helen Penraven had been placed in supposed safety by the old earl.

Waiting for no summons at the door, Rupert Dreadnought leaped the ditch, and dashing through the brushwood, made towards the house porch.

RUPERT DREADNOUGHT.

"WILL NOT SOME FRIENL TELL RUPERT I AM IN DANGER?" SHE CRIED.

He had no need to knock.

It was wide open.

It was easy to see that enemies hal been busy there.

On the floor, gagged and bound, were two men servants, while one lay dead in the entry.

The former were at once released and eagerly questioned.

 ONE PENNY THE TWO NUMBERS.

"Who has been here?" asked Rupert Dreadnought, as he helped one of the men to a chair.

"I know not who they are," cried the man, "for they were masked, and not one of their voices was familiar to me; but Mistress Penraven is gone—a prisoner—with them."

A muttered curse escaped from the lips of young eadnought as the man spoke.

"Are you certain of it?" he asked.

"Yes; I saw her struggling in the arms of a awny ruffian and rushed forward to aid her, when I was knocked down and gagged; while one of my poor companions, as you see, was shot down, and lies yonder. She screamed loudly, but it was all in vain. No help was near."

"And did she say nothing?—did she leave no message for me?" asked Rupert, distractedly.

"No; only as she was lifted up by her captor and placed before him on the horse, she cried out, in an agonized voice—

"'Oh! if Rupert were here! Will not some friend tell Rupert I am in danger?'"

Without asking more, Rupert seized a lamp from the hall table and passed up towards her room, followed by Allan of the Glen and two of the Mohocks.

They searched everywhere.

In vain.

In not one of the chambers was there the slightest clue to be found as to the identity of her captors.

However, on this point there could be little room for doubt.

It was a plan of Oscar Penraven, and it was he who must be discovered and punished.

Yet how fix the guilt on him?

That he *was* guilty there could be no doubt, however; and, after giving instructions to the serving-men what to do, Rupert led away his little band, and once more made his way towards London.

CHAPTER XV.

RUPERT'S DESPAIR—TOM THE WATERMAN—THE MYSTERIOUS CARRIAGE—THE SHRIEKS OF A CAPTIVE—TOM TO THE RESCUE.

THE feelings of Rupert Dreadnought, when he returned home to his quiet, deathstricken house and thought over the utter failure of his plan for rescuing Helen, I will not pause to describe now.

As may be imagined, they were intensely harrowin

At the very outset he was thwarted.

His father's express injunction was that nothing should be attempted until Helen was in safety, and the failure of the night's expedition, therefore, postponed indefinitely the opening of the first compartment of the IRON CHEST and the commencement of the first MISSION OF VENGEANCE.

However, there was nothing like despair in his heart.

Angry with himself and with circumstances, as he might be, he never for one moment faltered.

All he thought of as he rode home—all he thought of during the night and the next dreary morning, was how he could save Helen—where he could meet Oscar Penraven face to face, and wring from him the secret of her concealment.

It was a terrible thing now even to dream of delay.

Helen Penraven had been named by Oscar as his bride.

What villany might he not put in practice to secure the possession of her?

Force, of course, would be used; and without a single friend to aid her, or even give her advice, how could she be expected to go through the ordeal unscathed?

It was now that Rupert for the first time felt the loss of his father.

He had ever been accustomed to lean upon him, as it were, for advice, and it was indeed a change to miss his familiar voice—to miss his familiar face and form, and have to think and act entirely on his own responsibility.

"This night," thought he, "I will seek out Oscar's dwelling and force the secret from his dastard lips."

He little knew how useless on this occasion would be the endeavour.

In order to explain this we must carry our readers to a little hut on the edge of the river, where lived three persons who will play an active part in the development of our story.

These three persons were Mistress Braxley, her niece Agnes, and her son Tom—known at home and all along the shores of Father Thames as Tom the waterman.

Not that there was any speciality about Tom's watermanship.

There were plenty of watermen on the river, plenty of strong arms and willing hearts, but Tom had been called the "waterman" when first he dabbled, infant-like, in the muddy water, and tried to pull his father's huge oars, and so the name had stuck to him ever since.

There were plenty of "Toms" there and thereabouts, but there was only one "Tom the waterman."

And this one was a fine, tall, curly-headed fellow strong-armed and stout-hearted, the support of his widowed mother, the esteemed friend of his companions, the beloved of his cousin Agnes.

On the night of the abduction of Helen Penraven from Sandmount, Tom the waterman had been engaged very late.

A more than usually large number of persons had that night crossed from the Kentish side of the river towards the Tower, and more than usually mysterious had been their manners and their words.

Tom was used to mysteries.

His best customers were men running from the law or pursuit of various kinds, loving couples who were hastening from the anger of parents and cared not for the publicity of London Bridge, and masked and cloaked men who said little, paid well, and left strange doubts as to their occupation.

These latter had been his customers all that evening.

Four times his boat had been chartered, and each time two masked men had crossed the Thames.

His reputation must certainly have preceded him with these men, for although Tom expressed himself unable to accomplish so much work alone, they declined to allow him to seek help, preferring to assist him themselves.

With their aid, therefore, four journeys had been accomplished, and then a fifth journey brought over one man only—a tall, young, elegantly-dressed man, whose features, like those of his companions, were concealed by a mask.

The others, when they were landed, at once proceeded along the Essex Road.

The young one remained behind, and lighting a cigar, strolled away some distance beneath the shadow of the old houses, keeping as far as possible out of reach of all passers-by.

Tom the waterman was nearly worn out by the fatigues of the evening, and when the last passenger slipped a gold piece into his hand, he inwardly resolved that he would row no more that night.

Such, however, was not the intention of those who had employed him.

Just as he had moored his boat, and sat down upon the broad, dry steps, to take a whiff or two before entering his little home, the youngest of the masked men returned and spoke to him.

"Young man," he said, "we shall have need of your services again."

"I trust so, sir, since you pay liberally," returned Tom; "but not to-night."

"Yes, indeed, to-night," replied the stranger. "It is a lady who requires your aid, and you will not, I am sure, be so ungallant as to refuse her."

Tom laughed lightly at the tone in which the speaker addressed these words to him.

"Well," he said, "how long will it be before the lady will be here?"

"In two hours, so you have time for rest," returned the masked man. "Go, join your comrades in yonder tavern, and recruit your strength with rest and drink. I will apprise you when the hour arrives."

"Good!" said Tom, who, for a long time, had not made so fortunate an evening's work. "I will be here before the two hours, since you needs must have *my* boat, and row you across. Meanwhile, I will say good-night!"

The stranger nodded haughtily as the free-and-easy waterman walked away, and Tom, whistling to himself a merry tune, passed towards his mother's home.

He soon reached it, and pushing open the door, entered a small but comfortable room, where his mother and his cousin were seated by the fire, while near them was a table, with substantial viands yet untouched.

"Ah, dear mother!" he cried, as he kissed her cheek, and then saluted Agnes in a similar way; "waiting supper for me? That's too bad! I vow I won't touch a morsel the next time you act thus! Why, you two ought to be in bed, and not waiting up for a strong, hearty fellow like me, who can wait upon himself."

"Don't talk so, but eat, Tom," said his mother, kindly, as Agnes pushed a well-filled plate towards him. "Why, what's that, Tom—gold?"

"Aye, and plenty of silver with it," returned the young waterman, who had piled his night's earnings on the table; "and I've not done yet, for before I can turn into my bed this night, I've to ferry a lady over the old river."

"A lady at this time of night?" said Agnes, a pretty, bright-eyed girl of eighteen, with a well-turned, plump figure, and long, curling, dark hair · "what a curious thing!"

"Yes, it's altogether a curious thing," said Tom, who was eating and talking at the same time without raising his eyes from his plate. "The men that I've ferried over to-night are all masked, and seem full of money. I wonder what the lady's like. If she's handsome I'm safe to fall in love with her."

The blush on the cheek of Agnes Mayland as she murmured "Foolish fellow," told that she did not quite relish his joke; but Tom did not observe it, and rattled on accordingly, without intermission, in his cheerful jolly way until the clock struck.

He jumped up at once.

"I've none too much time," he said. "An hour's gone already. I'll run over now to the 'Three Sailors' and have a glass, and mind, when I *do* come back I shall expect to see all the lights out, and you two fast asleep."

Then the happy, genial fellow kissed his mother and cousin again, and went out into the night.

The "Three Sailors" was soon reached.

It was a little, low-pitched, oddly-built, but cleanly little tavern, standing not very far from the bridge, and just in such a position that Tom must see the return of the masked strangers with the lady, so he lounged near the door with some of his companions, and smoked, and drank, and listened.

He expected naturally that the mysterious lady, whoever she was, would come in a carriage, and his ears were opened, therefore, for the sound of wheels.

Presently they were heard, driving very rapidly, but they stopped suddenly, and all was again still.

Then came another sound.

A shriek, wild, piercing, prolonged.

"That was a woman's cry!" exclaimed Tom, whose gallant heart was at once moved; and, as he spoke, he sprang out, and glanced eagerly around him.

But nothing was anywhere to be seen.

"It's some poor thing cast herself off London Bridge, maybe," said one of his companions who stood near him.

Oh, no," said Tom the waterman, "my hearing tells me better than that. The cry did not come from that direction, but directly the opposite. Let's get some weapons, and wait here."

"Weapons!" exclaimed his friends, in undisguised amazement.

Tom's quick mind had at once realised the situation.

This cry was a woman's.

Might not she be the very one of whom the masked stranger had spoken?

Might she not be borne hither against her will?

"Yes, weapons," he repeated; "don't waste time in asking questions. Run in and get your oars and sticks, or anything. Depend upon it, we're wanted."

Tom, who was like a king among these rough river men, was at once obeyed.

In a few moments they re-appeared, armed with staves and oars, and hardly had they done so when there was a second loud and piercing cry, then a rush of feet, and the masked men who had crossed the river in Tom the waterman's boat, dashed from out the darker portion of the street, one of them bearing in his arms the form of a woman.

This was Helen Penraven.

"See, my friends!" cried Tom, as he rushed forward, "did I not say we were wanted?"

CHAPTER XVI.

THE FIGHT BY THE RIVER—OARS AGAINST SWORDS—THE CAPTURE OF THE BOAT—THE FLIGHT OF THE MASKED MEN—THE MYSTERIOUS WARNING.

"Save me! save me!" cried the wretched girl, as she saw in the dim, uncertain light the body of watermen advancing towards her.

"Curses on you, Frankland!" exclaimed the youngest of the party—the one who had remained behind; "did I not tell you to drug her food?"

"I will explain another time," replied the one addressed as Frankland; "here are the watermen; let us get quickly across the river, or her cries may arouse the neighbourhood. Quick!"

"Draw your swords!" exclaimed the young stranger; "these come as enemies. What means it? How now, Master Tom Braxley? is your boat ready?"

"No more this night for you!" cried Tom, boldly; "if I had known what evil I was doing, I would have lost my arm sooner than used it to bring you across the river to-night. Release that lady!"

"Insolent ruffian!" cried the masked stranger, drawing his sword. "What mean you by such words as these? Quick, to your boat! and if you do not want your tongue cut out, or your ears shorn off, be silent upon what does not concern you."

A derisive laugh from Tom was the only answer to this braggart speech.

Then, at a signal from him, the sturdy river men rushed upon the masked strangers.

But the latter were well prepared.

"Bear her to the boat!" shouted the clear, ringing voice of the leader. "We will cover your retreat. Keep back these insolent knaves," he added, "but let us have no unnecessary bloodshed. We must not have our names mixed up with street brawls."

The man who bore Helen Penraven across his shoulders had not now so much work to do.

There were no more struggles on her part.

The peril of her situation and the sight of the drawn swords, had made her swoon, and she lay a dead weight in his arms.

The other masked men formed before him, and as the river men rushed upon them with their oars uplifted, they were met by a stern resistance.

"On, on, my men, on!" cried Tom the waterman, beating down the sword opposed to him. "On, on, or we shall be too late! Drive them into the water!"

"By Heaven! this insolence surpasses belief!" exclaimed the young leader, as he fiercely rushed at Tom. "Are you mad thus to interfere with gentlemen? Quick, there, Frankland!"

As he spoke, the sword he had lunged so savagely at Tom's heart was dashed to the ground by a stroke of the oar.

The oar was then let drop, and Tom closed with his enemy.

The masked stranger was a powerful man, but he was no match for the young waterman, who soon held him on the ground at his mercy.

But the battle was a useless one.

The masked men had decidedly the advantage, and, although they gave way as they retreated towards the river's brink, it was but to cover their friends while they lifted the young girl into the boat.

As soon as they had succeeded in this manœuvre, the boat was pushed off, and the young leader cried, in a sneering tone, to Tom, who still held him—

"Now, then, my friend, is it murder you intend?"

"No," said Tom, releasing him, "but you, I fancy, intend worse than murder. Providence, unfortunately, did not aid us in rescuing yonder poor girl from your clutches; but, mark me, she'll escape you yet. If not, a terrible retribution is in store for you, as sure as Heaven is just."

Then, as the young masker sprang to his feet, Tom cried, turning to his men—

"Bill Flaxman, where is your boat? Let us pursue them."

And then, leaving the masked stranger to cross by the bridge, or as he best could, they rushed through the dry arch to the spot where Bill Flaxman's boat lay.

This boat was a long, sharp-pointed one, but it was capable of holding several men; and, in a few moments the skilled watermen had taken their seats, and were pulling with a will from the shore.

The others, however, were very far ahead, and were using the most strenuous exertions to reach the opposite shore, evidently being influenced by an intense dread of discovery and capture.

Tom soon saw that all pursuit was useless, and when half way across the river he gave the word to return.

They had hardly turned the head of their boat before they saw their enemy's wherry reach the opposite bank, and the captors of the young girl leap ashore and make hastily away.

When Tom and his companions returned to the spot they had left, the masked men were gone, and no one who was near could give any account of their whereabouts.

Tom was in no humour now to join his comrades in any further carouse, so he refused all inducements to retrace his steps to the inn.

Saying "Good night," therefore, he passed hurriedly towards his home.

His mind was strangely disturbed.

His thoughts were full of the lovely being he had seen.

In fancy he could again behold the sweet, appealing look she had given him when she cried—

"Save me—save me!"

Her voice, sweet and thrilling, seemed to penetrate into the inmost recesses of his heart, and he vowed that he would yet trace the enemies of the lovely unknown, or perish in the attempt.

He was so absorbed in these fancies that he was at his own door before he had any idea that he had travelled so far.

He was just entering, when a deep, sepulchral voice near him said—

"Beware, Tom Braxley, you have stepped upon a dangerous track; abandon it while you are yet safe."

He turned sharply to see who was the author of this mysterious warning.

But in that brief instant he was too late to learn much.

The words had been spoken quickly and sharply, and, as he turned, all he could see was a tall, dark figure in a cloak, gliding swiftly and noiselessly away.

He darted after it as it passed round the corner of the street, but, *when he reached the spot, it was gone.*

Tom was not reckoned to be a very superstitious man.

But, to say the least, this was far from being a pleasant adventure.

The whole evening had had its air of mystery about it.

What meant this last scene of all?

Who could be his mysterious adviser?

Tom had hitherto kept himself most wonderfully aloof from all kinds of intrigue.

Considering the curious character of some of those who had from time to time made use of his boat, it was indeed wonderful that he had been able to preserve himself so entirely from scrapes of all kinds.

And yet here was he, honest, prudent Tom Braxley, being dragged into the mazes of a mystery more intricate than all!

He turned into bed that night with a heavy heart, but his resolution was in no way shaken.

CHAPTER XVII.

A MEETING OF MOHOCKS—A RIVER SCENE—TOM THE WATERMAN FINDS A CLUE AT LAST.

We have said that after the failure of his first attempt at carrying out his dead father's wishes in rescuing Helen Penraven from the power of her cousin, Rupert Dreadnought—though not giving way to despair—was sorely angry and disappointed.

But he had not the slightest idea for a moment of giving up the chase.

Better it would have been in his eyes to have died in attempting to save his beloved, than live to see her the wife of another.

Better, by death, to cancel the vow of revenge which he had sworn, than live for vengeance alone, without the prospect of so sweet a reward.

The only friends who, upon the moment, he could depend, were Stanley Sherrington and his Mohocks.

THE CHIEF OF THE POISONERS.

These were desperate characters to mix up with, yet they had befriended him, and behaved as trustworthy comrades before.

Why should they not do so again?

So, in the evening, accompanied by Allan of the Glen, he made his way towards the old tavern where the Mohocks held their meetings.

Arriving here, he set Allan to watch at the door, while he, having given the pass-word, as conveyed him by Stanley Sherrington, advanced up a broad staircase, and made his way into a large room.

Stanley was in the chair, and, around him, sitting at little tables, drinking, smoking, and singing, were a number of young men, all belonging to the best classes of society, but debased and lowered to vulgarity now by excesses of every kind.

An insane notion that what they were banded together to perform was courageous as well as funny, led them into the most outrageous acts, but it was then only, of course, under the influence of drink that they were able to bring themselves to the commission of deeds which would have qualified any one of them in these days for Hanwell.

The entrance of Rupert Dreadnought, who was looked upon as a new member, was received with shouts of applause.

They little knew in what contempt he held them, or how eager he was to release Stanley Sherrington from their clutches, or, it is very probable, they would have commenced upon him the same style of attack that they practised upon their unfortunate victims in the street.

"Welcome, brother," cried one half-inebriated fellow.

"Hurrah! for the new Mohock!"

"Three cheers for the new cannibal!"

Such cries, amid shouts of mad laughter, greeted him, as he walked up to an empty chair near Sherrington, and sat down.

"Sherrington," he said, "can you come away? I want you."

Sherrington shook his head.

"No," he said, "I dare not."

"Dare not!"

"Yes, indeed. It is the correct word. If any here saw in me any signs of quitting hurriedly there would be a revolt."

"And what the consequences?"

"My death, perhaps."

Rupert smiled.

"You are jesting," he said; "you make your Society more terrible than it is."

"Not I," replied Sherrington; "it is a fact. In

their mad fury they would set upon me, and without, perhaps, intending it, they would accomplish my destruction. What you have to say you must reserve until presently. Is it important?"

"It is a matter of life and death."

"Then as soon as I can escape from them I will listen to you," said Sherrington; "they are bent upon a strange expedition to-night, and until that is over nothing reasonable can be done."

"And what is their purpose, then, to-night?" asked Rupert Dreadnought.

"You know well, of course, the pretty village of Twickenham?"

"I do."

"Well, there is a grand ball to be given to-night at Lord Hawksworth's. The guests are expected to leave the rooms about midnight, and most of them, in order to reach their homes, have to pass along Love Lane."

"And are these tó be the objects of attack?"

"One section of them. There are six young ladies, who will attend the ball, who belong to the school kept close to Hawksworth House by Miss Primrose. They will, of course, be escorted home by some gay gallants, and upon these it is proposed to make an attack. The young ladies will be seized, carried to the river side, and conveyed across the water in boats."

"But this is nothing better than murder," said Rupert; "in this cold weather, and with only their ball dresses on, they will die of cold and misery."

"Ah, well!" cried Sherrington, "I have done my best to dissuade them, but with no effect. I am bound by the oaths of the Society to aid them, and so I am compelled to take my share in all their foolish pranks. I shall do my best to prevent mischief. *You* will second me, I am sure."

Rupert Dreadnought started in astonishment.

"I!" he cried, "I! What have I to do with it? I shall not think of accompanying them in their mad expedition."

Stanley Sherrington leaned over him and whispered in his ear—

"Don't be mad, Dreadnought. Don't speak so loud. You are talking treason. You don't know what a desperate set of fellows you are mixed up with. They stick at nothing. You are one of us for the time being and cannot recede."

"Cannot! I fear them not," said Rupert Dreadnought. "Against such a set of inebriate fools my sword would be quite enough to clear my way."

"Yes, yes, but do not risk it," replied Sherrington. "I have an idea. We can rescue these girls."

"How? Tell me," eagerly asked Rupert.

"Listen, and then you must quit my side," answered his friend. "Full of drink as they are, they will observe us. We are going to take two boats on the river."

"From what starting point?"

"From London Bridge. Tom Braxley—Tom the waterman, as they call him, supplies them. We shall be rowed up the river to Putney, and shall arrive there about midnight. On our journey——By the way, before I say more, do you know Tom the waterman?"

"I have never seen him, but I have heard my father speak of him as an honest fellow," replied Rupert.

"He is," said Sherrington, "and not the one to aid in any madcap folly that is likely to end in bloodshed or disaster of any kind. Take him into your confidence. Remain behind when we land, and I will slip back to you. We together, masked, will lead the watermen to the rescue and save the girls."

"Good. I understand your scheme well."

"Say no more now, then. Ah! what means that? I fear even now we are suspected."

A tall, ill-looking young fellow of brutal appearance, heavy-browed, heavy-mouthed, and unlike altogether the sort of being one expects to find in circles of refinement, had left his seat a moment before, and in a low whisper imparted some information to those at the little tables.

Then he rose again and quitted the room.

Sherrington was not taken aback.

He was a good and cool hand in cases of sudden danger.

Rising to his feet, he cried—

"Gentlemen and brother Mohocks,—According to our rules our new brother here has to make his appearance three times at our club, and to partake in at least one adventure, before being elected. This is his second appearance, and having heard from me what is proposed to be done to-night, he has agreed to accompany us."

Loud cheers followed these words.

They had no idea what signification they had.

All they cared to know was that their new comrade was about to join them in their madcap excursion.

Whatever suspicion the one who had quitted the chamber had sought to rouse in their minds was now at once dispelled, and when he re-entered the clock's voice—telling them it was ten—closed all further conversation.

"It is time to start," cried Sherrington. "Drain your glasses, gentlemen, and prepare."

Inebriated as they were, they at once started to their feet, and within a few moments they had taken from a large cupboard at one end of the vast room a number of masks and weapons of various kinds.

In a few moments all were ready, and they sallied forth into the street.

At the door stood Allan of the Glen, who, at a whisper from Rupert Dreadnought, sprang away and disappeared into the house.

The night was a very fine one, and as they neared the river they could see the moonlight shimmering brightly and gracefully upon the tiny wavelets of Father Thames, and casting a kind of unknown splendour upon the roof-tops of old houses, which, in the merry sunlight, looked dark and dismal enough in very truth.

Underneath the arch of London Bridge, where, not long before—in fact not very many hours before—Tom the waterman had had his conflict with the abductors of Helen Penraven, the young fellow was waiting, with three comrades and two fine boats.

Neither Tom nor his friends had the remotest conception who their employers were, or it is questionable whether they would have cared to carry them, but as it was these young gallants were soon seated and the boats flying over the moonlit river.

Sherrington and Rupert Dreadnought sat close to one another, and near Tom the waterman, who could consequently overhear all their conversation.

"Tell me, Rupert," said his friend, in a low tone, what want you with me to-night?"

"I want your aid again to find Helen Penraven."

"Have you any clue to her whereabouts?"

"None."

"Then how do you expect to find her?"

"I come to you for advice," said Rupert. "Now, all *I* know is *this*. Helen was seized last night by a number of masked men, one of whom placed her before him on a horse and rode away with her across the moor. At the roadside inn they changed their mode of conveyance, and placed her in a carriage. They then dashed away on the road to London, and from that moment I have lost the clue."

Sherrington smiled.

"And how, think you," he said, "can *I* unravel the mystery?"

"I do not fancy you can," replied Rupert, "but among the desperate spirits who compose your club may be some friends of Oscar Penraven."

"This I will discover for you," said Sherrington "I can see your drift; and depend on me to aid you in everything which lies in my power."

It may be imagined with what intense interest Tom the waterman listened to this conversation.

Here, at length, was a faint clue to the mystery.

Here, at any rate, he had found one of the friends of the captive young lady, if he had not discovered her whereabouts, and he determined to communicate with Rupert directly they landed at Twickenham.

It was approaching midnight as they reached the shore and the young men landed.

"Let us go in couples," said Sherrington, "and hide ourselves in the lane. We shall in this way avoid exciting so much suspicion."

The Mohocks, who, on this evening, were under his direction, at once obeyed, and it was not long before Rupert and Sherrington were left alone.

As soon as the coast was really clear, Rupert turned to Tom the waterman.

"Tom Braxley," he said, "I believe you and your fellows are brave; my father has told me as much."

"Your father, sir!" exclaimed Tom, in surprise.

"Yes, Earl Dreadnought, who is now, alas, no more!"

"Is the good earl dead, then?" said Tom, sadly. "Yes, he knew me well; and you then, sir—that is, my lord—are his son?"

"Yes, I am his son," said Rupert; "but we have no time now to talk of my poor father. I and my friend are here to prevent the perpetration of a great wrong, and to prevent, maybe, the shedding of blood. Those persons whom you have brought here are the Mohocks. They are about to assail innocent and unoffending people. Will you aid us in preventing such an outrage?"

"Yes, willingly," said Tom the waterman; "but we have no swords."

Rupert gave a low whistle.

In an instant a dark form rose from the bottom of one of the boats, and in another moment Allan of the Glen sprang ashore with four swords in his hand.

"Here are your weapons," cried Rupert. "Be brave, and follow our directions, and you have nothing to fear."

Rupert was in the act of adjusting his mask when Tom the waterman touched his arm, and whispered, hurriedly—

"My lord, we have no time now, and in the fight we may be separated. Come to my house, near London Bridge, to-morrow night, at any hour you name (ask for Tom Braxley, and anyone will tell you where to find me), and I'll give you information about a certain lady."

"Helen Penraven!" exclaimed Rupert, in astonishment and excitement.

"I know nothing of her name," said Tom, "but I saw her carried away last night, and——"

"Now then," cried Sherrington; "now then. The clock has struck the quarter to midnight. We shall be late."

As he spoke, he advanced a short distance down the dark lane.

"To-morrow night at ten expect me," said Dreadnought, and then, with Allan of the Glen, they passed on rapidly after Sherrington.

The house of Lord Hawksworth was soon reached.

The Mohocks had reached the place before them, and were concealed behind the hedges and in dark corners, but Rupert Dreadnought and his friends remained in one body under the shadow of a large hayrick which stood at the corner of Love Lane.

It was not long before the unsuspecting company began to issue forth from the house where they had been enjoying themselves.

For some time no movement was made among the desperadoes.

Presently, however, there emerged from the house six young ladies, each leaning on the arm of a gentleman, while an elderly, prim-looking person brought up the rear.

Their appearance was the signal for a general rush, and a series of yells more worthy of demon from the infernal regions than of human beings.

"The Mohocks! the Mohocks to the rescue!" was the cry, which brought terror into every female heart, while it caused the gentlemen to spring aside and draw their swords.

As Sherrington had calculated, the defenders of the young girls were quite ready to do their utmost, but the swords they wore were but light dress ones, not intended for serious battle, and in a few moments they were driven off, and the ladies at the mercy of their insane tormentors.

Each one was seized in the arms of one of the Mohocks, who had just succeeded in imprinting one kiss on the cheeks of their unwilling captives, when a diversion occurred which they little expected.

A loud outcry was heard, and the shrill shrieks of women resounded along the river's banks.

They were not long, however, left in the hands of their tormentors.

"To the rescue, to the rescue!" and like lightning Rupert Dreadnought and his brave fellows rushed to the scene of outrage.

The Mohocks little expected this.

This was evidently an organised attack upon them.

Such a thing had never before occurred to them.

However, they resolved to stand it out, for though their acts were cowardly towards the defenceless they were able also to stand their ground against armed foes.

They had no chance, however, and this they saw at once.

Compelled, of course, to relinquish their fair prizes, they found themselves attacked not only by Rupert Dreadnought and his stalwart allies, but also by the gentlemen whose swords they had before beaten down.

It was of no use now shouting their rallying cry.

Little availed now the encouragement of leaders, and within a few moments it was quite evident that flight or surrender would be the next necessity.

A peculiar exclamation from one of them decided this question, and in an instant, without any intimation, they turned and ran, with three of their members badly wounded, and one of their number carried in the arms of his comrades.

"Now, ladies," said Rupert, raising his hat, "we can safely leave you."

"Oh, no!" cried one (whom he had snatched from the embrace of a tall Mohock), as she clung to his arm, "oh, no, do not leave us. See us to our door. They will return if they see you depart."

"We will see the ladies in safety," said Sherrington, and so, much to the chagrin of their gallants, the young damsels were escorted to their homes by our heroes, who had now removed their masks.

As they neared the door of the house, Rupert's companion spoke.

They were walking last, and as he turned to glance at her, the moonlight was full upon her face.

It was a lovely face, and as Rupert gazed down upon it, her eyes seemed to gleam through and through him.

"I know you!" she said.

"Know me!" he exclaimed, in unfeigned astonishment.

"Yes. You are Rupert Dreadnought," she said, still looking up into his eyes.

The voice she said this in was wonderfully low and sweet, but there was something in it which thrilled to Rupert's heart.

Not pleasantly—not with love's sweet pain.

No, it was an undefinable sensation—a sensation almost of alarm.

"And what is your name, my little fairy?" he said, leaning slightly over her.

"My name?—oh, that matters not," she said, with light laugh "I must not tell. We shall meet again."

"Your Christian name, then. That will not harm you."

"Rosalie."

Oh! if Rupert had but known who it was who leaned upon his arm—whose life he had saved—who was living among a number of innocent girls!

Rosalie St. Aubyn, whom Oscar Penraven had met at the Poisoner's Revel!

Little did he dream who it was whose arm hung so gently on his own!

He would have gladly attempted to discover the mystery.

He had not much time for further converse, however.

They had reached the door of the school; the mistress thanked them, the young damsels pressed the hands of their preservers, and they were gone.

Rupert Dreadnought little knew what strange tracks he had trodden in, but still the gleaming eyes and the strange beautiful face of the young girl haunted him as he went!

As they expected, they found on reaching the river bank that the Mohocks had taken possession of the boats, and they had therefore to proceed to the next boat-house and return to London in hired wherries.

"To-morrow night at ten, remember," said Rupert to Tom the waterman, as they parted for the night. "I shall be with you to the minute."

CHAPTER XVIII.

TOM'S HOME ONCE MORE—A DISAPPOINTMENT—A GOOD HEART—THE DARK RIVER—TOM AND HIS NEW PATRON GO ON A PERILOUS ERRAND—THE OLD RUIN—THE DANGEROUS ASCENT—ON THE BRINK OF A DOUBLE PRECIPICE—THE VISION OF BEAUTY — ALLAN'S MOUNTAIN EDUCATION COMES INTO USEFUL PLAY.

THE clock had scarcely struck the hour of ten the following night, when two figures, muffled in cloaks, knocked at the rude door of Tom the waterman's dwelling

Business had been very slack that evening, and Tom was indulging in his usual hearty supper, as Agnes opened the door.

Tom at once sprang up as he saw two figures, suspecting to see but one.

He was naturally somewhat alarmed, for the mysterious figure, which he had seen only for a moment upon the night of the abduction of Helen Penraven, had been flitting about the house, and he knew that his enemies were capable of any crime.

As he beheld the strangers, therefore, he advanced towards the door, with his hand on his long knife.

"'I AM HERE, DEAREST,' CRIED RUPERT."

"Who are you?" he cried.

"Do you not know me, Tom?" exclaimed the familiar voice of Rupert Dreadnought.

"Ay, I recognise you now, my lord," replied Tom; "but who is your companion?"

"One of whom you need entertain no fear, my worthy friend," said Rupert, as he entered the waterman's house. "He is known as Allen of the Glen."

He is a friend and faithful servitor of mine. Tell me," he added, as Allan entered, and Agnes closed the door behind him, "what is it you have seen since I saw you?"

"I saw one of the masked strangers pass the bridge this night," said Tom the waterman, "but he was on horseback, and I could not follow. However, it proves to me that it is on the other side of the water that their haunt is."

"True; but tell me, since you talk now in enigmas," said Rupert, "how much you know."

Brifly Tom the waterman told the story of the abduction he had witnessed.

There was no longer any doubt remaining in Rupert's mind.

The coincidence of time and everything tended to prove that the girl who had thus forcibly been carried off was Helen Penraven.

"By heavens!" cried Rupert, with blanched lips, "this is a terrible blow; this losing of all clue to her whereabouts."

"But why not go openly to your enemy and accuse him?" said Tom the waterman.

"It would be useless," said Rupert Dreadnought; "he would simply deny all knowledge of the transaction, and I have no proof by which to confute him."

"The lady, I presume, is some relation of yours, my lord," said Tom, almost nervously.

Poor Tom!

His heart was soft as his arm was strong, and the bright face of the girl whom he had attempted to rescue from the masked strangers had haunted him day and night.

Wild dreams of ambition floated before his mind, and he saw himself winning his way to glory for her sake.

So he listened eagerly for his reply.

"No," returned Rupert Dreadnought; "she is no relation of mine. She is dearer, nevertheless, than life. She is my betrothed bride, and, more than that, the care of her is left to me by my father as a sacred trust."

Tom's heart fell as Rupert Dreadnought spoke.

His vision melted away at once.

She the betrothed of the rich, handsome, daring, young lord!

Of what use, then, was his mad fancy?

"We will start at once, my lord," he said, as he turned away. "I know the spot where they landed, and from that point we must track them."

Very few preparations were necessary.

Tom was soon indued in his rough coat, and in a few minutes they had reached the side of the river, and were pulling rapidly across its dark waters.

The clue which they had to follow was certainly a very slight one.

But they did not despair.

The neighbourhood surrounding the place of disembarkation was a thinly populated one, and the appearance of masked men would doubtless have attracted considerable notice.

Pulling straight across the Thames to the point, they drew their boat under the shadow of an old building, and creeping up into the light, appeared as if rising suddenly from the water.

The thoroughfare was a narrow, well-lighted one, and they were just debating as to the best mode of procedure, when a man suddenly emerged from a tavern, and walked hurriedly away.

"My lord," cried Tom the waterman, excitedly, "my lord, let us follow that man. I am certain, though now he wears no mask, that he is one of those who were engaged in the carrying off of the lady."

"Lead on, then," said Rupert; "but please remember that I am plain Master Dreadnought."

"The title of Earl of Dreadnought, of which no man need be ashamed," said Tom, warmly, as they hurried on.

"Truly; but until my father's wishes have been carried out I will not assume it. But come, let us separate here. We may be suspected if he discover us following him so quickly."

The man, however, seemed entirely absorbed in his own meditations.

He walked on straight and rapidly, looking neither to the right nor left, until, reaching a turning partially enveloped in gloom, he darted round the corner.

In an instant Allan of the Glen was after him.

He was not lost to view, and when Rupert and Tom came up, he was seen entering the door of a large, gloomy-looking house.

Allan, who was crouching in the shadow of the street opposite when the portal was opened, saw that the hall was full of armed men.

It was useless, therefore, for the moment to attempt a forcible entry.

Indeed there was no proof that it *was* the prison where Helen Penraven was confined, or that Oscar was in any way connected with its inmates.

At present, all they were acting upon was mere surmise.

Chance, however, gave them a method of discovering the truth, which they would have been long, indeed, in finding for themselves.

The street in which the house was situated did not properly deserve such an appellation.

It was a rough-looking lane, whose roadway was cut up by heavy waggons, and where the houses, few and far between, had a dismal and deserted look about them, as if there was a curse upon the vicinity.

Next to the house where the man they were following entered, was a building half in ruins, which seemed to be leaning against it in its decrepitude.

Years before it had been destroyed by a fire, which had almost entirely gutted it.

Now little was left but the bare walls and a staircase, which wound its tottering way up to the summit.

"See," said Allan of the Glen, "see yonder ruin. We can climb to the top, make our way to the other house, and see whether we cannot effect an entrance. The lights are all at the top of the house, and the summit of the ruined building overlooks one window."

The plan was a good one, albeit less feasible to their minds than to the wild mountain boy who had leaped after the goats from crag to crag of his native hills.

However, there was not much room for hesitation.

Tom the waterman was still certain that he had

seen the form of the man before, and even to discover who and what this man was would be to advance one step further on the track of the mystery.

Allan of the Glen led the way, and with slow and cautious steps they began the ascent.

The staircase, left open for years to the winds and rain, was very rotten and shaky, and every now and then birds and bats, startled by the unusual sounds, swooped out of dark corners, and went soaring away with shrill cries.

But there was no fear of discovery.

Not a soul was moving in the lane or the dark, murky, misty land which stretched between the ruined house and the river, and unseen and in safety the three adventurers reached the topmost landing.

Here a difficulty presented itself.

The staircase ended here abruptly, and a wall of some height rose all around them.

What was now to be done?

"Let me mount on your back," said Allan of the Glen, "I am the lightest and most used to climbing, and the wall will bear me the best."

In a moment he was standing upon the strong shoulders of the Thames waterman.

Hardly had he done so when he uttered a cry of astonishment and glided down to his former position.

He had never seen Helen Penraven, but he had heard from Rupert a full description of her beauties.

"She's there!" he cried.

"What! Helen Penraven!" exclaimed Rupert.

"Ah, that she is, Master Dreadnought," said the Scotch boy, whose heart leaped with joy at the thought of having been the first to make the discovery, "she's there, unless my eyes very much deceive me; mount on my shoulders and see for yourself."

In an instant Rupert had mounted and ascertained that Allan of the Glen was in no way mistaken.

Opposite the wall against which he was leaning was a room brightly lit up by a lamp.

As *he* was, therefore, in complete darkness, he could see all that was passing within, in spite of the bars which crossed the casement.

Helen Penraven was indeed there, sitting near the table on which was the lamp.

She was leaning her head on one hand while with the other she was turning over listlessly the leaves of a book.

Rupert felt his heart leap within him as he dropped down again by the side of his companions.

"She is there," he said, in a voice of subdued excitement, "and we must speak with her, but how?"

"I can creep along the wall," said Allan, eagerly, "that is nothing to me."

"Where *you* go *I* can go," returned Rupert; "something must be done, however, to enable us to ascend without each other's help. A double weight might crumble away this wall. I think I see a method by which we can ascend singly."

Drawing his sword he began knocking away at one of the bricks, from which time and fire had crumbled away the mortar.

In a few moments the brick slipped from its place, and fell, with a loud plash, into some water at the basement of the building.

By this means he soon formed a means of passage to the top.

The enterprise was truly a perilous one, for the width of the wall on which they had to pass was only a few inches, and on either side was a sheer precipice some forty feet in depth.

In an instant Rupert made up his mind.

"Allan," he said, "that wall will not sustain both. I shall go alone."

The Scotch boy, with his adventurous spirit, had looked forward with pleasure to this hazardous enterprise, and was disappointed sorely at this speech.

"It would be less dangerous for me than for you, Master Dreadnought," he said.

"No," said Rupert, "you and Tom must remain here and watch. Helen is there and I must speak with her."

So saying he leaned over, obtained a footing on the wall, which swayed beneath his weight, and began his dangerous journey.

The distance was not great, but it was impossible to walk erect, for the bricks moved under his feet, and he was in danger each moment of being hurled to destruction.

Stooping, therefore, he contrived to crawl quickly over, and, reaching the other side, he raised himself up by carefully feeling the wall; and, grasping the bars, was safely within reach of the casement.

He was now only a couple of yards from where Helen was sitting.

"Helen," he said, gently tapping at the window.

The young girl heard the tapping, but not the voice, and did not move from her position.

Bats and night birds had been tapping at the casement all night long.

"Helen," he cried, in a louder voice, and again he tapped more strongly.

The young girl heard the voice this time, and started up in wonder and alarm.

Could it be a spirit that was addressing her?

She knew the voice well, but how was it possible that Rupert Dreadnought could be near her?

One glance at the window, however, was enough to show that he was there in reality, and she sprang eagerly towards the casement.

It was evident in a moment that it would be impossible to rescue her that night or to speak loudly, and in a moment Rupert took a desperate determination.

"Helen," he said, raising himself so that his face almost touched the window, "Helen, resume your seat and read your book as if nothing had happened. Then I will break a pane of glass with the point of my sword. They will enter, probably, to see what is the matter. I will conceal myself, and when they are gone we can resume the conversation."

Helen at once understood his meaning, and though her heart was beating wildly in her bosom, she resumed her seat.

Drawing his sword, Rupert then dashed it through the window, splintering it so that it appeared as if the wind, which was very high, had sent a stone through it from the summit of the old wall.

In an instant after—almost before he had time to sheath his sword—there was a light in the window beneath, which showed to the watchers above the forms of several men ascending a staircase.

"Have a care, Master Dreadnought," cried Allan, "the ruffians are ascending towards the room, and, as I live, the one who ascends first is one of those who attacked me in the 'Golden Acre.'"

"Hush!" cried Rupert, "and keep behind the wall. They can see you from the window."

Through the open casement Rupert could now hear all that passed.

The door was flung open violently, and a man entered.

"What was that noise, Mistress Penraven?" he said. "Were you trying to break from prison?"

"No, indeed, it would be useless," said Ellen, "surrounded as I am by ruthless ruffians. Some one has flung a stone through my window, or the wind has broken it."

The man grunted some surly reply, and approaching the casement, peered out.

All was as still as death.

"It's a bat or something has done it," he said; "it can't be mended to-night. Will you change your room?"

"No; I'll remain here. Draw the curtain across it. That will do for me. I like this room, for I can see the river, and some little sign of life."

The man said no more, but sullenly quitted the room, and in a few minutes the flash of lamplight on the ruined wall showed that he had once more descended the stairs.

A moment after, and Helen Penraven reappeared at the window.

"Rupert," she said.

His voice could now be heard distinctly through the open window.

"I am here, dearest," he cried; "your hand, my sweet one, that I may kiss it."

The plump little white hand was at once extended, and devoured with kisses.

"Now tell me," said Rupert, tenderly holding the hand within his own, "now tell me in what position are you. That ruffian cousin of yours told me that in two days you would be his bride."

"He lied to you, Rupert."

"Thank heaven it *is* so," returned Rupert Dreadnought. "But tell me what has changed his determination so suddenly?"

"Not his own will, you may rely upon it," said Helen. "It *was* arranged that to-morrow I was to be married to him."

"Forcibly?"

"Of course," said the young girl. "You could not suspect that I should yield, no matter what pressure was put upon me. I was to be kept here; a priest was to be brought to me, and in this room I was to be made his wife."

"Curses on him!" muttered Rupert, as the young girl paused, overcome by emotion.

Horror and disgust filled her heart even at the mention of the fate which had threatened her, and was now only put off for a time, unless her lover should be enabled to rescue her.

"Proceed," pursued Rupert; "I am eager to hear more. You have not yet told me why he delayed his hideous design."

"Last evening when he was in this room telling me of his determination a man entered—the dark-visaged ruffian who was here but now.

"He came in without knocking.

"Oscar turned savagely towards him.

"'How dare you enter this lady's room unannounced?' he cried.

"'*When we are sent we need no announcement*,' returned the man.

"In an instant Oscar's manner changed, and, as the man handed him a letter, he opened it eagerly.

"His face altered as he read, and his brow again became as black as thunder.

"'Accursed be this interruption to my cherished hopes!' he said. 'Why could not this letter have been sent before, or not at all? I have traitors somewhere about me, Marksby.'

"The man shrugged his shoulders.

"'If you think *I* am a traitor, prove it,' he said.

"'Oh, no; you value your life too much to run the risk,' said Oscar.

"'And,' replied the ruffian, bowing with every appearance of humility, 'I love my master too well.'

"A grim smile overspread the features of Oscar Penraven.

"Then he turned to me.

"'Helen,' he said, 'I am compelled to leave you. You were to have been my wife in two days. I am summoned away from your side for a week. During that time reflect on what I offer you. Wealth—distinction—the position of a queen in the place of a weary waiting for happiness with one who may die a violent death long before the conclusion of the time which he is compelled by his vow to wait.'

"I made no reply.

"But he could see how full of joy I was at his words.

"The short reprieve which he was giving me, was Heaven, compared with the horrid prospect which had opened up before me; and as he leaned towards me and imprinted a kiss upon my lips, I had no time to prevent him."

"It would have been his last moment had I been near," said Rupert, fiercely.

"He left me then," continued Helen, "and I have not seen him since."

"Oh! that I could release you now," said Rupert, "this may be but some ruse upon his part. How many guard this house?"

"It is full of armed men," replied Helen; "an attack upon it, unless you were in numbers, would be but a mad risk."

As she was speaking, Rupert, forgetful of the fact that he stood on so frail a support, tried the strength of the bars.

They yielded not.

They at least were set in solid masonry and he saw at once that any attempt on his part to wrench them from their holdings would result in instant death to himself.

So he desisted.

"I will return to-morrow night, dear Helen," he said, "with force sufficient to wrest you from your captors. In the meantime, dearest Helen, be firm. Let nothing force upon you a consent. Even if they declare us to be in deadly peril trust them not. Put your confidence in Heaven, my love, and all will be well. Farewell, dearest, I go now to hasten my preparations for to-morrow."

The little hand was again covered with kisses; and then, with another "Good-bye, God bless you," the lovers parted.

The young girl drew as near to the window as she could, and gazed out, as her lover gradually and carefully withdrew, along the trembling and treacherous pathway.

When he joined his companions, who were eagerly awaiting his return, he waved his hand once more to the gentle girl, as she stood in the casement, and then hurriedly descended the stairs.

Next night, at this hour, a red flame ascended to the sky, and the whole of the dismal and misty country around the deserted house was awakened for the moment into life.

But before we describe how this happened, and what hideous treachery caused it, we must follow Rupert, and then Oscar, on their night wanderings.

CHAPTER XIX.

THE INN BY THE RIVER—THE CONSULTATION—THE HAGGARD STRANGER—THE HORROR OF A MOMENT—THE STRANGE COMPACT.

HURRYING away from the old house, Rupert Dreadnought and his companions made their way into the high road, and, weary and agitated, entered a small tavern which stood near the river, and, indeed, close to the stairs which had served them for a landing place.

Here they ascended the stairs, and passed into a room which looked out over the Thames.

This was the public room, but at the moment we speak of it, it appeared to be tenantless.

Wearily they threw themselves down by the fire.

"We are on a strange adventure, Master Dreadnought," said Allan of the Glen, "and I fear that we are only at the beginning of it."

"Not so," cried Rupert, "we *must* bring it to an end. I cannot bear this suspense. I will either release her at once or I will die in the attempt. This week shall see her freed, or I shall never live to carry out my father's instructions."

"And where is this enemy, this Oscar Penraven, now?" asked Tom the waterman.

Before Rupert could answer, the door opened and a man entered.

"What are your orders, gentlemen?" he said, at the same time glancing uneasily round the room.

The tired travellers did not observe this movement, but at once ordered some wine, which was promptly brought.

The man hesitated after he had been paid the score, and looked earnestly at a dark corner of the room, which concealed the opening of a recess.

But after a moment's hesitation he appeared to change his mind, and thanking the guests for a gratuity given him, and bidding them ring if they required anything, he quitted the room.

The conversation was at once renewed, though in a lower key than before.

"You were asking where this Oscar Penraven was," said Rupert Dreadnought; "I cannot answer you. All I can say is that he has received a mysterious summons which compels him to quit yonder house for a time, and leave his prisoner in peace. To-morrow night I must arm my servants and attack that place."

ALLAN OF THE GLEN.

"Why not call in the assistance of the constables?" asked Tom.

"Because, legally, I have no right to interfere," said Rupert Dreadnought. "She is the daughter of Sir Robert Penraven, the guardian left for her by him is Oscar Penraven her cousin, and from him, therefore, I have no claim to take her."

"But you *must* take her, or she will be lost, whoever she be," said a voice close at hand.

It was a strange, sepulchral voice, and the three men started round simultaneously.

The speaker was stranger still than the voice itself.

He was tall and thin, his face was pale as death, except where the scars of ghastly wounds presented themselves, and his clothes, which clung to him with the peculiarly tight embrace which seems to denote poverty, were torn and ragged.

It was his eyes which gave tone and life to his being.

Red—gleaming—fierce—ravenous as those of an animal, they seemed as if they penetrated through and through those upon whom he gazed.

Rupert Dreadnought gazed in some wonder at the strange apparition which so suddenly appeared before them.

"Pray, sir, whom am I addressing?" he said, after a moment.

"An enemy of Oscar Penraven," the stranger answered, "one who will hunt him to the death."

"If you can destroy him why do you not do so at once?"

The ghastly apparition smiled.

"No," he answered, "that would not be revenge enough for me. I will follow him like his shadow. I will thwart his plans. Ever when the cup of happiness is close to his lips I will dash it from him."

Rupert gazed at him curiously.

Was he really what he seemed?

Was he in truth the enemy of Oscar Penraven, or was this simply a ruse to get Rupert into his power?

"If you are, indeed, Oscar Penraven's foe," replied Rupert, "then you and I are brothers in arms, if I may so speak. But in these times it behoves one to be careful. How do I know that what you say is true?"

"And how do I know that what *you* say is true?" said the mysterious stranger, with a smile.

"I did not express my feelings at first for your benefit," replied Dreadnought. "I knew not of your presence when I was speaking to my friends, whereas *you* volunteered *your* statement."

"True, true," replied the ghastly stranger. "You are young, but you are full of prudence. But come hither to me a moment and I will reveal to you what will curdle the blood in your veins, and at the same time will cause you to place that implicit faith in me without which it is impossible for me to do you any service."

Rupert rose at once, and was about to follow his strange friend to the other corner of the room when an idea struck him.

"Tom, and you, Allan, also," he said, "leave me alone with this gentleman a moment. Remain close at hand within call."

The stranger watched their departure, and then staggered to the door to see if they were listening.

"It is unnecessary," said Rupert; "they are honest men."

"I have found so few in my time," said the other, "that I doubt every one. However, I'll come to the fire (it's very cold), and we won't detain your friends long. In the first place, am I right in supposing that you are Rupert, or, rather, Lord Rupert Dreadnought, son of the late Lord Desmond Dreadnought?"

"I am."

"And did your father die a natural death?" asked the mysterious man."

"He died of old age."

The other shook his head.

"No, no," he said, "it seemed so, but such was not the case. He died of the mysterious malady that carries off all our rich people—*he died of poison!*"

"Poison!" cried Rupert Dreadnought, excitedly. "How know you this unless *you* were an accessory to the crime?"

A smile of scorn wreathed over the features of the stranger.

"If you are so hot-headed and suspicious," he said, "nothing can be done. In regard to your half accusation I shall say nothing except that it is absurd; and if I am to be met in that way I cease my speech with you."

The manner in which this was spoken convinced Rupert Dreadnought that he had been too hasty.

"Forgive me, sir," he said, "but the thought that my poor father had died of poison nearly turned my brain. Proceed, and I will not interrupt you. Are you certain of what you say?"

"I am morally, though not practically, certain," said the stranger, "but when I have told you my own story you will say that this moral certainty is as good as positive proof. Listen."

The strange and terrible story which he unfolded to Rupert Dreadnought I shall not here narrate.

Let it suffice that as he spoke our hero watched him with eyes full of a stony horror—a face pale as ashes—while ever and anon muttered ejaculations fell from his parted lips.

When the ghastly stranger finished there was silence for a few moments.

"This is horrible!—most horrible!" cried Rupert Dreadnought; "it seems almost incredible that in the heart of a populous city like London such terrible things could be. But so it is—you astound me, and all I can say is that, while believing all you have told me, I am, notwithstanding, confounded."

"I pledge my word that every syllable of what I have told you is correct," said the stranger; "but now I have told you—have trusted you before hand, let me ask you for a pledge of secrecy. It would ruin all my plans were it known that I was in any way cognizant of the fearful facts which I have narrated to you."

"I solemnly pledge to you my word of honour, as a gentleman, not to divulge a single syllable of anything which you have told me," replied Rupert Dreadnought; "but tell me by what name shall I know you, and where are you to be found?"

The stranger hesitated for a moment.

Then he said—

"You can call me Mark Redfern. Here, for the present, is my home. When do you propose to attack the house?"

"At ten o'clock to-morrow night," said Rupert; "this neighbourhood then is quiet. Most of its quiet inhabitants are then asleep, and we shall be for some time at least undisturbed."

Mark Redfern, as he styled himself, paused and reflected for a few moments.

"This is a very hazardous matter," he said; "it is an offence against the law, and you may get the constables against you as well as your enemies. But still there is great danger in delay, and I will not counsel it. Be here, if it is possible, at half-past nine o'clock, and I *may* have a plan to suggest. As you imagine," he added, with a smile, "my plans are generally quiet. I prefer stratagem to open warfare."

"Very good," returned Rupert Dreadnought; "I will collect my forces and bring them to the spot. I and my two friends will meet you here at the hour you name; and now adieu. Consider your secret still your own, with the exception of *one* thing—you will now have one who has vowed before Heaven to destroy Oscar Penraven, and who will risk his life with yours to carry out the Oath of Vengeance!"

Rupert then quitted his ghastly companion, and in a few minutes more he and his friends were crossing the cold river.

CHAPTER XX.

OSCAR PENRAVEN AND THE CHIEF OF THE POISONERS—A NEW OBSTACLE—THE STORMY SCENE—OSCAR'S DEFEAT—HIS TREACHERY OUTWITTED.

WE must quit Rupert Dreadnought for a time, and follow Oscar Penraven's steps as he left the old house where Helen was confined, and made his way towards the spot where the sender of the peremptory missive awaited him.

This was no other than the Chief of the Poisoners—the Head of the Society which was the scourge and terror of London.

It was to the house where the Poisoners had held their revel that Oscar now directed his steps.

He found the Chief waiting for him in the little room where he had heard for the first time of the treachery of Gascoigne.

The Chief was alone as Oscar Penraven entered.

He greeted Oscar cheerfully; but in his manner there was something which spoke either of anger or of doubt.

"You have sent for me," said Oscar, coldly.

He was there on compulsion; he was bound to do the bidding of his superiors, but there was but one thought in his mind.

This was the lovely bride which he had been forced to leave.

He looked upon her as his bride, for although there was no chance of her yielding to his wishes, he never dreamed that anything could step between them when he was willing to use any amount of violence to secure her.

"Yes," said the Chief. "I have in the first place an important communication to make to you, and on the other hand I have an important mission for you to execute for the Society."

Oscar bowed in acquiescence as he seated himself close to the President's chair.

"In the first place, you have deceived our Society."

The President said this in a solemn voice.

Oscar started.

In his own heart he was utterly unconscious—evil-minded as he was—that he *had* been guilty of deception.

"In what way?" he said.

"You have a cousin," returned the Chief, "named Helen Penraven?"

"I have."

"She is possessed of an immense property?"

Oscar smiled.

"I believe her to be penniless," he said.

The Chief of the Poisoners eyed him narrowly.

"You will swear that she *is* so," he said inquiringly.

"I will not swear that she *is* so," replied Oscar, "I will swear that I believe her to be so."

"You are in error, then," said the Chief; "she is heiress to a hundred thousand pounds."

Oscar was visibly moved.

He had never known the fact before; and it made him all the more desirous to hasten on his marriage.

"You surprise me," he said; "I had no conception of this."

"I believe you," said the President; "but I have another thing to add to this—the Society does not demand her death."

Oscar turned pale.

He had not even thought of this hideous alternative in regard to Helen.

"I love her," he said.

"For herself alone?" suggested the President, with a sneer.

"Yes, for herself alone. In a few days I hope to be her husband."

The President frowned.

"You forget one important fact," he said, "our members are none of them permitted to marry until they have done five years' good service to our cause. Your attachment to this Society is only of short duration; it dates, indeed, only two years back."

Oscar bit his lip.

He began now to feel the tyranny to which he had willingly, with his eyes open, subjected himself.

"Why," he said, in a tone of irritation, which he did not attempt to conceal, "why is this act of tyranny?"

"You forget your vows," said the President, ironically; "when you accepted the position you hold you did not speak of this as tyranny. But enough, the marriage is impossible. Her money is ours, it belongs to the Society."

"I say she *has* no money," returned Oscar, doggedly.

"She is your cousin, the daughter of your uncle. How could it be that he, with all his wealth, should leave her penniless?"

"The money you speak of is already in the hands of the Society," replied Oscar; "therefore my adopted father's wealth is all disposed of. Where can this money, then, come from?"

"It is through a private will known only to a few," replied the Chief of the Poisoners. "Listen to me attentively and you will hear a strange story.

"Sir Robert Penraven, your uncle, had a son by a former marriage.

"This son, a wild, harum-scarum fellow even in his boyhood, was shipped away to India (when your uncle desired to contract a second marriage) and placed under the care of a gentleman in Calcutta of the name of Radford.

"To this son your uncle has by a private will left one hundred thousand pounds, which sum he kept separate from the rest of his immense fortune.

"In the event of this son's—Richard Penraven's—death, the hundred thousand pounds comes to Helen Penraven.

"Now this Richard *is* dead."

"You have proofs of this?"

"Yes; but it will not do to allow the world to consider him dead. He must live again."

Oscar started.

He did not quite understand the drift of the Chief's words.

"I do not understand you," he said. "Will you kindly explain yourself?"

"I will," replied the President. "It is easy enough to do so."

"In the first place," he said, "this man being dead the money goes to Helen and we cannot touch it."

"Yes."

"If, on the other hand, he is not dead, we can."

"I cannot see it."

"Well, of course the real heir *is* dead," continued the President. "We give *you* the mission of discovering a new one. Nay, do not interrupt me. I can make all the plan perfectly easy, perfectly comprehensible.

"This Richard Penraven would, if he were now alive, be about eight-and-twenty. Now our object is to discover some one about this age, one who knows India, and one who would have no objection to aid you in the fraud. We have done all this for you. Such a man exists already in our Society."

"And who is it?"

"Alford."

This was the one who, it will be remembered, was speaking to Lesbia at the "Poisoners' Revel," described in my first chapter.

"Ah! I know him well," said Oscar, "he is just the man required. But since you are going to rob him of his inheritance as soon as he obtains it, what is his inducement to aid you?"

"Simply this," replied the President; "we shall give him ten thousand pounds out of the hundred, and, his identity once established, he will immediately come in for three other legacies of large amounts, which we will not touch."

"Does he know of this scheme?"

"Not a word. It is for you to make him acquainted with it."

"And the proofs of identity. Since the real heir is dead, how can you prove he is alive again, and how can you establish his identity?"

Oscar catechised his chief as severely as was possible.

He had no liking for the task that was set him—a task, be it said, from which he could not shrink.

"In the first place," replied the President, "I and one other, alone, know of the death of this young fellow.

"It was a disgraceful death, which alone, however, saved him from a shameful punishment.

"I, by accident, I need not say how, have become the possessor of the whole of the papers necessary to establish his claim to the properties.

"These I will place in your hands at once."

As the Chief said this he rose, and, approaching a bureau, took out some papers.

"Here," he said, returning to the table, "here is, in the first place, the certificate of his birth; here is a memorandum in his father's handwriting speaking of a peculiar birth-mark. Here is a copy of the will in the possession of Mr. Gregory Bramble, of 4, Grays' Inn Square, London; and here are correct copies of letters received by Mr. Bramble from your uncle, from young Richard, and from the gentleman in Calcutta in whose care he was placed. He has only now to present himself, with a forged letter of introduction from Mr. Radford."

"I see; and where is Alford now?"

"Here is his address."

"And what is to be *my* reward?"

"In that case," said the President, "I will see that the Society waives the celibate clause in your case, and you will be free to marry Helen Penraven when you choose."

"When, *as you fancy*, you have robbed her of all she is worth," thought Oscar.

"Very good," he said, aloud; "I will start on my mission at once."

He rose as he spoke, gathered up the papers, and saying—

"In three days I will report what progress I have made," quitted the room.

"He is an unwilling worker," said the President to himself, as Oscar departed; "but for his own sake he will work with a will."

CHAPTER XXI.

THE CURSE OF THE GUILTY.

The demoniacal smile which played on the features of Oscar Penraven as he left the old house by the river which had lately been the scene of mad revelry, showed plainly that he had some secret buried deep in his heart—some secret which not even the Chief of the Poisoners was a sharer in.

His plans, for the present, were entirely upset.

He had hoped, before many hours had passed, to clasp to his breast sweet Helen Penraven, either as his willing or his unwilling bride.

Now, however, it depended entirely upon the success of his mission whether she should be his bride or not.

With so sweet a prize in view, it may be imagined that he felt an inclination to deceive even the dread tribunal.

But this was a plan more easy to dream of than to realise.

Had Helen loved him, and been willing to become his wife, it would have been far different.

As it was, however, a bride who had been forced to his arms, would not be likely to do much to assist him, and he at once cast from him as impossible and absurd all attempts at deceiving the Poisoners.

Without hesitation, therefore, he proceeded towards the house where he expected to find Alford.

Alford was a strange man.

He had, as we have seen, a certain position among the Poisoners, and had been present at every revel which these demons in human shape had taken part.

He had brought money into the hands of the diabolical confederation.

Yet he subsisted only on rewards!

It was, nevertheless, in a comfortable room that Oscar Penraven found Alford sitting.

The latter started in some wonderment as Oscar entered.

"*The third hour and the Cross*," said Oscar Penraven, quietly.

Alford smiled.

"The hour of the Cross is far distant let us hope," he said. "I see you come from the Chief—not on any private errand?"

"You are right," said Oscar. "I come on strange and mysterious business."

"Sit you down by the fire, then," rejoined Alford, "take some of yonder wine—it contains none of our ingredients—and begin your story."

Oscar did as was suggested, and, in a few minutes, began his narrative.

The listener started at several points, but otherwise retained his composure, and did not speak a word.

Then he said—

"And what is the name of this person whom I am expected to personate?"

"Richard Penraven."

At these words Alford started visibly, and sprang with a ghastly smile from his chair.

GIVEN AWAY WITH Nos. 7 & 8 OF] [" RUPERT DREADNOUGHT."

"THE NIGHT DUEL."

RUPERT DREADNOUGHT.

"'I DEMAND THE SURRENDER TO US OF HELEN PENRAVEN!' CRIED RUPERT."

"Richard Penraven!" he cried.
"Yes."
"'Tis well; he shall be personated by me."
"'Tis to your interest to do so."
"I know it."

"You will find it somewhat difficult to personate Penraven, I should think," said Oscar. "However, I will do all that lies within my power to assist you."

Nos. 7 and 8. ONE PENNY THE TWO NUMBERS.

NOTICE.—With this Number is Given Away a Coloured Picture, entitled, "The Night Duel."

"Good! then, with the proofs you will give me, I shall be easily able to personate him, and obtain his wealth. I knew him so well that I am aware of all his peculiarities, his ways of speech, and his manners of life. Oh, doubt me not. I shall be successful."

"I fancy the scheme *is* well laid," replied Oscar, "and there is only one matter now to be settled. You must write me a letter, saying you are expected in London—say to-morrow—date it back a few days—ask me to call on Mr. Gregory Bramble, and so on, and I will take you on the second day to see him. But in regard to handwriting?"

Alford smiled strangely.

"Oh," he said, "I am an excellent imitator of handwriting. I fancy I shall have no difficulty in imitating that of Richard Penraven."

"And then the birth-mark? what about that?" asked Oscar.

Again that quiet, strange smile.

"That also can be managed," said Alford. "I don't do things by halves. Give me the papers; let me study them carefully, and by to-morrow you'll find me so transformed that you won't know me. But, by the way, I ain't specially liberally supplied with money at the present moment. You had better give me some."

Oscar shook his head.

"No," he said; "you are not doing this for me, but for the Society. You must apply to our Chief. It is for him you work; it is from him you must obtain the money of which I am to be robbed."

Alford mused a moment.

Then he said—

"This is a very pleasant little arrangement, I have no doubt, and, as far as I see, is likely to be very profitable, and so on, to me; but there is a very *un*pleasant and very *un*profitable affair mixed up with it, which none of you, perhaps, have looked at."

"And what is that?"

"*A murder.*"

"A murder!" echoed Oscar.

"Yes; I will explain to you briefly," said Alford. "When Richard Penraven arrived in India, he fell in love with a young girl named Rose Allerton; she was then only sixteen, and extremely beautiful. He married her, and within six months she fled with an officer. In the heat of passion, he gave chase, and meeting the seducer, shot him through the heart. The officer had a friend with him, who swore to be avenged. His vengeance was stopped by the news that Richard Penraven's body had been found in the river; but now, if I assume the character, I may also assume a most unpleasant responsibility. If I *am* Richard Penraven, I am liable to the deadly hate of this officer's friend; if I am not, I am an impostor."

"This I will represent to the Chief," said Oscar, "and since this will compel me to see him, I will also ask for the money. And now adieu till to-morrow night."

On the following evening Oscar presented himself at the appointed time.

Seated in a chair by the fire was a man of whom he had not the slightest recollection.

He was thin, pale, with a white, cadaverous face, short black hair, and no vestige of the luxuriant beard and moustache which were the characteristics of Alford.

Yet this *was* Alford.

Oscar for a moment was puzzled.

"You don't know me, I see," said Alford; "I think the disguise is good."

"It is perfect, and if it is like the original," said Oscar, "there can be no doubt about its success. *Your* identity is entirely sunk. But there is another difficulty, which has only just presented itself."

"And what is that?"

"There has just arrived in London an Indian nabob, who was once a bosom friend of Richard Penraven."

Again, this third time, the strange and satanic smile crossed Alford's face.

"Oh, he will be sure to know me. The story of my death can be easily explained to him. Well, and about this officer's friend—this one who has sworn my death?"

"If you allude to Colonel Dellmarr, he is in India," said Oscar; "it will take more than six months for the news to travel thither, and six months for him to come back to England. In the meantime, you will have secured the property and your reward, and resumed your former self."

"You are sure he is in India."

"By the last mail he was said to be far in the interior."

"*Very much so,*" muttered Alford to himself, with a peculiar intonation.

Then he added aloud—

"To-morrow, then, we will visit the lawyer and this nabob. Is he called Ramsetjie Jehador Khan?"

"The same."

"Where is he?"

"He is at a private house near Whitehall. I can give you the address to-morrow. I expect one at twelve; and in the meantime, farewell."

Alford watched him out with curious glances, and as the door closed, his whole face seemed to be lightened up with a new light.

"Oh, Heaven!" he cried, "I lived but for vengeance, and until now all chance of it has evaded me. Living near the one who deceived me—seeing her day after day, I have not dared to reveal myself—have not dared even to whisper the doom which is coming—coming inevitably for my enemies. Now all is changed. I shall soon handle a fortune which will enable me to punish the guilty, and then, Alford, even happiness may be yours. The curse I years ago called down upon the guilty is now about to fall heavily upon them."

CHAPTER XXII.

THE ATTACK ON THE OLD HOUSE.

Before we proceed to describe what success Alford attained with Mr. Gregory Bramble, we must follow once more the fortunes of Rupert Dreadnought, whose whole mind and soul was now wrapped up in the one idea—the saving of Helen Penraven.

It will be remembered that when Rupert parted with the strange, ghastly figure at the tavern, it was with an understanding that they should meet at the same place at half-past nine, and that those who accompanied Rupert should make their way towards the old house, and wait there for his coming.

Rupert was punctual to the hour, and found his strange and ghastly friend already waiting for him.

"Well," he said, "what cheer? Are your men with you?"

"Yes. They are waiting in the shadow of the old house," replied Rupert Dreadnought; "but is there any method of arranging matters without force?"

"I fear not; but I have contrived so that you will not be disturbed, I fancy," he answered, with a quiet smile. "Yet you must proceed as if you were unaware of this. Make as little disturbance as possible; and be as quick as you can, also, in your movements. One thing of importance, however, I have discovered."

"And what is that?"

"Oscar Penraven is not returned."

"That is well," said Rupert; "not that I desire not to meet him, but in such a position as this, it is best that he should be absent."

"Let us be going, then," said the strange man.

"Us!" repeated Rupert; "are you, then, coming?"

"I am," said the other, smiling. "I shall be glad to see the discomfiture of your enemies."

In a few minutes they were *en route* for the place of Helen's confinement.

Arrived here they made their way into the old house, where they found Tom the waterman, Allan of the Glen, Stanley Sherrington, and others waiting for them.

The first move to be made was to knock at the door of the house and demand to see Helen.

Rupert Dreadnought and Stanley Sherrington alone were to show themselves at the door, but if a refusal was given by those within, the others (who were to lie in ambush) were to rush forward and make a dash into the hall.

There was very little chance of their being able to make an entrance into the house by fair means.

But it was worth while to make the attempt.

With a beating heart, therefore, Rupert raised the heavy knocker of the door, and gave a loud and ringing summons on the iron plate.

In an instant the door was opened, but a heavy chain still crossed from the lock to the wall.

A shaggy head was protruded.

"What want ye?" asked the owner of the shaggy head, in a gruff and surly voice.

"You have a lady here—Mistress Helen Penraven—we desire speech with her."

The eyes of the shaggy-haired individual glared in fierce curiosity at the speaker.

"It is impossible," he said.

"Why so?"

"Because my master is from home, and we can't admit any one when he's away."

"Then you confess she *is* here?"

"Of course she is. She's here, and likely to remain so. Is that all you require?"

"Yes; and we *must* see her!" cried Rupert Dreadnought, angrily.

The man chuckled.

"*Must!*" he said. 'Oh, we don't know that word here. You *can't*, is my answer; so good-night."

Saying this, he was about to close to the door, when, according to a preconcerted arrangement, one of Rupert's men thrust the hilt of his sword into the aperture.

In an instant the man within the house saw that it was a preconceived plan to attack the house and release the prisoner.

A long, sharp cry rang out from the whistle which he raised to his lips, and in a moment more the hall was full of armed men.

Then followed a strange scene.

Not a blow was struck by one man on another, not a shot fired.

It was merely a struggle to reclose the door.

In this the attacking party had the advantage.

Those within had not anticipated any assault, while the besiegers had brought with them some axes, with which now they vigorously attacked the gate.

Allan of the Glen, with a short, stout hatchet, hacked and hewed vigorously at that point in the woodwork of the door where the bolt of the chain was fixed, and those within soon saw that it would of a necessity come to a hand-to-hand fight.

A few shots were now fired from the inside of the house, some at random through the door, and others through the open space right into the thick of the besiegers, slightly wounding more than one of them, but making no perceptible difference in the vigour of the assault.

At this moment, a number of dark figures, attracted by the noise of strife, made their appearance, and approached the house.

"We shall be foiled, after all!" cried Rupert Dreadnought, in a tone of disappointment. "Yonder come the constables."

The strange man whom he had met at the inn turned sharply round.

"Have no fear of them," he said. "I will arrange matters easily."

So saying, he darted away in the direction of the approaching figures, and was soon lost among them.

The constables stopped in a body, had, as it seemed, a hurried conference, and then moved rapidly away.

Whoever Rupert's new friend was, he evidently had power with *them*.

The woodwork at last, beneath the vigorous attacks of Allan and the others, gave way, and the door with a sudden rush burst inwards, disclosing a crowd of well-armed and resolute-looking men.

One of these advanced.

"Now then," he cried, "what seek you? Are

you mad, thus to attack a gentleman's house in the night?—or is your object plunder?"

"You have here a lady captive against her will," said Rupert. "I demand the surrender to us of Helen Penraven."

"Sir Oscar Penraven, her cousin, and our master, the guardian in whose care she has been left by his late uncle, is not here," answered the spokesman; "but he has left her in our charge, and with our lives we will defend our trust."

The man spoke with a bold eye, far worthy of a better cause.

It was evident the struggle would be a fierce one.

"You refuse even to allow me speech with her?" said Rupert Dreadnought.

"I do."

"Then your doom is sealed by your own hands," cried the young lord. "On, my friends, cut your way through them."

As he spoke, he rushed forward, and vigorously attacked the spokesman of the defending party.

No further words were exchanged.

Nothing was heard now but the clashing of swords, the hard breathing of the several combatants, the groans of the wounded, the cheering cries of leaders.

The attacking party were evidently the strongest, and by degrees the defenders of the house were driven back to the staircase.

The hall now presented a hideously changed appearance.

The balustrades and the furniture were broken, while men lay dying or dead upon a floor slippery with blood.

The longer the battle raged the more fierce became the combatants.

Their faces red with excitement, their eyes wildly gleaming, their fierce exclamations, made them seem more like demons than human beings.

Seeing that the contest was going so entirely against them, the leader of Oscar's men, who had as yet succeeded in escaping without a wound, in spite of the brilliant swordsmanship of Rupert Dreadnought, stooped down and whispered to two of his men.

They both at once darted upstairs.

At the first landing, however, they separated, one hurrying upwards towards the top of the house, while the other, taking a back staircase, descended to the basement, let himself out of a back window, and hurried across the dark, waste land which lay between the house and the river.

This one had gone for reinforcement, while the other had proceeded to the room where Helen Penraven was confined, and trembling with mingled terror and hope, as the sounds of deadly strife were borne to her ears.

Suddenly, in the midst of the combat, when the little band of besiegers were forcing their way up the side stairs to the first landing, a curl of thick smoke ascended from the basement, and rolled blindingly among friends and foes.

It was black smoke, mingled with a white, hot steam.

It told its own story.

The old house was on fire!

A deadly horror invaded the heart of Rupert Dreadnought.

The conflagration would quickly spread among the dry and rotting timbers, and, while they fought below, Helen, at the summit of the old building, would be completely at the mercy of the flames.

"Hold!" he cried in a loud voice. "This is madness. While we fight, the lady for whom we combat will die a terrible death!"

"Fear not," replied the leader of the defending party, savagely. "She will be saved. We see plainly through this ruse. Your men have fired the house. She will be all the more certain to escape your hands."

It was useless to argue with such a man at such a time.

"On—on, my friends!" cried Rupert, desperately. "One grand effort now, and we will drive these hireling hounds before us. On—on, for your lives, and for Helen Penraven!"

Incited by these words, and the example of their young leader, the besiegers concentrated their strength for a grand and final effort, although among the ranks of the combatants could no longer be seen the forms of Allan of the Glen or Tom the waterman.

There was nowhere to be seen any trace of them.

Cruel as were the thoughts which invaded Rupert's mind, however, he had no time to think of them, or to inquire if indeed they *had* met their death, or were fighting elsewhere, or had been carried wounded away.

Eagerly dashing onward, the gallant little band soon made good their footing on the landing, for the retainers of Oscar Penraven were fast losing heart.

Not only the smoke now, but the heat, betrayed the spread of the conflagration, and while Rupert and his friends had the street open to them and could fly at any moment, they were being driven to that portion of the building which was being rapidly seized in the eager maws of King Flame.

At every pause there was a quickly whispered conference.

But Rupert did not permit them much time for converse.

As they became less eager for the fray, so the eagerness of the victorious besiegers increased, until Oscar's men found themselves pressed up against a huge doorway which was burning to the touch.

"Surrender!" shouted Rupert, "further battle is a mad waste of blood."

He had hardly spoken when the door burst open as if rent by an explosion, and tongues of red and yellow flame lapped over the heads of the combatants.

Some of the unhappy men fell backwards amid the smoke and the steam and were suffocated, others ran to the staircase windows and threw themselves madly out.

Rupert, however, yielded not an inch.

"Now!" he cried to Stanley Sherrington, who had throughout fought by his side, "now to save Helen."

Stanley detained him.

"Stay," he cried, "it is madness to ascend higher. You will be going to certain death."

"Stanley," exclaimed Rupert Dreadnought, "I know not what you say. What if death does await me? If *she* is dead life is no longer of use to me. Follow or remain as you please."

Without waiting for further parley, he broke from his friend and rushed up the stairs, which were almost invisible for the dense smoke, in spite of the red glare of the flames and the light of the frequent lamps in niches of the wall.

He noticed neither the smoke nor the heat.

All he thought of was that his beloved Helen was above in extreme danger, and that, if he desired to save her, now was his only chance.

He was not long in reaching the top of the house, and here, of necessity, he found the atmosphere cool and refreshing.

The danger was below.

There all chance of escape seemed likely to be cut off.

Rupert cared not for this.

He knew well that the window of Helen's bedchamber overlooked the ruins.

There being now no danger in discovery, the bars could easily be forced from within, and he could bear her in safety along the wall to the ruins.

But he sought in vain.

Every room was empty.

The one where he had before seen her was the last he entered.

There was not even a trace of her.

The window was broken and the bars smashed away, but all was dark, gloomy, horribly silent without.

What could it mean?

What but that Oscar Penraven had received intelligence of the attack, and had carried away by the only means that was left to Rupert to secure her safety.

Vainly he sought and resought, vainly he cried aloud from the window.

There was no reply.

Helen was gone; and between her and him again a wide gulf was fixed.

He was in doubt as to whether or not he could make good his escape by the wall or by the staircase, when the question was decided abruptly for him.

There was a terrific crash—then a tremendous rush of smoke and flame.

The staircase had fallen in!

Rupert lost no time in making his way to the window and letting himself out; he crept swiftly, though carefully, along the wall.

It was not long before he descended the ricketty stairs and reached the front of the house, where his friends, huddled in a crowd, were wondering at his disappearance, and making conjectures as to his probable fate.

To his eager questions none could give a satisfactory reply.

No one had seen anything of Helen Penraven, and as for Allan of the Glen, he had been seen to stagger away as if badly wounded in the very beginning of the fray.

Of Tom the waterman no one had seen or knew anything.

TOM THE WATERMAN.

Rupert, sick at heart, turned away from the scene of strife.

After all this bloodshed, what had been achieved?

Helen was, to all appearances, more lost to him than ever.

As he moved away with such feelings as these in his heart, his ghastly friend of the inn clapped him on the shoulder.

"Rupert Dreadnought," he said, "never give way to despair."

"There is nothing else before me," said our hero; "Helen is lost."

The stranger bent forward and whispered in his ear.

Rupert started; the rich blood flew to his cheeks, and he cried in a loud voice—

"Friends, this way! Follow me!"

With these words he hurried along the dark street, and made his way towards the banks of old Father Thames.

CHAPTER XXIII.

A STRANGE DISCOVERY.

As we are now approaching the event which formed the great crisis of this part of Rupert Dreadnought's life, we will return for a moment to Oscar Penraven and Alford, and see how they fared with Mr. Gregory Bramble.

Exactly at the hour named Alford and Oscar presented themselves at the office of the lawyer.

Alford's disguise was exactly as it had been the day before, and Oscar could not but admire the wondrous change he had also made in his manner.

He seemed altogether a different person.

Mr. Bramble advanced towards Alford when he entered, and shook him with such cordiality by the hand that Oscar Penraven was taken quite aback.

"I am glad to see you, Sir Richard," cried the man of law, "*very* glad to see you! We had all given you up for dead."

"Yes, it was so reported," replied Alford. "The wish was father to the thought in many cases. But you see I *have* survived in spite of all."

"Yes, yes, I see, Sir Richard. Sit down, and I will explain what is to be done."

And the fussy little lawyer took his way back to the fire.

This conversation caused a strange sensation in the mind of Oscar.

The impostor, whom *he* himself was introducing, was spoken of as "Sir Richard."

The other words, he was helping another to step into his titles.

Strange to say, this thought had never before entered his mind.

But the fear it brought with it was only momentary.

What mattered it?

The money once secured, Alford was Alford again, and all would be well.

The story of the death could be reiterated, a clever impostor would be supposed to have carried off the cash, and so Sir Oscar would be Sir Oscar once more.

The lawyer and the supposed Richard Penraven had a very earnest consultation for some time.

This consultation surprised Oscar more than anything.

In every little detail of Richard's life Alford was well posted up.

He remembered his school days; his boyish pranks; his parting with Sir Robert, his father; his journey to India.

"He is a clever rogue," thought Oscar.

As for the lawyer, he expressed himself quite satisfied, mentioning only that two persons present at his birth would be forthcoming in a few days, and that they would end the matter.

"You are about as good an impostor as could possibly be manufactured," said Oscar, as they quitted the house, and walked in the direction of Alford's dwelling.

"You think so?" said the latter, with his quaint smile.

"Yes, I do, indeed; but how will you contrive about the birth mark?"

"I can arrange for that," he said, quietly. "You can have little faith in my cleverness if you fancy I cannot settle *all* the little details. However, there *is* one thing which is rather awkward—far more awkward than the finding of the birth mark."

"And what is that?"

"About the title."

"What about it?"

"How are you to arrange to recover it? I shall be called Sir Richard, no matter where I go."

"Ah! but we must make up some account of your death. That can be easily done, and then I shall be Sir Oscar again."

Alford smiled.

"Ah! I see you have thought of all likely difficulties. Very well; directly Bramble sends for me again I will let you know."

The coolness of Alford discomposed greatly the mind of Oscar Penraven.

He could not for the life of him determine its meaning, except that in some way or another he meant to act the part of a traitor.

One thing, however, he consoled himself with.

The loss of money by Alford's treachery would not fall upon him, but upon the Society, and the task of punishing him would also be the task of others.

On the second day after his interview with Alford and Bramble he received a letter from the former.

It was short and to the purpose:—

"MY DEAR COUSIN,—Please do me the favour of calling on me to-morrow at one, as I have affairs of importance to communicate to you.

"Yours sincerely,

"RICHARD PENRAVEN."

"Richard Penraven! confound the fellow," exclaimed Oscar; "but I suppose he must act thus to keep up the character."

Oscar was in no good humour.

News had reached him in regard to Rupert's doings at the old house which had roused his anger, the more so that he was unable at present to do anything against him.

He was eager, therefore, to rid himself of the business now on hand, which was of so little advantage to himself, and at exactly the appointed hour he made his appearance at the house of Alford.

He found that worthy sitting by the fire smoking, and still wearing the disguise which he had adopted since the commencement of the drama in which he seemed to play so willing and so capital a part.

"Good morning, cousin Oscar," he said, as young Penraven entered.

Oscar reddened.

"A truce to folly when we are together," he said. "I came anxious to know all the details of this business, for I have matters which will take me away shortly."

Alford pointed to a chair.

"Sit down, Oscar Penraven," he said, sternly, "and I will give you the details you require. They may perhaps surprise you."

Oscar sat down.

From Alford's manner he expected some strange revelation.

"In the first place," said he, "I have succeeded beyond all my expectations. The money is absolutely in my hands. I have so thoroughly proved to Mr. Bramble that I *am* the proper person that he has delivered over to me the entire control of the hundred thousand pounds which would have been my sister Helen's."

"Curse the fellow's impudence," thought Oscar. "His sister, indeed!"

But he did not interrupt him.

He was too anxious to hear more to do that.

So he merely said—

"Well, then, nothing remains to be done but to hand over to the Society ninety thousand pounds, reserving ten for yourself. This money would have been mine, but I regret it not, since by adhering to our rules a greater fortune still is mine."

"Stay," said Alford; "the Society will not have a farthing from me."

"Not a farthing! And pray why?"

"For a simple reason, because I do not feel disposed to part with what is my own!"

Oscar sprang up.

"This passes all bearing," he said; "you must be mad to think I would countenance such folly. If you intend to carry out this imposture thus shamefully for your own benefit, I shall so inform our Chief, and a terrible vengeance will be taken upon you."

Before Oscar could proceed to the door, Alford had sprung up, and, locking the door, put the key in his pocket.

His manner was cool and determined.

"Sit down, Oscar Penraven," he said. "You have not yet heard all, nor do you know yet the only terms upon which I shall permit you to quit this room. Waste no more time, but listen."

Oscar, lost in wonder, and seeing the uselessness of resistance, did as he was directed.

"Go on," he said; "play the farce out."

"You will find it anything but a farce," answered Alford. "The way I have disposed of my money is this (for I have already disposed of it); I keep fifty thousand myself, the other fifty I give to Helen Penraven. As long as she is *not* with you, or does not marry you, the interest of this money is at her command. If she marries Rupert Dreadnought, or any other person of whom I approve, she will have the entire fifty then, and in her own hands."

"And why, pray, have you made this arrangement, and why do you refuse to give up the money to those who have enabled you to obtain it?"

"Because of many things," returned Alford; "but first of all, *because I am in very truth Richard Penraven, your cousin!*"

Oscar fell back in his chair in utter amazement.

The manner in which the words were spoken was so impressive and so truthful that he could make no answer.

Was it indeed true?

Had this man been biding his time, and had they unwittingly helped the rightful heir to his property?

"Yes," continued Alford, "I came from India under a ban. I knew nothing of my father's will; I fancied that he deemed me dead, and that I must live a disguised and forgotten existence. I joined the Poisoners to watch you, not to betray or aid the Society. Now I relinquish it; my birthright is proved by your aid undoubtedly. My birth mark, known to many, has settled all in my favour. I *am* your cousin, Oscar, but from you and your friends I will defend my sister."

"Are you mad, or do you in truth mean me to believe you?" said Oscar, in wonder — half in fear.

"I speak the truth. I defy you to disprove it," said Alford (I must continue for the present to call him so).

"I shall so endeavour," returned Penraven. "I will not run the risk of death—a traitor's death, too —for your sake. I shall at once inform the Chief of the Poisoners of the failure of their scheme and your imposture, and leave them to deal with you."

Terrible, indeed, he intended in his own heart the punishment to be.

To permit Alford to live now would destroy all his hopes in regard to Helen.

Real brother or not, he had been recognised and welcomed by those who would certainly be taken as judges in the matter, and he would therefore have far more voice than he in the guardianship of Helen.

"Stay," cried Alford; "there is one thing more I have to tell you."

And as he spoke he walked to the locked door, and put his back against it.

"You are aware, Oscar Penraven," he said, "that I am a good shot?"

"I am."

"Well," he added, taking from his pocket a double-barrelled weapon, "you have your sword; but one step towards me, until I give you permission, seals your doom. You must swear to me, ere you quit this room, that for four days you will keep the truth from this Society. Refuse, and you die!"

"And think you," said Oscar, "that there is no punishment for such an open murder?"

Alford smiled.

"I should provide against that," he said; "when you were dead I should wound myself in the arm, and place your blood-stained sword by your side. I should then tell everyone that you had treacherously tried to assassinate me, and that I shot you in self-defence."

Oscar was in a complete trap.

There was no use in thinking of drawing his sword and rushing at his enemy.

Ere he could reach him the ball would have sped.

For once Oscar felt himself completely beaten.

"You have conquered by main force," he said. "I *must* make the promise."

"It is no promise," said Alford, sternly, "no such light thing that I require of you. You know the oath—the terrible oath you took when you bound yourself to the Society of Poisoners. You must take an oath quite as binding—quite as terrible. Repeat it after me."

Slowly and methodically Alford enunciated the words of an oath, from the breaking of which even a demon would have shrunk, and Oscar clearly and distinctly spoke them after him.

"Curse you!" he said, as Alford concluded, "curse you! I will yet be revenged for this."

"You may be," returned Alford, "but not in the way you are proposing to yourself. I have never betrayed the Society. I shall request permission to withdraw, and you will see how little then your anger will avail against me."

Oscar rose.

"I desire to hear no more," he said; "for four days you are safe. Now let me go, but remember my undying hatred will follow you for ever."

Alford unlocked the door and suffered him to go.

A smile of hateful anger and triumph wreathed itself over Oscar's pale lips, as he issued out into the street.

"I have promised," he said, "not to betray you to the Society. I have not promised *not to kill you with my own hand!*"

Then, shaking his fist savagely at the house, he departed.

CHAPTER XXIV.

ON THE TRACK OF THE CAPTIVE.

MY readers must by this time be anxious to know what has become of Helen Penraven, who so mysteriously disappeared on the night of the attack of Rupert Dreadnought and his friends upon Oscar's house.

Rupert, as may be imagined, was in a state of intense excitement and dismay upon discovering the disappearance of his beloved Helen, and the probable disaster which had befallen his two faithful servitors, Allan of the Glen and Tom the waterman.

All search for them in the vicinity of the old house was quite useless, for not a single clue could be found to their whereabouts.

So Rupert and his other friends returned dispirited and wondering towards Rupert's house.

As they approached, they saw that the large windows were full of light.

"Who can there be at my house?" said Rupert. "Since my father died the house has not been lit up so brilliantly."

"Let us hasten on and see," said Stanley Sherrington. "You seem so thoroughly surrounded by spies and enemies, that anything unusual seems to portend evil."

Hurrying on, they reached the door, and rang violently.

The servant who opened the door greeted his master with a glad smile.

"Allan is upstairs," he said, "with Mistress Penraven."

"Mistress Penraven!"

Rupert did not pause to ask another question.

These two words were quite enough to prove that all his hopes had been realised, and that Helen Penraven was safe, at any rate, for the time being.

Both Allan of the Glen and Tom the waterman were there, but although he saw this at one glance his eyes were only for his beloved.

At one bound he sprang to the side of Helen, and in an instant they were clasped in each other's arms.

Over this scene we draw a veil.

We need not describe the tears of joy that were shed, and the words of eternal fidelity exchanged, but we can say that the hearts of Tom and Allan were rejoiced to see the reunion.

At length Rupert Dreadnought remembered the friends who had brought about the happy event.

He sprang to his feet.

"Allan, and you, Tom," he said, grasping them both by the hand, "think me not ungrateful that I have not thanked you before. Tell me now, friends, are you wounded?"

"But slightly," said Allan, "and Tom has escaped unhurt."

"I was told that you were wounded, and staggered helpless out of the old house in the middle of the affray," said Rupert Dreadnought, "when the house was fired. I feared that both you and Tom and my dear Helen had perished. But tell me, how did you effect her escape? It seems truly miraculous."

From Allan's brief story it appeared that, seeing the slow progress of the contest in the entry of the house, and the smoke which told of the coming conflagration, they made a pretence of being wounded so as to avoid pursuit.

Hastening, then, to the ruin next door, they made their way over the ricketty wall, and, knowing how necessary haste was now, they both clambered over at once, and commenced an attack upon the bars with the axe which had proved of such assistance in forcing the outer door.

He found that the masonry crumbled beneath his heavy strokes, and it was not long before he was enabled to drag one of the bars from its place.

Two more quickly followed, and a third had but just shared the fate of the others, and been flung down the dark abyss below, when the burly ruffian whom Rupert Dreadnought had seen there before made his way into the room.

In an instant Allan had sprung through the window and confronted him.

Seeing Tom follow, the fellow was completely discomfited.

To resist was useless.

Fancying of necessity that he had only to deal with a lady, the man had sheathed his sword, and Allan's strong hand had clutched his throat before he had time to redraw his weapon.

"Yield!" cried Allan, with his sword at the man's throat. "If you permit us to bind you quietly no harm shall befall you; if you resist death is your fate. Quick! there is no time to lose."

"HE IS DEAD: THE ASSASSIN'S KNIFE HAS STRUCK SURELY," SAID THE MAN.

Under circumstances such as these, what could the man reply, but that he would do as they wished.

So he was at once bound, and in a few minutes the dangerous task of rescuing Helen was commenced.

It was indeed a perilous undertaking.

Even when one person was making his way over

the wall it staggered and shivered beneath the weight of him, and now it would have to sustain that of three persons.

Helen Penraven, however, was not one to risk the lives of others unnecessarily, and as soon, therefore, as they had succeeded in helping her out of the window, she passed along the wall by herself, grasping firmly the broad belt of the Scotch youth.

On reaching the street they were unable to find any trace of Rupert, and so they had at once made their way to his house.

The next thing to be done, now that Helen had been rescued, was to keep her in safety, and it was resolved that on the next day Helen should be taken to the house of Lady Claremont, a near relation, whose house was a kind of castellated mansion in a quiet suburb.

This plan was accordingly carried out.

On the following day the lovers, therefore, again parted, and Helen, whose departure from Rupert's house had not, apparently, been watched, was, for the time at any rate, in safety.

According to the arrangements, and the injunctions given him by his father, he was empowered now to open the first compartment of the IRON CHEST.

But, eager as he was to do this, anxious as he was to unravel the strange mystery, he was resolved not to risk the failure of this mission by being too precipitate.

He resolved, at any rate, to wait a few weeks in order to see if his enemies had watched his proceedings, and were in a position to take Helen once more from her concealment.

Then, if all went well, he would commence at once his mission of vengeance, and discover the FIRST SECRET OF THE IRON CHEST!

CHAPTER XXV.

MURDER!

RUPERT knew little what a strange chain of events was preparing to drag asunder all his cherished schemes.

He had truly a strong band of honest and earnest friends, but he had enemies against him in still larger numbers, unscrupulous, desperate, hungering after gold; seeming to love crime for crime's sake, and far more, therefore, to be dreaded in their doings than honest men.

It is in the track of these enemies we must now tread again.

More especially in the track of Oscar Penraven, whose first idea was the destruction of Alford, or, as he felt him to be, his supposed lost cousin Richard.

To permit him to live now was to risk ruin, disgrace, even death.

He could not return to the Chief of the dread Society with such a disjointed story as alone he could now unfold, kept as he was within a narrow limit by the fearful oath he had taken.

Strange was it, indeed, that this man who looked so calmly on death should hesitate at perjury!

The first thing which he did upon quitting Alford's house was to proceed to the house of the Poisoners in order to procure a disguise.

There was in the great mansion a room in which disguises of every conceivable kind were kept, and here he soon obtained one which exactly suited his purpose.

It was the disguise of an old beggar.

No one could possibly (no matter how clever he might have been) have recognised the dashing though stern-faced Oscar Penraven in the crouching, bent form that quitted the abode of the Poisoners.

Long, ragged locks fell over his shoulders; his features were unrecognisable in consequence of paint and false wrinkles, and heavy, jagged eyebrows, beard, and moustaches.

A long cloak full of holes hung in a slovenly manner from his shoulders, and his feet were almost shoeless.

His whole appearance was that of a wretched, decrepid, poverty-hunted old man.

Beneath this guise was a wrist of iron, an arm of steel, a hate as black as that of a demon, while beneath the wretched garments were weapons to destroy human life.

Confident that in such a guise as this it would be quite a matter of impossibility to recognise him, he made his way at once towards the street in which Alford resided, and hung about its skirts until evening.

He guessed that under present circumstances Alford would not go out much in the daytime, and that when he *did* go he'd be likely to try and quit the country.

Slowly the hours went by, and the assassin had nearly began to doubt that he should be able to clutch his prey, when the door opened and Alford stealthily made his appearance.

He glanced up and down the street, as if suspecting that his arch enemy would be on the look-out to destroy him.

The poor old beggar who emerged from the darkness and began shambling along the street, did not even attract a passing glance, and seeing that there was no one else near at hand, Alford at once emerged from the doorway and hurried away along the street.

Our readers must remember that no gas or even brilliant lamps of any kind were in the streets at this time to light the wayfarer.

It was a very easy matter, therefore, for the supposed beggar to make his way after his victim; and he was enabled also to go as quickly, the shadows of the high houses completely veiling him.

It many times occurred to him to rush across the street, and at once accomplish his revenge by plunging a dagger into the back of his unsuspecting enemy.

But there was the risk of failure and of di covery.

A loud cry at that early hour might rouse the neighbours, and he would either have to fly, perhaps, with his revenge half accomplished, or would remain to be seized and made prisoner.

So he waited patiently until at last, at the angle of the street, Alford halted.

There were three streets joining here, and he glanced anxiously up each.

Then seeing no one approach, he made his way across the street to a spot where a glowing light, looking merry and cheerful in the darkness, showed the point where a tavern offered its hospitable shelter to the tired and thirsty traveller.

Here he entered, and after speaking to the landlord, passed into an inner room.

Oscar remained outside.

Many persons paused and looked at him.

But not one suspected him.

His disguise was complete, and not a few who departed from the house of entertainment slipped alms into his outstretched hand.

Alford, meanwhile, when he entered the inner chamber, found in it but one man, who greeted him cordially.

This stranger was dark and swarthy, and both by his dark skin and his peculiar features seemed to speak of Indian blood.

"Well, Richard, or rather, Sir Richard, I should say," he cried, with a smile, "you have come at last. I had begun to think that some untoward event had occurred to keep you back."

"Not so," said Alford. "I have delayed in order that my doings may not be watched by my enemies."

"And are you sure you have not been observed now?"

"Certain."

"That is good. And now sit down, have some wine, and tell me what are our plans."

"I shall not remain long," replied Alford, as he sat down by the fire, "for I have much to see to, and to-night I wish to see my lovely Lesbia."

The half-caste smiled.

"You still love her then," he said, "and yet she is a poisoner."

"By name only," returned Alford. "She was inveigled into the Society, and she has never in any way aided it."

"There you are wrong," said the other; "she is present at their balls, at all their meetings; she knows well who they are and what is their mission, yet she is friendly with all. Ah! Penraven, you see with the eyes of love, or rather love blinds you."

"No; I understand her better than you," said Alford; "but never mind; every man has his infatuation. I have mine, and that is Lesbia. But come, we will drop her name and speak of our plans. You were always a cynic in love matters, Najid, and so it's of no use trying to persuade you of anything."

Najid laughed as he poured out some wine.

"Call me what you like," he said, "but you'll find me right in the end. But as you say, we'll talk of business. When do you propose starting?"

"To-morrow."

"And have you arranged the money safely?"

"I have. Everything is arranged in such a manner that as far as my fifty thousand pounds is concerned no one can touch it without my sanction."

"And Helen Penraven—your half-sister, what of her?"

"Her money is so settled that if she is forced into a marriage against her will, it cannot be touched by her husband. And feeling sure, therefore, that all my wishes will be carried out as I wish, I shall leave London with greater pleasure. To-morrow we will quit this country together, and at Paris I shall remain a month. By that time a letter will have left England, addressed to my old enemy, warning him of my presence in England. At the end of the month, therefore, I shall start for India and we shall pass him on the road."

"And shall I meet you here to-morrow night?"

"Yes, Najid; at the same hour as I came to-night horses shall be ready at the door for both of us. We will then lose no time in reaching the coast, and proceeding as secretly as possible across the channel."

Other little arrangements were entered into, a few more glasses of wine indulged in, and then the two friends parted.

It was getting late now.

The tavern was just closing as Alford left, and the streets were empty and dark.

The pretended beggar, too, was nowhere to be seen, but in reality he was not far off.

Under the shadow of the opposite houses, however, he still lurked, and when Alford moved away, he followed.

Now the time was approaching.

Alford was now nearing a part of the town which was but thinly inhabited, and unless he soon entered a house he would, in the course of a few minutes, be out in the open country, a dark, dismal part, too, where murder would very easily be accomplished.

So on went the victim, and on crept the assassin, noiselessly, surely, in his steps.

Presently the houses became fewer, and the trees more frequent, and after a time the road merged into a country lane.

Now was the moment.

With almost noiseless, cat-like steps the murderer crept on.

Alford, wrapped in dreams of bliss with Lesbia, heard nothing, for the assassin made his way along the soft ground, and only a slight rustling and crushing of leaves betokened the presence of any-one or anything near Alford.

The latter noticed this not, for the wind was sighing round him, and boughs were creaking, and leaves from evergreens falling and tapping on the crisp ground.

In an instant, in the hushing dark, the assassin was upon his victim.

The bright blade gleamed aloft, and descended like a lightning flash upon Alford's back, crashing in between the shoulder blades, and drawing from the unfortunate being one loud, prolonged shriek of agony.

Just as this terrible cry awoke the stillness of the night, and the murderer was kneeling to make sure of his victim, there was a shrill voice near at hand.

It sounded like the hooting of a night bird, but it was evidently only a good imitation of such.

As Oscar felt the pulseless heart, the cry was answered by another as shrill, and then two men sprang from out the hedge.

One of these was Stanley Sherrington.

Oscar waited not to give a second blow, but darted away ere the new comers caught sight of him, and rushed rapidly in the direction of the city.

They had heard the cry of agony which had proceeded from the mouth of the wounded man, and Stanley's companion, drawing a dark lantern from his pocket, directed its rays full upon the spot where the body lay upon its back, just as the murderer had turned it over.

He knelt down, gently raised him, and placed his hand then upon the heart.

"He is dead," he said; "the assassin's knife has struck surely."

CHAPTER XXVI.

TOM THE WATERMAN ON THE TRACK.

The escape of Helen Penraven from the old house by the river was well known now to Oscar, but the business which he had had in hand for the Chief of the Poisoners had so thoroughly taken him off the scent, that he had no conception as to her having been taken to the residence of Lady Claremont.

Having thus lost the clue, it became necessary for him now either to punish Rupert, or, by getting him and his friends into his power, wrest from them the secret of her whereabouts.

It may seem strange that one possessed of the black heart and evil mind of Oscar Penraven, could entertain such a resolute feeling of love for Helen.

But it was *not* love properly so called.

There was no pure affection in his soul.

It was a wild passion, heightened to greater intensity by Rupert's love for her, and his own determination that he of all men should not possess her.

He admired her beauty, but he also admired the beauty of Rosalie St. Aubyn.

From this latter he preserved, as a profound secret, the knowledge of his love for Helen Penraven.

Rosalie, lovely and young as she was, had a fierce and terrible mind—an implacable spirit of revenge—a resolute will—and even if she had cared nothing for Oscar, would have been stung to madness by the idea that he was forsaking her for another.

Little did Oscar imagine what a terrible Angel of Retribution he was raising up!

In his own heart his plan was easy and definite.

He would snatch Helen from the arms of Rupert, even if death was the consequence.

Better death for her, than happiness with his hated foe; and then there would be happiness for him with Rosalie.

A desperate game this, Oscar, to play with two women!

It was on the evening of a dark day, some three weeks after the attack on the house and the murder of Alford, that Tom the waterman made his way towards the house of Rupert Dreadnought.

He had been sent by Rupert on a mission of trifling importance; and as with the answer he entered the old porch, he came face to face with a burly ruffian, whose face he seemed to recognise.

It was not a pleasant face by any means, or a pleasant-looking person altogether.

He was a stout, ill-dressed, swarthy, ragged-haired fellow, with a huge scar on his forehead, hardly concealed by the hat he wore slouched over his brow, and an animal, famishing look in his eyes.

A second glance convinced Tom where he had observed him before.

It was at Oscar's house.

He could be on no good errand, that was very certain, unless, indeed, he came, as was likely with a ruffian such as he, to betray his master.

However, as he had issued from the house quietly by the door, Tom did not accost him, but hurrying up the steps, knocked at the door.

"Who was he who just passed out?" he asked eagerly of the domestic who answered his summons.

"A messenger from Stanley Sherrington."

"And is Master Dreadnought at home?"

"He is not; he has gone to Master Sherrington's."

Tom waited for no more.

Without saying a word to the astonished servant, he dashed down the steps, and followed in the track of the ruffian.

The latter, who had either no necessity or desire to hurry himself, was soon overtaken.

Tom's wish, however, was to follow him until he reached a lonely spot.

There might, indeed, be no time to waste in delays; but it would be more dangerous still to be precipitate.

So he kept his quarry in view.

Presently the fellow dropped into an ale-house.

"Good," thought Tom; "this is all the better for me. If he drinks hard, he will be more readily my prey."

Tom the waterman had, since a boy, been celebrated among his companions for his wonderful powers of imitation.

He could, after once being in the presence of a person, imitate the gait, the manner, the voice, to a nicety, and he had often kept his friends in a roar by his peculiar skill.

This skill he had never yet put to any purpose save that of amusement.

Now he resolved to put it to good account in the unravelling of what he felt sure was a mystery affecting Rupert Dreadnought's safety.

The ruffian in pursuit of whom he was did not remain long in the ale-house.

In that time, however, he had imbibed sufficient to give an additional redness to his features and an unsteadiness to his gait.

Humming to himself the refrain of some Bacchanalian song, he now, at a more rapid pace, took his road into a lonely and dark portion of the city.

Here Tom followed him up closely, and at length, as they neared a dead wall, he sprang forward.

The ruffian, however, had just caught the sound of his approach, and darting on one side he had time to draw his knife before Tom was upon him.

The face of young Braxley was strange to the villain.

"What want you with me?" he cried, loudly, and in a swaggering tone.

"A word or a blow—which you please," said Tom.

"The word first, then."

"Good. You come from Oscar Penraven?"

"You lie," returned the bully; "but if it were so, what is it to you?"

"Much, as you will find to your cost," replied Tom. "I am the friend of Rupert Dreadnought, sworn to aid him and protect his interests. You have taken to him a letter purporting to be from Stanley Sherrington."

"Well."

"It is not well!" cried Tom, boldly; "it is a forgery!"

The bully laughed loudly.

"You have settled it so," he said, "therefore I will not gainsay you; but you have *not* seen the letter, and cannot, therefore, know what it contained."

"Enough," cried Tom. "I can waste no further time in bandying words with you. I know full well that no letter from Stanley Sherrington would come to Rupert Dreadnought through your hands. Tell me at once whence came you, and whither Rupert Dreadnought has gone, or I shall cut out your lying tongue!"

The ruffian laughed loudly.

"Ha, ha!" he said, "you boast well. Well, I refuse. Come, put your threat in practice!"

In an instant Tom rushed forward, and the two men were engaged in a fierce combat.

It was a desperate, deadly struggle — truly hand to hand.

There were no swords' lengths here; but knife to knife, stabbing, hacking at one another.

Both were adepts in the art; but Tom's head was cool, his arm strong, his footing sure, while the bully's brain was excited by drink, and, besides the fact that he was fighting for hire, his legs were far from being under his control.

It soon became evident, both to attacker and attacked, that the bully was losing ground.

Frequent wounds, too, although each slight in itself, told upon his strength, and as his blood flowed, and he grew weaker, Tom pressed him more hotly and more hotly, until at length, staggering back quickly to avoid a stroke, the ruffian fell to the ground heavily.

Tom could now have easily dispatched him.

But his object was not to kill.

It was to gain the secret where Rupert had been inveigled, and to save him.

Instead, therefore, of at once stabbing his adversary to the heart, as he could have done had he felt disposed, Tom the waterman threw himself upon him, and knelt on his chest.

"Now," he cried, "tell me what I require or you die!"

As he spoke, he pressed the point of the knife upon his throat.

The man uttered no sound.

There seemed to be in his mind a sullen determination to resist.

"Speak, I say!" cried Tom again, "speak, or you die!"

As he said this, he pressed the point so hard against the ruffian's throat that the steel entered the flesh.

Resolute as the man had been before, this changed entirely the state of his feelings.

"Stay!" he cried, as his blood began to flow afresh, "stay! I will tell you all. Suffer me only to rise."

The conqueror withdrew the point of the knife.

But he was not foolish enough to acquiesce in the request of the ruffian.

STANLEY SHERRINGTON.

"No," he said; "you must remain as you are until I know all. Even then you will remain my prisoner. Quick! speak!"

The man, in spite of the helpless position he was in, muttered a curse between his teeth.

But he at once recognised his danger, and saw the peril of delay.

"I was sent by Oscar Penraven," he said, "to inveigle Rupert Dreadnought to his house."

"Which house?"

The man hesitated.

"Quick! tell me," said Tom, once more applying the sharp point of the dagger to his throat

"I have to break a fearful oath," muttered the man; "but for the sake of dear life I suppose I must do it. Rupert Dreadnought is by this time in the hands of the Poisoners."

"Of whom?"

"The Poisoners, of whom Oscar Penraven is one."

"And where is their home?" asked Tom, as a new light dawned on him. "Quick! I have no time to inquire further now. Tell me, where is this house?"

Pressed thus, the man soon informed Tom of the exact spot where he could find the house, gave him the password, and full information of everything.

Having thus satisfied himself on the points upon which he was most concerned, Tom searched the ruffian, took from him everything which could in any way be converted into a weapon, and then, still holding him by the arm, rose to his feet.

"Now," he said, as he drew a pistol from his belt, "now, if you attempt to escape, or to excite the attention of any passer-by, I shall blow your brains out!"

The whole affair had happened very quickly, and it was in a surprisingly short space of time that they stood at the door of a house where resided one of Tom's oldest friends.

He was a strange-looking customer, this friend; short, thickset, and powerfully built.

We have met him before when the watermen had endeavoured to save Helen Penraven.

It was, in fact, Bill Flaxman.

In a few words Tom explained all.

It was indeed a matter of life and death.

The delay of half-an-hour might prove fatal to Rupert Dreadnought.

"But this fellow?" said Flaxman, "what am I to do with him?"

"He is worthy of no consideration," he said. "I will tell you."

He leaned forward and whispered in his friend's ear.

The latter started.

"It is a horrible punishment," he said.

"Not too horrible for a ruffian such as this—a poisoner—an assassin! Quick! we have no time to lose."

Hurrying the wondering ruffian along a passage, they emerged in a back yard, and crossing this, ascended a few steps, and entered an outhouse, which had the appearance of a disused stable.

Here they opened a dark lantern, and the prisoner guessed at once the doom to which—for a time at any rate—he would have to submit.

Fixed in the wall by powerful iron staples was a stout chain.

For whatever purpose it may have originally been placed there, it certainly had the appearance of one of those chains which are used to fasten murderers in the worst of prisons.

For an instant his glaring eyes were fixed upon his foes.

He was evidently measuring their strength and his own.

There was now no drunkenness left in him.

His desperate fight and his wounds had succeeded in thoroughly sobering him.

Suddenly, therefore, he dashed forward, unarmed as he was.

But it was in vain.

It was but a sudden effort, and the two captors had him soon again upon the ground.

Here Tom held him with a pistol to his forehead, while his friend fetched the key of the great iron hoop which was to be fastened to his leg.

"There is one thing more," said Tom, "which I must know."

"What is it?" asked the man, who was now gasping for breath after his severe struggle.

"Your name?"

"Jack Gradley."

"Good!" said Tom, "and now let me give you one warning. I am going, at the peril of my life, to release Rupert Dreadnought from the hands of Oscar Penraven. If I return not by to-morrow morning—if, in fact, through any false information of yours, I should fall this night, my friend, who now approaches, will take his revenge upon you."

"I have told you all," said the man, who now seemed paralysed by a deadly fear. "I know not what they intend to do with them. You must enter the house privately with the key you took from my pocket, and wait in the large ante-room till Sir Oscar calls you. That is all I know."

It did not take long to fix the heavy fetters upon the leg of the prisoner, and in a few minutes he was chained to the wall.

He glared terribly, with a mad stare, at them, as they left him in utter darkness.

Then he began to leap wildly, desperately about, in a way which threatened to drag the staple from the wall.

"Oh, if I could only escape now," he muttered, as he gnashed his teeth, and the white foam gathered on his lips, "I should have a splendid reward and a glorious revenge!"

CHAPTER XXVII.

THE DOOM OF RUPERT DREADNOUGHT.

The writing of Stanley Sherrington was far from being a peculiar one.

In fact, in those days writing had not become the art it is now, and there was a greater similarity than now exists between the writings of both rich and poor.

The wording was so exactly what would have been Stanley's under the circumstances, and the whole tone of the letter was so exactly what his writing would have been expected to be, that there could not reasonably arise in Rupert's mind any suspicion of foul play.

The appointment was made at the meeting house of the Mohocks; past events were spoken of and certain little matters alluded to which completely put Rupert off the scent of suspicion.

"Bring Allan of the Glen with you," said the letter, as it wound up, "as there may be tough work to do to-night."

As the letter contained this intimation, neither Rupert nor Allan, as may be imagined, forgot the precaution of being well-armed.

As Stanley Sherrington had on so many occasions befriended them, both master and servitor imagined that he intended to ask of them a favour in return, and they went, therefore, prepared to grant it to the full.

The night was, as I have said, a very dark one, and just such a one as they might fancy Stanley Sherrington would choose for an adventure, either of gallantry or revenge, and they advanced along the streets, scarcely taking the precaution of looking out for enemies.

Before reaching the meeting place of the Mohocks they had to pass an awkward and perilous-looking spot.

There were no lights anywhere to be seen, and for several hundreds of yards a number of ruined edifices, relics of the old fire of London, raised their gloomy and jagged walls against the sky.

It was here that Oscar Penraven had prepared his trap.

Suddenly, when they least expected it, there was a rush of feet, and before they could understand what it all meant, and even see who or what were their assailants, a sense of insensibility came over them, and they knew no more.

When they recovered they were in a strange room bound.

It was a place without any window, with a door which apparently had no lock.

Rupert Dreadnought was the first to wake from his unconsciousness.

His companion, Allan of the Glen, was seated in a large chair, with his hand bent down over his chest.

Rupert himself was also seated in a chair of luxurious dimensions and make, from which he had no wish to move.

There was, in fact, a lassitude over him that prevented for the moment all idea of rising.

When, however, he did try to do so in order to endeavour to rouse Allan, he found that his feet were confined in such a manner that he could not move from the spot.

"Allan," he cried, as he once more relapsed into the seat, "Allan, awake!"

The Scotch boy started, and then sprang up.

He too, however, was confined safely by his legs, and fell back in his chair helplessly.

"Where are we, I wonder?" he said. "They seem to have left us our hands free, and our swords by our sides."

"That is in mere ridicule of our misfortunes," said Rupert. "These iron bands which confine our legs prove too certainly what deadly enemies surround us. For myself I trust in Heaven always, but we are nevertheless in a terrible predicament. I care less for myself than for you, who are only their enemy because you are my friend."

As he spoke there was the sound of feet approaching, and the door opened suddenly.

Oscar Penraven and Rupert Dreadnought met now for the first time face to face.

Behind him was the Chief of the Poisoners, with about a dozen armed attendants.

All, with the exception of Oscar, were masked.

The first impulse of Rupert Dreadnought was to spring to his feet and draw his sword.

But, as if he had anticipated this movement on his part, Oscar advanced quickly to the centre of the room, and pressed his foot violently and with a sudden jerk upon one of the planks of the flooring.

In an instant the chairs upon which both Rupert and Allan were seated became instinct with life.

A huge eagle's head rose as if by magic from the back of the chair, while from the sides rose talons, which seizing the unfortunate captives by the head and arms, kept them down with irresistible force, in such a position, that they could move neither to the right nor the left.

When this had been effected, the Chief of the Poisoners advanced towards the captives.

"Rupert Dreadnought," he said, "in the name of Oscar Penraven and our great convention, established for the purpose of rescuing Society from wealthy reprobates—from the CURSE OF RICHES—I am about to ask you a few questions."

Rupert made no answer.

"In the first place," continued the Chief, "I demand to know where is Helen Penraven?"

A derisive smile crossed the features of Rupert Dreadnought.

"I refuse to answer," he said. "No matter what torture you put me to, I shall never consent to permit her to fall into your hands."

"There is worse still than that," continued the Chief; "but remember that we do not torture. Torture to a brave man is nothing. DEATH is the best punishment of all. DEATH, which cuts you off at once in the midst of youth. DEATH, which takes you from all you love. DEATH, which——"

"You need say no more," returned Rupert. "DEATH also re-unites us to friends—eases our sorrows—releases us from man's tyranny and cruelty. No fear of this will make me do anything you desire. I have no dread of death, or of your Society!"

"Your doom, then, will be a far more terrible one than you imagine," said the Chief of the Poisoners. "*By a subtle essence, which we shall administer to you, you will be deprived of all power of speech and motion. You will then be placed in a vault, where two men will watch you night and day. No food will be given you, and you will in two weeks cease to exist. During this time you will be asked, twice in each day, whether you consent to our terms. By your eyes you will be able to express 'yes' or 'no.' And now for the terms upon which your safety can be secured. In the first place you must disclose the place of concealment of Helen Penraven; in the second place, you must deliver over to the Society two-thirds of the property left by your father; in the third place, you must swear that you will never, to any one, under any circumstances, reveal the proceedings of this night!*"

The Chief paused.

His stern eyes were fixed upon the unfortunate prisoners.

On Allan's face was expressed nothing but astonishment.

His brave heart, like Rupert's, knew no fear

On the face of Rupert there was the supremeness of contempt, mingled with the despair which no one could avoid feeling under such circumstances.

"I refuse again," replied he. "Nothing will induce me to be a traitor, or to give up the mission which was left to me by my father. Helen Penraven was left to my guardianship. I will protect her, or I will die in the attempt. My fortune is hers, if I die; and as for betraying the proceedings of this evening, if Providence does aid my escape, I shall do my best in every way to make them known to everyone, and to destroy your infamous companionship!"

A grim smile wreathed itself over the lips of the Chief.

"You will make one more martyr to human obstinacy," said he. "Oscar, sound the bell."

Oscar drew near the fire-place and pulled a rope.

A loud, gong-like sound resounded through the building.

Then the door opened, and six men appeared robed in black.

At the head of this sombre procession was a man dressed in exactly the garb in which the villain had been dressed who had brought the false letter to the house of Rupert Dreadnought.

In his hand he carried a black bottle.

A bottle of iron!

The object of this instrument was easily apparent.

Containing as it did the deadly liquid of which the Chief of the Poisoners had spoken, it could be introduced into the mouth of a victim by force and could not be broken.

"Advance," said the Chief of the Poisoners. "The prisoners are ready."

The man, scarred, dirty, with his ragged red hair, advanced towards Rupert Dreadnought in the first place.

Then he bent over the captive and placed the bottle near his lips.

"Villain," said Rupert, "you will repent this."

"Hush," whispered the man in an almost imperceptible tone. "I am a friend. It is I, Tom the waterman. I can say no more. Drink."

"What say you?" asked the Chief of the Poisoners.

"The prisoner spoke," replied Tom, in a voice which was a splendid mimicry of the dark-browed ruffian's tones. "I know not what he says, but I believe it to be something against the Society."

Rupert spoke no more.

He was wrapped in astonishment.

But still he believed the speaker.

Tom's natural voice was too much opposed to the surly tones of the other whom he represented, to permit him to be mistaken.

A whirlwind of thoughts rushed through Dreadnought's mind.

How had Tom entered the very heart of the Poisoners' citadel?

What was he doing there?

What chance had he among such a set of villains?

These, and a hundred more ideas, entered Rupert's brain, but he nevertheless recognised in this hour of danger the wonderful interposition of Providence, and believing in Tom as he would have believed in a brother, he drank as directed.

Here Tom whispered, as he poured the liquid down the victim's throat—

"In ten minutes you must assume insensibility."

Then he moved to the side of Allan of the Glen.

"Drink," he said.

"You may force it down my throat," returned Allan, who, of course, had not heard Tom's words of warning, "but I will not drink willingly."

"Hush!" said Tom to him, as he had said to Rupert, "hush. I am Tom Braxley. Drink!"

Allan, who was not quite so convinced of Tom's fidelity as Rupert, glanced quickly at his master.

"Drink," said Rupert. "*I* have done so. Be as brave as I am, and be assured that those who *dread nought* can safely fight against the world."

The tone and the look were enough for Allan.

With an inward prayer that Providence would one day restore him to Mary Macpherson, he allowed the iron bottle to be placed between his lips, and drank.

"Farewell," said the Chief of the Poisoners, turning towards the door.

Then the gloomy procession once more moved towards the door, which opened as if of its own free will, and allowed them to pass like noiseless spirits out into the dark passage.

Oscar was the last, and the look he cast back ere he disappeared Rupert never forgot.

CHAPTER XXVIII.

THE APPOINTED HOUR.

TOM the waterman, in his new character of Jack Gradley, was, of course, compelled to quit the room at the same time as his new masters.

But his actions already were enough to show that, bad as the position of our hero was, he had, notwithstanding, a good friend near.

It was but a shadowy hope of safety, however, even now, for how long Tom would be able to keep up the illusion it was a matter of difficulty to determine.

In a nest of villany such as he was now, where all around him moreover were strangers, what numberless chances there were of discovery!

"Allan," said Rupert, as soon as they were alone, "be careful what you say. No doubt there are plenty of means by which spies can overhear our conversation; so mention nothing which can harm us or our friends. We shall be saved."

"I believe it," said Allan, "though, to tell you the truth, Master Dreadnought, I feel strangely bewildered by all that is passing round me."

"Ah! what is that?" exclaimed Rupert, suddenly.

Well he might ask.

As Allan had uttered his last words, the whole room shook violently, and gradually but surely the flooring of the room had begun to sink.

Rupert had heard of such things as these, but in such modern times it seemed truly a romantic idea to believe them possible.

However, there was now no doubting that such things were.

The windows, and then the high edging of the floor, sank out of view, and still they descended.

This descent was almost noiseless.

Down—down went the flooring, with only the slight jarring of a chain to show by what agency it moved.

A colder air was soon diffused around the captives, showing that they were gradually approaching underground regions, and then the descent stopped.

Around them now were dark stone walls, humid and gloomy, while a barred window was seen close by one of the dark arches which supported the walls.

While they were wondering what next would occur, and whether the carpeted floor would remain there with the vast expanse of emptiness above them, they saw a trap-door opened, and three men appear.

Now was the critical moment!

Neither of those who appeared was Tom the waterman.

These were paid ruffians; and both Rupert and Allan saw that they had a difficult part to play.

The ten minutes mentioned by Tom the waterman had now elapsed, and they must, therefore, pretend to be insensible.

When, therefore, the men approached, they permitted them tc remove their bonds, without moving either to the right or the left, and without even moving their eyes.

The ruffians, who were under the influence of drink, would scarcely have been able to notice them even had they been less expert in their acting.

Rudely undoing the bands which confined them, they first raised Rupert and then Allan, and carried them through the trap-door, down a short staircase into the room below.

This was their place of doom.

RUPERT DREADNOUGHT.

THE LIVING TOMB.

As soon as they were both at the bottom of the steps, the floor upon which they had descended once more began to ascend, and when it had risen into its former position, they found that they were in a chamber whose only furniture was a table, two chairs, and a long, tressel-like apparatus, like that which is used to support coffins.

Upon this now were a matress, a blanket, and a velvet pall edged with white.

The only thing which gave any shadow of comfort

to the room was a large fire, which blazed merrily up a broad and ample chimney.

As soon as the moveable ceiling had settled into its place, the men raised Rupert and Allan, and placed them side by side on the tressels.

Over them they then placed the blanket and the velvet pall, and this done, they took from the cupboard a number of altar candles, and lighting them, placed them in rows on both sides of the bier.

This was, of course, to enhance the horrors of the situation; and to anyone who had no shadow of hope —who had no friend near—the appearance of the whole place was certainly enough to rouse horror and dismay.

As it was, however, although thus buried in the bowels of the earth, neither of the prisoners despaired.

They remained quite still, while one of the men quitted the chamber, and left the others sitting by the fire.

One of these presently went off into a sleep, as could be told by his loud snoring, leaving his companion to watch.

It was now that the first suspicion of foul play entered the minds of the captives.

A drowsiness irresistible came over them, and in spite of all they could do they were unable to keep open their eyes.

Even now they were afraid to destroy the plan of their unknown friend by speaking, and so silently they lapsed into sleep.

CHAPTER XXIX.

THE MYSTERY.

When they awoke again, a dark form was bending over them.

This was Tom the waterman, still in his disguise.

"You have deceived me," said Rupert Dreadnought. "You told me to assume insensibility, while in fact you produced it."

"I did so for a good purpose, Master Dreadnought, as you will soon know. It was necessary for you to be silent for two days. I did not desire you to be put to such a terrible test as that of having to keep silence for such a time."

"And have we been here two days?"

"Yes, two days and two nights," replied Tom. "It was necessary that you should remain so until I became one of the watchers, in order that you might learn from me the only method of escape. Here is wine; quick! drink it."

Eagerly the two prisoners drank up the generous liquid.

Then Tom bent over Rupert, and detailed to him his plan.

This plan, strange, mysterious, perilous as it was, we shall not detail here.

The workings of it will be seen throughout our true but wonderful history.

Suffice it to say that the prisoners joyfully listened and acceded to it, and when Tom departed they had little doubt of their escape.

About the fall of night one of the watchers approached them.

He held in his hand a lamp, which he raised high above the heads of the two captives.

"Do you consent?" he said, as Rupert fixed his eye firmly on him.

There was no reply.

To answer verbally would be, as Rupert well knew, to destroy entirely the great plan which Tom the waterman had concocted.

"If you consent, close your eyes," said the man again.

But the eyes remained open.

"Well, well," said he, as he removed the light and returned to his seat, "these mad people will die like the others, I suppose. It's no business of mine."

But it *was* the business of the other watcher, who was no other than Tom the waterman.

He kept his eyes closed, but he slept not.

His thoughts were too busy to permit him to slumber.

He kept a careful watch, not over the prisoners, but over his companion, now and then pretending to move uneasily in his sleep, and casting an eye upon the man.

He was waiting his time.

As soon as the other began to show signs of drowsiness, nodding in his chair, and jumping up suddenly as if to rouse himself, Tom pretended to wake from a heavy slumber, and said, yawningly—

"You can have your turn now, I've been dreaming ugly things, and don't care about sleeping again."

"No wonder *you* dream ugly things," said the other; "with all the blood *you* have on your soul, I wonder you can bear to sleep at all!"

Tom smiled.

He had, he knew, taken upon himself the similitude of a ruffian, but he was unaware, till now, that this ruffian was one who was unpopular among his fellows.

However, he did not make any reply.

It might have been dangerous so to do, and he therefore held his peace.

His companion, meanwhile, having delivered himself of his sentiments, appeared satisfied, and coiling himself up, so to speak, before the fire, lapsed, in a very few minutes, into a heavy slumber.

Tom waited until he was sure of his man, and then rose.

Approaching a cupboard, he took from it some viands and some wine, and drawing near the strange bier, he whispered—

"Here is food. Quick, eat; you will have need of it."

The two strangely imprisoned men rose from their recumbent positions, and eagerly devoured the somewhat scanty meal which Tom the waterman was enabled to provide for them.

This they did with all the haste possible, and then resumed their former positions.

They had stronger hope now.

Yet, what a mystery came next.

* * * * *

The appointed time passed.

The hour came—the final hour when Rupert Dreadnought and Allan of the Glen had to give in their adhesion to the wishes of the dread Society in whose power they were, or die a quiet yet terrible death.

In the room in which upon a former occasion they had assembled to try Gascoigne the traitor, the terrible tribunal were assembled.

Around the table were gathered masked men, whose eyes, the only visible sign of life, glanced eagerly and wonderingly at their Chief.

There were some there who had never assisted at a similar ceremonial; but all were aware that something extraordinary was about to happen.

When all had assembled and the doors were closed, the Chief of the Poisoners rose, and commanding silence by a wave of the hand, said—

"As we must expect in all great ventures, we have met with a signal failure.

"At least, if we have not already failed, I expect every moment to hear that we have done so.

"Both Rupert Dreadnought and his retainer remain obstinate.

"They seem to prefer death to yielding to us the property which by right of victors belongs to us."

As he spoke there was a knock at the door, the announcement that a messenger desired to be admitted to the august tribunal.

"Enter," said the Chief, in a solemn voice.

The door opened and one of the watchers entered.

"What news bring you?" asked Oscar.

"They are dead!"

"Dead!" exclaimed all present, in tones of astonishment.

"Yes," said the man, "their forms are not only cold and rigid, but show already signs of decay. They must have been dead some time."

A frown gathered on the brow of the stern Chief.

"Who has been watching?" he asked; "those who had the care of the prisoners should have been able to tell when the awful change came."

"They watched zealously," returned the man, "but as the prisoners could not speak, they had no means of ascertaining when death came."

The Chief thought a moment.

Then he rose again.

"Friends," he said, "let us descend and gaze upon our enemies."

The masks rose at once, and, preceded by their Chief, filed out of the room, and entered the chamber where stood the two spring chairs.

At a signal the floor began once more to descend, and when it had reached the bottom they passed through the trap-door down into the dark vault.

All there was very still and solemn as the moveable ceiling returned to its place.

The high altar candles burned around the bier with a dim light, and on the bier lay TWO DEAD BODIES! their faces partially concealed by a heavy cloth.

There was no doubting the fact that they were dead.

The glassy eyes, the changed complexions, the ghastly pallor, the rigidity, the whole air and manner of them, proclaimed too thoroughly the fact of dissolution.

One glance the Chief gave at them, and then he turned to Oscar Penraven, who stood next to him, and whispered some words in his ear.

Oscar, after one more glance at the inanimate forms, quitted the Chamber of Death; and, after a few moments, the side of the vault opened as it were like one large wall.

Four men then advanced to the bier, and raising it on their shoulders, bore it quickly away.

The whole of the masked men followed until they arrived in a huge vault.

Here they halted; the altar candles were placed in niches round the walls, and the bier having once more been laid down, the men proceeded to raise some of the huge flagstones of which the flooring was composed.

There seemed very little difficulty in this, for the stones were lifted rapidly, as if they had been accustomed to be raised often.

When about six had been taken up, there appeared a black surface, which soon proved to be an iron slab, with a huge keyhole at one end.

To this the Chief of the Poisoners, who seemed anxious to keep up the solemnity of the occasion (although the impression was to be made upon his friends, and not his enemies), advanced, with measured tread, and taking from his pocket a large key, opened the lock of the mysterious slab, which fell downwards with a dull sound that echoed through a large black vault below.

A stifling vapour ascended hence.

The vapour of death!

Who could gaze down into this dark abyss of crime without a shudder?

It looked what it was.

A receptacle for hidden villanies!

The men now, at a sign from the Chief of the Poisoners, raised the bodies one by one, and descended the steps which led down into the gloomy abyss.

Then, with no funeral service read over them, the dead were placed in niches in the wall—coffinless, uncovered, save by their own clothes, with their swords by their sides, and their daggers in their girdles.

After this the black slab resumed its place, and the Chief of the Poisoners, raising his hand, said—

"SO PERISH THE ENEMIES OF THE CONVENTION!"

A smile of satisfied hate crossed the lips of Oscar Penraven, as they turned away.

"They are dead," he said. "My uncle's wrongs are avenged. I no longer live for vengeance, but for myself."

He forgot that if his enemies were dead, there were Avengers who would demand from him a terrible account.

END OF BOOK I.

BOOK II.

THE FIRST SECRET OF THE IRON CHEST.

CHAPTER I.

THE STRANGE MASTER—THE MYSTERIOUS MEETINGS—THE OLD HOUSE IN NEW HANDS.

IT was about a month after the strange and horrible events narrated in our last chapter that a change of great importance took place in Rupert Dreadnought's house.

One day there was extraordinary bustle.

A man arrived in a carriage, entered the house, though a stranger, with the air of one in authority, and in the course of a few hours the servants began to quit the place.

Before evening the place was empty, the shutters were closed, and no signs of life were visible in any part of it.

So it remained for a week, though it was evident that people were eagerly watching it, for relays of patrols passed to and fro incessantly.

As the darkness of the seventh night, however, fell over the city of London, a carriage again drew up to the door of the old house.

From this descended four men and a woman.

The former were all masked, the latter deeply veiled.

They entered hurriedly, by means of a key—the door closed—the carriage drove off—and all was once more as still and sombre as before.

On the next day, however, the windows were all opened, and the house resumed something of its former appearance.

A new batch of servants made their appearance—all strong, hearty fellows, as able to wield a sword as to perform menial offices—and it was currently reported in the neighbourhood that the old house had got a new brave master, though everyone regretted the departure and strange disappearance of the last scion of the House of Dreadnought.

The new comer, that is to say, the one who took possession of the house, was a dark-skinned man, apparently about thirty years of age, with a heavy moustache and beard.

His figure was tall and commanding, his face noble and expressive; his air and carriage altogether that of one used to command, or, at least, one who considered himself to have a right to command.

There was a certain sternness about him which did not detract from the general amiability of his manner, but which showed that his life had a solemn purpose in it.

On the evening of the second day all the inmates of the house—retainers and others—were gathered in the banqueting hall of the old mansion.

At the head of the table sat the stranger.

On the board near him were those who had come with him—the three men and the veiled lady.

Two of the four men were strange-looking beings—ghastly, scarred—seeming as life's struggle had been with them a hard and a terrible one.

The other strong, hale, and hearty.

The lady, veiled as she was and dressed in deep mourning, was yet one easily recognisable.

It was Helen Penraven!

The retainers, if so we may term them who stood round, were, as I have said, all good, stout fellows, and seemed to take a lively interest in the proceedings about to commence.

When all were gathered together, and the doors closed, the one who sat at the head of the table rose.

"Friends," he said, "we have met here for a sacred purpose.

"Combinations have been made against us, and these combinations we must meet by others.

"We are here, then, to vow eternal enmity and vengeance against the foes of Rupert Dreadnought, and to swear moreover to carry out to the best of our power the mission left him by his father, and which we have before this engaged to carry out.

"Will you all, without reserve, swear to devote every energy of mind and body to this task?"

"We will," replied all.

"Then," continued the speaker, "repeat these words after me. 'We swear in the sight of Heaven to devote all energies of mind and body to the task of destroying Oscar Penraven and the hideous Society with which he is connected; to risk life willingly for this purpose; to follow implicitly the instructions of our leader in this and in the unravelling of the strange secrets of the Iron Chest. And as we fulfil faithfully our vow, so may Heaven have mercy upon us.'"

Slowly and solemnly the speaker enunciated these words, and slowly and solemnly all those present repeated them after him; Helen Penraven rising and speaking with the rest, her sad face beaming with the glow of enthusiasm.

The strange speaker continued—

"And now, friends," he said, "since you have taken this all-important oath, let me ask you another question. Are you satisfied with the leader you have had? are you content that I should continue to hold my position as your chief?"

"Yes, yes," was the answer on all sides, "we desire none better."

The speaker bowed.

"Good," he said; "then I will endeavour to fulfil faithfully—as I will at the peril of my life—the task imposed upon me. This day week meet me here again, and I will lay before you all I know in regard to the strange and mysterious secret contained in the first compartment of the Iron Chest. Now, for the t me, farewell."

The assembly, including Helen Penraven, then quitted the room, and the master of the house remained alone.

When they had all gone, he rose and stood by the fire for a few moments, wrapped in deep thought.

Then he raised his hands, took from his head the wig which covered his own natural hair, threw back the flowing locks to their original position, and stood there, though darkened artificially in complexion, the same Rupert Dreadnought that had dared, and had sworn to dare in the future, a thousand dangers to perform the mission left to him by his father.

"Time will yet prove," he said, "that the small but brave and willing band that surround me will prove more than a match for the combination of villains who meditated giving to me and mine so hideous a doom. Now, courage, Rupert—the FIRST SECRET OF THE IRON CHEST MUST BE REVEALED!"

LESBIA.

CHAPTER II.

THE FIRST SECRET.

IT required some degree of courage on the part of even Rupert Dreadnought to begin the unravelment of the complicated mystery which was his legacy.

It was of course the first step in the weaving of a strange web of destiny that he was about to take. Yet it was not exactly a feeling of alarm that invaded his heart; it was a sensation of awe—respectful awe, at thus once more opening up the secrets of the beloved though stern old father who was now gathered to his ancestors.

It seemed like opening a vault to open that old bedchamber once more.

Since the day of the funeral the door had never once been unlocked.

And now as, lamp in hand, he turned the key in the lock, and pushed open the portal, the cold air rushed upon him as from the depths of a charnel-house.

The light waved as he held it up, and threw quivering and fantastic shadows on the walls.

But Rupert's heart failed not, even though the bed stood there white and cold, just as it had been when the grand old earl drew his last breath of life.

Advancing boldly, he closed the door behind him, and, locking it, placed the lamp on the table, lit the tall wax candles which were affixed in candlelabras depending from the walls, and in a few moments a bright and comfortable light was diffused over the apartment.

Then taking the key from his pocket, the key which in the early part of the evening he had dug up from its mysterious receptacle in the old vault, and advancing to the rose-bedecked pillar and counting ing carefully, he found out the centre flower.

Pressing this hard he was soon rewarded by the sight of a wide panel, which opened swiftly, and revealed a dark interior.

He then—ere he trusted himself to a darkness which might launch him to the same doom as that which had attended the midnight robber—returned to the table, and taking the lamp, carefully examined the opening.

It was no illusion that greeted his eyes.

It was not this time an apparent fathomless abyss, but a large closet, in the centre of which was the IRON CHEST.

Gloomy and mysterious it looked, with its black sides, unrelieved either by glittering fastenings or brass nails.

As far as was possible with an inanimate object it seemed to tell you that it was the repository of strange and sacred mysteries.

With a beating heart Rupert Dreadnaught knelt down, and, putting the key in the lock, turned it eagerly.

The contents of the chest were covered with a red cloth, and, on removing this, he exposed to view two rusty swords lying crosswise over each other.

On the point where they crossed lay a skeleton hand grasping a roll of paper, while in one corner was a cambric handkerchief, which had once, evidently been steeped in blood.

After gazing for an instant in awe and wonder at the sight before him he took the skeleton hand, and, removing from it the roll of paper, he unfolded it.

The manuscript was in the handwriting of the old earl, and ran as follows—

"MY DEAR BOY,—You already know my story and I shall not, therefore, need to remind you of any of the circumstances which formed the curse of my young days.

"You will find this paper clenched in a skeleton hand.

"This hand belonged once to the murderer of a dear friend of mine.

"This friend had always doubted the sincerity of Richard Penraven, and once had the courage to say so in public.

"This was when I was away from England, and when Robert Penraven began to circulate the report of my death.

"He boldly asserted that Penraven lied.

"This he did before a number of Penraven's friends.

"The companion of the villain who knew all the truth was at first confounded, fearing no doubt that my poor friend, Henry Fortescue, had proofs of my being alive.

"Finding, however, that it was not from proof but simply from conviction that my friend spoke, Penraven's friend, Robert Redlock, renewed his swagger and openly ridiculed the idea.

"'I tell you,' said Fortescue, fiercely, 'that you lie. Dreadnought lives.'

"In an instant there was an uproar, and urged on more by the eagerness of his friends than his own wishes, Redlock challenged him.

"There was talk of a meeting in the early morning.

"But friends made up in clamour what was wanting in real impatience; and the morning was voted accordingly too far distant.

"'Now, now is the time.'

"'There's no time like the present.'

"So a space was cleared, the doors were locked, and the two angry men faced one another.

"There was no chance of foul play on the part of Redlock and his friends, and numerous friends of Fortescue were present who would soon have stopped anything of the kind.

"I need not describe the duel.

"It will suffice to say that Henry Fortescue was no mean swordsman, and that, as he ran his sword in, it caught his adversary's wrist, and severed it completely from his arm.

"You will observe it is the left hand.

"Nevertheless, the duel was over.

"Redlock could no longer engage in any combat, disabled as he was, and accordingly Fortescue was declared the conquerer, and carried away as soon as possible by his friends.

"Months passed.

"During this time Fortescue had heard nothing of the man who had lost his hand in the foolish encounter, and who undoubtedly had acted in all he had done at the instigation of Penraven.

"During the sixth month, however, there was a change.

"Without absolutely seeing anything, Fortesoue felt himself watched.

"Wherever he went there seemed a shadow by his side.

"And at length this shadow took substance.

"Fortescue was walking with me (after my return to England, and my discovery of Penraven's treachery), when the darkness overcame us just in a suburban lane.

"It had been very stormy all day, and now a heavy mass of grey cloud obscured all glimpse even of the the setting splendour of the sun.

"What came, came so suddenly as to be almost indistinguishable.

"There was a sudden cry, Fortescue fell forward, and I saw a man *whose left hand was gone*, rushing away with a long and dripping knife clutched in his right.

"I just caught a glimpse of his face; but as I was about to fly towards him, Fortescue caught my cloak, and I tripped.

"'Don't leave me,' he said; 'I feel I am dying, and have but few words to say. It is Redlock who has murdered me. Avenge me!'

"He grasped my hand, glanced once with a look of wondrous friendship in my face, and then—all was over.

"I carried his body to the nearest house, and then made an attempt to trace the assassin.

"It was in vain.

"I have never seen him since, though I know he lives.

"He will be, when you read this, about five and forty years of age, with a long hooked nose, piercing small black eyes, a broad-built, heavy frame, a thick, repulsive mouth, and *remember he has but one hand!*

"The task of destroying this man I leave as a heritage to you.

"Unless you discover certain proofs of his death, remember that you must never cease from the search.

"REMEMBER YOUR VOW!"

"I will accomplish it," said Rupert, "so help me Heaven!"

And on that day week, when his friends assembled, the same vow again ascended to Heaven!

CHAPTER III.

RED LIGHTS ON THE DARK RIVER.

IT was about a week after this that Tom the waterman rowed across the river a man who was wrapped in a cloak, and whose features, although he wore no mask, were quite undistinguishable, in consequence of his hat being slouched down over his eyes.

What he could see of the stranger's face was white and ghastly, and his eyes glared fiend-like from beneath beetling brows.

The few words he said, however, were of kindly import, and he paid liberally when he reached his destination.

He had taken Master Tom's boat from the stairs close to the house of the Poisoners.

Of this circumstance, however, the young waterman had taken no notice, although when he returned he cast a look of inquiry and hatred as he remembered the fearful scenes through which—in its gloomy depths—Rupert had been subjected.

He was just meditating thus, when he fancied he saw a red light flickering in one of the windows.

For a moment he took no further notice; but presently his attention was irresistibly drawn to it, for this time a crimson glow pervaded the chamber and shed its light far over the waters.

Tom's heart leaped joyfully.

"The place is on fire," he said, "and the villanous brood will at length be destroyed."

He resolved in his own heart that nothing should be done by him to render any assistance to the hideous crew who were the scourge of London, and he accordingly simply rested on his oars, and gazed at the strange scene before him.

It was not long before greater indications of a terrible conflagration were apparent.

The red glow, which had only shown at intervals, now became a steady light, and lurid flames thrust their forked tongues upwards towards the sky.

Out of the casements they came, mingled with smoke and steam, and soon the entire building was wrapped in the consuming element.

Nothing for a long time could be seen but the fierce tongues of fire.

Clouds of sparks, like red snow-flakes mounting heavenwards; huge beams, swaying about in fiery tangles; windows crashing out; old pictures shrivelling to destruction; cold statues, warmed, as it were, into life by the hot embraces of the Fire God!

Soon, however, the scene changed.

A fire is always attractive.

In these days it is pre-eminently so.

In those days it was more so still.

Remembering the terrific conflagration which, but a few years ago, as it were, had devastated a great portion of London, the citizens flocked eagerly to the scene of such a fire as this.

Soon, therefore, in every available corner in the streets adjoining, and in the large open space before the building, an immense crowd was assembled, and, little knowing what a villanous crew they were helping, they began exerting themselves to the utmost to save the inmates.

The latter, strangely enough, had not yet shown themselves.

All seemed tired of life.

"This is a queer affair," said one man to another, as they hurried up with a ladder; "there doesn't seem anyone in the place."

"Oh, that can't be," returned his companion, "for it was a short time since, passing by this house, I saw numberless figures at the windows, and heard the sounds of revelry."

Seeing the crowd, and rightly imagining that he might learn something and see something which would be of service to his master, Tom the waterman landed, and made his way in among the throng.

As he landed there was a sudden outburst, a sudden roar from the huge assemblage.

Well it might be so.

At three of the windows appeared some human beings, who at first, in the glare and the smoke, were unrecognisable as male or female.

In a few minutes more, however, two of them were seen to be women.

In the eyes of a crowd women in danger are, of course, terrible objects of interest; and for a few moments all present were paralysed with fear.

The very desire to aid them seemed to interfere with their power to aid.

Then, with a sudden cheer, they burst away, and within a short time three long ladders were brought up to the spot.

It was just at this moment that three horsemen appeared on the scene, who, though disguised in cloaks and masks, were still recognised by Tom the waterman, who at once advanced towards them.

"Master Dreadnought," said he, in a low tone, as he approached, "the nest which has harboured our enemies so long will at length be destroyed."

"Aye, Tom; but the evil brood may yet escape. They have, perhaps, by this time, escaped by the river gate."

"There are some yonder," said Tom, as he pointed upwards.

Rupert glanced in the direction which the young waterman indicated, and, as his eyes fell upon the forms of the women standing in the glare of the furnace within, he uttered a cry of wonder, alarm, and anger, as it were.

What was to be done?

Was he, known and appreciated as he was by all his friends for bravery, was he to stand by and see the destruction of two women, who might be innocent of all knowledge of the brutal traffic of the Poisoners?

He strained his eyes upwards; but their features were, of course, utterly undistinguishable amid the smoke.

As he gazed the ladders were placed in position.

They had been taken at random, however, and they were now found to be short.

A man dashed forward with a shorter one.

"Who will mount and carry this up?" he cried. "They can be saved by this."

The man stood still as he spoke, not offering to work himself.

This was more than Rupert could stand.

"Come," he said to Tom the waterman, as he leaped off his horse, "come, let us ascend. If we err in saving them, we know how and when to retrieve the mistake."

In a few moments—sooner, indeed, than it takes to write these lines—the brave young earl had seized the ladder and was mounting the long one, with Tom the waterman close behind him.

On reaching the top spoke of the ladder, he fixed the small one securely so that the other end touched the window sill.

"Now then, Tom," he said, "hold this with all your strength. I will ascend."

He had no sooner done this, however, than the man who was the third of the group seized one of the females in his arms and rapidly descended.

The woman whom he left behind was evidently insensible, lying in her ball dress helplessly, with her head upon the window sill.

As soon, therefore, as the first couple had descended, Rupert Dreadnought rushed upwards and seized the fainting female in his arms.

He had no time or opportunity of observing her features now.

Whoever she was, she was at any rate a woman, and he had come to save her; so folding her gently though firmly to his breast with his left arm, he began steadily to descend, amid the loud cheers of the multitude.

The descent was by no means an easy one.

Flames, red and threatening, were bursting

the lower windows, and almost completely enveloped the ladder and those who descended.

Bravely, as on a former occasion Allan of the Glen had borne Helen Penraven from the old house, did Rupert Dreadnought now pass through the fire with his burden, precious to him because of its being of the sex of the one he loved.

As soon as, amid deafening plaudits, he brought her to the ground in safety, he bore her away from the crowd towards a hostelry close at hand.

Here he quitted the press of curious people, and bore the woman he had saved at the peril of his own life up into a room, whither Tom the waterman accompanied him.

"Quick," said Rupert to the waiter, "quick, some brandy! The heat and the fright have cast her into a dead faint."

"She is very beautiful—very beautiful," said Tom, as he gazed upon her.

Truly she was.

Dressed, as she was, in the costume of the ball, all her lovely shoulders and her round, dimpled arms were bare; deadly white now, like her bosom, where rose-buds nestled upon mounds of snow.

Her eyes were closed; but her pretty mouth, her rounded cheeks, her long, drooping lashes, her lustrous hair, gave promise that when they did open, two orbs of dazzling beauty would be revealed.

Yet Rupert Dreadnought did not for a moment answer Tom's words of admiration.

His eyes, truly, were fixed upon the lovely vision before him.

Yet he appeared not to see it.

At length, just as the waiter entered with the brandy, he said—

"This lovely creature can never be a Poisoner. I know the face well. Where have I seen it? Ha! I know it now; it was she whom I rescued from the hands of the Mohocks. She was at the boarding-school; she has no doubt been lured in some manner into this den of iniquity."

As he finished speaking, the eyes of the lovely being, who had taken some of the invigorating draught, slightly opened.

It was, indeed, Rosalie St. Aubyn who lay before him!

She gazed for a moment wonderingly at the masked stranger who leaned over her, and then her eyes closed again.

For a few moments she remained thus; and then a shuddering sigh shook her soft bosom, her eyes once more opened, and she slightly raised herself, while a sweet blush as of maiden modesty overspread her face.

"Where am I?" she said, in a sweet voice. Then she added, rising with a pretty start, and with an admirable assumption of terror, "Am I free from those horrid wretches who inveigled me to that house?"

"Yes, fair lady," said Rupert, "you have escaped from them. With the aid of this brave fellow I contrived to rescue you from the flames, and I will, if you desire it, see you safely home."

The lustrous, voluptuous eyes of the beauty were fixed upon the speaker as he said these words.

"We have met before," she said.

"We have," he said, feeling, as she looked at him the same glow of excitement, the same apprehension of coming evil, that he had experienced before. "I remember your face well."

"And I, strange to say, remember your voice," she said. "This is the second time that you have saved my life. May I not know the name of my preserver?"

"Not at present," said Rupert. "I have my reasons for keeping it secret for the present. Some day, no doubt, we *may* meet under other circumstances, and then my name shall no longer be kept from you. But now, fair lady, shall I conduct you to your own home?"

Rosalie thought a moment.

He had asked an awkward question.

"No," she said, "I think, if they can accommodate me here, I will sleep here to-night. Will you kindly ask them? In this guise I should scarcely dare to return at this hour."

The thought now, for the first time, struck Rupert—how was it that in such a place as the Home of the Poisoners she should have been attired in all the voluptuous undress of the ball room.

"How was it," he asked, "that I found you in such a house dressed for a ball?"

"That is easily explained," she said. "I was in the very heat of the dance, when, feeling faint, I asked my partner to lead me into the conservatory.

"No sooner had we entered the moonlit house of flowers than I felt him press something over my face. I lost consciousness, or rather the power to cry out and resist, and in a few moments I found myself in a carriage, being whirled away towards London.

"I then quite lost my senses, and I knew no more what happened to me until I found myself in a room with a number of masked men.

"There was apparently to be some kind of trial; but what it was I never had the opportunity of knowing.

"Before scarcely a word was spoken there was a loud outcry, and a man, bursting into the room, proclaimed the fact that the building was on fire.

"In an instant all was confusion.

"The masked men sprang from their seats, and in a few moments I found myself alone.

"They knew the means of escape.

"It was not so with me.

"The building and everything in it was perfectly unknown to me; and when I fled from the room, I found myself at the top of a staircase, up which the smoke and flames were rolling in thick volumes.

"Naturally I fled upwards; but when I reached the room where you found me, I was enveloped still more in the fire, and I swooned."

Rupert believed, to a certain extent, this strange story; but he received it with reservation.

He had been so utterly deceived in so many things, that he was not only resolved to be cautious, but he also felt an instinctive drawing back, as it were, a disinclination to believe as he had been accustomed to believe.

"You know, of course, the person who so treacherously inveigled you from the ball-room?" he said.

"Yes, well—his name is——"

"THE MOHOCKS DASHED MADLY AT THE TWO FRIENDS."

Rosalie stopped suddenly.

This time there was no acting. She really had been upon the point of committing an error.

She turned her look of blank dismay into one of arch pleasantry in an instant, with the skill of an accomplished actress.

"You forget one thing," she said, while a smile wreathed itself over her pouting lips.

"And what is that?" asked Rupert Dreadnought.

"You reserve your name from me—I must be equally reserved with you," replied the lovely deceiver; "but pray ascertain now for me if I can remain here for the night."

Rupert descended to speak to mine host, and in a few minutes returned with the news that the best room would be got ready for her reception.

"And now," he said, "I must quit you; I have other work to do ere I retire to rest. Farewell."

He bowed over her hand, as he took it gently.

She gazed at him earnestly; her eyes gleamed; her bosom rose and fell in soft undulations with the violence of her emotions.

"We shall meet again," she murmured, this time in genuine agitation.

"Assuredly," said Rupert, "though when it would be difficult to say."

"Well," added Rosalie, "since you have not disclosed your name, and my name also is unknown to you, let us at least have some password by which we may recognise each other again. I have it. It is for your ear alone."

Rupert bent down, and her little hot lips were placed close to his ear.

"The password shall be 'Love and Night.'"

Rupert laughed lightly.

"Good," he said; "I will keep it secret, though, doubtless, ere long you may meet me unmasked, when you will recognise me without its aid. And now, fair lady, adieu once more."

He pressed her hand slightly again, and then quitted the room.

"That lady's in love with you," said Tom the waterman, as they descended the stairs.

"Her manner seems truly strange," said Rupert Dreadnought; "but I do not fancy that it is love by which she is actuated."

He was wrong, and Tom was right.

Strangely enough, Rupert Dreadnought had raised in the bosom of this evil-hearted woman a devouring passion, which utterly obliterated all thoughts of Oscar Penraven.

When Rupert had quitted the room she sank back upon the couch, pressing her hand over her heaving breast, and murmuring in low but resolute tones—

"I love him—I love him! He must be mine!"

CHAPTER IV.

THE FIRST GLIMPSE OF THE ENEMY.

On leaving the tavern where he had placed Rosalie St. Aubyn, Rupert at once hastened back to the scene of the fire.

The conflagration was now at its height, and out on the river the waves rolled like blood.

The flames were ascending eagerly and triumphantly now with a roaring sound, as if proclaiming their victory; and, as the great crowd gazed at the scene, the roof fell in, and a myriad of sparks of fire floated upwards towards the starlit heavens.

It was quite impossible to render any assistance in extinguishing the flames in the building itself, for they had far too firm a hold; but it was possible to prevent its spreading to any alarming extent, and workmen were employed now in pulling down an old, half-ruined edifice that joined it at one end.

At this point, where the noise of the hammers and the picks could be heard even above the roar of the fire, the largest and most eager crowd was now collected, for the fire had not yet reached this point, and it became a matter of interest to see which could work quickest, the workmen or the devouring element, which, in spite of the jets of water continually cast upon it, was gradually, but surely, approaching the spot.

Among the crowd here, too, were to be seen many well-dressed men, who conversed eagerly together in low tones, and who seemed most eager to watch the result of the conflagration.

Near these Rupert and Tom (their other companions having ridden off) placed themselves.

Instinctively our hero felt that these were in some way connected with the Society of Poisoners who had attempted his death, and from whom he and Allan had so miraculously escaped by placing the dead bodies of the two keepers in their places.

"Tom," he said, in a low tone, "I feel certain that these men who are talking so eagerly here have something to do with the Society of Poisoners."

"They seem very much interested in all that is going on," said Tom; "they little think how near them stand the men who killed their keepers, and deceived them into burying the wrong men."

"Hush!" said Rupert; "let them not hear our voices. Ah! what is that?"

As one of the men in front of them raised his arm to point out something to his companion, something gleamed brightly in the light of the fire.

It was not a sword point, neither was it a dagger.

It looked rather like a hook of steel, such a hook as is placed at the end of an arm *from which the hand has been cut off.*

A thrill passed through the frame of Rupert Dreadnought.

The man of whom he was in search had lost his left hand.

Here was one whom he already suspected to be one of the Poisoners.

Could this be the man?

Could this be his enemy, brought thus almost miraculously before him?

His blood coursed more quickly through his veins, and he resolved at once to discover the truth.

Moving forward, he suddenly, as if by an accident, pushed up against the man, who turned round quickly, so that the full glow of the firelight was on his face.

"Your name is Redlock!" cried Rupert in an instant, as he seized him, and gazed full into the features, which, through his father's description, he now recognised fully.

The man glanced at him in wonder and some alarm.

"Who are you?" he cried; "and why do you thus madly assail me?"

"I am Rupert Dreadnought, son of the old earl," said our hero, "and the avenger of Fortescue. Come quickly with me."

A shudder passed through the stranger's frame, and he attempted to wrench himself from the grasp of his assailant.

"You are insane," he said, "thus to assault a stranger in the street. My name is not Redlock, and I know nothing of you or those of whom you speak."

A fierce fire glowed in Rupert's eyes.

"Come with me," he said, in a stern undertone; "I have something most essential to speak about to you. Come!"

At this moment a shrill, wild cry arose from a hundred throats.

"Run for your lives! Save yourselves!" were the words which could be distinguished, amid the hoarse shouts of men and the shrill screams of women.

And then a huge rafter, balancing itself for a moment warningly on the summit of the wall, toppled over into the space which had so lately been filled by an excited and bustling crowd.

As it was, they were not all able to escape, and the end of the beam just caught the tail of the flying crowd, crushing down two or three as they sought vainly to struggle through the mass of humanity before them.

In an instant, Rupert felt himself wrenched violently away from the man he so longed to attack, and when the beam had fallen, and the crowd had flowed back, as it were, into its former position, Redlock, if indeed it was he, was no longer to be seen.

"Dastard!" muttered Rupert, angrily, to himself; "but he shall not escape me. I have seen his face now, and it is more than ever vividly engraven on my memory. Strange that he should thus be thrust in my way only to escape once more, as if to show me how difficult is the path marked out for me. Never mind. The vow I have sworn I will carry out, and the more willingly when I think of Helen, the lovely prize I shall win in the end."

As these thoughts found vent in a low whisper to himself, as it were, he felt a hand suddenly clapped upon his shoulder, and turning round he beheld Allan of the Glen standing near him with a flush of excitement upon his handsome face.

CHAPTER V.

THE NIGHT DUEL IN THE STREETS OF LONDON.

"QUICK, quick, this way, Master Dreadnought," said Allan, in a tone of intense agitation.

"Why, what is the matter, Allan?" asked Rupert; "you seem out of breath."

"Stanley Sherrington is awaiting you. Oscar Penraven is near at hand, and you have a chance now of meeting your enemy face to face."

Rupert's heart leaped in his bosom at these words.

He had indeed met Oscar face to face.

But it had been when he had been helpless either to avenge the past or to defend himself in the present.

Eagerly, therefore, he turned to Tom the waterman.

"Come," he said, "let us hasten. My enemy awaits me, and while I contend against him, you and my other friends must watch and see fair play. Quick, come."

With flushed cheeks and eager steps Rupert Dreadnought followed the steps of Allan of the Glen, and in a few minutes they had emerged from the dense crowd and reached a spot where even the blaze and roar of the conflagration could no longer be seen or heard.

Here Allan led them into a tavern, where they found Stanley Sherrington and another awaiting them.

"Allan tells me Oscar is near at hand," said Rupert Dreadnought.

"He is," replied Stanley Sherrington; "he is in this very building. He and a number of those who have escaped the destruction of the old house are at the present moment making merry in an upper room, little dreaming that we are here. We must watch their departure and destroy him."

"There must be a fair fight," returned Rupert Dreadnought. "Villain as he is, I will not have it said that the assassin's knife put an end to his infamous life. No, my own good sword, backed by my good cause, will be enough for me. But are you sure they are still here?"

"I am."

"And in which room are they?"

"That above us."

"Good; then we can watch their movements, and they cannot well escape."

They had not long to wait.

They had scarcely finished their second glass of wine, when they heard the sounds of steps descending, and going to the door, they beheld Oscar and his friends pass out.

"Now, then," said Rupert Dreadnought," let us follow at once."

Within a few moments they had sallied forth, and as they did so, the bright glare of a lamp at the corner of a street showed to them the friends separating and going different ways.

Oscar and one friend then passed down a street, and Rupert's mind was at once made up.

"Sherrington," he said, "you accompany me. This duel to the death shall be a fair one. Oscar Penraven has one friend only with him, so also will I. You, Allan and Tom, can return home. Come, Stanley, let us hasten onward."

There was no time for much consultation, so they advanced at once, and after following their enemies until they reached a spot somewhat more secluded than ordinary, they advanced quickly and challenged their enemies.

Oscar and his friend turned quickly.

He had been during months past the victim of such constant mishaps and attacks, that it was with some alarm now that he heard the challenge given in a strange voice.

When he turned to face the stranger who had shouted "Stand there, on your life!" in so resolute a tone, he failed entirely to recognise his adversary.

He had no conception that Rupert Dreadnought lived.

It was not a matter of surprise, in fact, that he should have been satisfied of his death, when the last view he had imagined himself to have taken of him was in a dismal vault, where altar candles burned near a bier, and cast their uncertain light upon the face of the dead!

"Who are you?" he asked boldly.

"I am one you little expect to see," returned Rupert Dreadnought. "I have met you now face to face. You have a friend with you; so also have I. We have time and opportunity. Old scores, therefore, can be paid, and the vengeance I have long sworn against you and yours can now be accomplished!"

Confident as Oscar Penraven was that Rupert Dreadnought was numbered with the dead, the words of the stranger were utter riddles to him.

"I know not what you mean," he said. "I know not your face—your form—your voice. You are following some shadow."

"Oscar Penraven," said Rupert, in a stern voice, "think not so to avoid a meeting with me. No doubt, after the murderous efforts you have made against me and my friends, it will astound you to know that we are living; but fortune has favoured me—Heaven has protected me. Behold, Oscar Penraven, your sworn enemy, Rupert, Earl of Dreadnought!"

Oscar started back in utter amazement as our hero uttered these words.

"Cast aside your disguise," he said, "and let me see your face. You ask me to treat you as an honourable man. Let me do so, as I am willing; but let me know with whom I am fighting."

"I have already told you," replied our hero; "I am Rupert Dreadnought; does not that suffice?"

"Show, then, your face. Rupert Dreadnought is dead. I saw his dead face; I was present at his burial."

"You lie!" exclaimed Rupert, "I live."

And as he spoke he flung aside the hat that covered so completely his features, and disclosed the well-known though darker countenance of Oscar's foe.

Oscar was no coward.

We have before seen this.

When Gascoigne the spy had been left to him to destroy, he had not shrunk from his fearful task.

So he eyed his enemy boldly, though his heart leaped and his face turned deadly pale for mere astonishment.

"Strange, indeed, this," he said; "you must have risen from the dead! But fear not, I will fight you. This is too dark here for you or for me. Let us go on to yonder square; or stay rather. Yonder come two watchmen. We will enlist their services."

His voice was free from all fear.

He spoke boldly and coolly.

"Good," thought Rupert, "he will not shirk his duty. I shall obtain my revenge."

The watch, seeing four men evidently bent upon fighting, thought it a good opportunity for a little bluster.

"What is this? What have we here, gentlemen?" cried a fat, fussy little party with a red nose. "We can have no combats and blood-shedding in the streets."

Rupert seized him by the arm as he spoke.

"How far are we from the watch-house?" he asked, sternly.

"Some mile and a half," said the Charlie; "but come, young sir——"

"A truce to folly," exclaimed Rupert Dreadnought; "open your lanterns; stand yonder and raise them aloft, so that we can see to fight. Quick, we have no time to lose."

The watchmen looked from one to the other in utter wonderment.

"But indeed, sir," exclaimed the one who had not yet spoken, "this is against the law; we really must——"

"Hold your tongue," said Oscar, "or you may chance to have it cut out. I will now stand in line, so that will do. Now then, Rupert Dreadnought, I am ready."

The watchmen saw that all resistance on their part would be simply folly.

So they yielded gracefully.

Their lamps were opened and raised on high.

The bright swords of the deadly enemies were drawn and crossed, and in the middle of the dark street the duel began.

Duels with swords have been so often described that it would be useless again to enter into every detail.

But this was a curious one in every way.

Besides the fact that it was taking place between the heirs of two deadly enemies, the circumstances which surrounded it were strange.

The fact of it being fought boldly in the open street, where all such meetings were strictly forbidden—the fact of the very custodians of the public peace being compelled to be unwilling aiders and abettors in the transaction, made the whole matter out of the way and unusual.

Neither of the combatants, however, seemed influenced by the peculiarities of the scene.

They thought of nothing but attack and defence.

The one was thirsting for revenge.

The other was resolved now, once for all, to rid himself of a foe who was continually dogging his footsteps, and rendering every hour of his life a terror and a misery.

So every lunge was deadly; every parry was given and watched with eager eyes.

Both of them had been brought up with a purpose.

One to avenge, the other to destroy.

Both, therefore, were good swordsmen, and for a long time there was but little perceptible difference in their positions.

Presently, however, both warmed to their work.

Their blades flashed brightly in the light of the lamps, and they advanced and retired rapidly and eagerly, while spots of blood upon the pavement showed that wounds had been given and received on both sides.

Seeing his adversary's blood flowing, Rupert Dreadnought became more desperate, and attacked him fiercely, never for one moment, however, losing his presence of mind, or suffering his hand to become unsteady.

Gradually now Oscar began to yield ground, and as he did so, the face of his second became dark, and he half drew his sword from his scabbard.

Stanley Sherrington was eagerly watching his movements, and as he saw him thus preparing for an attack, he advanced towards him.

"Stay," he said, "stay. We came here to be witnesses of a fair fight. If you interfere, I have a sword, and can interfere also."

The other eyed him for a moment angrily, but after reflection returned his sword to its scabbard.

"No," he said, "we will not fight now. Whatever happens we will be but spectators, and can settle our quarrels after."

While they had been speaking, the battle between Oscar and Rupert had waxed fast and furious.

Huge drops of perspiration fell from the faces of the combatants, while their shirt-sleeves were stained heavily and darkly with blood.

Their eyes gleamed savagely.

Their swords writhed like gleaming serpents.

Then they stood closer to one another.

All danger was forgotten.

All they thought of was that they were deadly foes, and that their business was to destroy each other or perish in the attempt.

To the wondering eyes of the two watchmen it seemed at length more like a stabbing-match than a duel, so quickly did the blades dart to and fro.

Then at length there was a brilliant pass, a sharp cry, and the contest stopped.

RICHARD PENRAVEN.

Rupert Dreadnought stood firm, while his adversary fell back into the arms of his second, the blood pouring from a large wound in his chest

Rupert was drawing his sword back to give a final thrust, when the second raised his hand deprecatingly.

"It is not needed," he said. "He is dead!"

Whatever Rupert's intentions were, now he was utterly unable to carry them into effect.

There was suddenly a wild and unearthly yell—a crowd of dark figures came dashing round the corner, and in an instant the Charlies were on their backs and their lamps extinguished, while Rupert and Stanley Sherrington found themselves surrounded by a shrieking mob of bacchanalian revellers.

The new-comers were no other than the Mohocks.

"What have we here?" shouted one, in a drunken voice of solemnity. "A duel in the streets of London! This cannot be."

And ere Rupert was aware of it, a bag of flour was dashed in his eyes, and one of the maddened drunkards rushed head foremost at him.

Eluding this drunken imitation of a battering-ram, Rupert leaped aside, while his would-be assailant, catching his head against a post, fell stunned and bleeding to the ground.

This was the signal for a desperate outcry on the part of the Mohocks.

They were unused to find themselves worsted in these mad scenes, and to see one of their number stretched apparently lifeless on the pavement drove them in their state of inebriation to a state bordering really on madness.

Wild cries filled the air—unearthly shrieks, like those of some savage tribe.

Swords were drawn, and, regardless of all else but their determination to avenge themselves for the discomfiture of their comrade, they dashed at the two friends.

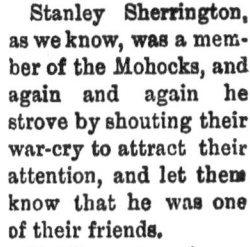

Stanley Sherrington, as we know, was a member of the Mohocks, and again and again he strove by shouting their war-cry to attract their attention, and let them know that he was one of their friends.

But it was in vain.

They were thoroughly exasperatod, and would listen to no reason.

Wild cries resounded around the open space.

"Death to the Night Prowlers!"

"At them—at them!"

"Blood for blood!"

"Down with them!"

"The Mohocks for ever!"

This last cry was fatal to their chances of success.

People had looked out from their windows when the other duel was proceeding, but they had taken no notice.

They were used to such scenes as this; but, when they heard the name of Mohocks shouted out, they recognised a common enemy.

In a few moments, therefore, doors were opened, and men, with swords drawn, were seen rushing from their houses in their knee breeches and shirts.

They were only just in time.

Drunk as they were, they were still more than a match for the two friends, one of whom was tired already with the severe struggle with Oscar Penraven, and though they had their backs to the wall, they were becoming thoroughly exhausted.

The wounded Oscar and his friend had, during the fray, disappeared entirely from the scene, for when the lanterns of the Charlies had been extinguished, the open space was enveloped in utter darkness.

It may be imagined, therefore, what difficulty there was in distinguishing friends from foes; but those who issued from the houses, being all in their shirt sleeves, were at length enabled to arrange themselves on the side of Rupert and Sherrington, and then the tide of battle turned.

Those who had so suddenly and opportunely appeared on the scene were nothing but citizens, unused to the use of swords, but the name of Mohock seemed suddenly to turn them into soldiers.

They had all grievances against these prowlers of the night.

Some had been brutally attacked, some had wives and sisters who had been insulted, and they had now an opportunity of revenging their wrongs.

The Mohocks were taken utterly by surprise. Drunk as they were, they yet saw that they had fallen among the Philistines, and they gathered themselves as it were together.

But they were no use against their more sober assailants.

Gradually they were compelled to give way, and at length the shrill note of warning from their chief warned them that they were to disperse.

They made now but a feeble resistance, just making one stand and then breaking away, as they had done upon the night when Rupert and his friends had saved from their clutches Rosalie St. Aubyn and the other young ladies from Primrose Academy.

Their enemies, when they had defeated them, did not think it worth while to pursue, but suffered them to escape, while a shout of derision followed them.

The results of the enemy's proceedings were eminently unsatisfactory.

He had indeed seen the wounded Oscar fall back into his friend's arms with the blood pouring copiously from his breast.

Yet he had had sufficient experience in the manner in which even from the most deadly scrapes clever men could escape, that he was far from being satisfied that even now Oscar Penraven was safely disposed of.

He himself had made his way out of the very jaws of death as it were, from the very grave over which his enemies had rejoiced, and it was there fore unsafe for him to believe in the destruction of an enemy upon whom he had not seen the evidences of decay surely creeping.

"We have yet more work to do," said he to Stanley Sherrington, as they thanked their strange friends, and sheathing their swords, made their way from the scene. "I believe not in Oscar's death until I have seen his utter destruction."

"The past justifies you in saying so truly," said Sherrington; "but if we follow up this night's adventure we may yet carry out our design before we had hoped to do so. To-morrow we will pay a visit to the old ruin, and see if there is any clue to be there discovered."

CHAPTER VI.

A STRANGE VISIT.

Among those who exhibited most interest in the events of the past evening, where, on returning home, Rupert Dreadnought narrated them to his friends, was one whose red wig and peculiar caste of appearance altogether denoted a disguise.

The most interesting portion of the evening's proceedings to him, however, seemed that in which Rosalie St. Aubyn was concerned.

At the mention of her name he started, and an unwonted fire gleamed in his eyes, which seemed all the more fiery in comparison with his ghastly face.

"You call her beautiful?" he said, as Rupert finished speaking.

"I do, indeed," said Rupert. "Perhaps, if we except Helen Penraven, I never saw so loveable a face."

The other smiled.

"Ah," he said, "no doubt you are right. Her face is lovely, but I have learned to fear beauty. And has she succeeded in her desire?"

"What desire?"

"The desire to make you love her."

"No, indeed," said Rupert; "though were I inclined to be conceited, I should say she had conceived a strange passion for me. No, no, the woman does not live who can wean my affections from Helen Penraven."

Soon after, the one who had taken so great an interest in the conversation rose, quitted the room, and, arming himself, issued forth into the street.

Meanwhile, Rosalie St. Aubyn retired to rest almost immediately Rupert Dreadnought quitted her presence.

At three o'clock that morning we find her fast asleep in the bed.

She looked most beautiful now, for her eyes were closed in a calm and pleasant sleep, and their evil gleaming could no longer be seen.

The heat of the weather had caused her to throw off some of the bed-clothes, and her white shoulders and rounded arms, therefore, were visible as they had been when she had first appeared to Rupert Dreadnought in her ball-dress.

A beautiful flush was upon her cheeks, her parted lips disclosed two rows of pearly teeth, while her lustrous hair fell in wild profusion over her heaving bosom.

She was lying thus when her window suddenly began to be opened from without.

The new-comer had evidently no desire to be detected, for he proceeded to his work slowly, gently, and methodically.

Gradually, therefore, the sash was raised, and presently a man peered in.

He was masked, but the little that could be seen of his features showed that it was the pale man who had suddenly quitted Rupert Dreadnought's house not long before.

He glanced eagerly round the room, which was enveloped in partial gloom, a lamp half turned down, on the table in the centre of the chamber, casting but a feeble radiance over the objects around.

Then his eyes were rivetted for a moment on the figure that occupied the bed.

A gleam as of fire appeared then to shoot from his distended orbs.

It was the fire of revenge!

There were no gleams of love or passion in them.

It was the flame of fierce hate and cruel vengeance that lit them up, and made him mor-

quickly and with less caution make his way into the room.

Then he closed the casement by which he had entered, turned the lamp up to its full height, and approached the bed.

Here he stood, and gazed for a moment at the picture of beauty before him.

"Beautiful demon," he murmured; "no wonder is it that people are deceived by you; no wonder that your lovely form has led men on to their destruction. No more shall it be so; no more shall you revel in the belief that you are far beyond the reach of the avenger's arm. You shall know, and tremble as you know, who is on your track."

As he spoke, he laid his hand on the fair sleeper's shoulder and shook her gently.

She shuddered slightly, and then her eyes opened, and she gazed wildly round the chamber.

In another instant she had sprung up in the bed, and a scream was about to issue from her lips, when the new-comer placed his hand over her mouth, saying sternly—

"One word and your life is forfeit."

"What want you here?" she cried, in a tremulous voice, as he removed his hand, still not daring to scream in face of the gleaming knife which he held close to her throat.

"I have come to speak with you, and to warn you," he said.

"To warn me! How came you here, then, and who admitted you?"

"I admitted myself through yonder window," he said; "what I have to say must be said in secret, and I desired no one to know of my coming."

"Your purpose cannot be a good one," she said, "or you would not come through the window like a thief in the night. But whatever you have to say, say quickly, for I have no desire that you should be found in my chamber at this hour of the night."

"Who more right than I?" he answered.

Then he added aloud—

"You are luring another into your deadly coils. This night I have discovered it."

"Of whom speak you?" she said, while her features became deadly pale.

"I speak of Rupert Dreadnought," he answered.

"And who spoke to you of him in connection with me?"

"He himself."

"And does he love me then, and are you a woman, that you are jealous?"

She said this eagerly and then sneeringly.

A smile wreathed itself over his lips.

"He loves you not," he answered; "he loves another; but tell me, you know Alford?"

"I do. He is dead."

"He is not."

"You are wrong. He was killed by Oscar Penraven."

"So Oscar thought. He was wrong. He lives still. I am he."

So saying, he withdrew his mask, and revealed the pale and ghastly features of the man whom Stanley Sherrington had taken for dead.

The features of Rosalie St. Aubyn underwent pleasureable change as he did this.

"Why do you come thus mysteriously," she said, "since you are one of us, and since you and I have always been friends?"

"We are friends no longer," he said, sternly; "I will not kill you as you deserve—I will not cast shame on your name, as I could, by opening this door and calling in the people of the house. I will only enjoy the great triumph of telling you all I know, and how utterly and miserably your plans will fail in the future."

Rosalie St. Aubyn gazed at him now in real amazement.

He had always been on terms of friendship with her.

What could have made this change?

She was a vain woman, full of the consciousness of her glorious beauty, and she did not remain for many moments in doubt.

He loved her; he was jealous of her passion for Dreadnought.

"What has changed you thus?" she asked, as her eyes assumed a softened expression.

"I will tell you my reasons afterwards," he said; "now listen while I crush your hopes one by one. In the first place, you have cherished a mad hope that Oscar Penraven will make you his wife."

"He has sworn it."

"He means it not," returned Alford; "he loves Helen Penraven, and is pledged heart and soul to her. He means no marriage to you."

A flush of anger and irritation crossed the face of the lovely woman.

But she betrayed no further her emotion.

"He is welcome to wed whom he pleases," she said; "I love another. This is no sorrow to me."

"Be it so," said Alford, "though I believe it not. In the second place, your name is not Rosalie St. Aubyn, but Lady Richard Penraven."

It was now that the first evidence of intense agitation betrayed itself.

The woman's body became, as it were, convulsed; her mouth opened, and she clutched the bed on both sides of her, sitting up erect and staring at Alford with wildly glancing eyes.

"Madman!" she murmured after a moment, "what fool's tale is this you repeat?"

"What makes your heart palpitate with dread—what makes you turn sick with fear—what crushes your hopes for ever?" said Alford, triumphantly. "I am Rupert Dreadnought's friend. I know, and he knows, your story, although he does not as yet know your identity with Lady Penraven, or rather the Mrs. Richard Penraven of the scandal."

"And you are going to tell him, I suppose? You are going to enlighten him when it *can* be no interest to you to ruin me," said Rosalie St. Aubyn, bitterly.

"Excuse me, you are wrong," returned Alford; "I am *not* going to tell him."

"Then, what *do* you mean?" she said. "I confess myself at a loss to understand you."

"I will let your passion for him increase; I will even, if I can succeed in doing so, induce Rupert Dreadnought to lose his fealty to his real mistress and love you. Then will my moment of triumph come," he cried, raising his hand aloft. "Then, when you imagine your best hopes realized, I will disclose the whole story of your infamy; how your husband——aye, madam, interrupt me not—I *will* speak; how your husband rescued you at the early age of sixteen from the companionship of villains; how he married you; how you fled from him after a long period of devotion; how he met your betrayer; how he shot him to the heart, and how you left India for England to seek out another victim to deceive and destroy. And he can also tell more."

"What mean you, most sapient historian?" said Rosalie, who had by this time recovered, by a violent effort, all her composure.

"He can tell how the husband, who was said to have destroyed himself by casting himself into one of the deep and swiftly-running rivers of India, followed his wife to England; how he watched all her movements; how he saw her on the point of inveigling his friends; how, at the last moment, he met her face to face, and, taking off his disguises one by one, thus, and thus cried—'Behold the one you thought dead—the one who lives to punish and avenge!'"

As he suited the action to the word, and threw his wig and false moustache and beard on the floor, the fair demon, as he had termed her, uttered a cry of fear.

No wonder was it.

The one whom she had wronged and fondly imagined dead and out of her way, had suddenly reappeared to thwart all her plans.

She seemed thoroughly paralysed.

"You are mad," she said. "Who are you who thus take the semblance of the dead to extort from me money or a confession?"

"Rose Allerton," returned Alford, sternly. "You know me well. your husband, Richard Penraven. You guess your future from the fact of my reappearance."

There was now a moment of intense silence, during which the husband and wife, long separated, gazed at each other in silence.

Then, there was a sudden start, a dash forward, and Alford staggered back, pressing his hand to his brow.

Then, as he essayed to utter a cry, he gasped fo breath and fell heavily on the floor.

What had happened?

CHAPTER VII.

THE SECRET CONCLAVE—THE CHAINED MADMAN—THE TERRIBLE FIGHT.

BEFORE continuing Alford's adventure in the tavern where he had so adventurously entered in search of Rosalie St. Aubyn, we must return to Oscar Penraven, and narrate the circumstances which followed his duel with Rupert Dreadnought.

The wound he had received at the hands of our hero was a most severe one.

It had passed through his shoulder, the fleshy portion of which it had torn open; but nevertheless it had not passed through such a portion of his body as to render the injury a mortal one.

His second carried away the wounded man to the nearest tavern, where he was soon in the hands of a skilful doctor.

His swoon lasted a long time; but towards morning he opened his eyes and glanced round him in surprise.

He naturally had expected, when the cold steel had plunged through his body, that he should never again open his eyes upon this world, and now that he found himself in bed in a dark room he naturally reckoned upon finding himself in the hands of his foes.

"Where am I?" he said, in the loudest voice he could assume.

A man crept up to the bed.

It was his second—Mark Forrester.

"Ah! Mark," said Oscar, "are you there? This is indeed a a surprise. I had reckoned myself with the dead."

"You are worth many dead ones," said Mark, with a cheering laugh; "your luck is too good to give them a chance of disposing of you."

He was right.

A strange destiny seemed to watch over the young reprobate.

It seemed, truly, as if fortune were assisting in the exact development of the mission given him by the old earl, as if young Rupert's sword was fated to destroy Redlock ere it could succeed in doing more than wound any other.

It would be useless to describe minutely the convalescence of Oscar Penraven.

It will suffice to say that it was a somewhat long and tedious matter, but at the end of the time care and fresh air restored himself entirely to his old vigour.

His hatred now redoubled against Rupert Dreadnought, and he left his sick room vowing unceasing vengeance against his hereditary foe.

During his illness the Poisoners had not been idle.

Their residence in the very heart of the city of London had certainly possessed great advantages, but it had also its disadvantages.

It was in the centre of action, but then also it was capable of being unceasingly watched.

It was resolved, therefore, to move entirely from the metropolis, and as they had plenty of agents at command, they were not long before they pitched upon a suitable locality.

It was some distance down the river, on the Essex coast, close to the river. It was always convenient to be near the swift flowing waters of the river, as it enabled them to bear away their booty—to carry the bodies of murdered victims and cast them into the centre of the stream, as well as to go and come without attracting notice.

While they had been in search of their new domicile, they had many secret meetings in the vaults of the old building, which had not been touched by the devouring element that had otherwise destroyed the abode of crime.

They came under cover of the dark night, and were thus unnoticed by any.

Again and again they had endeavoured to ascertain the cause of the calamity which had so utterly destroyed their old place of concealment.

But in vain.

Whoever was their enemy, he had taken his measures well, and had left behind him not the slightest clue to his whereabouts

RUPERT DREADNOUGHT.

"STAND BACK!" CRIED LESBIA, "THE FIRST MAN WHO APPROACHES DIES."

It was in the dark vault where they held their meetings prior to making their way to the old house on the Essex side of the river that Oscar Penraven made his first appearance after his illness.

He was welcomed with acclamations by all as a kind of martyr to the cause and was raised by general accord to the position of one of the council of the Society.

The office of the council was far above that of the other portions of this hideous community.

They had power over all the others, were able to send them upon any mission, and were entitled, moreover, to a larger share in the disposal of the riches acquired by murder and crimes of every hue.

The failure of the scheme in regard to Alford did not detract from Oscar's reputation.

He had fought well for them, he had done his best, and if he had failed he had done only what others had done before him, and had spilled his blood in their behalf.

It was with utter astonishment that they learned from him the fact of Rupert having escaped from the deadly trap that had been laid for him.

How he had done so was indeed to them a perfect mystery; but this mystery they determined at once, if possible, to unravel.

"Let us open the Death vault," said the Chief of the Poisoners, "and see who lies in their places. There must have been murders done, if no treachery was afloat."

The vault in which the two friends had been supposed to have been buried after their long and ghastly imprisonment had not been touched by the fire.

They adjourned, therefore, in a body to the place where they had seen the last of their enemy and Allan of the Glen, and proceeded to raise the stone.

There beneath the slab were two bodies enveloped in their winding sheets.

Their faces could not at first be distinguished, but on removing the clothes from their features, they started back in astonishment.

The faces they saw were not those of Rupert and Allan, but those of the two men who had been set to watch them.

How they had been placed in the vaults, and how they had been killed, was still a matter of mystery.

But one thing was still evident.

There had been a traitor in the camp.

"There will be another fearful ordeal for someone to go through," said the Chief of the Poisoners. "If our present terrible rules do not keep our Society from treachery, then we must invent some torture more terrible and desperate still, which will wring with horror the heart of him who is seduced into treacherous actions. Come, let these men rest in peace; they died in the execution of their duty. We will return to our place of meeting."

They had not again taken their seats more than a few minutes, when there was a rushing noise along the passage, and then a rattling as of iron being dashed again and again along the stone pavement.

Accompanying this was a sound as of successive shrieks and groans from someone in mortal agony, and then a heavy substance came dashing up against the door.

One of the assemblage at once opened the door, when a strange object presented itself; a man with long matted red hair, wild eyes, and haggard face; a man attenuated by long illness or long confinement in an unwholesome atmosphere; a man whose clothes were torn, and to whose limbs a long chain was attached.

His eyes had a ravenous look in them, like those of a wild animal, and as he entered the council chamber he cast a look of idiotic savageness around.

Then he broke into a maniacal laugh, and with a wild bound mounted on the table.

Here he danced and screamed like one bereft of his senses, and madly flung his arms about.

It was some time before they could recognise the strange being.

But at length Oscar Penraven cried—

"It is Jack Gradley, one of our keepers. What can this mean?"

"Gradley," said the Chief, "whence come you?"

The madman glanced at him vacantly for a moment, and then broke into a wild laugh.

"Ha, ha!" he cried, "hell is around me now! The demons surround me—the wild shrieks of the fiends ring in my ears. Avoid thee—avoid thee, satan!"

As he said these words with frantic emphasis, he swung the heavy chain round his head and struck out madly at those around him.

Then he remained stiff and motionless as a statue, with eyes starting from his head like one lost.

"This man is the one, and the only one, who can elucidate the great mystery," said the Chief of the Poisoners, "and he is mad. What is to be done?"

"I will speak to him," said Oscar. "Let us approach him. Draw your swords, and let me have room to escape from his mad efforts, should he be roused again to his insane condition."

The assembled men did as he desired, and formed in a circle round the table, where the infuriated wretch crouched as still and as mute as an image.

It seemed absurd to take precautions against such a being.

He seemed now in a state of harmless idiocy.

But Oscar knew that he was not to be trusted.

Drawing his sword, he approached stealthily and warily.

As he did so the poor maniac drew back a foot, uttering a noise like the growl of a beast.

"Fear not," said Oscar Penraven; "I desire not to harm you. Answer me, Jack Gradley, do you know me?"

The man shook his head.

Evidently he had no recollection of him whatever, and yet on a dark night he had found his way to the old house of the Poisoners.

"Where have you been?" said Oscar.

The maniac grinned.

"Ha, ha!" he shouted, "ha, ha! I have escaped. Oh, it was a fearful place! cold, very cold. The sun never shining. All wind—chill wind, and no sunshine. Rats to keep you company, and men to mock you! Oh, it was horrible—horrible!"

"The poor devil has suffered much," said the Chief of the Poisoners. "This Rupert Dreadnought and his friends, who set up for humanity, have allowed a fine specimen of it to escape. Speak to him again, Penraven."

"Gradley," said Penraven again, "speak to me. How came you to leave us? Tell me; I am your friend."

As he spoke he held out his hand.

The maniac misunderstood the motion.

To him it seemed the movement of an enemy, an in an instant he darted back, raising his chain abov his head, and uttering a sharp hissing noise, like a monkey in a rage.

The chain was a formidable weapon with heavy links, and the madman raised them apparently without any difficulty, and in an instant commenced his attack.

He gazed round savagely upon all, but Oscar Penraven was his special mark.

He appeared to see in him a likeness to one of his keepers, and he darted at him with fearful malevolence.

"Ha! ha!" he shouted, as he swung the rusty iron links round his head, "ha! ha! once I feared *you*, now I am free; it is you who fear me!"

The sword which Penraven carried was no use in parrying blows from such an awkward, and at the same time heavy, weapon as that used by the maniac, and the only way, therefore, in which he contrived to elude the fierce swinging blows was by stooping suddenly.

"He must die!" said the Chief of the Poisoners. "It were better for him to quit life than to live on; and, moreover, if we allow him to depart he may partially recover his senses and betray us. At him, my friends, cut him down!"

The poor wretch semed to understand in some degree the cruel hands into which he had fallen, and drew back into a corner, gibbering like a wild beast.

Oscar Penraven, who was nearest to him, commenced the attack, and was seconded by many others.

But for a long time the madman held his own.

It was really difficult for the men, numerous as they were, to get near him while he remained in a corner.

But his discretion did not last long.

Suddenly seeing, as he fancied, an opportunity, he rushed forward, and, swinging the chain savagely round his head, dashed one of the Poisoners to the ground deluged in blood.

It was this moment that Oscar Penraven chose to settle the matter.

Drawing his sword back he grasped the hilt firmly and drove it through the madman's heart.

With a wild shriek the poor wretch fell back—his eyes glazed, and then he staggered dead upon the floor.

"There is another victim to our enemies," said the Chief of the Poisoners; "more than ever now will our vengeance follow our destroyers. Friends, we will bury this wretched being, and let that be our last action in this house. We will leave it this night for ever. In future it will be as a spot accursed—a memory only of our wrongs."

Wrongs!

The direst villain of the age, the curse of London, preached to his hideous flock about his wrongs!

Within half an hour a grave had been dug, and the remains of the unfortunate maniac had been deposited therein.

Then the ghastly assemblage broke up, and the old house was deserted by them for ever!

CHAPTER VIII.

THE SUBTLE ESSENCE.

When Alford fell to the ground in the room where Rosalie St. Aubyn had been carried by Rupert Dreadnought, she sprang out of bed, and after slipping on a few articles of clothing, stood and gazed at him.

"He thought to triumph over me," she murmured, "but he is conquered. He should have known what it was to raise up the demon in me."

Then a strange and inexplicable change came over her.

She looked down upon his haggard visage—his ghastly features—his attenuated form, and a feeling of compassion entered her heart.

She remembered him as the love of her youth—the man who, in the prime of his manly beauty, had won her heart—who in the old times had been the admired of all.

And there he lay now, poor fellow, stricken by her misdeeds—helpless through her wickedness—at her mercy!

What advantage should she take of him?

Should she not rather try to persuade him?

Should she not rather try to make him remember old times, and forgive her for the great love she once bore him?

Foolish woman!

She forgot that the greater the love the greater the hate!

It was well, however, for him that she did not indulge in such thoughts.

It saved his life.

Going to the bell-rope, she pulled violently, and the chambermaid appeared after a moment.

"What is the matter, my lady?" she said, starting in wonder as she saw the lady standing in partial undress, with her hair falling wildly over her white shoulders, and her features expressing the intensity of her agitation, while lying on the floor was Alford, still pale and motionless.

"My husband here, pursued by ruffians, has entered my room by the back window," said Rosalie. "He seems dying. What hour is it?"

"It is now five in the morning," replied the maid-servant.

"Good," said Rosalie; "then let a carriage be fetched at once for us, and we will return to our own house."

The girl stared at her in wonder.

"Had I not better fetch a doctor?" she said.

Rosalie frowned.

"Do as you are bid," she said; "I understand my husband better than you. He is suffering from faintness and weakness, that is all. By the time you obtain the coach he will recover."

What she could not do by force she had resolved to do by stratagem.

The girl said no more, but retired slowly from the room.

Well she might wonder.

The whole affair was a mystery.

When she had assisted in undressing Rosalie St. Aubyn, the latter had told her that she had resolved to remain all night, and perhaps the following day.

Now she was going suddenly, and more than this, there was now in her room a strange man, who seemed to be in the last agonies of death.

The girl was of an inquisitive turn of mind, and she resolved therefore to see if she could discover anything by a little eavesdropping.

So instead of going at once down stairs, she lingered near the door, which she only half closed.

Peering through, she saw the strange woman kneel down, draw something from her bosom—a small bottle, apparently—and pour a liquid into the mouth of the insensible man.

The effect was magical.

It seemed scarcely to touch his lips before he opened his eyes and stared round him.

It was a wild, half-maddened stare.

Then he closed them again, and murmured in a low voice—

"Where am I?"

The strange woman stooped down and pressed her lips to his brow.

"Poor Richard!" she murmured.

Then she said, in a louder tone—

"You are with friends—fear not."

The girl, on seeing this, and hearing these words, considered that there was no immediate necessity for her interference, and moved away.

In about a quarter of an hour she returned, and knocked gently at the door.

As she entered the room Alford was seated in a chair, apparently sensible, for his eyes were open wide, and his colour somewhat restored.

Rosalie St. Aubyn was standing by his side, as if she had been tending him carefully.

A sweet smile played over Rosalie's face as the young girl entered.

It was, indeed, no guide to the fierce passion which was agitating her breast.

"If you can oblige me with a cloak to wrap around my shoulders," she said, "I will pay you well for it."

"I will do so," said the girl, who, like others of her class, was by no means averse to making money, "I will do so. The carriage is ready, and I will procure it for you at once."

The promise of reward having enlivened her footsteps, she soon returned, bearing a heavy travelling-cloak, and, Rosalie having given her a handsome gratuity, she led the way down to the coach.

Alford appeared to the unsophisticated girl to be quite recovered from his swoon.

His eyes were open; his colour, as I have said, was restored, and he walked without much difficulty as he leaned upon the arm of his fair companion.

But she little knew the subtle essence which had instilled this seeming life into his otherwise senseless body.

It was the deadly poison which the Poisoners' Society alone knew of.

Like the *Aqua Tofana* of old Rome, it was an indefinable essence, only that, while the one killed, the other annihilated reason only; made the brain, in fact, stagnant, while the rest of the body preserved its power of motion.

They passed slowly down the stairs, and entered the carriage.

Rosalie waited for a moment until the door of the tavern was shut, and then, leaning out of the carriage window, she said to the coachman—

"To Granville House, Putney."

The coachman at once ascended the box, and drove hurriedly away in the direction indicated.

During the journey not a word was spoken.

Alford remained perfectly still, and, in fact, in the same position as when he entered the coach, until they reached their destination.

The carriage stopped at a house of dark and gloomy exterior, surrounded by heavy pine trees.

Rosalie assisted Alford out with every care and tenderness, and the man still walked on as in a dream.

A slight tap at the door was sufficient to obtain admission, and, as it opened, an elderly servant showed himself.

He expressed no surprise on seeing his mistress enter in so strange a garb, or with so strange a companion.

He simply bowed in a stolid kind of way, and at a sign from Rosalie, took Alford's arm, and led him up the stairs.

Here, had he been in the possession of his senses, he would have seen that he was in a large room, elegantly furnished, but with barred windows.

"See that he is put to rest and has all he wants, Martyn," said Rosalie to the man. "Although he is now like many before him, he is no enemy."

And so she left him.

Mad, foolish, wicked woman!

In her own hard, cruel heart, blackened by a purposed indifference to crime, she saw not the fearful injury she had done to him.

No enemy!

No savage tortured by another could have felt more terribly vengeful in his heart against his foe than was Richard Penraven against her.

CHAPTER IX.

A DEADLY CONFLICT.

On the following evening Rosalie St. Aubyn visited her prisoner.

He had recovered his senses partially during the morning.

The drug was of the same nature as that which had been administered to Rupert Dreadnought and Allan of the Glen by the conspirators, and he was only able, therefore, to move about in a dazed kind of way, able indeed to glance out of the barred windows, and move about the room.

Towards evening he was well enough to eat a meal, and, after he had partaken of a few glasses of wine, and some food, mechanically, as would an automaton, he sat by the fire, looking vacantly into it.

Now and then a gleam of consciousness seemed to come across him, and he would start and raise his hand to his brow.

But then the old gloom seemed to settle once more upon him, and he would sit still again, and gaze, like one distraught, into the flames.

Presently the door opened, and Rosalie St. Aubyn entered, her splendidly rounded form cased in a robe of black velvet, so tight as to show every outline of her superb contour.

She closed the door gently, without taking the precaution of bolting it, and approached her prisoner.

She knew well he was in no condition to enable him to make his escape.

"Richard," she said, in a gentle voice, "do you know me now?"

He gazed vacantly at her a moment.

Then she held to his nostrils a bottle containing a strong aromatic liquid, and he seemed to revive from his lethargy, shivering violently and gasping for breath.

He glanced at her then in surprise and wonder.

"You here!" he said. "I thought I was dead. Where am I now?"

"You are in *my* house."

Alford shuddered.

"In your house!" he murmured. "Why did you not let me die while insensibility held me in its chains, rather than bring me here to endure a long misery?"

"Such is not my wish," replied Rosalie St. Aubyn. "I desire not to torture you. You are wrong there—cruelly wrong. I want to make a compact with you."

"As to what?"

"As to our behaviour towards each other in the future."

"Well, and what want you?" said the helpless man, shivering. "I am cold; give me wine."

Rosalie rose, and, pouring out a large bumper of wine, gave it to him.

He drained it in a draught.

"Now," he said, "I am better. Answer me."

"Listen then," she murmured, "and I will explain. I married you, did I not, when I was a mere child?"

"Yes, if you call it childhood to be sixteen—to be a woman full of passions, and daring enough to break hearts and laugh at the ruin you make."

"Stay, waste not the time in recriminations. I have much to say and much to do. Admitted, I was sixteen. I did not love you. You persuaded me into marriage against my will.

"For a long time I strove to be a good and true wife to you.

"But I could not.

"I saw others happier—I heard others more joyous—*you* led me into the society of men whose only enjoyment in life was to fascinate and destroy. I *was* fascinated—I *was* destroyed. You killed my destroyer. I hated you for it then—I thank you for it now."

"Well, and what now?" asked Alford, as Rosalie St. Aubyn paused for a moment.

"I love another."

"I know it—Rupert Dreadnought—but it is useless. I have sworn to be his friend; no matter who may be the one who endeavours to injure him, I have sworn to befriend him. Never shall he who — my best friend—who has been instrumental in saving my life—be induced for a moment to fall into such a deadly snare as that you desire to set for him."

Rosalie eyed him with a hateful look in her eyes, as she answered—

"Cannot you forget the past? Can you not, at least if you *will* remember, think that your own folly in marrying me so young was an excuse for my mad folly also? Cannot you think of me as a stranger, and let me go my own way unmolested. I know you love another; I will place no obstacle in the way of your marrying Lesbia Howard; but on that condition I must act as I please with Rupert Dreadnought."

"Never!" said Alford, "never! Though here helpless, in your power, I will never consent to degrade myself by such a compact. Were you a stranger to us it would be just the same—I should think it my duty to warn Rupert against you."

AGNES MAYLAND.

The gleaming hate in Rosalie's eyes became more intense as he spoke.

"Is this your resolve?" she hissed, as she leaned her beautiful form over him.

"It is—in the face of all dangers—yes."

"Then you must die," she said, and again the fatal handkerchief was pressed to his nostrils.

This time it did not take so great effect as it had done at the tavern.

He lapsed into helpless immobility, but he had still the power of hearing and seeing.

He was, in fact, in the same condition as Rupert and Allan of the Glen had been in the old house by the river.

As soon as she saw the condition into which he had passed, she moved towards a secretaire, and drew from it a small dagger, fine at the point like a needle.

With this she approached Alford.

"Now," she said, "I will give you one more chance. You cannot speak, I know, but you can express yes or no by your eyes. What I wish you to express is this—that you swear never to molest me again, no matter under what circumstances—never to interfere between me and Rupert Dreadnought—never, in fact, to treat me otherwise than as a stranger. Promise this, and you are free on the instant—refuse, and you die now. If you wish to say 'yes,' close your eyes."

But the brave man was not dismayed.

He looked her boldly in the face.

Not a sign was there of yielding.

"Good!" said Rosalie. "You have sealed your own fate."

And as she spoke, she began slowly unfastening

the doublet of the helpless man, so as to be certain that the fatal instrument would reach his heart.

But Providence still watched over him.

Just as the wretch was about to plunge the knife into his heart, the door was burst violently open and a woman entered.

A deep veil obscured her features, but this was at once thrown aside, and disclosed the features of Lesbia Howard, radiant with triumph.

The knife dropped from Rosalie's hand.

"Ah!" cried Lesbia. "I am just in time wretched woman!"

"How came you here?" cried Rosalie, white with rage.

"I heard that Alford was in your power."

"Where?"

"I tracked you to the tavern. They told me of the strange man whom you had claimed as your husband, and with whom you had gone away—he in a helpless state. I knew well who it was by description, and I readily guessed that your country house would be the place to which you would take your victim."

"What right then have you here?" said Rosalie, defiantly. "This man *is* my husband!"

For an instant Lesbia was staggered.

This man her husband!

If this were true, then she was the infamous, faithless woman who had crushed Richard Penraven's life.

The woman, who really loved him, recovered herself, however, in a moment.

"If it be so," she said, "I should, if I were you, be ashamed to own it. But, nevertheless, husband or no husband, you have no right to murder him, and here I take my stand to defend him."

As she spoke, she took from her bosom a pair of small, finely-chased pistols.

A look of scorn passed over the lips of Rosalie St. Aubyn.

"What care I for your threats?" she said. "In an instant I can call to my aid a dozen servants, who will turn you from my doors or destroy you at my bidding."

Lesbia's courage did not for a moment give way.

The man who was more to her than all the world besides, was lying there helpless in the power of his greatest enemy, and if she was unable to deliver him it mattered not to her whether she lived or died.

Rosalie St. Aubyn was unprepared for any display of desperate courage on the part of her antagonist, and Lesbia's next speech took her completely by surprise.

"I fear you not," said Lesbia; "the man whom you have yonder helpless in your power is the only being in the world whom I love. If you slay him, you take from me all my happiness in life. As, therefore, I know that, if I leave him in your power, you will kill him, I will swear this, that if you attempt to cry out I will fire."

The resolute woman, as she spoke, held one of her pistols in a direct line with the head of her enemy.

There was no mistaking the courage which beamed from her eyes, and was evident, in fact, in her every attitude.

"What want you, then?" asked Rosalie.

"You have the courage to murder; have also the courage to defend yourself. Take that pistol, while I retain this, and let us fight."

"You are mad!" said Rosalie. "Duels are for men—not women."

"Nevertheless," said Lesbia, "I am determined that it shall be so. Accept my terms, or you will die like a dog."

Rosalie gazed once more at the woman who addressed her thus with all the boldness and resolution of a man.

She saw in the face of her adversary not a sign of relenting, and she reluctantly, therefore, took up the pistol.

As usual, her heart was full of treachery, and she, therefore, resolved if possible to take a base advantage of her brave enemy.

"Well, then, since you are resolved," she said, "I must agree."

Then suddenly, when Lesbia least expected it, she raised her pistol and fired.

Fortunately for Lesbia, Rosalie, in her trembling eagerness for murder, took but an unsteady aim, and the ball which was intended for her heart passed harmlessly by.

A deadly whiteness passed over Lesbia's face, her eyes shot fire, and, with a quick but steady hand, she raised her pistol and fired.

Rosalie St. Aubyn had no time to avoid the shot, and as the smoke cleared away, Lesbia Howard saw her enemy falling back, with blood spurting from her bosom.

As she fell back, the door was dashed open, and a man rushed in.

A man about five-and-forty, with blue eyes and fair hair, and with but one arm!

"Oh! Redlock," murmured Rosalie St. Aubyn, as she sank down upon the couch, "I am dying!"

"What does this mean?" he cried, rushing forward, and catching his mistress in his arms. "This is murder!"

"No murder," said Lesbia, proudly; "see the pistol still in her clenched hand. On my part, at least, it was a fair duel."

"Let her not escape," said Rosalie, in a faint voice, as Redlock handed her some wine. "Let her be confined in a barred room, and see that this man has no access to her."

"Fear not!" said Lesbia, as Redlock rushed to the door, after seeing that his mistress was safe on the sofa, "fear not! I shall attempt no escape. I came to save that man, and if I cannot do so I care not for life. Do with me as you will!"

Redlock passed out to call the servants, and send one of them for a doctor.

In an instant Lesbia sprang up—rushed to Rosalie—snatched the pistol from her grasp, and then approached Alford quickly, loading the two weapons meanwhile.

"Alford—Alford!" she said, shaking him, "wake—wake! Have you no strength to rise and aid in your own deliverance? Rise—rise! I entreat you. I am here to save you! It is Lesbia, your own Lesbia, who speaks!"

It was in vain she tried this.

He was powerless to rise, and she might as well, in fact, have appealed to a stone statue.

The man who had not been awakened by the report of the two pistols could not be roused by the mere voice of the one he loved.

She had hoped, wildly, for a moment that she could have awakened him—placed in his hand a loaded pistol, and that they could thus have fought their way out of the house.

But this hope was nipped in the bud as Alford looked at her, wistfully, without being able to speak to her, and make her understand by any gestures his utter helplessness. Her bosom heaved, and the tears flew to her eyes.

But she quickly dashed these aside.

This was a time for courage, not for tears.

Thrusting the pistols into her breast, she raised the attenuated form of Alford in her arms, and, approaching the door, was about to pass out, when Redlock appeared, followed by several men.

Drawing one of her weapons again, she stood before them blazing with fierce anger and resolution.

"Stand back," she cried, "stand back! The first man who approaches dies!"

There was a momentary hesitation on the part of the men.

There was no doubt in their minds as to one fact.

One, at least, of their number would fall before that pistol held so steadily by that little white hand.

However, this hesitation did not last long.

"Come on, my men," cried Redlock. "Let us not be startled thus by a woman. The pistol has been discharged; fear not."

The men at this made a dash forward, and Lesbia, aiming at Redlock, fired.

The ball missed him, but took deadly effect upon a man behind him, who fell with a loud shriek into the arms of his comrades.

The diversion caused by this bold act gave the brave woman time to draw the other pistol from her bosom and again confront them.

Redlock himself was staggered by this display of courage and precision.

But he was, nevertheless, a determined and resolute man.

When Rupert had accosted him in the street the name of "Dreadnought" had for a moment paralysed his strength, but here there was no such cause.

"Come," he said, "come on, my men; let us make another attempt. On, all at once, as I bid you."

They quickly and bravely did as they were bidden, and again the fatal report rang out, the bullet sped, and another of the attacking party fell.

She made a dash forward now in the frantic hope of escaping amid the confusion.

But it was all in vain.

She was but one against many, and she had the weight of a man in her arms.

Her courage, kept up to this moment, now at length gave way, a deadly sickness invaded her heart, and had it not been for those around her, Alford would have been dashed down the steep staircase.

"You will be punished terribly for this," said Redlock, as he seized her and bore her back into the room; "you will be denounced to the Society."

Whatever idea this presented to the mind of the listener, it was evidently one of horror, for a shudder passed through her frame, and she sank down into the chair nearest her.

"I care not," she said, in a low voice; "if he is in your power, I have nothing to live for. What have they done with him?"

"Ask not; he will die; but you, you will, as I have said, be denounced to the Society; and you know what terrible doom will follow that."

Again the shudder came, and the chill at her heart, and she sat still, saying nothing.

In a few more moments Rosalie faintly opened her eyes, and asked Redlock to approach.

He at once approached her.

"Take her away to the fifth chamber," she said; "let her not remain here while the doctor is here. Quick, I feel very faint; more wine, more wine."

Whatever position Redlock held in the household of Rosalie St. Aubyn, he seemed very eager to obey the behests of the wounded lady, and he obeyed with the utmost alacrity.

He brought her the wine, assisted her while she drank it, and then, approaching Lesbia, said—

"Now then, follow me."

His voice was harsh and stern.

From him she knew she could expect no pity.

So she rose slowly.

One glance again she gave at Alford, helpless, motionless, all but his wistful eyes.

"And will you not tell me what you are going to do with him?" she asked again.

"I have answered you once," replied Redlock. "I can say no more."

She saw it was utterly useless to ask more, and so in silence she followed her conductor.

He led her up two flights of stairs, and emerging upon a broad landing, unlocked the door of a room, into which he motioned her.

Resistance being utterly useless, she entered.

It was a place over whose portal should have been written, as over the Hell described by Dante in his "Inferno"—

"Abandon hope all ye that enter here."

It was a dark, gloomy chamber, to which the light only came through a small barred window.

The walls were of a colour which appeared black, and there was no fire-place in which the cheerful companionship of a bright blaze could be secured.

She made no remark, however, but passed in and took her seat upon a chair.

She had not been in this gloomy abode more than a few moments when a wild cry of agony assailed her ears.

The sound reached her, not through the doorway nor the window, but from some other opening in one of the walls behind her.

Glancing round her, she saw a recess covered over by a black curtain.

She at once rose, and, approaching the spot, drew aside the curtain, and beheld a sight which filled her with astonishment.

Sloping down from the room in which she sat, was a wide, smooth shaft of wood, and up this came the agonizing cries of a man.

She soon recognized the voice, and trembled to her heart's core as she listened.

It was Alford who spoke.

"Oh, great Heaven!" he was saying, in a half-suffocating voice, "why not have left me as I was, in a state of insensibility, and not have roused me into life again that I might suffer thus!"

Then there was a stifled shriek, and all was still again as death.

In vain she listened for further sign of life, and at length, weary, dispirited, and fearing she knew not what, she seated herself by the little barred window

CHAPTER X.

THE MYSTERIOUS VISITOR.

We must leave Alford and Rosalie St. Aubyn for a time, and return to other personages in our story.

Allan of the Glen, as has been shown, was one of the most active friends of whom Rupert Dreadnought could boast.

While Alford and the other mysterious man, who was now one of Rupert's friends, worked their ends by intrigue and subtlety, he and Tom the waterman and Allan fought against their enemies by sheer pluck and strength, combined with the use of ordinary common sense.

It is of Allan of the Glen that we must now turn more particularly.

He, of course, as one of the most persistent and energetic champions of the young earl, was now marked out by the Poisoners for destruction.

He knew, of course, to a certain extent, in what a perilous position he stood.

But no thought of danger made him swerve from the path which he had marked out for himself—the path of unswerving devotion to the man who had saved his life.

It was with confidence the most implicit that Rupert Dreadnought left his house in charge of Allan whenever he had occasion to go abroad alone.

It was one evening that Rupert Dreadnought had gone out with Tom the waterman that Allan remained in Rupert's bed-chamber, according to his master's direction.

It had been a bright day, and the evening had dwindled gradually away from twilight to darkness so gradually that Allan scarcely noticed the change, but sat there by the glowing embers, never even troubling to light his lamp.

He was sitting thus, when the door opened, and a servant entered, bearing a letter.

"This is for Mr. Dreadnought," said he; "see that he has it, Allan."

"Leave it there; it will be quite safe," said Allan of the Glen; "I shall remain here awake until he returns."

"Shall I light the lamp?"

"Yes; but turn it down," said Allan. "I like this twilight; it brings back old memories."

He sat here for another half-hour thinking of the Hidden People, of his lost Mary Macpherson, of the strange father who had so mysteriously taken him from friends only again to desert him, when he fancied he heard the door open.

He listened and looked, but saw nothing.

Satisfied that the sound was no delusion, he rose, and going to the door found it slightly open.

But that was all.

Everything outside was still.

Along the broad old corridor, moonlight streamed in ghastly bands, and lay quivering on the waxed floor.

Gentle breezes rushed in from a half open window, but that was the only sound.

Satisfied now that he had made a mistake, he returned to his seat, closed the door, and walked back towards his seat.

As he did so, he turned up the lamp and glanced at the superscription of the letter.

It was in a pretty female hand, one that Allan had often seen before, the hand of Mistress Helen Penraven.

A sigh escaped his lips as he thought of his own lost love, and then he reseated himself before the fire, and once more relapsed into his reveries.

Thinking of bonnie Scotland and his bonnie lassie he at length lapsed into a refreshing sleep.

He dreamed a strange dream.

Dreams, be it said, are always strange, always wild and mysterious.

This was no more so, perhaps, than dreams usually are, but throughout its entire length it was Rupert Dreadnought who was in danger.

No matter in what position Allan himself was in this wild vision, a dark cloud seemed to hang over and shadow the fortunes of Rupert.

It was while dreaming thus that he awoke with a start.

He rubbed his eyes, looked round him, saw that the lamp was burning low, and that the fire was nearly out.

Scarcely had he come to the full consciousness that he had been dreaming, when a shadowy form left the dark gloom behind the head of the bedstead, and darted towards the door, which Allan now saw was half open.

Seizing the first weapon he could see, which happened to be a short dirk, and casting aside, as it were, his drowsiness, he dashed after the intruder.

But he was too late.

Quick though he was, the fugitive was quicker.

Guilt, and a desire to preserve a strict incognito, lent wings to his feet, and ere Allan was within three yards of the window, he had swung himself out, dropped into the darkly-wooded garden and disappeared.

"AS THE UNKNOWN FLED, ALLAN STAGGERED BACK IN TERROR!"

Allan was not slow to follow his example.

But it was all in vain.

The gardens, even in those days, were not very large in that part of the city, and Allan had soon explored every portion of them.

The fugitive, whatever his errand had been, had disappeared, and Allan of the Glen was compelled to return, baffled and angry, to his chamber.

As he did so, his first idea was to see if the letter was safe.

It was in its former position.

He took it up, and in an instant he saw that some villany had been at work.

The handwriting was still that of a lady, but it was not Helen's, though it was an excellent imitation of it.

For a long time Allan thought and pondered.

What new trap was this?

Into what fresh snare did Rupert's enemies design to drag him?

He felt certain that the letter now in his hand was not from Helen Penraven, and yet he hesitated to open it.

If it contained any appointment which was on the face of it a trap to ensnare his master, he had resolved to act as Tom had done, adopt a disguise, and foil his enemies with their own weapons.

He could personate Rupert, dress himself in his clothes, and incur the risk, whatever it might be, to save the one who had saved him.

Still it was not the act of an honourable man to break open a letter, no matter what he suspected to be in it, and at length he cast it down on the table again, and with a sigh resumed his seat.

Honour prevented his aiding his master.

He was saved from much debate upon the subject by the entrance of Rupert himself.

Eagerly he seized the letter, but Allan of the Glen detained him.

"Stay, Master Dreadnought," he said, "that letter is an imposture if it seems to you to come from Mistress Penraven. I have a story to unfold—a confession to make, too, for I have slept at my post."

Rupert smiled.

"My friend," he said, "you cannot be expected to watch at all hours. But quick; tell me the story, for I am all impatience to see what this letter contains."

Briefly Allan told his tale.

"Curses on this midnight intruder!" cried Rupert. "He has taken Helen's letter, then, and in that, no doubt, she has mentioned her address."

As he spoke, he opened the letter.

Well he might start with astonishment as he read its strange contents.

It ran as follows—

"One who loves you, and has your interest at heart, begs of you not to disregard the request made in this letter. At ten o'clock to-morrow night a man will await you on the second arch of London Bridge. You know him not, but do not fear to meet him; his desire, as mine is, is to save your life. Remember the watchword, 'Love and night.'"

It was, then, from Rosalie St. Aubyn.

Knowing not her name, he yet well remembered the password.

Could it be that the woman whose life he had saved at the peril of his own was now endeavouring to betray him?

"No he could not believe it.

"I shall keep the appointment," he murmured, and as he said so, his eye caught a postscript, hurriedly added, in a fainter ink—

"I know well your story. I know that you have repeatedly been the victim of conspiracies and attempts upon your life. Still, keep this appointment. You will perhaps give greater credence to my words when I tell you—when I openly confess to you that the man whom you are to meet holds a high position in the terrible Society which has so long been a scourge to London!"

Rupert Dreadnought started in astonishment.

The confession before him was indeed a strange and unexpected one, coming as it did from the lips of so fair a being.

That she was the writer there could not be much doubt, for no one but himself and she knew the password.

"Pray do not go," said Allan of the Glen, as his master told him of the contents of the missive. "Let either I or Tom, or both together, go instead of you, and learn from the lips of this stranger what he requires of you."

"No, no," said Rupert. "I have good reason to believe that this appointment is not a snare, but one that I ought to keep. I shall go."

"You will at least allow us, or me, at any rate, to accompany you?"

"Yes," said Rupert, "you can accompany me if you please. That will be quite sufficient."

"You may think so," thought Allan, as he quitted his master's presence, "but I will see that you are not deceived."

In the wonder excited by the strange epistle, Rupert Dreadnought had forgotten one thing.

Helen Penraven's letter was in the hands of Rosalie St. Aubyn's messenger, and in that letter her address was given!

CHAPTER XI.

THE MEETING ON OLD LONDON BRIDGE.

On the following night, at half-past nine, Rupert Dreadnought and Allan of the Glen quitted the old house, and made their way slowly towards the place of meeting.

They watched carefully to see if any spies were about, but not a soul was in the street.

Evidently those who expected them, friends or enemies as they might be, made sure of their coming.

It was a somewhat cloudy night, though the moon showed itself at intervals, and when they at length reached the bridge, it was veiled in heavy darkness.

"Now," said Rupert, "you must leave the rest to me, Allan; fear not; if he attempts any treachery I will at once put you on the alert."

So saying he walked rapidly onwards, followed by Allan, who, though keeping at some distance, watched his every movement, and had his sword well loosened in his scabbard.

The person who awaited the arrival of Rupert Dreadnought had been there some time when the young earl approached, and at once advanced to meet him.

To anyone who had seen him once before, he could easily have been recognisable.

He was none other than the man with the red gleaming eyes, who had so alarmed Rosalie St. Aubyn at the meeting which I described in the first chapter of my story.

He was wrapped now in a large cloak, but he had no farther disguise.

"You have then come to time," said he, as he advanced so suddenly as to startle our hero.

"I always keep my appointments," said Rupert Dreadnought. "This is truly a strange one; but tell me what is its object?"

"We are unobserved," said the stranger; "therefore we can speak freely. You are aware who I am?"

"Yes; the letter disclosed to me the terrible fact of your connection with that society of monsters which has been the scourge and terror of London."

The stranger's brow darkened.

"I have come here," he said, "as a friend, and therefore I have a right to demand some courtesy. I have come here to save your life."

"You expect me to believe you, when I know that my father fell a victim to your hideous fraternity?"

"I do expect your belief in me," returned the stranger, "for one simple reason."

"And that is——"

"Because I have a debt of gratitude to pay you —a deep debt of gratitude."

The stranger's voice trembled as he said the words.

"Gratitude to me!" exclaimed Rupert Dreadnought. "What mean you? I know you not!"

"You do not, but I know you well," returned the other. "You met one evening, not very long since, a youth who was being beset by enemies. You saved his life at the peril of your own, and he is now in your service. That youth has noble blood in his veins, and his father—were he alive—would invoke blessings on your head for rescuing his child from the daggers of low and cruel assassins."

"Of whom do you speak?" said Rupert.

"Of Allan of the Glen!"

Rupert started.

Well he remembered the story which the young Scotch boy had told of the strange father, who had rescued him from the dominion of friends only to discard him and place him under the care of highland robbers and outlaws.

What connection had this man with him or with them?

That was the question he desired at once to solve.

"Who are you, then?" he asked.

The stranger smiled.

"It is not for me yet," he said, "to disclose that secret to you. Time may come when I may consider it safe to do so. But it is sufficient now that I tell you why I desire to save your life."

"Yes; tell me quickly now how my life is in danger, and how you propose to save me from it."

"I will. The Society of the Poisoners," said the man, as he drew Rupert Dreadnought further into the shadow, "reckons among its numbers no more respected member than Oscar Penraven."

"He is just the villain to suit them," said Rupert. "It was he who incited them to the murder of my father."

"You have twice laid your father's death at the door of our convention," said the stranger. "It is false. He died by a natural death; at any rate as far as Oscar and the Society are concerned. We had no hand in it. This I can swear. But to resume Oscar Penraven is your bitterest foe."

"He is, as I am his."

"True. Then it follows that in Oscar Penraven you have an enemy to be feared."

"No, not to be feared; an enemy to be watched and punished."

"We waste time in choosing words," said the stranger. "Let me proceed, for my moments are precious. There is no doubt that within a month you must fall a victim to the Poisoners. They are all to a man sworn to destroy you."

"They tried once," said Rupert Dreadnought, "and I was rescued out of the very jaws of death."

"Yes, but that time they had a reason for deferring your death, and they consequently aided in their own defeat. This time they will adopt the means, sure and undiscoverable, by which all their other victims have fallen."

"Granted that I recognise the danger," said Rupert. "What is the remedy?"

"You must join our Society. You must——"

"Never!" exclaimed Dreadnought, impetuously.

"Stay, stay. Ere you speak rashly, listen to all I say. I ask you not (and recollect that in asking you I am acting entirely for myself and the fair lady who loves you)—I ask you not to join the Convention in any active way. I simply ask you to take the oaths, to swear not to betray the secrets of the Society, to become a member of it in name only, and I will then give you a password which will be your protection everywhere."

The man's manner was so earnest and sincere that not for a moment did Rupert Dreadnought doubt that his hideous proposition was made to benefit him.

It was a madman's idea of rewarding an honest man, but it was preferred in that form.

"I thank you," said Rupert; "no doubt you have made this proposition to me in all sincerity, but I cannot and will not accept it. No matter to how little extent I was implicated in the doings of your Society, I should still consider myself culpable. I should be tacitly aiding by the mere fact of not betraying. No; I thank you for your wish to serve me, but I cannot accede to your plan."

The stranger heaved a deep sigh.

"I regret this the more," he said, "because another whom I wish to serve is included in the fatal list."

"And who is that?"

"You call him Allan of the Glen."

As he spoke the stranger's voice faltered.

"Ah! he is my faithful servant. I have more, it seems, than myself to defend."

"He was with you when you so miraculously made your escape from the vaults of the old house by the river."

"He was."

"He also then knows our secrets. Can you wonder that he is included? But mark you," and as he spoke the stranger pressed Rupert's arm. "I am, or, rather was, his father's friend, and though I am one of the Convention, I wish to save him. Give me, at least, the chance of trying whether he, too, is as obstinate as you are."

"He is here, not many yards distant from this spot," said Rupert.

"He is here!" exclaimed the stranger, excitedly; "Let me then see him."

"You can do so," said Rupert. "Here, Allan!"

His clear voice had scarcely rang out over the waters of the dark river when Allan of the Glen sprang forward, sword it hand.

Hearing Rupert's voice, he naturally supposed that danger was near, and rushed forward as for a rescue.

"Nay, Allan, there is no danger," said Rupert Dreadnought; "I called you simply because my strange friend here desired to see you."

"To see me!" said Allan of the Glen. "Whom, then, I have offended?"

The stranger gazed at him for a few moments fixedly.

There was a dreamy, far-off look in his face as he did so.

He seemed to be recalling old memories long buried.

"Young man," he said, "you have, as you are aware, offended the Convention."

"I know of no Convention," he said.

"He alludes to the Poisoners," said Rupert Dreadnought, "those whom, by almost a miracle, we were enabled to escape from."

"How, then, have I offended them?"

"By the simple act of escaping. But listen; this person has a strange and momentous question to put to you."

"And, mark you," said the man, "I ask you to permit him to give me an answer without in any way biassing his opinion."

"Good," said Rupert; "I will not interfere with him. Speak on."

The tall, commanding figure of the stranger moved nearer to Allan, and took his hand.

"Young man," he said, in a voice which betrayed some emotion, "I was the friend of one whom, if he had been here now, you would have obeyed—I mean your father. In his name, therefore, I conjure you to give credence to what I have to say."

He then briefly, but with emphasis, made to Allan the same offer that he had made to Rupert Dreadnought.

But it had the same result.

The young man, staunch and true as the young earl, refused at once.

"Horrid as the proposition you make me is," he said, "I believe you make it out of true friendship; but I must decline it."

A great struggle seemed taking place in the other's breast.

He made no reply.

"Why do you not yourself leave the terrible Convention," said Allan; "you could then aid both me and my master."

A look of horror overspread the stranger's features, and he raised his hands shudderingly.

"Talk not of it—it is impossible," he said; "nothing but death can release me from a convention to which I am pledged, not only by terrible oaths, but by being implicated in awful deeds. No—no—if this is the only way in which I can serve you, I cannot serve you at all. But oh! Allan, consider—consider the danger you are in."

"Providence and my good sword will protect me," said Allan; "I can make no compacts with the devil."

At this moment a long, shrill cry was wailed out over the river.

The stranger, over whose face a cloud had passed as Allan spoke, started as he heard this cry repeated.

Then, as if acting under the influence of a sudden impulse, he darted forward, and whispered four words in the ear of the astonished youth.

Then he fled away, and Allan of the Glen, as he saw him disappear amid the shadows, staggered against the wall of the bridge, saying in hollow accents—

"My father! My father!"

Seeing the condition of his companion, and hearing words which, under the circumstances, were of such fearful import, Rupert Dreadnought darted after the flying figure of the stranger.

But it was quite in vain.

The irregularly-built old houses on the bridge precluded any moonlight from descending to the thoroughfare; and indeed, from the manner in which the unknown had departed, it seemed as if he had disappeared into one of these.

Which of them, however, Rupert could not tell.

After a few minutes' fruitless search, therefore, Rupert Dreadnought returned to the side of his companion, who had now to a certain extent recovered himself.

"What ailed you but now, Allan?" he asked.

"A dreadful discovery, Master Dreadnought," returned Allan of the Glen, in a hollow voice, "that man—one of the Chiefs of the Poisoners—declares himself to be my long-lost father!"

CHAPTER XII.

REDLOCK, THE ONE-HANDED.

We must leave Rupert and Allan to make their way home from London Bridge, while we return to Lesbia and Alford.

It will be remembered that when my readers last saw them, a wild and piercing shriek of agony had resounded through Lesbia's room, and that then Alford's voice was heard from below pleading for mercy.

Naturally enough it occurred to Lesbia that it must be something grave in the extreme which would wring from a strong man's lips the cry she had heard, as well as the plea for mercy.

She was correct in her surmise.

They had released him from the influence of the fatal draught, only apparently to increase his misery and suffering.

As soon as the doctor had appeared, and had attended to the wound inflicted upon Rosalie St. Aubyn by Lesbia's pistol, and she had received stimulants which somewhat revived her, she sent for Redlock.

The man of medicine had ordered that she was not for some time to be moved, and coverings were laid over her, therefore, upon the sofa where she had been first placed.

"Bring Alford's chair near to me," she said; "then make him drink a reviving draught. I wish to speak to him."

"If I do so he will escape," said Redlock.

"Not so; see that his arms and legs are well secured ere he drinks," said Rosalie.

For some reason or another Redlock performed her every bidding with the most abject show of haste and obedience.

He seemed a perfect slave to her will, and hastened to quit the room and return with cords, as if he were bent upon doing a favour to himself.

Though the chair in which Alford had been replaced by Lesbia after her ineffectual attempt to save him was in no respect similar to that in which Rupert had been seized by lion's claws, it was of such a shape that, when his arms and legs were tied, it was quite impossible to move.

But a few moments were required to render him a helpless prisoner.

Then the draught was given him, and in an instant a tremor, a strange thrill passed through his frame, and opening his eyes he gazed earnestly around him.

Rosalie motioned Redlock then to depart, and he quitted the room at once without hesitation.

"Richard," said Rosalie, "the one you love has been here."

"I have seen her; I know all," returned Alford; "she tried to save me."

"She did; and she is now in my power," returned Rosalie, with a vindictive smile.

A smile crossed Alford's face also.

"You dare not harm her," he said; "she is, like you, one of the Society. Your oath precludes you from harming either me or her."

REDLOCK, THE ONE-HANDED.

"And yet she has harmed me. You rave," she said, sneeringly; "the Society does not protect one more than another. Lesbia Howard assailed me. I can show the wound she inflicted upon me."

"Yes, in a fair duel."

"Oh, duels between women are not recognised," returned Rosalie; "at any rate I can end this discussion readily. The Convention may not recognise the right of one member to punish another in private; but supposing that, that one is helplessly in my power. Suppose the Society knows nothing of it, and suppose the heavy clay encloses the dead body of a victim destroyed in secret. What then? Who is to tell the Society?"

"I acknowledge that you can do murder," said Alford, "but you cannot do it single-handed, and there are traitors everywhere who will afterwards betray you."

"True; but remember that Lesbia Howard is no real member of the Convention. She was forced into it; under fear of death she was compelled to take the oath. She hates all there save you. I can denounce her to the Society as a traitor."

For the first time emotion was visible in Alford's face. His pallor increased to a perfect ghastliness, and he bit his blue lips.

"I have moved you, I see," returned Rosalie. "Now I am going to renew our conversation. Lesbia, in one way or another, is absolutely and entirely in my power, and in that way, if in no other, perhaps I can find a way to your heart."

"Of what, then, do you wish to speak?" said Alford, coldly.

"Of Rupert Dreadnought," she answered.

And then, as before, she spoke of her intense passion for the young earl, and besought Alford never to reveal to him her follies and her crimes.

It would be waste of time to repeat her arguments here.

What she said was an impassioned repetition of what she had said before at the tavern where Alford had paid his midnight visit.

But it took as little effect.

He listened to her in silence, with a sneering smile upon his lips, and, when she had finished speaking, he was as stony as before.

"Well," she said, her heart feeling a freezing sensation within itself as she gazed upon the man sitting there immovable as a statue, "well, have you nothing to say?"

"Nothing but what I said before—that I refuse," returned Alford, severely. "The oath that I made when I was left by you for another I will keep, in spite of the world."

Again there was a passionate appeal.

She would have thrown herself on her knees had she been able, but her wound prevented her, and she could only look her anguish and her eagerness.

But it was all in vain.

Alford was resolute.

He was determined not to yield, even in the face of the utmost peril, and in his stern face Rosalie read the hopelessness of further persuasion.

Her brow grew dark as night.

Then she raised her hand feebly and pulled a bell-rope.

After the delay of a few minutes, Redlock reappeared.

This delay was necessary to him to enable him to calm himself, to smooth down his features, to change the intonation of his voice.

Unseen by either of them he had been the witness of all that had taken place; he had eagerly drank in the words of both, and his brow had grown dark as night as he had listened.

"What," he murmured, as he heard Rosalie's avowal of her love for Rupert Dreadnought, "what!

after all this striving, after all this slavish obedience, shall I lose my prize at last? No, no! Rosalie St. Aubyn shall be mine, or she shall be no man's. I will spoil her pretty scheme."

When he entered the room, however, not a sign of emotion was visible upon his face.

"I find this man obstinate—utterly so," said Rosalie; "place him in the vault."

Redlock bowed, and, re-approaching the door, called for the attendants, who, to the number of six, entered the room.

They then unbound Alford from the chair, leaving his hands and ankles still tied, and then lifting him in their arms bore him from the room.

They carried him at once to the basement floor, then down a murky, damp-smelling staircase of stone, and then halted at the door of the vault.

This they opened, and, ere he had any notice, hurled him, with jeering laughter, into what seemed a black abyss.

It was at this moment that the wild cry escaped him as he found himself, bound and helpless, falling among jagged stones.

Redlock turned fiercely towards the half-drunken crew as they closed the door of the vault.

"Fools!" he cried, "did you receive instructions to act thus?"

"No," said one of the men, in a swaggering tone, "no. But we know right well that when anyone is placed in the vaults it matters little whether he comes forth alive or dead."

"You lie!" said Redlock, angrily, "and have, moreover, exceeded your duty. Enter again, and see that no evil befalls him."

As the somewhat disconcerted men turned to do as they were bidden, he retraced his steps, and made his way towards Rosalie's room.

He was madly eager to tell her all he had heard, and to learn his fate.

CHAPTER XIII.

IN WHICH REDLOCK RECEIVES AN UNEXPECTED CHECK.

Rosalie St. Aubyn's wound was a serious one, and it may well be imagined that it was with no degree of pleasure that she saw Redlock again entering her room.

The loss of blood, and the sudden shock, moreover, had severely tried her nerves, and she was just lapsing into a state of slumber when he came in.

She looked up somewhat startled, and, seeing who it was, she frowned.

"What want you now, Redlock?" she said. "Have my orders been carried out?"

"They have," he answered, closing the door, and approaching her. "I have, in fact, more than fulfilled your instructions."

"You have not killed him?" she cried.

A peculiar smile flitted over Redlock's face as she said this.

"No," he said, "as regards Alford your orders have been obeyed. I spoke in regard to myself. I have been playing the eavesdropper."

Whatever colour had been left in Rosalie's cheeks faded away at this announcement, given as it was in a tone of deep meaning.

"And pray, sir," she said, "pray what have you gained by your treachery?"

"You use a wrong term," he said, "it is *not* treachery. Were I desirous of betraying you I should not come to you with a confession of what I had done. But as to *what* I learned it was knowledge that will be of the utmost use to me. In the first place Alford, or rather Richard Penraven, is, it appears, your husband."

"Well."

Redlock's eyes gleamed fiercely.

"You confess it boldly, then?"

"Of what use is it to deny it? You heard all."

"How then——" he began; then he interrupted himself saying, "yet stay, I will first say that I heard also your declaration that you loved Rupert Dreadnought. How does this tally with the hope which you have always held out to me?"

The eyes of the young girl, as he spoke, naturally took in the whole appearance of this man who set himself up as Rupert Dreadnought's rival.

Redlock was a man of some five and forty years, and looking older.

His figure, broad and set; his face, here and there, seamed with scars; his whole demeanour that of a coarse and brutal person; while, on the other hand, there was the vision in her mind of Rupert, young, handsome, elegant.

Redlock, though he kept his features under control, saw her action, and readily guessed her meaning; but he awaited in silence her reply.

"It does not affect anything I have said or promised," she said, sullenly; "Rupert Dreadnought is, you *know*, an enemy to the Society; by inducing him to love me I can lead him into a trap and destroy him. You are too impatient; how can I be your wife while Alford lives?"

"Then, if I destroy him, will you swear to be mine at once?"

The girl thought a moment.

"I do not wish him destroyed," she said musingly. "I wish him to release me from the bond that connects us, and set me free to marry whomsoever I please."

"You love him still then?"

"No, no; but I remember that I owe him much; that he was a friend as well as husband, and that I betrayed him—outraged his best feelings—trampled on his honour, and I will not fill up the catalogue of my evil doings by shedding his blood. No, no. We will compel him to yield all claim to me—to leave England, and then I can be yours; but not till you have assisted me in snaring Rupert Dreadnought. Had you no other proof of my love for Rupert being assumed, you should know that no woman ever loves where she is despised as he despises me."

This, in spite of her weakness, was said with some degree of energy.

But her manner did not deceive Redlock.

He saw at once that it was put on, and he resolved to deceive her, as she was deceiving him.

Madly—passionately in love with her as he was, this man of many crimes only saw one way of securing her to himself.

His plan, which flashed with lightning speed through his brain, was one of duplicity and crime.

He would free Alford, that he might proceed at once to Rupert Dreadnought, and inform him of the schemes of Rosalie; he would then dispose of Alford also, by murder or otherwise, and through this crime wade his fearful way to the love of the one who now regarded him with contempt.

"Good," said he, concealing his real feelings; "you may depend upon my assistance, but I cannot see why you should wish to spare Alford."

"I have told you."

"Yes, but in this case he is your worst enemy. It is incomprehensible."

"Not to me," said Rosalie, shuddering. "I have committed many crimes, but I shrink from this. I remember the time when I loved him, and I cannot—will not—consent to his death until nothing else will avail me."

"Good," said Redlock, taking her unwilling hand, and raising it to his lips, "good—we will work together in this, and as soon as all is accomplished you will be mine?"

"Yes; I have promised."

And ere the words were scarcely formed, or, rather, ere their echo died away, she had formed in her own mind the resolution.

"This Redlock becomes importunate. When he has aided me in bringing Rupert Dreadnought to my feet, *he must die.*"

On quitting the room of the woman with whom he was so madly infatuated, Redlock, who had constituted himself a kind of *major domo* in this mysterious house, proceeded to every part to see that all was safe—that all the doors were locked, and that no prying retainers were about.

Then, in pursuance of his plan, he proceeded first to the room in which Lesbia Howard had been imprisoned.

He tapped gently at the door.

Lesbia was not asleep.

In such a house she feared to sleep, and, even if she had under other circumstances been inclined to do so, the cry of despair which Alford had uttered still rang with a dismal echo in her ears as to preclude all idea of rest.

Naturally enough, she feared to open her door at Redlock's summons.

"Who is there?" she asked, timidly, as she approached the door.

"It is I, Redlock."

"What want you?"

"I desire to speak with you a moment. Quick! open, it is important!" he cried, in a tone of eagerness.

The key without was useless to him, for she had shot a bolt within.

What was she to do?

She was safe apparently until morning.

Why not remain so?

"Speak as you are," said Lesbia. "I fear to open the door, knowing you to be my worst enemy—knowing how I tried but now to take your life."

"Fear not," whispered Redlock. "I come to save you; I swear it."

There was silence, and he continued—

"I give you five minutes to consider. I cannot say more here. If you will not trust me I shall go and leave you to your fate."

Lesbia thought a moment.

If this man really was there for an evil purpose; if he came there, in fact, as the emissary of Rosalie St. Aubyn, he could burst open the door.

So, after a few instants' reflection, she turned the key in the lock.

Redlock glanced round him, and entering with stealthy steps, closed the door behind him.

"I do not wonder at your hesitation to open the door," he said. "It was simply natural. But when I tell you that I come to save Alford, you will doubt no longer."

Lesbia gazed earnestly into his face.

"To save him?" she said, eagerly. "Oh, could I think this true!"

"It *is* true," answered Redlock. "I will save you both, but on one condition only."

"And that is——?"

"That neither you nor Alford disclose to a living soul the manner in which you contrived your flight. You must swear this."

"Yes; I will swear it," answered Lesbia. "There *can* be no harm in such a promise."

"Indeed, no," responded Redlock. "I have my reasons for acting as I do; what they are, matters not to anyone, but I have no harm in store either for you or the one you love."

"I swear it, then," repeated Lesbia; "never to a living soul will I divulge this secret."

"Good," said Redlock, as he motioned to her to approach the spot where the mysterious shaft descended. "You see this sloping shaft?"

"I do," said Lesbia; "and from the bottom of it I heard Alford's voice raised in pain."

"Yes, the brutal fellows cast him in headlong upon the jagged stones. I am now about to descend to the vault where he is concealed, and explain to him what I have explained to you. Then, when I call to you, descend the shaft fearlessly. It is of polished wood, and you will descend quickly and safely."

One glance of doubt overspread the features of Lesbia Howard.

Was this a trap to induce her quietly to descend into the living tomb that contained Alford?

Redlock understood her meaning at once.

"You still doubt," he said. "You tell me that even from this place you could recognise Alford's voice?"

"Yes, at once."

"He then shall bid you descend when all is ready," said Redlock; "he would never lead you into danger. And now, for the moment, adieu. Remain here and listen for a voice."

Redlock then stealthily opened the door and closed it after him, while Lesbia crouched down near the opening of the shaft, and listened.

CHAPTER XIV.

THE VAULT—THE COMPACT—THE CONFLICT AT THE DARK GATE.

When Redlock descended to the floor of the vault in which Alford was confined, he found that two men (whether or not ordered there by Rosalie St. Aubyn, he knew not) were seated, or, rather, half-lying near it.

One of them was already in a deep slumber, but the other was making pretence to be on the watch, in spite of his numerous potations.

When, therefore, Redlock approached the vault door, the custodian caught him by the leg.

"What have we here?" he cried, as he turned the light of his lantern upon Redlock's figure. "Ha! Redlock."

"Yes, Redlock," said the one-armed man. "What then? Give me the lantern. I have a message from Mistress St. Aubyn to our prisoner."

The man hesitated, but after a moment delivered up the light without a word.

Then, as Redlock entered, and closed and bolted the door after him, he shook his companion rudely until he woke him.

"Rouse up, Jack," he said, in a hurried whisper, "rouse up. There's some devilment up here, I think. Quick! follow me."

"Why, what's the matter, think you, Bob?" growled the other, who was in no way pleased at being thus roused from his sleep.

"Mistress St. Aubyn has been for some time in a sound sleep," returned the other, addressed as Bob, "and Redlock, I verily believe, is prowling about for his own purposes. She will pay well if we thwart any secret design of his. Come, let us hasten away. I'll show you where to watch."

Thus incited, the man rose from his recumbent position, and hurried away with his companion, who, in spite of the drink that was in him, had had the shrewdness to detect in Redlock's face the signs of some hidden purpose.

When the latter entered the vault, and allowed the full light of the lantern to play upon the walls of the subterranean apartment, it disclosed a strange scene.

The place looked more like some underground spot beneath an old abbey or church, than a room under an ordinary house.

There were huge, rough-edged stones about, and here and there among them grinned the skull of some victim, whose other bones helped to aid in the confusion of the various portions of the vault.

It looked like a dead house, or an adjunct to a dissecting-room, rather than what it was, and the ghastly figure that now presided over it gave to it a more than ever unearthly and hideous aspect.

When Alford had been so hastily and brutally cast in by the myrmidons of the fair demon of the place, he had fallen face forward upon the jagged stones, and both his hands and his features were besmeared with blood.

He was now seated on a huge stone amid a pile of human bones and rubbish, and, as the light of the lantern fell upon his gory features, Redlock started at the sight.

Hastily, however, he recovered himself, and approached the prisoner.

"Alford," he said, in a low tone, as he drew from his pocket a flask of brandy, "Alford, I am come to save you. Drink."

Alford made a gesture of repugnance.

"No, no," he said, in a low and painful voice; "I have already had enough experience of your drinks. What want you with me?"

"I am come to save you," repeated Redlock. "Listen and I will tell you how."

He then briefly explained to him the same which he had explained to Lesbia.

Alford listened with greater incredulity than even Lesbia had done.

He knew nothing of the shaft, or the proximity of the one he loved.

"Yours is a specious tale," he said; "how can I be certain that you are not deceiving me?"

"Ask Lesbia Howard herself. See here. Call to her up this shaft, and she will descend to you. I desire to be revenged upon Rosalie St. Aubyn; is not that enough to persuade you that I am in earnest?"

Alford, without further delay, rose in spite of his great weakness, and, approaching the shaft, called loudly the name of Lesbia.

She instantly recognised the voice.

"I will come," she whispered down the shaft, and in another moment the sound of some one descending was heard.

Another moment again, and she was clasped in Alford's arms.

"Now," said Redlock, "have I deceived you?"

"At present—no," answered Alford; "but until I breathe the fresh air of Heaven, I cannot be expected to believe you. However, give me the brandy; I am too weak to do anything without some kind of stimulant."

He took the flask, and drank a deep draught.

"And now," he said, "where is my sword?"

"You shall have mine," returned Redlock, as he unbuckled his leather belt, and handed Alford the weapon. "Now hear me. I shall now lead you by a subterranean passage to a spot where you will find yourself on the verge of the high road. Having done so much I can do no more. There may be spies watching you, but I cannot aid you, for to allow Rosalie St. Aubyn to know that I aided your escape would be to bring ruin on all my plans. You have a good sword, and you have one with you who has the courage of a man. You can safely trust to her. See, Mistress Howard, here is a pistol. I am aware that you know how to use it."

"Aye, I know well how to use it," returned Lesbia, meaningly, "and if treachery be intended, I shall willingly risk my life in a conflict."

Redlock then placed in her hand a large chased pistol, and saying—

"Now follow me,"

Led the way to a corner of the vault which was mmersed in the deepest darkness.

RUPERT DREADNOUGHT.

"'YOUR WILL IS LAW,' SAID OSCAR, BOWING."

PLACING his hand upon a certain spot in the wall, he gave a slight pressure.

A rumbling noise followed, and a portion of the wall slowly receded, leaving an aperture large enough to permit of the passage of an ordinary-seized man.

Through this aperture the three passed, and found themselves in a damp, narrow passage.

Redlock led the way along this, until they came to a door, which he opened.

"See yonder," said Redlock; "there is the spot towards which you must make your way. Draw your sword, and keep yourselves on the alert, for you know not what spies Mistress St. Aubyn pays to watch her residence."

Redlock held the door open until the fugitives had passed through.

Then it noiselessly slid into its place again, and they were alone.

They paused not to utter a sound now, but quickly hurried on towards the spot where the glimmer of light gave token of an opening into the free air.

After a few minutes' walking along a sloping ground, they reached it.

"Now then," said Alford, "we must be careful!"

The opening was covered with densely growing twigs and undergrowth, and the keen edge of Redlock's sword had to be used to cut this away.

He did this as noiselessly as he could, and in a few moments they were standing on the outside—free!

But Redlock had told them the truth.

There was danger lurking near at hand.

No sooner had they issued from the gloom of the subterranean way than there was a scuffling of feet, and two men rushed forward from behind the shadow of the heavy trees that here overshaded the high road.

These were the men who had been watching at the door, and had seen Redlock enter the vault.

"Stand and surrender!" cried the man who had been called Bob.

A mocking laugh escaped Alford's lips.

"Escape thus far, and then yield!" he said; "no, no, you must be mad. Never will I yield. Death may overcome me, but if that does not overtake me, never will I submit to be a prisoner again in yonder house of crime! Stand aside there and let us pass."

As he spoke he advanced boldly, sword in hand, and Lesbia also, levelling her pistol, followed bravely by his side.

There was not a moment of hesitation on the part of the men.

They had a grudge against Redlock, who was, as may be imagined, no gentle master, and they knew well that the discovery by Rosalie St. Aubyn of any treachery on his part would be the signal for his ruin.

With this incitement, as well as the expectation of a handsome reward, it may be imagined that they thought not of danger.

Lesbia, who had already seen two men drop before her death-dealing weapon when endeavouring to save Alford from Rosalie, was loth again to shed blood, and as her adversary advanced she held her pistol straight towards him, but did not fire.

"Back," she said, "or death will be your portion."

But the man was not to be alarmed even by such boldness as this.

He advanced steadily and suddenly; making a lunge with his sword he endeavoured—not to wound his fair adversary—but to dash aside her weapon.

In this, however, he failed, and the leaden messenger of death sped on its way.

Not fatally this time, however.

It took effect in his left shoulder, wringing from him a cry of pain, but otherwise not disabling him so far as to prevent a continuance of the combat.

The ball being now spent, Lesbia clubbed her pistol, and awaited thus the arrival of her adversary.

But she was not sufficiently used to conflicts to render her courage of any further avail; and in the space of but a few minutes, she was on her knees at his mercy.

He had no desire to kill.

His object was to bind her, and carry her back into the house a helpless prisoner.

Meanwhile, Alford had by far the best of the battle.

Added to his brilliant skill as a swordsman, there was his determination to escape, and gradually but surely he drove back his enemy, wounded and dispirited, towards the open highway.

The minions of the fair demon were making a final effort, when there was a rush of feet along the subterranean passage, as well as the sound of horses' feet along the high road.

A reinforcement of four ruffians came leaping out of the underground way, and at once fiercely attacked Alford, who found himself now sorely beset on all sides.

But there were friends as well as enemies in sight.

No sooner had the villanous crew issued forth into the night than the horsemen, whoever they were, drew nearer, a dark form leaped up towards the villain who was assailing Lesbia, and, with a loud cry of agony, he fell prostrate upon the ground.

A long knife had been, with unerring certainty, plunged into his back.

A dark face peered down over his form, and, after a moment's scrutiny, the friend who had arrived so opportunely raised Lesbia from the ground, and untied the bonds which already confined her legs and arms.

Then Alford saw who it was.

It was his Hindoo friend, Najid.

In a moment after the liberation of the young girl, he was in the middle of the fray, which had not progressed long before the horsemen whom they had before heard arrived upon the scene.

Comprehending instantly the state of affairs, the newcomers, who were two in number, at once leaped from their saddles, and drawing their swords, ranged themselves on Alford's side.

The men who thus had so opportunely arrived were Rupert Dreadnought and Allan of the Glen.

Alford's heart leaped as he gazed upon the noble countenances of these two youths, beaming with enthusiasm.

There seemed no doubt now as to the issue of the conflict now that their stalwart arms were ranged upon his side; and seeing that Lesbia had now fled out of danger, he redoubled his efforts.

In the midst of the affray he had remembered the promise he had made to Redlock, and saw that if either of the men who had first attacked him were allowed to escape, they would be certain to betray him to Rosalie.

Glad enough, therefore, was he to see the first villain dispatched by the ready knife of Najid, and he with eagerness sought to destroy the second.

He was saved the trouble.

Allan of the Glen saw at once that Alford's adversary was no mean swordsman; and as he leaped from his horse, he thrust his gleaming blade through the back of the man, who fell to the earth with a loud cry of despair.

"Mount," cried Rupert, as he still pressed onward, "and we will place the lady before you. There is no need of your aid to thrash these cowardly miscreants."

Alford, for Lesbia's sake, could have acted on the suggestion, but he had no idea of leaving his brave preservers to punish his enemies alone.

He, therefore, ran to Lesbia, bade her mount one of the horses and be ready to accompany him, and then he rushed back to the scene of conflict.

It was soon apparent, however, that the myrmidons of the Convention had had enough.

Seeing the fate of their comrades, they gradually withdrew towards the mouth of the subterranean passage, and then, turning, fled at full speed into the house.

For a few moments Rupert hesitated.

"I have a good mind to remain and set fire to the house," he said; "these dens of iniquity should be rooted out of the land."

Lesbia clasped her hands, and cried with a shudder.

"Oh, no, no," she said, "not that; anything but that. You know not——"

A hard grasp upon her arm restrained her from further speech.

"You forget," whispered Alford, as he leaped upon the crupper of the horse, "you forget that what you were about to say would amount to a forfeiture of your promise to Redlock. We have promised, and, though he is a villain, we must keep that promise, or we cannot hope to succeed. Come, Dreadnought, let us hasten away. I am faint and ill, and eager, moreover, to save Lesbia. We know not how soon we may be beset by larger numbers."

After a moment's hesitation, Rupert Dreadnought and Allan mounted their horses, the latter taking Najid up behind him, and they were soon speeding away on the road to London.

And (the two villains being dead) no one through all this suspected Redlock of any complicity in the escape of the prisoners.

CHAPTER XV.

IN WHICH OSCAR PENRAVEN IS ENABLED TO DO HELEN A SERVICE.

Lady Claremont, at whose house Helen Penraven had been left by Rupert Dreadnought, was a lady of high aristocratic blood, and among the lower orders was no favourite.

The Claremonts had fought at Marston Moor against the friends of the Commonwealth, and among those who still retained a slight tinge of the old Puritan blood, she was, as may well be imagined, anything but a favourite.

There was not a few of these Puritanical people in England, and more especially in London, at this time.

As London is now the centre of Liberalism, it was then the centre of Rupublicanism; and many a time did the Lady Claremont, now a widow, hear deep groans and hisses as she entered her rich carriage.

Her husband had been a fervent believer in the rights of the Stuarts, and in her they saw his representative, though, truth to tell, it mattered not to her whether George or the Stuarts were on the throne.

At the time of which we are writing the spring had come in chill and damp, and provisions were terribly dear.

Angry words had been spoken; remembrances of the old civil war were brought forward; once more the "accursed" name of "aristocrat" was whispered low, as in Paris some seventy years later.

The authorities took little notice of it.

They regarded the riotous cries they heard as only the result of hunger, and disdained to regard them as implying anything serious.

Hunger was the creator of a terrific Revolution and a twenty years' war not long after; but the distress in London never approached in its dimensions that in Paris in 1789, nor were the English aristocracy to blame, as were the French.

It was on the evening of a cold, miserable day that Helen Penraven and Lady Claremont were seated in the drawing-room of Claremont House.

Lady Claremont, a lady on the verge of fifty years, was reclining near the window.

They were talking of Rupert Dreadnought, whose arrival they momentarily expected, when suddenly Helen started.

"Hark!" she cried. "What is that?"

Lady Claremont ceased speaking, and both listened.

At first the sound that met their ears was like the far-distant murmuring of the sea; then it swelled in volume as it came nearer, and took the form of the loud and hoarse voices of men raised in anger.

"What can it mean?" said Lady Claremont, shudderingly. "And see that red light—what is that?"

They both sprang up, and, approaching the window, gazed out.

A red light was certainly glowing in the sky.

It was the fiercely-flickering light of a huge conflagration.

The mob had risen, the riots had begun! They were setting fire to the houses!

Helen Penraven had, in her early childhood, heard rumours of terrible doings in the times not so very far removed from those in which she lived—doings which presaged the downfall of the Stuart dynasty and the rise of daring old Noll.

No wonder, then, that she experienced a deadly chill of the heart as she saw the red flames lapping up towards the sky and heard the mutterings of the angry populace.

"What are they going to do?" she said, turning to Lady Claremont—"what does it all mean?"

"They are hungry and unreasonable," said Lady Claremont. "They will, no doubt, in their mad fury, attack the houses of everyone whom they consider to be their enemies. We must prepare for them."

So saying, she rang the bell, and, in a few moments, a man servant appeared, looking white and scared.

"What is it, my lady?" he said.

"The populace has risen for some mad purpose," answered Lady Claremont; "see that the iron shutters are closed, and every preparation made for defence. Be quick, that there may be no chance of the wretches entering."

The man bowed, and hastened away, without speaking, to obey the orders of his mistress, and in a short time the house was in a state of defence, which it would have been difficult for a crowd to have forced in unless they had persevered for hours together.

The preparations were not made too soon.

Hardly had the great chains and bolts been shot into their places, than the roaring, yelling crowd rushed into the open space in front of Claremont House, and began anew their game of pillage.

"See! here is the house of old Claremont!"

"Down with the Claremonts!"

"Down with the robbers of the poor!"

Such cries, and others more terrible still, were yelled out by the hoarse throats of the crowd, and, within a few moments of the time when they entered the open space, the attack had begun in real earnest.

In order the better to see during their hideous work of destruction and revenge upon an innocent woman for the fault of her forefathers, they lit a huge bonfire in the front of the house, made of the straw, and hay, and furniture, which they had dragged from the bakers and corn-shops, and soon, through the cracks in the iron shutters, could be seen the reflection of the ruddy light.

Then came showers of stones, and the heavy blows of sledge-hammers on the door.

The women clung to one another in terror, as well they might.

The yells and mad rage of the crowd without showed plainly what destruction, reckless destruction, was in their thoughts.

Helen Penraven herself was unknown to the mob, but the very fact of her being a friend to Lady Claremont would, she knew well, be enough to condemn her.

"Bread! bread! Give us bread!" shouted the mob.

And then some of them, more desperate than the rest, came rushing with a huge scaffolding-pole, which they used as a kind of battering-ram against the door, which soon began to give way.

It was at the moment when it was just yielding, and when the women were giving themselves up for lost, that the door opened, and Oscar Penraven entered.

In an instant a wrong view of the case entered Helen's mind.

She seemed now to appreciate the whole of the desperate scene.

The mob were but blind instruments in the hands of her worst enemy.

The place seemed to swim round with her; she faintly murmured Rupert's name. And, overcome by the terror of the situation, she swooned away.

Oscar Penraven rushed forward and caught her in his arms.

"I will save her," he said, as he bore her towards the door.

Lady Claremont had never set eyes on him before.

"Stay!" she cried. "Who are you?"

"Oh! there's no time for babble," he cried; "it is enough that she is in danger, and that at the peril of my life I am here to save her."

And without deigning further words, he rushed away.

Hurrying down the stairs, he made his way to the rear of the premises, and through the little gate in the garden.

Here his carriage was waiting.

To hail the driver, open the door, and deposit the form of his fair and inanimate burden within, was the work of an instant; and, giving the man some hasty directions, he entered, and the coachman, hastening his horses into a galop, turned the corner just as Lady Claremont, led by a man-servant, reached the corner of the avenue.

"It won't do to stand here, my lady," said the man, as he caught sight of the fast-receding carriage; "that stranger has got away with Mistress Penraven safe enough, and now we must take care of ourselves. If they get hold of me or you, they may kill us. I know a hiding place."

Starting off with him, Lady Claremont soon found herself standing outside a building which was in the course of construction, not far off.

Standing outside until some of his fellow-servants came up, he assisted her into the area, and in another moment they had, luckily unobserved, found a safe refuge, for a time at least, in the cellar, between a pile of timber.

Meanwhile, Rupert Dreadnought had heard of the desperate scene that had been enacted, and, with Stanley Sherrington and a small number of friends and retainers, well armed, came gallantly on towards the house—the mob giving way before them—and succeeded in reaching within fifty yards of it just as the door gave way before the continued battering of the beam, and the thronging crew began pushing and crowding in.

There was no time for hesitation.

The watchmen had long been disposed of by the populace, the soldiers had not yet arrived, and so, getting his men into line, Rupert ordered the mob to fall back.

His orders were laughed at, and a volley of stones followed the derisive yells and cries which greeted him.

"All right, friends," he said, "we will fire on them. That will bring them to reason. Fire!"

A volley was immediately poured in among the crowd from long horse pistols, shooting down several of the foremost rioters.

"On them, boys! Drive them back! Charge!" shouted Rupert, and, waving his sword, he rushed forward, followed by his men.

Stones, bricks, and every sort of flying missiles came hailing down upon them, and one of Rupert's men fell.

But the rest still pressed boldly on, encouraged by the cheers and gallant words of their bold leader, by whose side Allan of the Glen and Tom the waterman were conspicuous for their determined bravery.

They gained ground step by step until they had nearly reached the house, when the mob, now desperate, made a determined stand, having been reinforced by a number of men armed with muskets which they had stolen from neighbouring gunsmiths.

Rupert's position was now critical in the extreme.

It was impossible for his handful of men, plucky as they had proved themselves to be, to stay long against such odds, and he began to fear lest he should be obliged to retreat and leave Helen in her danger, when he heard a loud shout behind him.

Turning quickly round he beheld to his delight a large body of soldiery charging through the streets.

Again facing the mob he shouted—

"Once more, men! Charge them home! down with them! Follow me!"

A volley of fire-arms, stones, &c., were hurled in defiance, but none of his men were hit, and with renewed energy they pushed onward, while, the soldiers now coming up, the mob gave way at last and took to their heels in a panic.

By this time flames were issuing from the top of Claremont House, and scores of people, men and women, were in the lower part engaged in carrying off the valuables and wantonly destroying what they could not take away.

As soon as he could, Rupert mounted the steps, and, with his friends, rushed into the house, forcing aside the mad crowd within in a wild search for Helen.

But it was in vain.

Neither Lady Claremont nor Helen Penraven were there, nor was there one to tell how and whither they had gone.

CHAPTER XVI.

HELEN IN DANGER.

Helen for some time remained in a state of unconsciousness upon the carriage-cushion where Oscar Penraven had placed her, and, as soon as all danger of pursuit had passed, Oscar turned to her, and raising her from her recumbent position, seated himself by her side, and taking her hand in his, commenced gently chafing it, in the hope of restoring her to consciousness.

As he looked into her face, whose loveliness seemed rather heightened than diminished by the deadly pallor which pervaded it, the feeling which had so long animated him assumed its sway in a greater degree than ever.

He had intended to have tried, by restoring her to her friends, to endeavour to do away with the evil impression he had before inspired, but now his old evil wishes predominated again.

Fate having thrown her once more into his hands, he would be losing a golden opportunity should he restore her.

He had rescued her from a dreadful fate; should he, now that the object of his mad passion was in his possession, run the risk of again relinquishing her?

No!

He would not!

Fate had given her to him, and his she should be

THE ATTACK ON CLAREMONT HOUSE.

Having arrived at this conclusion, and made up his mind what course to pursue, he leaned from the open window of the carriage, and spoke hurriedly to the driver.

The man, without a word, increased the already rapid speed at which they were going, and altered his course, while Oscar, drawing down the silken blinds of the coach, supported Helen in his arms, and gave himself up to planning the details of the scheme by which he hoped to secure his object.

Within a few moments, however, Helen began to show signs of returning consciousness.

She heaved a deep sigh, the colour began to return slowly to her lips and cheeks, and the lovely blue of her eyes was becoming visible through their partly opened lids.

Oscar started when he witnessed these indications.

He knew well that should she awaken, she would never consent to continue the journey which he contemplated.

Another moment, and she would be once more herself.

In possession of her senses she would listen to nothing from his lips.

What was to done?

For an instant an expression of disappointment flitted over Oscar's face.

Then suddenly, as if struck by a bright idea, he brightened at once, and, quickly placing his hand upon his breast, he smiled with satisfaction, as it pressed against some hard object concealed in the inside pocket of his coat.

Quick as lightning he drew forth a small phial containing a colourless liquid, and, drawing the cork with his teeth, he poured a portion of the contents upon his handkerchief, and placing it against Helen's face, allowed it to remain there until she had inhaled the fumes of the liquid for some minutes.

He then gently withdrew it, and gazed anxiously into her face.

The colour had partially returned to her cheeks, tinting them with a flush as delicate as the first faint streakings of dawn.

Her eyes were once more closed, her bosom rose and fell with her gentle breathings, and her features wore an expression of calm and tranquil repose.

Oscar saw this with the most intense gratification.

His rapt gaze remained rivetted upon her pure, unconscious loveliness, until his whole frame became agitated by the intensity of the feelings which filled his being.

Her lovely head lay pillowed on his arm, which half encircled her, and, with eyes aglow and flushed cheek, he stooped his head towards her face, and pressed his lips passionately to hers.

"Never," he said, aloud, as he raised his head, "never shall Rupert Dreadnought possess so much loveliness as lies here now in my arms."

The carriage rolled swiftly and smoothly along until it arrived at a plain, rustic gate, which stood at the entrance of a long but narrow avenue, shaded on either side by rows of majestic willows, whose drooping branches met overhead and formed an arch of brightest green.

Along this avenue they proceeded until they arrived at a broad lawn, around which a wider road, also shaded with willows, led to a large, old-fashioned house, before the wide porch of which the carriage stopped.

Before Oscar could alight, an old female servant made her appearance at the head of the broad flight of stone steps.

"Here," said Oscar, as he opened the carriage door, "here, come and help me to take this lady out."

"A lady!" cried the woman. "Lord sakes! so there is, and as pretty as a picter. Why, she's fainted clean away."

"Yes, she has been in great danger and much frightened," said Oscar. "Let us get her in at once."

Helen was soon carried in and upstairs into a large and elegantly furnished room in the front of the building, where they laid her on a sofa, and after some little time she returned to consciousness.

Pressing her hand to her throbbing brow, she gazed around her distractedly, and said softly—

"Where am I?"

Then, ere the old woman could reply, the dull heavy expression of her eyes left them, and, starting suddenly up, she exclaimed—

"How came I here? Now I remember. The mob—the yells—the oaths—the thunderings at the door—the dreadful fear that overcame me. But who brought me here? Where is Lady Claremont?"

"Don't look so scared, child," said the old woman. "Master Oscar Penraven brought you here in a coach, and told me to take good care of you as you'd been in danger."

"Master Penraven! And where is Lady Claremont?" asked Helen.

"I don't know," said the woman; "only when you came here you had fainted clear away."

Helen rose, and approaching the window gazed out, and started in surprise as her eyes fell upon the broad lawn, the tall trees, and the artificial lake—a scene which plainly told her that she was far from the crowded city.

She stood a moment as if in doubt whether what she saw was real.

Then turning, she said—

"What place is this?"

"It is the Willow House."

"Whose is it?"

"Master Penraven's."

"Where is he? Let me go to him at once," said Helen, angrily. "This conduct is shameful."

"Well, I'll lead you to him in a moment," said the woman; "but just take a glance at the mirror, and see how disordered your things are."

Helen did, and seeing that her radiant curls had escaped from their confinement, and fallen in heavy masses over her shoulders, she opened a dressing-case standing on the table in search of a comb.

As she did so, she saw a small phial containing a red liquid.

Instinctively she clutched it, and raising it, read the one word on the label—

Poison!

Glancing in the mirror, and seeing that the woman was not watching her, she quickly concealed the phial in her bosom, and having gathered up her tresses, was about to quit the room, when a knock came at the door, and after a moment Oscar Penraven entered, and beckoned to the woman to quit the room.

"I am glad to see you recovered," he said.

"Where is Lady Claremont, and why am I alone?" returned Helen, without noticing his words.

"Because I could only save *you*, and I brought you thus far that you might be out of the way of the furious mob. When I looked behind for Lady Claremont she was beyond my reach, and not a moment was to be lost. If I had left you to save her, you would have been sacrificed. Let us hope her servants succeeded in saving her."

"Again I say why am I here? Was there not, in all the vast city, any place where I should have been as free from danger as here?"

"No; the excitement was widespread," said Oscar. "The mob infested a dozen different positions of the town, and no one could tell where its fury might fall. No place was safe, and so I brought you here. Fear nothing! I have sent already for Lady Claremont."

"Then, till she comes, leave me," said Helen, firmly.

"Your will is law to me," he answered; "but you have little faith in my honour."

"I shall have more faith in it if you withdraw at once from this chamber, and leave me to myself." said Helen.

Oscar hesitated but a moment.

Then he bowed deeply.

"As I have said, your will is law," he answered. "Farewell, then, until Lady Claremont arrives!"

"Or until you send me safely to her care," replied Helen.

Penraven made no reply, but, turning away, quitted the chamber.

CHAPTER XVII.

THE MIDNIGHT INTRUDER.

As soon as Oscar had left her, Helen flew to the door, and after securely locking and bolting it, threw herself upon the sofa, and gave way to the grief and tears she could no longer control.

She had no faith whatever in the assurances Oscar had given her of Lady Claremont's safety, and the fears, too, she entertained in regard to herself by no means abated her excitement.

She could not but see in all Oscar's actions a design to force her into the hateful marriage with himself which had long been her horror.

Why else had he brought her so far?

Why to this lonely place, where there were none but his own servants, the willing slaves of his will, no doubt?

As these thoughts filled her mind, her tears abated, and her grief gave place to a wild, uncontrollable longing to fly and make her way somehow back to the city, and seek to end the suspense she felt, no matter what danger she risked.

She rose, and paced the room with heaving bosom and distracted looks.

The night had now fallen, and, as she stepped from the room out upon the wide balcony that surrounded the house on three sides, and looked towards the city with longing eyes, she saw the sky lit up with a red, lurid glow, and ever and anon could catch the distant sounds of bells, and a dull, heavy roar, which came borne to her ear across the country by the wind, showing that the riots were still going on, and that the work of robbery, destruction, and perhaps murder, was not yet complete.

Turning at length from the contemplation of this scene, with all its terrible and sickening suggestions, she once more entered the room, where her ears were startled by a tapping at the door.

She made no response at first, but at length the tappings increased to loud knocks, and she heard the old woman's voice calling—

"Here, mistress, open the door. I bring you a lamp and some supper. It is only me, I assure you."

Thus assured, Helen undid the fastenings of the door, and the old woman entered, bearing two lighted wax candles and a tray, upon which were set out various articles of refreshment.

"Now, my dear lady," she said, in a coaxing voice, as she sat the tray down upon the table, "now, my dear lady, you must be faint and hungry; do try and eat."

"No, thank you, I require nothing," replied Helen Penraven.

"What, not eat!" cried the woman. "I never heard tell of such a thing. You needn't be frightened to taste them. I cooked everything myself. Just look at that boiled chicken!"

"You're very kind," said Helen, smiling, "but I require nothing."

"What! can't I do anything for you?"

"Yes, one thing," said Helen, seizing her eagerly by the hand.

"What's that? I'll do it if I can."

"Assist me to leave this place," said Helen—"show me some way of escape from this house."

"Why, Lord 'a' mercy, my lady!" exclaimed the old servant, "why do you want to get away? Nobody'll hurt you here. Where do you want to go to?"

"To London."

"Oh! my lady, that's not possible. It is a long way off; the roads are as dark as pitch, and full of rioters. You'd be running right into the lion's mouth. Never fear, no harm shall come to you while I'm here, I'll promise. Come, do eat something; you'll be ill."

"Thank you for your kindness," said Helen, "but it is not possible. I could not force myself to eat; but I see the dangers you speak of, and shall remain."

"Well, then, I'll lead you to your bedroom," said the old woman, taking a lamp from the table.

"No, no," said Helen; "I will not leave this room. I feel safer here. Good-night. I would rather be alone."

"Good-night, then," said the servant, and in a few minutes she had quitted the apartment, and Helen Penraven was once more left to her own thoughts.

The words of the woman had to a certain extent re-assured Helen, so far as any danger she might have feared for herself was concerned, for she felt as though in any emergency she might rely upon such poor protection as she could offer.

With heavy heart, however, she once more sought the balcony, and turned her longing eyes towards London.

Once the thought entered her mind that she could succeed in stealing out of the house unobserved, and fly from the place.

But where could she go, and what other grave dangers might she not encounter in her flight?

She knew not the road by which she had come.

There was no other human habitation visible to her sight, and the high road was, as the old woman had said, teeming with rioters, who, no doubt, were by this time in a state of insolent drunkenness.

What insults and shame might she not be exposed to on such a journey, on a dark night such as that which now spread its mantle over the country?

She, therefore, reluctantly was compelled to give up all idea of flight, at any rate for the present.

If Oscar Penraven really did intend to inform Lady Claremont of her whereabouts, there would at any rate be a change for the better within a few hours.

At last, worn out with grief and care and the

anxiety she had gone through, she re-entered the room, and closing the windows as well as she could, and securely fastening the door, she threw herself on the sofa, and exhausted nature yielding, she fell into a fitful sleep.

From this she was awakened by the sound of someone cautiously opening the window at the further end of the room.

She started up at once into a sitting posture, and gazing in the direction from which the sound proceeded, saw by the faint light of the candle the figure of a man emerging from the balcony.

Thrusting her hand into her bosom, she grasped the phial she had concealed there, and rising to her feet, exclaimed—

"Who is there?"

"Do not be alarmed, it is I," a voice responded, which she recognised as that of Oscar Penraven, who now moved towards her with rapid steps.

"Begone!" she exclaimed; "leave me on the moment, for I swear that if you advance a single step further I will drain this phial, which contains a deadly poison, to the very dregs. I am in earnest. If you would not have murder on your soul, stand back!"

Penraven, who had advanced within a few paces of her, paused instantly.

Helen stood with one hand extended towards him, as if to wave him away, while with the other she raised the poison towards her lips.

There was a pause for a few moments, during which Oscar gazed on her with mingled fear, surprise, and admiration; but at last recovering from the shock her words and actions had given him, he exclaimed—

"In Heaven's name hold your hand! You are mad. I come not to harm you."

"Then why are you here at all?" cried Helen. "Why do you steal upon my seclusion, in the dead of night, like a thief, if you mean no harm? Your words and acts are at strange variance."

"Because I am mad!" replied Oscar, who, if he was able to entertain no other pure feeling, was at least sincere in his love for Helen; "because I could not resist the temptation to be near you, even while you slept unconscious of my presence!"

"I will hear no more!" she cried, sternly. "Begone!"

"Nay, listen to me!" he exclaimed. "Do not turn from me or drive me hence, but hear me."

"I will *not* hear you!" she exclaimed. "What can you say that will excuse your cowardly act in dragging me here—separating me from those I love, and whose life is far more precious to me than my own—under the false pretence of saving my life, only to doom me to a fate worse, ten thousand times, than death itself? I know well that you will do anything to force me into a marriage with you. But you do not know me! My life is nothing to me, and if you dare attempt to come near me but one single step, I will keep my word, and end it at once! The sin be on your head, not mine."

"By Heaven!" he cried, "you do me wrong! No thought of wrong has entered my heart. If you would but listen to me—if I could but picture to you the pure and holy feeling with which your beauty, purity, and virtue have inspired me, you would be more ready to pity than condemn me. If I have done you wrong in bringing you here, the wrong ended with that act. You have misjudged me. You have mistaken the truest and purest love man ever felt for woman for base passion! I brought you here that I might tell you of that love—that I might kneel at your feet and beseech you to bless it with your own!"

"You confess this," said Helen, "and yet tell me that your love is pure! Do you pretend to forget that I am the betrothed wife of your greatest enemy? Do you not know that I have sworn never to be your wife? I will not listen to another word, for every one you utter is an insult. I feel myself as much the wife of Rupert Dreadnought as if the ceremony had already been gone through. Once more I bid you leave me. Your carelessness has given me a weapon in this little phial, which makes you powerless to harm me!"

"Do you refuse to listen to me in my own defence," cried Oscar, "and thus condemn me unheard?"

"Yes, when I cannot listen to you without dishonour."

"But you may. Even if you were Rupert's wife, you are free."

"What mean you?"

"That Rupert Dreadnought is dead!"

"Dead!"

"Aye, dead! While you were his betrothed wife, you would have deemed each word I spoke an insult, and would have driven me from your presence with scorn and contumely. Now you are no longer bound, and I am free to declare my deep—my lasting—my unconquerable love!"

"You have invented the story of his death to deceive me," cried Helen, "thinking, in your vanity, that if I believed it I should listen to your vows, and be willing to rush into your arms. But I believe you not. Rupert Dreadnought is *not* dead! My heart tells me so!"

"I tell you he *is* dead. He was killed when the crowd burst into the house."

"I believe you not! Leave me!"

"Oh, woman!—angel!" cried Oscar, with outstretched hands, "you know not the feelings with which you inspire me! My love is free from every taint of grossness—it pervades my inmost soul. It is not force of impulse, it is the offspring of respect. It springs from admiration of your mind—your soul—which gives loveliness to your form. It is not wild and transient, but firm and lasting, and will live upon the slightest hope. Oh! deign to say one word of hope for the future. I will imperil my life by breaking terrible vows I have made. I will leave all and follow you. Only speak to me!"

"DISMOUNT, AND FIGHT FOR YOUR LIFE," CRIED RUPERT.

As he spoke with all the fervour of his warm nature, he had kept his eyes fixed on Helen, who, as she listened, so far forgot the fear which until now had prompted her to watch his movements, that she allowed her hands to fall by her side, and removing her gaze from his face, suffered her eyes to search the ground.

Oscar saw this, and quick as lightning he rushed

forward, threw himself at her feet, and seizing the hand which held the poison, grasped the phial, and cast it behind him to the furthest end of the room, where it was shivered against the wall.

Helen started back in sore affright, and would have fled, but Oscar held her hand so tightly in his own that she could not withdraw it, when, in a voice of tremulous fear, she cried—

"Unhand me, or I will alarm the house!"

"Nay," exclaimed Oscar, producing a pistol from his breast, and forcing it into her hand, "here is another weapon more powerful for your defence. That poison you could but have used against yourself; this you can turn upon my heart if by word or deed I give you cause to fear, or but offend you with a look. See, I am entirely—absolutely, at your mercy. Decide my fate—you cannot misjudge my purpose now. I am kneeling at your feet—my very life at your disposal, imploring you to accept my love—to be my wife if Heaven ha removed the barrier between us."

He paused, and Helen stood gazing at him with heaving bosom and wondering eyes.

At length she was about to speak and bid him rise, when the sound of voices and footsteps fell upon her ears, and with a bound she sprang towards the door, which was shaken violently from without, while a voice demanded admittance in loud and agitated tones.

CHAPTER XVIII.

FLIGHT.

In Helen's mind the loud clamouring at the door announced the arrival of friends.

To Oscar's calmer brain it was only a premonition of danger.

"Who is there?" he demanded, in a loud voice, at the same time gently preventing Helen from withdrawing the bolts of the door.

"It is Redlock," said a voice. "I have important news."

"Quick, Helen," said Oscar, in a low tone, "retire behind those curtains, where no one can see you. These men must not know you are here."

"No; I will remain and demand their protection," returned the young girl, standing resolutely before him.

"For Heaven's sake be not so mad!" cried Oscar. "These are ruffians employed by a society to which I am bound by terrible oaths. They must not see you here; you run the risk of insult."

"Quick! quick!" cried Redlock, in a tone almost of anger. "What delays you?"

"He is Rupert Dreadnought's deadliest enemy—Redlock the One-Handed," said Oscar, sternly, as he began to unbolt the door. "Whatever happens is your fault, not mine."

These words were so evidently dictated by sincerity that Helen no longer hesitated.

She heard without the tramp and oaths of a number of men, and, hurrying across the room, she concealed herself behind the heavy curtains near the casement of the balcony.

Then the door was thrown open by Oscar, and Redlock rushed in, followed by a crowd of men, eager and excited.

"What on earth ails you, Redlock?" cried Oscar, as he gazed on the white and ghastly features of the one-handed man. "You look, truly, as if you had seen a ghost."

"This is no time for jesting, Sir Oscar," returned Redlock; "if I am white, it is because I and my fellows here, too, have rushed hither in such eager haste."

"And what ails you, then?"

"I come to apprise you that Rupert Dreadnought and his men are on your track, and——"

A smothered exclamation of delight from behind the curtain restrained him.

"What was that?" he said. "There's someone in the room!"

"No, no," returned Oscar, hurriedly, "it was the wind that stirred the casement. Proceed."

"Well, it is no matter of mine if there are listeners as long as you vouch for their truth," continued the one-handed. "Well, as I was about to tell you, Rupert Dreadnought and a large number of men are on their way hither. Those among the crowd who have refrained from drink, have eagerly enrolled themselves under his banner, for he has denounced you as a Poisoner—one of the Chiefs of the Poisoners—and the mob have commenced to shout out—'Death to the Poisoners! they have robbed us of our money and our bread! death to the enemies of the poor!'"

"And how know they their way hither?" asked Oscar; "this house belongs not to the Poisoners; this is my private house."

"I saw how that was done," returned Redlock. "When Rupert and his men, with the aid of the soldiery, drove the mob out of the house of Lady Claremont, and had, in vain, searched for Helen Penraven, a man from the crowd sprang forward, and seized the bridle of the horse upon which Dreadnought rode.

"Rupert at once imagined that it was the first signal of a general attack, and was about to cut him down.

"The man, however, held up his unarmed hand, crying—

"'Hold! You seek Mistress Penraven?'

"'I do,' said Rupert, lowering his sword.

"'Then follow me,' returned the man. 'I know where she is confined. She is in the hands of Oscar Penraven, one of the Chiefs of the Poisoners.'"

"Curse him!" murmured Oscar Penraven. "He must be some traitor. Could you not see his face?"

"Yes, I saw his face, and should know it again at once," said Redlock; "but it is not one which is familiar to me. However, the words he spoke were caught up by the crowd, and the cries I have before told you of were yelled from a hundred mouths.

"'Do you swear you are not deceiving me?' asked Rupert.

"'I do swear!' replied the man.

"'Then lead on. Let us at once advance!'

"Then Rupert, with his own friends, and nearly a hundred of the rioters, started on their road hither."

"A hundred, say you?"

"Yes, full that number, and, excited by the recent events as they are, they are no mean adversaries."

Oscar remained for some minutes deep in thought.

What was to be done?

He had in his house only a handful of men, and these were ill armed.

He had no conception of being able to withstand any attack.

The house was a private one, and only known to a few persons as in any way belonging to him.

"We cannot withstand any attack here," said Oscar. "They will destroy us like rabbits in their holes. How far distant are they now?"

"Not far. If you go out on the balcony you can see the lights of their torches and hear the shouts of the rioters," replied Redlock.

Oscar moved hastily across the room and gazed out towards London.

Redlock was right.

The advancing crowd were not more than a quarter of a mile distant.

He could hear the confused murmur of their loud voices, like the far-off murmur of the sea, and see the flickering of their torches.

"Curse them!" he said, as he brushed by the curtains, behind which was standing Helen Penraven with a bosom heaving with a fervent hope of rescue. "They will be here before we can make good our retreat, if we go not at once."

"And whither do you propose to fly?" asked Redlock, in surprise.

"To the ruins of the old Abbey—Cronmess Abbey. Go quickly below, see that the postern is opened, and return instantly. I may then have something in which you can assist me."

Redlock saw the necessity of haste, and, though somewhat curious to know for what mysterious purpose Oscar desired to be alone in this hour of danger, he hastened away and closed the door after him.

Oscar then immediately drew back the curtains and bade Helen come forth.

"You have heard all," he said, sternly, as he saw by the bright light in her eyes and the tremulous motion of her breast how full of eager hope of rescue she was.

"I have," she said. "Yes, I have heard that Rupert is coming. Let me stay to meet him. You told me he was dead, and if you mean truly to give me up to Lady Claremont, you will not detain me longer."

"Helen Penraven," said Oscar, quickly, "this is no time for argument. Every moment my enemies are drawing near. Into Rupert's hands you shall not fall again; sooner would I see you stretched dead before me. You have only one minute to decide. Either consent to go with me this instant peacefully, or suffer the indignity of being bound and borne forcibly away."

Delay was everything to Helen.

Already she could hear the sounds of the approaching crowd.

If she could but hold out, Rupert would soon be there. So she determined to brave all risks.

"I will not go quietly," she said.

"Very well," said Oscar, "then you will have to be bound with ropes. You have, while you have been with me, been treated with every respect; now if you submit yourself to the rudeness of strange hands, and oblige me to have you forcibly bound, it is your fault, not mine."

Helen had no idea that he would proceed to that extremity, and still refused to yield.

"I care not," she said. "Do as you please."

With a muttered curse, Oscar quitted her side, and, proceeding towards the door, shouted for Redlock.

In a few moments the one-handed ruffian made his appearance.

"Is all ready?" he asked. "For there is no time to lose. Ah! a lady! I had thought so."

"Yes, all is ready, save one thing," said Oscar. "She refuses to go quietly. Bring up some rope and tell Lambert to come up with you. She must be bound and borne away in the next few moments, or we shall be too late."

"You are right," said Redlock. "Already the crowd is within a stone's throw of this house."

And with that he sped away.

Not yet did Helen Penraven yield.

Oscar had placed in her hand a pistol, and she resolved to brave it out as long as she could.

"You have armed me against yourself," she said, as she raised the weapon; "the first one who lays a finger on me dies."

A cruel smile played over the features of Oscar as she spoke.

"You have a weapon truly, but it is harmless," he answered. "Think you that I would have trusted in your hands a weapon with which you could have destroyed all my long-conceived plans? No; you are in my power. I have behaved towards you like an honourable man, and yet you will not trust me further."

One glance at the pistol told her how she had been deceived.

There was no flint in it.

With a cry of anguish she flung the weapon down, and sinking into a chair, cried—

"Oh! villain, villain—perjured villain!"

At this moment Redlock appeared, accompanied by the man whom Oscar had sent for.

"Now, then," he said, "be quick. Our enemies are at the door; quick, bind her, and follow me."

The sight of the man as he advanced towards her at once altered Helen's resolution.

She could not dream of struggling in the arms of two such ruffians.

So she rose with dignity.

"I am conquered by your villany," she said; "I must yield, and will go with you. But remember that your conduct now is so thoroughly distinct from your professions but a few moments ago, that I shall always hereafter know how to estimate the value of your words."

As she moved towards the door there was a roar of many voices, and a loud knocking at the outer gate.

One wistful glance Helen cast towards the open window.

Then she prepared to yield to her fate, and, with a bosom heaving with sorrowful emotion, she followed Oscar.

The villain was only just in time.

As he descended the stairs and made his way through the stone court to the postern, the summons at the front gate was repeated still more loudly, and loud and angry voices demanded admittance.

CHAPTER XIX.

THE FORCED MARRIAGE.

"Now," said Oscar, as they hurried through the postern, and made their way through the wooded country at the back, "now I shall be able to prove to you that all my seeming harshness is only the result of my love. Before to-morrow night I myself will deliver you into the hands of Lady Claremont."

"I cannot believe," said Helen, who was now in tears; "this is only some fresh phase in your villany. I will believe nothing."

"My actions, then, shall prove it," said Oscar. "Come, give me your hand; it is dark, and the road is new to you."

Oh! how bitter were the young girl's reflections, as they passed along that dark path.

Here she was being hurried away by the one whom, of all others, she hated, while only a few yards from her, as it were, was the one to whose bosom she longed to be clasped.

But it was no use repining.

The only thing now to be done was to dissemble and try her utmost to escape.

The Abbey ruins were soon reached.

They were undistinguishable in the dark night, except as a mass of rugged masonry; but Oscar seemed to know his way well, and they were soon descending some rough stone steps leading to an underground vault.

Here Oscar showed Helen a rough, rude bench, gave her his cloak, and bade her sleep while he watched.

This command she resolved not to obey; but tired Nature was too much for her, and she at length relapsed into slumber.

About eight in the morning they were joined by Redlock, who narrated to Oscar and to Helen, who awoke at his entrance, the events of the preceding night.

Rupert Dreadnought and his men had entered the house, in spite of all protest, and searched everywhere.

They were utterly astounded on finding that the bird had flown.

They resolved, however, to keep watch for some time, and see that no communication was had with anyone.

After some hours, however, they went away, thoroughly convinced that they were on the wrong scent, and vowing vengeance against the man who had led them there.

This Redlock had heard from another.

He had concealed himself in the woods, and had not ventured near the house until he knew for certain that all were safe out of it.

"But," he added, when he had concluded his tale, "it is not safe to remain here, or to return to the Willow House. Why do you not——"

Helen heard no more.

The rest of the sentence was whispered so gently as to be inaudible.

Whatever it was, however, that Redlock said, it caused Oscar to start and glance at Helen, with a peculiar look which made her tremble.

"Yes, yes," he said, "I will take your advice. This evening we will quit this place, and proceed to the house of Sir Houlston Redclyffe. You, in the meantime, must proceed to London and endeavour to discover where Lady Claremont is, in order at once to request her to join Mistress Penraven. Return now to the Willow House, procure some refreshments for us, and give instructions that a carriage is to be waiting at eight o'clock on the highway yonder near the gate."

At eight o'clock the carriage came round as arranged, and, reluctantly, Helen took her place in it, while Oscar took his place by her side, and directed the coachman to drive on rapidly.

It had grown very dark, and they were proceeding at a rapid pace, when the driver suddenly slackened speed, and, opening the little window in the front of the carriage, said, in a voice of alarm—

"We are pursued!"

Oscar listened.

The sound of horses' feet was plainly distinguishable.

"Turn to the left," cried he, "and drive at full speed."

The window was once more closed, and, obeying his master's instructions, the man turned sharply to the left, and drove away at a headlong rate.

Farm-houses, villages, they passed, never once stopping until the steam from the horses obscured the glass of the windows, and the people, as they gazed, thought the horses were running away.

Helen's heart turned faint, and she grasped his arm tightly.

Her face was absolutely ghastly as she turned and gazed at him.

"You are deceiving me," she said.

"In what way?"

"This is *not* the road to London; you promised me, when we left the Abbey ruins, that you would take me somewhere near London, where I should soon be with Lady Claremont."

"It is true; we *are* still going in the direction I indicated, but, as you yourself heard, we are pursued, and I have been compelled, therefore, to make a detour to the left."

As he spoke they turned again to the right, and up an avenue of lofty elms leading to an old house.

Helen could not see where they were until they were close up to the door of the building.

Then, however, when she looked out, her idea of treachery was confirmed, and her heart beat wildly with emotion.

As Oscar leaped out of the carriage, and bade her alight, she cried in a voice which trembled with mingled fear and anger—

"Oscar Penraven, you are again acting the part of a villain. What place is this?"

"A house where I must hide for a short time—say an hour—until I can baffle my pursuers. Come, let us enter quickly."

"I shall not enter here," said Helen, firmly.

Oscar waited for nothing further.

Seizing her in his arms, before she was aware of his intention, he bore her from the carriage, hurried up the steps, and entered a room in the rear of the building.

There was now no longer any room for doubt.

She had been entrapped once more.

"Sir," she cried, as, panting from her vain struggles, her every limb palpitating with her efforts, she sank upon a chair, "what am I to understand from this?"

Oscar smiled.

"That by a clever ruse, Helen, I have again secured you," he said.

"Wretch, perjured wretch!" she murmured.

"I can afford, Helen, to bear your compliments for a time," he answered; "I trust, however, that time will change you. In two days I shall return to London, taking you with me as my wife."

Helen eyed him contemptuously.

"That can never be," she said.

"To-morrow morning a priest will be in attendance here, and unite us in the bonds of marriage. On the following morning we will return to London. For the present, farewell; the room next to this is your bedchamber; you will find all you require, for I gave strict instructions that your comfort should be attended to, and a supper be prepared for you. Adieu, fair one, adieu for the present."

So saying he bowed and quitted the room, locking the door on the outside.

When he had gone Helen rose to reconnoitre.

The chamber in which she had been placed was fitted up as an elegant sitting-room, and the bed-room into which it opened was equally luxurious.

Yet the prospect which met her eyes as she gazed out of the casement was anything but inviting.

Nor did it accord in any way with the luxury of the interior.

The moon was shining now with unwonted brilliancy, and as she gazed out she could trace the outline of a ruined wall, and the shattered relics of what seemed a chapel.

"In the morning," she thought, "I shall be able to discover the features of the place before he comes."

She partook sparingly of the delicate viands provided for her, and then threw herself on the bed without undressing, and after carefully locking the bed-room door, to snatch, if possible, a few hours' repose.

It was quite evident to her that Oscar did not anticipate any very determined resistance on her part, or else on his next visit he did not purpose coming alone.

On the table, where her supper had been spread, knives had been placed.

One of these, a long-bladed one, with a sharp point, she secreted about her person, and then lying down, as I have said, she slept until the first rays of morning burst into her room.

She then rose eagerly and looked out.

On one side rose the ruins of an old chapel, next to which was the house in which she was, and which appeared to be coeval with it.

Around them the grass grew in wild luxuriance.

Evidently the place had long been uninhabited.

But what struck Helen with some degree of wonder was the fact that beneath her window she could see a deep stone passage, or, rather, the commencement of a series of stone passages resembling cloisters.

Why the idea occurred to her she knew not; but unconsciously she seemed to connect these cloisters with the hope of escape.

How she was to reach them she knew not.

The window was far above the level of the ground, and to reach the intended place of concealment seemed impossible.

Yet she could not banish the idea from her mind that amid these dark and gloomy passages, which seemed to wind and twist around house and chapel, she should find her safety.

As she turned from the window she started back in surprise.

All vestiges of the supper had disappeared, and a breakfast was ready. No knives, however, were on the table.

THE RETREAT OF THE POISONERS.

This time they had evidently thought of the imprudence of supplying her with weapons of defence, and had, perhaps, missed the knife she had secreted about her person.

She searched round and round the rooms, but could find no outlet.

Yet the doors were still locked, and no one had evidently tampered with them, as the bolts were still there.

No one appeared till ten in the morning, nor, indeed, did she hear the slightest sound in the house.

As a neighbouring clock struck the hour, a loud knock was heard at the door.

"Who is there?" cried Helen.

"It is I," replied Oscar.

"I shall not undo the door."

He had locked it on the outside, but she had shot the bolts.

Oscar laughed.

"It is vain for you to endeavour to keep me out,

Helen," he said; "if you refuse to unlock the door, I and my friends will break it open, and that will prevent your having any privacy in your apartments."

Helen saw it was in vain to resist.

She unlocked the door.

Oscar entered, followed by five gentlemen, or, rather, men dressed in the garb which is supposed to be the attire of gentlemen.

When they had entered, Oscar relocked the door.

"Allow me, Helen," he said, with a nonchalant impertinence which was infinitely provoking, "allow me to introduce you to the Reverend Edward Tyrell. He has attended at this hour and place for the purpose of uniting me to you in the holy bonds of matrimony."

The Reverend Edward Tyrell was a man about the medium height, with large, bland eyes, a bland smile—a bland style of manner and appearance altogether.

He smirked benevolently at Helen, placed his hand on his heart, and after a low bow turned to Oscar.

"Sir Oscar," he said, "I trust you have with you the licence."

Oscar drew from his pocket the requisite document.

"Here is a special licence, Mr. Tyrell," he said; "read it, and then commence the ceremony at once."

The clergyman took the paper, and read it.

While he was doing so, Helen rushed up to his side.

"Oh, good sir!" she said, "if you are indeed what you seem to be, save me from these men. This perjured wretch—the chief of a society of assassins—is one whom I loathe and hate. I will never be his wife. I am here by force. You dare not perform a ceremony which would be a mockery and a sacrilege."

Mr. Tyrell's pale face grow a trifle paler as he turned to Oscar.

"Sir Oscar," he said, "this is quite a new feature in the case. I cannot perform such a ceremony as this. I cannot marry that young lady to you against her will."

Helen murmured her thanks, and clung to him as if for protection.

Oscar frowned and pointed to the licence.

"Is that licence in due form?" he asked, sternly.

"Yes, quite; but then—"

"What you now say is quite sufficient," interrupted Reginald; "that licence directs you to marry the persons named in it at any hour and place. Is it not so?"

"It is; but——"

"Do your duty then."

Tyrell handed him back the licence.

"I refuse to proceed," cried he, firmly.

Oscar drew from his breast a loaded pistol.

"I will have no trifling," he said, fiercely; "I have not brought you here to make a fool of me. Proceed, therefore, or I will blow your brains out."

The savage tone in which these words were uttered, left no doubt on the mind of the unfortunate man that Oscar would carry out his threat.

What was he to do?

He was surrounded by five men, all evidently bent upon carrying out this compulsory marriage.

He turned to Helen.

"My dear child," he said, "I have a family dependent on me; I cannot, for their sakes, afford to die thus unprepared. You must forgive me if I am forced to read the marriage service."

Helen saw that all was now over.

She sank down and wept bitterly.

"Heaven protect me," she murmured, as the clergyman began to read the service.

And so it proceeded.

Oscar gave the responses, while Helen still knelt and wept, her whole person convulsed with agitation.

As he finished a triumphant smile passed over the face of Oscar Penraven.

"Mine at last!" he whispered in her ear, as he raised her from the ground.

She made no reply, but shrank from him and sat down in a chair by the window.

The clergyman followed her.

"My dear child," he said, "my name is Tyrell; I live at the rectory about a mile from this. Trust in me. I have done a wrong action to save my life. I will sacrifice my benefice if necessary to undo the evil."

"Now," cried Oscar, "let us have the certificate."

"I have no form with me," returned the priest.

Oscar uttered an oath.

"You must make out one on paper, then," he said; "I warrant me no attempt will be made to dispute the marriage."

The clergyman did as he was desired, but Helen refused to append her name to it.

Oscar was about to drag her up to the table when, springing up, she drew from her bosom the long sharp knife, exclaiming—

"Come not near me, or I will bury this knife in my breast."

"No matter," he said, "it is as well as it is. The hour will come when you will be glad not to have this marriage disputed."

He then whispered a few words to his friends and turned to Tyrell.

"You must remain here awhile," he said. "It would be unsafe for me to trust you abroad; I should have the neighbourhood about my ears. To-morrow you shall be released; until then I assign you a room n my house."

The clergyman turned pale.

But he made no reply.

He saw, in fact, the utter uselessuess of resistance.

Oscar then approached the door and said—

"Follow me."

Then, as if he had forgotten something, he approached Helen and whispered in her ear—

"Expect me, my dear bride, early this evening."

These words produced the most sickening feeling in her breast.

She had just strength to stagger across the room, as Oscar and the five men left it and locked the door; then everything seemed to rise and swim around her.

The furniture, the floor itself, appeared rolling like the billows of the sea.

After this all consciousness left her, and she fell on the floor in a dead faint.

How long she remained in this condition she knew not.

When she recovered she was lying on the bed in the adjoining room, while on the table were preparations for dinner.

As she rose, she caught sight of a piece of paper on one of the plates.

She snatched it up eagerly.

It was a rough scrawl, evidently in a female hand, and ran as follows—

"The gentleman who married you to Sir Oscar Penraven this morning, says that, if you escape, you are to go to the rectory. On the left side of the bed is a brass knob, which——"

Here the note broke off.

Evidently the writer had been disturbed.

Eagerly Helen ran to the place indicated.

There *was* a brass knob, but it seemed fixed in the solid wall.

She pressed and tried to turn it, but all without avail.

Then, at length, when she was about to give up the attempt in despair, it slid on one side, a door opened, and she almost fell into a dark abyss.

She looked up and down on either side, but she could see nothing but darkness.

Was this an attempt at murder, and if so, who was the would-be assassin?

CHAPTER XX.

ON THE TRACK OF THE GUILTY.

To depict the feelings of Rupert Dreadnought when he found Oscar's house empty, and, in spite of the numbers at his back, could do nothing to save Helen Penraven from her worst enemy, would, indeed, be a difficult task.

He was, as it were, thrown back upon himself.

While Helen was in danger, he was precluded from following up the clue to Redlock's whereabouts, and the work of vengeance was indefinitely postponed.

His marriage with Helen, moreover (even if she could be saved from Oscar) could never take place until after he had fulfilled the five missions which formed the substance of his life work.

The possession of this beautiful creature was what he lived for.

What would his feelings have been could he have known that she had been absolutely united to Oscar Penraven in the bonds of wedlock?

On the evening following the attack on Lady Claremont's house—that is, the evening when Oscar inveigled Helen away with him in the carriage—London had resumed somewhat of its former quiet aspect.

The authorities had taken prompt measures.

Soldiers patrolled the streets, and the people, who, on the night previous had relieved their anger, had been supplied with something to supply their appetites and relieve their hunger.

On this evening Rupert was sitting writing, when a servant entered with a letter.

The superscription and the contents were both written in a strange hand, and the letter ran as follows:—

"I am aware, of course, that you regard as a traitor and deceiver the man who led you from Lady Claremont's house to that of Oscar Penraven. You are wrong. I am that man, and I acted for the best. Oscar Penraven *was* the one who took Helen from Lady Claremont's, and it was to his house in the country that he bore her. He escaped with her that night when he found you at his door clamouring for admittance; but whither he has gone now, I know not. I did not present myself with this for two reasons; I have no desire to be known, and, moreover, I have no doubt you would assail me as a traitor. However, to prove to you I am not, I will give you a second piece of information that will be useful to you. You are in search of one named Redlock. Go to-night or to-morrow night at ten to the sign of the 'Three Neighbours' in Crane Street, and you will see him. He will come forth a little after ten *alone*. I need say no more."

There was no signature, and the handwriting was very strange.

Rupert placed it on the table before him, and, for a time, gave himself up to thought.

Was this a genuine friend who wrote to him in this strange way?

It was evident that, whoever it was, he knew exactly the state of his feelings in regard to Redlock.

Should he trust him?

He took but a short time to consider.

Yes; the case was desperate; he *would* trust him.

The time now, however, was nearly the appointed hour; eager, therefore, as he was to encounter the one who was specially marked out by his father for vengeance, he resolved to defer all attempts until the following night.

The hour soon arrived, and without insinuating to anyone whither he was going, he buckled on his sword—*the* sword which the IRON CHEST had yielded up to him as the instrument of revenge—and sallied forth into the night.

He went out so quietly that no one knew of his departure, or, in spite of his marked reticence, Allan of the Glen would have followed him.

Allan had sworn never to desert him in danger, and he was resolved to keep his vow.

On this occasion, however, he had not the opportunity given him, for when he knocked at Rupert's door, and, receiving no answer, entered, he found the room deserted, and a few lines hurriedly written on a slip of paper on the table.

"Do not be alarmed at my absence; I am upon a special mission. If I meet an enemy it will be but one, and you need, therefore, fear nothing. I shall probably be home ere morning."

Meanwhile, Rupert made the best of his way towards Crane Street, and arrived there just before the clock struck ten.

The "Three Neighbours," where he was told to watch for Redlock, was an old-fashioned inn, with a solitary lamp swinging over the doorway and diffusing only a dim light around.

Opposite was an archway leading to some outbuildings, and here, accordingly, Rupert Dreadnought posted himself.

He had not long to wait.

Redlock, a few moments after the hour had tolled, appeared with a friend at the doorway.

Here they paused to speak a few words; the friend then went in and Redlock passed away alone.

A thrill passed through Rupert's heart as he saw him depart.

"Now, then," he said to himself, "the beginning of the end approaches."

Then he loosened his sword—THE SWORD OF VENGEANCE—in its scabbard, and followed in the wake of his enemy.

Redlock was so thoroughly immersed in his own thoughts that he would not have noticed the approach of a more clumsy pursuer than Rupert.

The latter, however, kept steadily on his way, never once making a false step or permitting his shadow to fall where it could be observed by his enemy.

As luck, or, to him, ill luck would have it, Redlock had a desire that night to visit Rosalie St. Aubyn, who was now certainly well recovered from her wound, and was able to move about.

Redlock, however, had been so engaged in other ways that he had had no time to pay her a visit, and he, on this evening, resolved to do so.

His way, therefore, led not through the crowded streets of London, but through country roads, for Rosalie was still residing at her country house.

He, therefore, soon after quitting the sign of the "Three Neighbours," passed into the courtyard of another inn, rang a bell, and within a very few moments was supplied with a horse.

It was now a desperate game.

If Rupert permitted this man to quit the place on horseback, he would certainly lose him for the time.

He resolved, therefore, to chance it.

Drawing his hat down over his brows, and raising the collar of his cloak, he rang the bell, crying in a loud but altered voice—

"Ostler."

Redlock's horse was already being saddled.

Another ostler bustled out.

"I want a horse," said Rupert, in an undertone; "I want one saddled instantly in order to follow yonder gentleman."

"You are a stranger to us," said the man; "you will, of course, leave money."

"Yes, yes," said Rupert, quickly; "here is a purse of gold, only be quick."

The word "gold" acted magically.

The man hastened in to count the money, but not before he had given orders to a man to hasten the saddling of a second steed, which was ready just as Redlock mounted and rode out of the yard.

It was not Rupert's policy now to seem too eager, and he, therefore, allowed his arch-enemy to ride out of the place before he made any attempt to approach his horse.

When, however, he had ridden for some yards down the street, Rupert leaped into the saddle and followed.

Redlock soon saw that someone was on his track, but perhaps from the same reasons which actuated Dreadnought, he did not attempt to come to an open rupture in the street.

He kept on, therefore, at a moderate pace until they passed out into a more open part of the country, when he put spurs to his steed and began galloping rapidly.

Rupert followed at the same pace, and they soon found themselves in the open high road, fringed by the budding trees.

Now came the trial.

Redlock had no wish to be overtaken, and finding now that he was really pursued, he gave the reins to his horse, and dashed away at a headlong rate.

Rupert was, of course, not slow in following his example, and at once a tight race ensued.

Both horses were of good mettle considering that they were hired, and for a long time it would have been a matter of difficulty to know which had the best of it.

Presently, however, Rupert began to overhaul his adversary, and that too pretty visibly.

It was no very great distance now to the house of Rosalie St. Aubyn, and Redlock, therefore, who was determined not to be overtaken, made now the most frantic efforts to escape.

But it proved in vain.

After rattling over Driftwood Bridge, and reaching a wider part of the highway, they came alongside, and Rupert cried in a loud and resolute voice—

"Halt! or I fire."

Reluctantly Redlock drew rein.

"Who are you," he said, "who thus stop people on the high road? If your object be robbery, you have stopped the wrong person."

"My object is *not* robbery," answered Rupert Dreadnought, sternly; "it is vengeance."

"Who, then, are you?" exclaimed Redlock, in wonder.

"I am the son of him whose friend you murdered," replied Rupert, raising his pistol, and presenting it at Redlock. "I am Rupert Dreadnought, son of Earl Dreadnought, the avenger of Henry Fortescue. In my father's chest—nay, interrupt me not—I found a skeleton hand—*your* hand; I found also the sword with which you murdered Fortescue. That sword I wear now to avenge him. Dismount and fight for your life!"

The words were uttered in a stern voice, that left no doubt as to the determination of the speaker to carry them out to their full meaning.

"This is no fair duel; this is an attempt at assassination," said Redlock. "Why not appoint a time and place where we can meet with seconds and settle this matter properly?"

"*You waited for no seconds when you murdered Henry Fortescue*," returned Rupert, sternly; "therefore, do as I desire or die."

RUPERT DREADNOUGHT.

"IN AN INSTANT REDLOCK WAS AT HIS MERCY."

Redlock saw now that there was no use in delay. "Good," he said, "since you insist upon this combat, I agree to it. We will fasten our horses to yonder tree and try the issue."

In an instant both had dismounted, and passing over the velvet sward which at the side of the road divided the highway from the hedge-row, they fastened their horses by the bridle to a tree that

ONE PENNY THE TWO NUMBERS.

overhung the path, and returning to the centre of the opening, crossed swords.

"Now then for justice and for vengeance!" cried Rupert, as the sword of Redlock crossed the blade which had entered the heart of poor murdered Fortescue.

The moon, which shed its pale brilliance on the scene of strife, perhaps never shone upon two faces more lit up by fierce passion—the one the passion of anger and fear, the other the passion of resolute justice and revenge!

It was a fight to the death!

Both were eager for each other's destruction.

Any one could have seen this from the fierce and angry glare of their eyes, and the muttered exclamations which escaped their lips.

At length it was evident that Rupert was gaining the advantage.

This was no sooner observed by Redlock than he brought a peculiar mode of conflict into play.

He parried the blows with his iron hook, while he contended with his right, and began sorely to perplex his young adversary. But not for long.

Rupert Dreadnought soon got used to his peculiar mode of behaviour, and aimed to disable the left arm of his foe.

In doing this, at length his sword got entangled for an instant in the iron hook and sleeve, and, suddenly wrenching it on one side, he seized his enemy's sword-arm in his left.

In an instant Redlock was at his mercy, and his sword was drawn back to deal the death blow, when the one-handed man cried—

"Hold! You would save Helen Penraven. If I die the secret shall die with me!"

The magic name of Helen stayed the hand of our hero.

"Drop your sword," he said, "and I will release you. If I find you are deceiving me, I will take no unfair advantage of it, but will fight this fight over again."

Somewhat amazed at this proposition, the one-handed man dropped his sword, and, in an instant, Rupert Dreadnought released his hold upon his wrist.

"Now then, speak," he said, sternly, "and to the purpose."

"As I said before," returned Redlock, "you desire to save Helen Penraven?"

"I do."

"Shall I tell you more? Your father instructed you to destroy me, no doubt, but he also said that you were to attempt nothing while Helen was in danger. Is it not so?"

"You are right," said Rupert Dreadnought; "but how did you receive this knowledge?"

"That is a secret which I shall keep to myself," returned Redlock; "but I know this, that by this time, if I am not mistaken, Helen Penraven is the wife of Sir Oscar."

"The wife!" gasped Rupert.

"Aye!—in name at least. I know well his plan—believe me, or believe me not, as you please."

Rupert now was full of intense emotion.

He sheathed his sword.

"Quick—quick!" he said, "tell me where she is concealed."

"Excuse me," said Redlock, "that is my only safeguard. I will conduct you thither, but rather than reveal the place to you now I will renew the fight."

A hundred thoughts rushed through Rupert's mind at once.

What should he do?

He had sworn to slay this man—the sword of vengeance was even now at his side, and yet if he were to slay him he should, perhaps, lose for ever the chance of saving Helen.

Yet was he but trifling with him? Was he but leading him into some ambush?

"Redlock," he said, "how do I know you are not betraying me?"

"I can only reiterate what I have said," returned Redlock. "I can only swear that I know Oscar's plan. His scheme was to take her to a certain place, obtain a special licence, induce a clergyman to perform the marriage ceremony, and return to London on the following morning. Whether you believe me or not, I cannot help it. I only say that I can lead you to the place where they are—you may take as many persons with you as you please, but all I advise you to do is to be quick, for, by this time, if Oscar's plans have been carried out, Helen Penraven is his wife!"

"Quick, then!" said Rupert; "let us mount the horses and start at once."

This was soon done, and in another moment they were speeding away along the road to London.

CHAPTER XXI.

THE CHARNEL-HOUSE.

We must now return to Oscar's house.

There appeared, as I have said, no outlet to the room in which Helen Penraven was immured.

In the dark chasm which opened before her, when she pressed the brass nob in the wall, there seemed no staircase or means of exit whatever.

Did the person who wrote the mysterious note desire to destroy her?

The tone of it precluded the idea.

And then, again, it appeared certain that this was the only method by which the attendant who brought her her meals could enter.

She crouched low on the floor, and glanced down

Her eyes had deceived her.

What she had thought to be an abyss of darkness was merely a landing, surmounted by a black door.

When she had become accustomed to the dim light, she observed a handle.

Turning this she pushed the door open and found herself at the top of a flight of steps.

Hastily closing both the doors, she hastened down, and was soon among the cloisters.

Dark and gloomy enough they appeared, but yet not dark enough.

In the twilight she [illegible] the risk of being discovered.

Where should she hide?

After tremblingly glancing around her she saw beneath one of the archways a door, and resolving to enter here at all hazards, she tried to push it open.

It yielded to her touch.

But the sight that met her eyes was one which would have appalled anyone engaged in a less important enterprise.

Heaps of bones lay around.

Bones of every shape and size.

Here a skull—here an arm—here a thighbone—here a rib.

Such a place would scarcely have been selected by any one under any circumstances, and, though running from a fearful peril, Helen felt a creeping horror in her limbs, and retreated.

But then what could she do?

Was not her danger great?

Was she not alone in the house—alone, indeed, as regarded friends?

Would she not, in a few hours, receive a visit from one who now claimed to be her husband, and who was aided by unprincipled men?

Would she not, by returning to that room, or showing herself in the cloisters, where she might be dragged back, be sacrificing for ever her hopes of happiness?

The sound of approaching footsteps determined her.

She entered hastily.

The only fastening to the door was a hasp for a padlock, but the padlock had long ago been taken away.

Seizing one of the small bones, she hastily placed it in the hasp, and concealed herself by crouching behind a huge heap of bones.

But the sound died away in the distance, and no one came.

Then a new idea struck her.

Might there not be some other outlet?

Eagerly she sought round the damp and dirty vault.

No sign of a door was visible, and a long and weary search ended in her being compelled to sit down, breathless and discomfited, upon the stones.

A gloomy afternoon had passed into grey twilight, the grey twilight had passed into a dark night, when Helen, trembling with cold, and tormented, too, by the pangs of a hunger she could not appease, heard angry voices without.

They were the voices of Oscar Penraven and Lambert.

The thought immediately occurred to her that, as the door was not closed before, and there was no visible mode of egress, the fact of its being now shut might excite suspicion in their minds.

Quickly, then, she arose, rushed to the door, and took out the piece of bone.

Then she regained her corner.

The voices became more distinct.

"How can she have fled," said Oscar, as they halted near the door, "is a mystery. She cannot have found the brass knob, and the window was unopened."

"Have you searched both rooms well?" said Lambert.

Oscar replied impatiently—

"Yes, yes; there is not a corner in either chamber I have not ransacked. She must be out here somewhere."

Lambert laughed drily.

"Perhaps she's in the bone-house," he said; "let's go in."

"No, it is not likely she's there; the sight of the hideous relics would alarm her."

"Not in such a case as this," returned Lambert. "She's evidently resolute against having anything to do with you, and would, I think, gladly accept death if she had to choose between it and you."

Oscar took no heed of the bad compliment thus paid him.

"Well, then," he said, "we will begin with the bone-house, as it is the first of the vaults. *We can close them up as we proceed and thus make sure of her!*"

Close them up!

What words of horror were these?

Words implying nothing less than a long, lingering, terrible death by starvation!

Death but a few feet underground beneath the hum and busy life of the world!

Death, when those who loved her were seeking her, and might walk unheeded over her living tomb!

Death, just as life was young and hopes were brightest!

They approached.

She feared no longer the dead, but the living.

Down over her, therefore, she dragged the huge pile of bones until they covered her everywhere, and the relics of mortality touched her very lips.

The first horror gone, they alarmed her no longer.

Poor remnants of lives long lost, why should she fear them?

The hearts which had once beaten within those frames, what had they not suffered? What anguish had they not endured before they shuffled off this mortal coil, and fled away to other realms of existence!

The two men of crime entered.

In Lambert's hand was a lantern.

The bright light from the bull's eye flashed hither and thither over the dark and murky walls like a jack-o'-lantern, showing here a furrow made by decay in the old walls—here a brick displaced—here a skull, grinning alone in a corner—here a skeleton lying in grim silence on the oozy and uneven ground.

Lambert laughed coarsely.

"This is a pretty place for a bride to hide in on her wedding night," he cried. "I doubt very much if we shall find our bird here."

Even Oscar shuddered.

A terrible dread invaded his heart at the thought that to avoid him the girl he had so much outraged had hidden herself among those grinning skulls.

"You are right," he said, "quite right. Helen would never conceal herself in such a place as this. Come away!"

Lambert drew him back as he was moving off.

"We are less likely to be overheard here than anywhere else," he said, "so let me ask you one or two questions. Depend on it those skeletons, of which you seem so much afraid, will not resume their flesh to attack you."

"Speak on!" said the young man, impatiently

"You speak your own thoughts, not mine, when you talk of fear."

"In the first place, then," said Lambert, "what about this parson?"

"I do not understand you."

"What are you going to do with him?"

"Leave him here."

"What, to die?"

"No; he will find some means of escape. But before we go we will slip beneath the door the key of his room. He will find it in the morning, and, by that time, all will be well. But come—let us be going. While we remain here the girl may escape. Let me but find her now," he added, with a muttered curse, "and she will have but a sorry wooing of it."

They then quitted the bone-house, and secured the door without by fastening the bolts.

Helen's heart sank within her.

"Heaven help me!" she said, as she disengaged herself from the skeletons and emerged from her terrible hiding-place; "Heaven help me and guide me from this place."

There was, indeed, but a dreary prospect before her.

On the one side starvation, on the other the love of Oscar Penraven.

Of these two she greatly preferred the former.

CHAPTER XXII.

AN UNEXPECTED DELIVERER.

Another day passed.

On the night following the evening of her escape, Helen Penraven, wearied and faint, fell asleep.

She awoke in the morning racked with the terrible torments of a fierce hunger, to find not far from her side a jug of milk and a piece of bread.

Some one, then, had discovered her hiding-place.

Whether it was friend or foe she could not tell, but it certainly seemed unlikely to be the latter.

Any companion or parasite of Oscar Penraven would have dragged her forth into the light of day to a doom more terrible than death.

After satisfying the cravings of her appetite, she rose and approached the door.

It was still fastened, and the bone she had replaced before retiring to rest had not been touched.

There was a mystery here.

There seemed no outlet, and yet some one had not only seen her, but had entered and supplied her with food.

But the very mystery seemed to console her.

The same unaccountable secrecy had hovered over her dwelling in the old house.

So, as I have said, another day had passed away.

Night once more veiled everything, and deeply veiled it too.

Helen could see the light through the chinks of the door, and so, as evening closed over her, she knew it by the fading away of even the muffled light within her dismal cell.

During the day, and more especially the afternoon, he had heard voices without, and among them she seemed to recognise the voice of Oscar Penraven.

In the old house, too, there were murmuring sounds as of people hurrying to and fro, and discussions in angry tones.

But as night closed in, there was a lull over everything, and the place appeared to be deserted.

It was about nine o'clock, and Helen was in that state of dreamy reverie that she might almost have imagined herself to be asleep, when she heard a noise above her head, which caused her to start and look up.

It was difficult, indeed, to distinguish objects in the darkness, but as far as she could tell it seemed to her that a face was peering down at her through the muffled light.

Suddenly a swinging lamp of peculiar construction was let down to the ground by a string.

Then she could see two feet and a pair of legs, which she could just distinguish as those of a female.

Then appeared the body, and a girl of some nineteen years of age dropped to the ground.

She was a pretty girl, with a pleasant, happy face.

It was Agnes Mayland, Tom the waterman's sweetheart.

She smiled sweetly as she entered.

Then she gathered together a pile of skulls and bones, so as to form a seat, and sat down.

"Well, here I am," she said.

"Yes, I see," said Helen, smiling, in spite of herself, "and tell me why?"

"I am come to save you. Do you see that hole up there where I came through? Do you think you could scramble up there?"

Helen looked up, and saw that there was a rope hanging down.

"Yes," she said, "I think I can climb up."

"Well, you can take your time," responded Agnes; "they are all gone."

"Are you certain?"

"Yes—yes—they are gone—every one of them, and if you follow me I'll save you."

So saying, she, without further parley, clambered up the rope, and in a moment after Helen followed her.

Though not quite so active as Agnes Mayland, she was soon at the top, for the girl was there to aid her ascent.

As soon as she had squeezed herself through the narrow opening she rose to look around her.

It was a strange place in which she found herself, the interior of an ancient church.

Around her, jagged and decaying, were the walls of some edifice, in which, at one time, hymns of praise had risen to Heaven.

Above her, the eternal skies, forming for a time its roof, smiled down, as it were, upon the relics of man's frail creation.

And the still night air told her of the liberty she inhaled at every breath.

On the cold stones she knelt and prayed earnestly for a few moments; then she turned to Agnes Mayland.

"And who are you," she said, "who have done me this unexpected kindness?"

"I am Agnes Mayland, the cousin of Tom the waterman. Master Dreadnought knows him well."

"Yes—yes," said Helen, "I know him well, too. Many a time his brave arm has been raised against my enemies. But how, in the name of wonder, did you come here?"

"Well," returned Agnes, smiling, "it is a curious story. I was staying with some friends at a farm-house near, when I heard that a gentleman of the name of Penraven had taken this old house, which for some time had been untenanted; I heard, too, that he was going to be married, and wanted a maid-servant. One of the girls at the farm wished to go, but I was determined to find out the mystery, and so, by a little gratuity, I was enabled to go as the young girl's substitute. It was I who wrote you the note, but I was interrupted and could not say more. Now let us hasten, for fear any one should be on the watch."

They had soon set out on the high road, and after showing to Helen the way to Mr. Tyrrel's house, Agnes kissed her warmly, and returned towards the farm-house.

Mr. Tyrrel's house was situated about half-a-mile beyond the old ruin which Oscar Penraven had rented.

The Ruins, as this place was called in the neighbourhood, had not been inhabited for years, and when Lambert made so sudden an offer for it, it was at once accepted.

The edifice had originally been a Catholic church, and the house adjoining it had been set aside for the residence of the priests.

"MY MISSION IS FULFILLED," SAID RUPERT.

Both, however, had been nearly destroyed by fire, and had never been restored.

Mr. Tyrrel, as I have said, was a married man, and he was under the thumb of his wife.

What Mrs. Tyrrel said was right, and had to be done, no matter how much it affected the reverend gentleman in purse or feelings.

Equally, it may be imagined, that what Mrs. Tyrrel did not like, Mr. Tyrrel dared not do.

When, therefore, Helen arrived at the door of the rectory, she was ushered at once into the presence of Mrs. Tyrrel, who sat be-ringleted and be-ringed in her arm-chair, which, for want of a better, was her throne.

She surveyed with much mental disturbance the face and form of the beautiful girl, both begrimed with dust.

"Who are you?" she said, sternly.

She always disliked pretty girls.

Helen told her story.

Mistress Tyrrel eyed her superciliously.

Such was a rule; she, in fact, delighted in saying that she was a check on her husband's rash charity.

When Helen had finished, she waited a moment and then said—

"And do you expect me to believe this most extraordinary story?"

Helen flushed crimson.

"Certainly," she said, with quiet dignity, "I claim your belief."

Mistress Tyrrel smiled.

"My husband," she answered, "has just left for London. He would certainly have mentioned the case to me if it had been a deserving one. I must beg you, therefore, to excuse me if I decline to have anything to say in the matter."

Faint and weary, Helen turned from the door.

What could it mean?

Had the clergyman, who had seemed so kind to her, deserted her at the last moment?

What was she to do?

She had not a penny, not an idea of the road, not a conception of the distance she would be compelled to walk before she reached London.

Nevertheless, weary as she was, and dark as was the night, she resolved to make inquiries at the nearest house, and commenced her journey at once.

As she had so resolved, she heard footsteps approaching, and fearing every one now, she turned in alarm.

It was a woman with a baby slung at her back.

Helen waited for her to come up.

"Which is the way to London?" she asked.

The woman gazed at her in wonder.

"London did you say, mistress?" she asked.

"Yes."

"Well, then, you're coming straight away from it. But it's a long way; you can't be going to walk it."

Helen smiled sadly.

"Yes, indeed I am," she answered; "I'm obliged to do so. I've no money—no friends here, and until I get to London I've small hope of getting either."

"I'm going part of the way," said the woman; "I'll put you on the road."

So they plodded on together.

She need not have blamed Master Tyrrel for anything that had happened.

Shortly before evening Oscar Penraven and Lambert were in earnest conversation in the room next to that in which he was imprisoned, and through the thin partition he could hear all they said.

"There is no doubt," said Oscar, in a tone of vexation, "that Helen has somehow or another escaped."

"Certainly she is gone," said Lambert; "that girl, Master Penraven, was never meant for you. She has escaped you in every way. It has all been your own fault, however, for you have had her in your power half-a-dozen times."

"I'm not such a villain as you are," said Oscar Penraven; "besides, I love her truly, and took no advantage of opportunities. However, she is no doubt by this time in London. We must follow. Go and see if all is ready."

They were, of course, utterly unconscious that the clergyman could hear what they said.

He heard all.

He heard, too, a stealthy step creeping along the passage and stopping before the door.

A chill pervaded his form.

What did this mean?

Did they intend to murder him?

His suspense was of short duration.

There was a rustle on the floor, and then his eager eyes caught the glistening of a key.

He seized it eagerly.

"They are going away," he thought, "and are leaving me the means of escape. Heaven be praised."

He listened again.

He heard them depart; he heard their voices lessen in the distance and their carriage roll away along the hard road.

Then all was still.

Only a short time he waited to be certain he would not be discovered.

Then he unlocked the door, and went out softly.

There was no need for precaution.

It was quite evident that the house was entirely deserted, at any rate for the time; the doors were wide open, the outer door ajar; everything denoted a hurried departure.

With a heart full of gratitude for his own escape, and the signal failure of Oscar Penraven's schemes to ruin for ever the happiness of Helen Penraven, Tyrrel issued from the house, and made his way home.

He was satisfied, from the conversation which he had overheard between Lambert and Oscar, that the young girl had escaped, and was now on her way to London, or perhaps at his house.

When, therefore, he arrived at the rectory, he merely asked—

"Has any one been here?"

"No one, sir," said the servant.

Then he entered the presence of his august wife, listening calmly to her reproaches for his conduct in remaining absent a whole night (he a minister of the gospel, too); and then stating quietly that business of an important nature demanded his immediate presence in London.

To London, therefore, he proceeded at once, with the intention of handing over to justice, if possible, those estimable friends, Lambert and Oscar Penraven, and also to discover what proceedings were necessary to annul the marriage, such as it was, between Oscar and Helen.

Meanwhile, Helen plodded on.

The woman who was with her had come many miles, and when they reached Sainton, a little village some four miles from the ruins, she entered an ale-house to have some refreshment.

Helen hung back.

"Why don't you come in?" said the woman.

"I've no money," returned Helen, in a low voice.

The woman laughed.

"It ain't to be supposed you have any," she said, "after going through all you have told me. Come in, and share with me what I have."

So they went on together until late at night, when they slept in a barn.

In the morning they parted.

"My husband is working at Exham," said the woman, as she left her companion, "and I'm on the tramp to meet him. Here's a shilling, if that'll help you."

She placed it in Helen's hand, and made off before Mistress Penraven could make any comment.

Helen watched along the road—watched her until she faded away and disappeared in the distance, just as she must now fade and disappear for ever from our story.

Then once more she went on her lonely way, thinking how hard the world must be when she, innocent and pursued by deadly enemies, could find no help.

But so it was.

Against her claims to aid, the hearts of all seemed closed.

Some sneered, some laughed at her, some insulted, none helped.

No one cared, as it appeared, to waste upon her a kind word, much less a kind action.

Some looked from her pretty face to her torn and dirt-stained clothes, and regarded her as the authoress of her own misfortunes.

Some shut their doors rudely in her face—others scouted her.

All combined to drive her well nigh to despair.

Yet she went resolutely on.

On—on! though the weather was cold, and the wind howled dismally, and the storm clouds gathered over her head.

On—on! though her legs trembled beneath her, and her tongue clove to the roof of her mouth, and her heart was faint and weary!

On—on! without food—without a word of kindness—almost without hope.

On—on! until passing from the high road along a bridle path, she found herself suddenly in a churchyard.

The church itself was ruined, but the tombstones still clustered round it.

It was a dreary place to stop in, but she could go no further.

Fainting with cold and hunger, and almost too desperate to know what she was doing, she sank down upon a mound, and lost all consciousness.

Picture her to yourselves, fair readers, whose

homes in these courting days are lit by the smiles of husbands, or fathers, or brothers!

Picture her to yourselves as she plodded on through starless nights and sunless days; and then think what were the feelings of her desolate heart when she lay down to die upon that churchyard mound beneath a black and stormy sky!

CHAPTER XXIII.

ON THE WRONG SCENT.

It will not surprise those of our readers who are acquainted with the character of Redlock, the one-handed, to know that in his heart of hearts he intended to deceive Rupert Dreadnought.

There was a curious mixture of feelings in his mind.

In the first place, Rupert Dreadnought was, as he himself declared, his natural enemy—his hereditary foe.

In the next place, he had a wish for him to be taken out of the way of Rosalie St. Aubyn, either by fair means or foul.

Loving Rosalie as he did, the assassin of Henry Fortescue saw, of course, in Rupert a formidable rival in his affections.

And yet to destroy him would take him out of the path of Oscar Penraven, who was another rival.

Better was it, then, to permit Rupert to discover Helen, and marry her; or if Oscar *had* married her, to wait and ascertain the fact before destroying Rupert.

In this, however, he did not see his way clearly.

To lead Rupert Dreadnought to the house which Oscar had chosen as the scene of the false marriage, would be to permit Oscar to know of his treachery, and this would, therefore, be courting destruction for himself.

What, then, was he to do?

The traitor soon decided.

He would lead Rupert to London, suggest the propriety of procuring the assistance of his friends, and then, while he was arranging matters, he could make good his escape.

"We must hasten on," he said, as he rode along by the side of his companion, "or we shall be too late. This evening was the time fixed by Oscar Penraven for the solemnization of the marriage ceremony; and, unless some strange accident has occurred to assist her, Helen Penraven is by this time his wife."

A thrill of terror and mad rage ran through the person of Rupert Dreadnought as Redlock spoke.

"By Heavens!" he cried, "if she *is* forced into this union with a man whom she hates, there is no punishment that I shall consider too terrible for him. On—on! let us spur forward!"

"You had better seek the assistance of your friends," suggested Redlock, as they sped onwards at a still more rapid rate; "*he* will not be there single-handed to meet you, and it will be of no avail for you to proceed thither alone. You understand, of course, how far our compact extends. I'll lead you to the house, but my sword will not be drawn against my friends."

"Good," said Rupert, "I will take your advice most certainly. Oscar will find that there are bright swords and strong arms always ready to defend me and mine."

After a rapid ride they reached Rupert's house, the bell of which our hero rang hastily and loudly.

No one in the house had expected the return of the young earl before morning, and it was, therefore, with some degree of surprise that the servant who put his head out of window saw Rupert standing at the gate.

In a few minutes after the gate was opened, and our hero and his father's foe entered together.

It may seem strange that Redlock should thus deliberately put his head in the lion's mouth, but the truth was that from all he had heard of Rupert's character he felt not the slightest fear of treachery.

Dreadnought might be a terrible and uncompromising enemy, but he was also an honourable man.

In a few moments Allan of the Glen and four of Rupert's servants were dressed and ready to start, while, within a quarter of an hour, all were equipped and mounted.

A sharp look-out had been kept on Redlock, and when all were ready he was placed in the centre.

Then he gave the word, as a direction which way they were to go, and off they started.

My readers already know how Helen Penraven escaped from the hands of Oscar Penraven, and that by the time Rupert was on his way she was already beyond his reach.

We will not, therefore, linger too long on the details of this journey.

Suffice it to say that the golden streaks of morning were inundating the country side as Rupert and his friends, with their captive guide in the midst, drew up for refreshment at a roadside inn.

"Are we far now from our journey's end?" said our hero, turning to Redlock, as they drew rein.

"We are not," replied the one-handed. "Yonder, among the trees, some mile distant, is the spot."

As he pointed to a place where the bright rays of morning were tipping the summits of the trees, a bright thought suddenly struck him.

He would deceive Rupert, and so avoid, also, the consequences of what he most dreaded, the anger of Oscar Penraven.

He knew that near the house which had been selected by Oscar for his nefarious purpose was another, inhabited by two old maids.

He would point *this* out to Rupert as the one in which Helen had been confined, and he trusted to his own cleverness to entirely deceive him.

"I am all impatience," cried Rupert, as his friends were quaffing eagerly the ale, so cool and refreshing after their long ride. "It is but a mile more; let us ride as for our lives."

So on again they dashed.

In a very few moments they reached the house.

"Now, then," said Redlock, in a voice of sincerity, "now, then, I beg that I may be acquitted of all blame. *This* is the house, but I know nothing of how many men Oscar Penraven has with him. As to that you must, of course, accept the responsibility."

"I am willing to do that," said Rupert. "But the house seems quiet enough."

"That, of course, is on purpose to throw you off the scent," said Redlock. "Two old women are there who pretend to be owners of the house, and who will deny all knowledge of the matter. You, of course, understand how to dispose of them."

"Yes, yes," said Rupert. "Now, then, Allan, follow me."

A loud knock at the door brought to an upper window an old lady, who poked out her head enveloped in a frilled nightcap.

"What do you want, master?" she asked, in a trembling voice, as her eyes fell upon the group of mounted and armed men.

"Instant admittance," cried Rupert. "Open the door, or we shall break it down."

"Certainly, certainly, you shall be admitted, gentlemen," said the old lady, who, of course, having nothing whatever to do with Oscar or Helen, was in a state of utter bewilderment, and closing the window, she hurried down.

In the few minutes which elapsed, however, two things had been done.

In the first place, a boy whom the old maids kept to do odd jobs was dispatched by a back way across the fields to the parish constables.

In the second place, a couple of huge bloodhounds, which were kept for the defence of the old ladies and their property, were let loose in the hall.

It was a rather dangerous experiment thus to act, for the old women knew nothing of the errand upon which Rupert and his men were paying them so early a morning visit.

But the looks of the party were so fierce, that they had put them down at once as highwaymen.

Presently the door opened a few inches, a chain being kept up, but the aperture being sufficient to show just the faces of the two desperate bloodhounds.

"Now, gentlemen," said the old lady, in as firm a voice as she could command, "now, gentlemen, what is it you require?"

"I desire to see Sir Oscar Penraven," returned Rupert Dreadnought; "I have come here for the purpose of rescuing from his clutches the young lady whom he is holding here by force."

"You are talking to me in riddles," returned the old lady, eyeing him in intense surprise; "I know of no such people."

"I anticipated that such would be your answer," returned Rupert Dreadnought, "but it will not suit me. Open the door; I intend to search the house. And, if you set any value on the lives of those dogs of yours, remove them, or they will be shot."

The parish constable's house was not very far distant from the house in which the old ladies resided, and they, therefore, resolved to make as much resistance as possible and delay, so that there would be a chance of a rescue.

"You must either be mad, or you must intend to rob my house," replied the old lady. "I shall, therefore, refuse to open the door. Burst it open if you please, but do not expect that I am going to yield without a struggle."

Then in an instant the door was flung to, and they were once more on the outside.

In an instant Rupert dismounted, as did the rest of the troop.

One man was left with Redlock, to see that he did not effect his escape, and the others immediately commenced an attack upon the door.

Allan had brought his hatchet with him, and, as he had done once before, he soon began to make an impression upon the woodwork.

The deep growls of the bloodhounds could be heard as the work proceeded.

But they were undismayed.

Again and again, taking it in turn, they drove the sharp steel into the woodwork, and soon they had made a hole sufficiently large to allow a man's hand to be inserted and the bolts withdrawn.

The old ladies had not counted on this.

They began, seeing the daring way in which the assault was being made, to suspect that really some mistake was being made, and one of them—the younger of the two—once more approached the door.

"Gentlemen," she said, "I feel certain that you are making some error. If there was a man in the house, do you suppose he could be such a coward as to leave us here helpless? He would come to our assistance."

"Believe not a word they say," whispered Redlock.

"You may be telling the truth in this respect," replied Rupert Dreadnought; "there may now be no man in the house, but that is no reason why Helen Penraven should not be here. I have reason to know that she *is* here, and I *will* release her or destroy the place."

"I solemnly declare," said the ancient dame, "that we know not what you mean."

There was such an air of sincerity in her voice and manner as she said this that she, for the moment, convinced Rupert.

He turned to Redlock.

"Are you certain that we are at the right place," he asked, "or are you deceiving me?"

"Considering," replied the one-handed traitor, "that I never came here with Oscar, I cannot swear that he came to this spot at all. All I know is, that this was the place he told me—this was the place he hired—this was the place to which he ordered his coachman to drive when he carried off Helen Penraven. More I cannot tell you. I am not deceiving you, but if you believe so I am in your power, and you can act as you please. I think I should indeed be mad to attempt it under present circumstances. Search the house and see for yourselves."

"THE LANDLORD, SEEING THE LADY, IMMEDIATELY OPENED THE DOOR."

Urged on thus by the traitor's plausible words, Rupert returned to the shattered doorway and drew from his belt a double-barrelled pistol.

This he levelled at the dogs, who were now baying savagely and leaping up at the aperture.

There were two reports, and then the two faithful creatures were stretched dead on the floor.

To undo the bolts within was now no difficult matter, and in a few minutes the party of besiegers stood within the hall.

In spite now of the tears and remonstrances of the old ladies, who were nearly terrified out of their lives, they were seized and bound, and left in a room in the basement while a vigorous search was made throughout the building.

"You'll be punished for this," sobbed one of the poor old creatures, as Rupert quitted the room. "I've sent for the parish constable."

"Good," said Rupert; "we must then be all the more rapid in our movements."

Every nook and corner of the place was soon searched.

But, of course, nothing was found.

Not a trace was to be seen of any female inhabitant, save the old ladies, and not the slightest sign, moreover, of any secret doors or passages.

"I have been deceived or *you* have," said Rupert to Redlock, as he descended to the hall; "but what have we here?"

"It is, I suppose, the parish constable and his friends," said Redlock; "I saw them hurrying along the road. We had better mount and ride away. If there has been any mistake, it might prove a somewhat awkward affair."

There was no doubting the wisdom of these words.

Deceived or not, there was no use in remaining, and the idea of being arrested and locked up in a country gaol was infinitely revolting to Rupert's mind.

Besides, what time would not be lost before he could prove the truth of his story?

"Mount, my friends," he said, pointing to the crowd, who were now not many yards from the front gate. "Mount, and let us be off."

"But the two old ladies," suggested Allan.

Rupert smiled.

"We will leave the parish constable the task of seeing to their comforts," he said. "At present freedom is everything to us, and yonder crowd seem evidently inclined to dispute it with us."

It was a strange rabble that the parish constable had brought with him.

Having an idea that one of the most daring bands of highwaymen then known in England had gathered round the house of the old ladies—feloniously and murderously intent—he had not deemed it prudent to rush to the scene of action with the aid only of his two assistants.

He wisely imagined that any daring knight of the road would simply laugh at them.

He had, therefore, enlisted the sympathies as well as the persons of a number of valiant citizens, who now, to the number of at least fifty, were approaching, armed with sticks, and old muskets, and pitchforks, and divers other weapons.

Rupert and his friends had but time to mount and reach the front gate, when the throng of people surrounded it.

"Now, then," cried he; "I fear we have made an error, and we must not be taken. Do not, however, hurt these people unnecessarily. Strike with the flat of the sword, and ride them down, but do not kill."

Drawing their swords, they struck the spurs into their horses' flanks, and dashed forward.

But they were met with a most vigorous resistance.

"Seize the thieves! Capture the highway robbers and murderers!" cried the parish constable flourishing his sword, but wisely keeping in the background.

Those who were behind and safe, therefore, pushed and pressed on those in front, so that the points of some of the pitchforks entered the horses' chests, and made them plunge and heave like mad things.

"Now, then," cried Rupert, and with the flat of his sword he struck the foremost man on the side of the head, and sent him sprawling on the ground.

His fall was the signal for the utter defeat of the rabble.

Upon him fell several others, among them the parish constable, and, putting spurs to his horse, Dreadnought leaped clear over the fallen group.

His friends were not slow to follow his example, and, amid the yells and screams of the disappointed crew, they were seen cresting the hill, and dashing away on their return journey.

CHAPTER XXIV.

SAVED.

Before following any further the fortunes of Rupert and his friends, we must introduce our readers to a man who is hurrying along the road towards Essex from London.

As the moon breaks from behind a cloud just as he enters St. Luke's churchyard, a short cut to the high road, and inundates the ruins of the edifice, destroyed by a recent fire, we see Tom the waterman.

As he passed beneath the ruins of the church, he saw something in the moonlight lying on a mound—the mound of a newly-made grave.

He stopped still and gazed at it.

It seemed like the form of a woman.

He approached, therefore, and spoke.

"My good woman," he said, "tell me what is the matter."

There was no answer, and kneeling down, there fore, he took her hand.

It was cold and clammy.

He raised her up then, and the moonbeams fell full upon her face.

"Great heavens!" he cried, "it is Helen Penraven, and she is dead."

She did, indeed, seem dead.

A livid pallor had overspread her features, and her limbs appeared rigid.

But Heaven had ordained it otherwise, and saved her for many more trials.

Her eyes slowly opened, glanced at Tom, and then with a shudder she closed them once more, as if to shut out a dream of horror.

The scene was scarcely one calculated to reassure her.

The sky was grey and monotonous.

On one side rose the ruins of the church, shattered by a conflagration and blackened by smoke.

Round them were the tombs, white and grey with

time, and here and there leaving a slant from the subsidence of the earth.

In the darkness she did not recognise Tom.

"I am Tom the waterman; don't you know me?" he said.

A faint smile passed over her lips, and her eyes again opened.

"I am cold and hungry," she said; "I feel as if I were dying."

Her words were uttered in a whisper—a low whisper, like the voice of one in the last stage of life.

Gently he raised her up, and set her up with her back against a tombstone.

Then, drawing a flask from his pocket, he poured some brandy down her throat.

This had the desired effect of reviving her, and she staggered to her feet.

"I will try and walk now," she said.

"It is quite useless," replied Tom; "I will carry you to the nearest inn, where you can obtain refreshment and repose also for the night."

He took her up in his strong arms as he would have done a child, and bore her away through the tombs.

Many times during that strange journey he stopped and listened, and hid himself and his charge in shadowy corners.

He thought, naturally enough, that treacherous enemies might have pursued her, and be even now on the watch.

The noises which alarmed him, however, were but the voices of the night; the sighing of the wind; the swaying of the trees; the creaking of the branches.

At length the welcome light of an inn appeared in view.

This was the spot where Tom had originally intended to rest for the night before pursuing his journey by the stage coach towards the very spot where Rupert and his men had so recently been, though with a far different purpose.

He was on the road to join Agnes Mayland, his sweetheart, at the farm, where, as we have said, she had been stopping with some friends.

Now, however, all his plans were changed.

Pledged as he was to aid Rupert in all his plans, his duty to Helen Penraven demanded that he should abandon his journey for the present, at any rate, until he had placed her safely in the hands of her friends.

The inn was closed when he reached it, for Helen was a weighty burden to carry so far, but the landlord, seeing him bearing the form of a lady, apparently insensible, immediately opened the door.

"An accident, sir?" he inquired, in a kindly tone, as Tom entered and sat down on a bench.

Tom placed Helen by the side of him on the bench, and said—

"No, not an accident exactly. This lady, the betrothed wife of a gentleman I know, has lost her way, and is cold and hungry. Let her have a hot supper and a warm bed, and I will pay."

"Good!" said the Boniface, as he closed the door. "There is a large fire in the parlour yonder. Take the lady in there, and I will rouse up my wife."

Tom gently helped Helen into the parlour, which, though roughly and uncouthly furnished, was at any rate warm.

A cheerful fire blazed in the grate, and, seated by this, Helen narrated the events which had brought her to this sorry pass.

"Cheer up, Mistress Penraven," said Tom, as the landlady appeared, bearing some hot soup and some other warm comestibles. "To-morrow I'll take you to Dreadnought House."

"But the marriage—the marriage!" said Helen, shudderingly. "Oh, how I dread to see Rupert."

"The marriage!—a fig for it!" said Tom. "Don't distress yourself about that. It's no marriage at all, and can be set aside directly. Eat your supper, mistress, and get to bed, or you'll be tired to death by the morning."

"Yes, I will try and eat if you will join me," said Helen, with a pleasant smile.

"With pleasure," said Tom, "for I'm very hungry, too, I can assure you."

And so Tom the waterman and the daughter of the baronet sat down together to their meal, after which the landlady took her to a bedroom, where a nicely warmed bed was provided for her accommodation.

But any hopes as to her speedy recovery were destined to be nipped in the bud.

The morning found her in a low fever, unable to raise her head.

She was feverish and helpless, and sometimes even incoherent in her talk.

Poor Tom felt quite in a dilemma.

"What am I to do?" asked the brave, simple fellow of the landlady.

"Well, you can't do anything," said that worthy lady, with a smile; "if you know her friends you'd better go and tell them at once. She *must* stay here."

"That *will* be the best," said Tom. "I'll start for London at once. You have a horse, I suppose, to let me?"

"Yes, my master'll let you have his own nag," said the woman; "and, meanwhile, I'll send for the doctor."

"Thank you, thank you many times for your kindness," said Tom, as he turned to seek the landlord. "Master Dreadnought will reward you handsomely."

Then a sudden thought struck him.

"Stay," he said, "I have forgotten one thing. Whoever comes to see her *without me* (except, of course, the doctor), don't you admit him. She has just escaped great danger at the hands of lawless men, and they are most probably in pursuit of her."

"Never fear," said the landlady. "I see you're kind to the lady, and she knows you. I won't let anyone else come near her."

Within three hours Helen, who had fallen into a heavy slumber, awoke to find Rupert and Lady Claremont sitting by the side of her bed.

About this part of my story I will not linger.

It will suffice to say that it took but a short time to restore Helen to health, and that it was not long before she was enabled to return to London.

The question then came where would she be most safe?

Lady Claremont's home was certainly not the spot which could be chosen as a place of refuge; and it was suggested by Tom the waterman that she should adopt a disguise, dress herself in humble habiliments; in fact, assume the position for a time of Agnes Mayland, and remain in quiet seclusion at his mother's house.

This, as a most sensible solution of the difficulty, was at once accepted by Rupert Dreadnought.

"But," said Tom, "there's a much easier way out of this, Master Dreadnought."

"And what is that?"

"You love Mistress Penraven, and she loves you. Why not marry her at once?"

Rupert smiled.

"Tom," he said, "your solution of the difficulty is one which I would gladly accept. But it is impossible."

"And why?"

"Can you ask me when I have explained to you that at my father's deathbed I took a solemn vow never to marry Helen until I had fulfilled every mission left for my fulfilment in the Iron Chest. The very first of the five missions is not yet accomplished."

"Ah, well," said Tom, "of course it's not *my* place to advise you; but if it were *my* case, and Agnes Mayland, my cousin, were the one in danger, I'd marry her first, and fulfil the missions afterwards."

Helen was, on the very evening of her return to London, transferred to her new quarters.

Willingly, indeed, she went, although to such a humble home.

After all she had been made to suffer, it seemed to her a palace.

Another matter also came to light as soon as Helen was restored to health.

Rupert then learned how utterly he had been deceived by Redlock, and he at once dispatched Allan of the Glen to the house of the old ladies with a handsome compensation for all injuries received, accompanied by such apologies that the ancient dames were compelled to receive the matter agreeably.

These matters having been settled, the hour approached for vengeance upon Redlock.

The one-handed was still a prisoner in Rupert's house; and on the evening after Helen's removal to Mrs. Braxley's, Rupert resolved to bring matters to an issue.

CHAPTER XXV.

IN WHICH REDLOCK FIGHTS HIS LAST BATTLE.

It was in the large banqueting hall of Dreadnought House that Rupert awaited the entrance of Redlock, the man with whom he had now to fight a duel to the death.

Redlock entered with a pale face, but yet not one in which any emotion or fear was visible.

When the door closed behind him, and he found himself alone with Rupert Dreadnought, Allan of the Glen, and Tom the waterman, he folded his arms, and, looking round with a sneering smile, said—

"Well, am I brought hither for execution?"

"You know well that you are not," replied Rupert Dreadnought. "You are come here to fight a fair duel, although, considering that not many days ago I held your life absolutely at my mercy and gave you but a reprieve, I might commence from the point where I held my sword at your throat."

"And pray where are my seconds?" said Redlock. "Is it fair that you in case of need should have two friends here to aid you, and I be alone, to die, perhaps, unnoticed? What is my guarantee that if I get the best of the fight I shall have fair play?"

"I told you upon a former occasion," returned Rupert, sternly, "that you waited not for seconds when you murdered Fortescue. However, I will not be hard upon you to such an extent. If I can have any proofs that my messenger will not fall into any ambush, I will send to some friend of yours and let him be present."

For an instant the face of Redlock brightened.

But only for an instant.

In this concession there was only hope of justice, no hope of safety.

"Well," he said, "send for my friend. I will give you the address now. But it is some distance hence."

Rupert saw through this ruse at once.

It was a pretext for delay.

"If you have no friend near at hand," he said, "I shall not send. This night must decide between us. I can see in your suggestion a plan for deceiving me, and, after the manner in which you betrayed me in regard to Helen Penraven, it is not likely I shall trust you."

"Be it as you please then," replied Redlock; "I have no friends near save those who would come rushing here in a body. Promise me two things. First, if I succeed in destroying you, I may go scot-free."

"I promise; and the second demand?" said Rupert Dreadnought.

"Is, that if I die, my friends may be allowed to know how I fell. If yours is a just cause, you should not be ashamed to tell the vengeance you have taken."

"Be it so then," said Rupert; "write upon a piece of paper the name and address of the person, and give it to Allan yonder. Then both he and my other friend there will retire and leave us alone with locked door. The odds will then be even."

Redlock advanced to the table, where stood the materials for writing, and hastily wrote out a name and address.

Then he placed the paper in the hand of Allan of the Glen, and turning, faced Rupert, sword in hand.

"Now," he said, in as firm a voice as he could command, "I am at your service."

Allan of the Glen and Tom the waterman then retired from the room, and Rupert proceeded to the door to lock it.

As he did so his back was turned towards Redlock.

In an instant the treacherous villain conceived an idea worthy of his antecedents.

If he could thus, unawares, slay Rupert, there were no witnesses to know whether it was in fair fight or not.

Suddenly darting forward, therefore, he made a

lunge just as Rupert Dreadnought had turned the key in the lock.

He missed his aim, however.

The sword only grazed Rupert's left arm slightly.

"Treacherous villain," cried our hero, starting round and eyeing his adversary fiercely. "Well do you carry out your murderous character. But, by heavens, you have committed your last assassination. I feel within me the strength and determination to destroy you. This sword I hold in my hand was once red with the blood of Henry Fortescue, my father's friend—you will now see how, whetted with the blood of the murdered, it will find the heart of the murderer! Come cross swords. My brain is on fire. I can brook no further delay."

His words but expressed his looks.

Disgusted beyond endurance by this last attempt at treachery on the part of Redlock, his eyes shot fire, his features assumed a deadly pallor, and his lips, too, were white and quivering

He was in a fierce passion, but yet his hand trembled not.

His nerves were firm for the battle.

Redlock seemed to read his own fate in the eyes of his adversary as they crossed their swords.

Still he resolved to fight to the death.

A strange fortune had saved him from destruction before in the lane.

Some accident might occur again.

It was no duel this.

There was but a momentary pause, a measurement of distances, and then Rupert's blade was uplifted, and the fight began.

Even now Dreadnought showed his strict adherence to justice.

Redlock had but one available arm, and was, therefore, to a certain extent at a disadvantage.

He accordingly drew his left arm behind him, and displayed only the right, filled, as it was, with the *sword of vengeance.*

I cannot describe this duel at any very great length, as in its general details it would be but a recapitulation of many others I have described before.

After many desperate lunges had passed, however, Rupert's sword traversed the fleshy part of Redlock's right shoulder, and at the same time Redlock's sword wounded Rupert in the left.

Both staggered back badly wounded, but Rupert had, of course, the advantage.

His one-handed foe saw this, and redoubled his efforts, knowing that after a short time the wound would stiffen his right arm, and entirely disable him from further useful exertion.

Rupert's sword seemed, however, to flash hither and thither like lightning.

His style was far too brilliant to enable his adversary to wound him, and Redlock was compelled to keep on the defensive.

As this idea penetrated his brain, he trembled.

There was Death in the thought!

Delay was useless.

To act on the defensive was simply to prolong the fight, for out of that room Rupert Dreadnought had sworn that both should not pass alive!

Nerved to desperate and reckless exertion at this, Redlock began to fight like a madman, his strength every moment becoming less and less.

Suddenly the sight of something inspired him with fresh energy.

In backing from one of Rupert's rapid lunges, his eye fell upon a pistol lying upon a table in a corner of the room.

To a treacherous mind such as his the idea at once occurred—

"Here is life and liberty. I will shoot him before he can have the chance of finding me at his mercy."

So when Rupert rushed forward and made his next pass, Redlock withdrew, and dashing back, seized the pistol, and cocking it, levelled it at Rupert's head.

All this was done so quickly that Rupert had no chance of preventing him, and the report and the crash of glass behind him was the almost instantaneous sound which followed.

HELEN SEEKS REST IN THE CHURCHYARD.

The ball had whizzed by his ear, and crashed through the lofty mirror behind him!

Redlock stood aghast at his failure, the exploded pistol still in his hand.

Slowly Rupert put his hand to his belt, his eye still on his enemy.

Then for the first time Redlock saw that he had pistols in his belt.

"Murderer!" cried Dreadnought, in a voice of thunder, "I have given you every fair chance; I have treated you as an honest foe, when you have acted the part of an assassin! Now die the death of a dog!"

He raised his pistol as he spoke, took deliberate aim, and ere the trembling villain could speak, the weapon belched forth its flame, and the ball went crashing through his skull.

Rupert paused not to look at him, but unlocked the door and admitted Allan and Tom, and, drawing them to the body, which lay prone upon its face, he said solemnly—

"MY FRIENDS, YOU ARE WITNESSES! MY FIRST MISSION IS FULFILLED!!"

END OF BOOK II.

BOOK III.

THE SECOND SECRET OF THE IRON CHEST.

CHAPTER I.

IT was with a feeling akin to awe that Rupert Dreadnought looked forward to the opening of the second compartment of the Iron Chest.

The terrible punishment which his father had caused him to inflict upon Redlock, made him fear lest the second mission might be of the same nature.

However, whatever it might be, he was bound to perform it.

He had sworn to carry out whatever behests his father might give him.

So a week after the death of Redlock—after, in fact, the body of the traitor had been buried—Rupert once more made his way to the room in which was the IRON CHEST.

With a tremor at the heart, he placed the key in the lock, and opened the strange receptacle of secrets.

The second compartment having been arrived at, he found lying before him a large parchment, tied with red silk, and directed to himself.

Opening it with eager hands, he read as follows—

"MY DEAR SON,—Again the sword of vengeance must be drawn.

"Fear not that I shall ask you to shed blood without due cause.

"A vow which I took myself, and had not time to carry out, I have left to you, and by all your hopes of salvation you are bound to carry it out."

Rupert paused a moment.

A tremor invaded his limbs.

What dreadful thing was coming that the old earl thought it necessary to remind him of his vow again?

But the vow had been taken, and he was bound to fulfil it.

So, summoning up his courage, he proceeded.

"In the second vault, on the left-hand side of the subterranean passage beneath the church of St. Andrew's, Chichester, you will find an empty stone coffin.

"In that stone coffin one of my dearest friends, a cousin, was murdered.

"Lured there by his younger brother to search for a pretended treasure, he was suddenly attacked, and, after receiving a heavy blow from a mallet, was forced by his unnatural companion into the coffin.

"There he died of suffocation, and his younger brother, and the man he had brought with him to aid him in his hideous work, locked the vault and left him.

"The younger son, who was at least twenty years the junior of the other, now, of course, inherited the estates, for after a few days the vault was unlocked, and in the search the body was found.

"How he got into the coffin was, of course, a mystery, but, at any rate, the desired end was attained.

"He was dead, and the next heir was, of course, a wealthy man.

"The death-bed confession of the minor villain made me acquainted with the horrid deed, and it was then I heard that, as he was being forced into the stone coffin, he uttered my name.

"I at once considered that he had appointed me his avenger, and for twenty years I have sought the assassin in vain.

"His name is Hugh Dalrymple, and you will know him, perhaps, by the following description:—

"He is very tall, over six feet, and broadly-built.

"His eyes are black and piercing, his voice harsh and dissonant, and his hair is generally worn in tangled masses over his shoulders.

"An aquiline nose gives a peculiar character to his face, while across the right cheek is the deeply-marked scar I gave him when we had our only combat.

"He is now about eight and thirty.

"I have sworn that he shall be laid in the coffin where his murdered brother was suffocated by his unnatural hands, and that in that very vault he shall meet his doom.

"This oath you have now inherited from me. See that it is performed to the letter.

"R., EARL OF DREADNOUGHT.

"6 Oct., 1712."

"Thirty-eight in 1712, and it is now 1714," murmured Rupert Dreadnought, as he threw down the parchment, and leaned back in his chair; "he is at the present time, then, forty."

Then he remained for some time lost in deep reverie.

Here was another vengeance to accomplish—another life to take!

A bitter sigh escaped his lips as he thought of these sad tasks which were left to him to fulfil.*

* My readers may, perhaps, be inclined to think that this part of my story is exaggerated. But it is not so. In Corsica and Sicily *vendettas* of far more terrible extent are frequent, and considered perfectly legitimate and even necessary.

But there was no chance of escaping the evil.

He had sworn, and his vow must be kept.

As on a former occasion, he, on the following day, collected his friends together, and narrated to them the discovery he had made.

Allan of the Glen was the most attentive listener of all; and when Rupert Dreadnought had completed his account, he sprang to his feet.

"Master Dreadnought," he said, excitedly, "I will take the responsibility of this mission from your shoulders."

"What mean you?" asked Rupert Dreadnought in surprise.

"I know this man. I am certain, from the description you have given of his voice and appearance, that he is one whom I met in the streets not many nights since—who insulted and struck me, and was carried off by his friends before I could resent the affront. Leave this task to me Your sword has already drank too much blood."

"True, true," said Rupert, with a slight shudder at the words which so expressed his own feelings; "but I have sworn with my own hand to accomplish this vow, and I must give it to no one else. I will accept your assistance as ever, but that is all."

To this Allan of the Glen was bound to yield, at any rate in appearance.

It was only in appearance, however.

Inwardly he resolved that if he could contrive to obtain the time and the opportunity, his own sword should reach the dastard heart of the man who had struck him and fled.

CHAPTER II.

ON THE TRACK OF THE GUILTY.

NOT far from London, on the road that leads from Finchley, stood a building which was more a castle than an ordinary mansion.

It stood on the edge of the high road, with a broad deep ditch running like a moat round it—a wide bridge of planks spanning this, and being capable of being withdrawn if required.

The windows on the basement were mere loopholes, like those of a prison, while those above were barred so as to prevent any escape or entrance.

Round the summit of this mansion, which was flat, ran a stone balustrade, built like ramparts, and here on the evening on which I introduce the spot to my readers were walking two ladies.

The one was about five-and-thirty, tall, finely-moulded and well preserved, the other about eighteen.

The former was the mistress of the house, the latter her handmaid.

There was a striking contrast between the two.

The one, as I have said, was tall and well preserved, with a fine sweep of limb, a stately walk, dark eyes, dark hair, and a proud air of superiority about her—the consciousness of wealth and station, perhaps, too evident.

The other was fair and rosy, with blue eyes, golden hair, and an exquisitely-proportioned figure, just indicating the budding bust and the pretty, rounded shoulders of sweet maidenhood.

"Mary," said the lady, as she leaned languidly over the balustrade, "he is long in coming. The evening shades are falling fast, and yet all along the road from London I can see no sign of his horse. Fetch me a chair."

The girl at once obeyed, and in a few moments she had placed her mistress in a chair, settled a shawl around her shoulders, and was standing silently by as she gazed out over the changing landscape. Presently she turned.

"Mary," she said, "I doubt if he will return to-night. I will remain here till dark; but before I rest to-night I desire to see Lady Clanberris."

"There is danger in that, my lady," said Mary. "Suppose my master were to return and find her here; you know how he would storm and rave."

"Ah, yes; but I will run the risk, Mary," returned her mistress. "I have waited too long already. My heart is longing to hear news of——"

She stopped, and a bright blush overspread her features.

But the maiden had seen it, and interpreted it aright, although the lady had not mentioned the name for whom her heart was longing.

Who it was our story will explain in due course.

"It is a lonely path to Clanberris House," said Mary, with a shudder, "but I will go."

This hint did not take any effect upon the lady, who was evidently deeply wrapped in the thoughts of the intended visit of Lady Clanberris, and the news she would bring her of some one whose name she could not utter.

There was a far-off look in her eyes as she gazed out over the hushing landscape, and she turned suddenly round to Mary, as if she had not heard her words.

"Be sure," she said, "to be careful. If my husband has not returned I will leave the flag flying on yonder staff. The moon will be bright to-night; if you are late, and if you see no flag flying, you must return. Go quickly, Mary, and that necklace you so coveted yesterday shall be yours."

A bright flush surmounted the girl's cheeks at these words, but it gave place to a pallor and a moisture of the eyes as she turned away

Alas! the thought occurred to her—

"Of what use are ornaments to me who have none to love me?"

The road to Clanberris House was truly, as she had said, a most lonely one, leading along a narrow, rocky pathway, and over a heather-covered heath, where very few pedestrians were ever seen.

However, she had traversed it on many occasions before, and though now she felt a kind of presentiment that something unusual was about to happen, she went on courageously.

Hurrying along, she reached Clanberris House ere the dusk had much deepened, and was soon admitted into the presence of the lady whom her mistress was so eager to see.

This lady, though also beautiful, offered a marked contrast to both Mary and her mistress.

She was about thirty years of age, neither blonde nor brunette, having blue eyes and dark brown hair, with a good though scarcely fair complexion.

"Well, Mary," she said, "what brings you hither over the lonely moor to-night?"

"It is over that lonely moor that I wish your

ladyship to accompany me," returned the maiden. "My mistress wishes urgently to see you."

"Is your master from home, then?" said Lady Clanberris, in surprise.

"Yes, and she does not expect him to return to-night. The flag on the flag-staff on the summit of our house will be flying as long as he is absent. So there is no danger of our making an error."

"Good," said Lady Clanberris. "We will go at once then. I have important news for her, and no doubt she is eagerly expecting me."

In a very few minutes, Lady Clanberris had seen her husband, and, muffled in a heavy cloak, had passed out into the dusky night with the young maiden, who, still impressed with the idea that something unusual was about to occur, was glad enough of a companion.

The shades of evening had now begun to fall more heavily upon the already sombre heath, and objects were not plainly visible.

Hedgerows and trees looked like misty rows of men, while over the short heather a white fog began to rise.

Mary clutched at her companion's arm tightly, regardless of all distinctions of rank, and the two women hurried on like frightened things.

Half-way was an old wooden bridge spanning a narrow stream, and they had just begun to ascend the slight incline which led to it, when two men rushed from behind a hedge, and stood before them.

They were broadly-built, burly, ragged ruffians, evidently intent on plunder, and their appearance, armed, as they were, to the teeth, was certainly not such as to reassure two terrified women.

"Now, then, my pretty ones," said one of them, addressing both unceremoniously; "now, then, my pretty ones, let us have all your money and jewels, and be sharp about it."

Lady Clanberris was equal to the emergency.

She saw at once the utter uselessness of resistance.

They were wholly in the power of these lawless men, and to resist would only be wilfully subjecting themselves to indignity.

So, without a word, she divested herself of all her ornaments, and took from her pocket a tolerably well-filled purse.

"Here," she said, "take these; my companion is but a servant, and has no money or jewels with her. Take this, and let us go in peace."

As she spoke, the men rushed forward, and seizing each of them round the waist, dragged them apart.

"We don't want any of your nonsense," said one; "it's only a game to save your money. But it won't do for us. She doesn't look like a servant."

While both gave vent to the most piercing screams of distress, the men began to search them roughly.

But not for long.

The shrill cries for help prevented them hearing the sound of a horse's feet, deadened as it was by the turf, on which the steed was proceeding rapidly, and before they were aware of it a horseman dashed up and sprang from his saddle.

"Ha! now then, villains!" cried a loud voice, as he darted on them, sword in hand, and wounded one of them severely. "What mean you, thus molesting ladies on the high road? Stand, cowards, and defend yourselves!"

But they were not, by any means, disposed to act on the defensive.

Bullies as they had proved themselves towards women, they were cowards now even before a single brave man, and, releasing their victims, they darted through the hedge and dashed away at full speed in the darkness.

As they did so, Mary, alarmed beyond her power of endurance by the scene through which she had passed, fainted, and would have fallen to the earth had not the new-comer caught her in his arms.

"Here, madam," he said, addressing Lady Clanberris, "here is a lantern in my belt. Open it and throw the light upon this lady's face while I administer to her a little brandy."

The lady was not slow in obeying his behests, and in a moment the bright light of the lantern was turned full upon the pale features of Mary.

As it did so a wild cry of delight escaped the lips of the young man.

"By heavens!" he said, "it is Mary Macpherson, my long-lost Mary!"

Allan of the Glen and his mountain-love were once more united.

The brandy which he administered in a few moments restored her to herself, but when she opened her eyes and beheld the features of her lover, she shuddered and closed them again, as if she imagined herself in the realms of spirits.

"Fear not!" said Allan, upon whom the movement was not lost; "fear not. It is, indeed, Allan, your own Allan; tell me, tell me, do you love me still?"

Then the beautiful eyes were opened again, and the soft arms were flung around his neck, and Allan and Mary were now clasped to each other's breasts.

Allan was the first to realise the fact that the situation was in no way interesting to Lady Clanberris.

He quietly disengaged Mary's arms from around him.

"Mary," he said, "whither are you going? I will see you safely to your destination."

"Not very far from this," she said; "we have only to reach Dalrymple House."

Allan started.

"Dalrymple House!" he said. "To whom does it belong?"

"To Sir Hugh Dalrymple," replied Lady Clanberris. "But now, my noble preserver, let us hur forward, for the night is coming on apace."

To describe the effect produced upon Allan of the Glen by her words would be impossible.

RUPERT DREADNOUGHT.

"ALLAN STAGGERED FORWARD WITH A GROAN!"

It seem truly as if the age of miracles had returned.

It was but a few days, as it were, before this meeting, that Rupert Dreadnought had learned the second mission which his father imposed upon him; and now—unless there was a strange coincidence of names—Allan had already discovered the lair of his enemy.

The heart of the young Scotch boy beat high with joy.

He had asked Rupert to be allowed to take upon himself the fulfilment of this mission, and had been refused.

Rupert could not blame him if, having his enemy, as it were, in his clutches, he did his best to destroy him.

Smothering as well as he could, therefore, the emotion which stirred his heart, he answered—

"Let me precede you. The way is very dark and lonely, and those ruffians may yet be inclined to return. Or stay; if you and Mary mount the horse I will lead him."

This suggestion was at once put into execution; and, having assisted them to the saddle, Allan of the Glen, still sword in hand, led the way, under their directions, towards Dalrymple House.

Presently they came in sight of the gloomy old building.

"We are safe," cried Lady Clanberris. "See, the flag is waving in the breeze. Sir Hugh is absent. Let us press forward."

The horse accordingly was allowed to trot along the now even road, and in a few minutes the wooden drawbridge was reached.

"Now, my preserver," said Lady Clanberris, "I must leave you. I am compelled to enter this house by stealth. You cannot enter!"

"Cannot enter!" echoed Allan.

Knowing, of course, nothing of the circumstances, he had anticipated naturally that he would be received into the house as the preserver of the lady and her companion, and that he would thus be able to learn important particulars regarding Rupert's enemy.

As he echoed Lady Clanberris's words, therefore, he turned towards Mary Macpherson.

"Allan," she said, "it is now too late to explain anything. Believe me, she is not ungrateful, but every moment she remains here is fraught with danger to her. To-morrow evening at eight meet me by yonder oak tree, and I will explain all. For my sake, Allan, ask no more now."

He could not, of course, refuse anything to her, and so, kissing her ripe, red lips, he bowed to Lady Clanberris, and leaping on his horse sped away.

He was disappointed, and yet he had, in very truth, no reason to be so.

He had truly not been permitted to enter the house, but he had most unexpectedly discovered the whereabouts of his master's new enemy.

With this, therefore, he was tolerably satisfied, and looking forward to the following evening, when he should meet alone the one he loved, he put spurs to his horse, and hastened onwards on his journey.

CHAPTER III.

LOVE'S MYSTERY.

As soon as the forms of Allan of the Glen and his horse had faded away in the distance, Mary Macpherson took the hand of her companion, and led her along a narrow path which skirted the moat.

For a short distance this path was open enough, but it presently led beneath tall and heavily foliaged trees.

Only a few yards along this path did Mary proceed, before she stopped at a spot where the earth had been cast into the moat, and dammed its waters.

Here, across a narrow wall, as it were, of hardened clay, they passed, and found themselves at a small gate.

No need was there to knock or ring here, for Mary Macpherson had left it ajar when she started from the old house.

They were soon, therefore, within the precincts of the old house itself.

"Hist!" said Mary, as they reached the bottom of the spiral staircase which formed a kind of secret mode of entrance to the chamber of Lady Dalrymple, "we must be very careful now, for we may be watched. *My* absence may have been observed, and from that other things may have been suspected. You know that Lady Dalrymple is watched—has treacherous spies in her house, and anyone who is known to be friendly to her is subject to the same suspicion."

Lady Clanberris made no reply, but clasping the young girl's hand firmly as in acquiescence, followed her up the stairs.

In a few moments they had reached the apartments of Lady Dalrymple, apparently unobserved.

It was only apparently, however.

As they passed up the dark stairs, an old and long disused door had been stealthily opened, and a pair of gleaming eyes watched them.

Only for an instant did they show.

One glance apparently was enough.

The door was closed noiselessly, and the two women passed up, imagining themselves to be unobserved and unsuspected.

Lady Dalrymple greeted her visitor eagerly.

Throwing her arms round her neck she kissed her fondly, saying—

"How good—how kind of you to come and see me so late. Have you news for me?"

"Yes, great news," returned Lady Clanberris; "are we quite safe from intrusion?"

"Yes," said Lady Dalrymple, who was now evidently under the influence of intense excitement, "yes. Look once more, Mary, to see that all is closed, and then we can talk."

The two ladies sat down in the centre of the room on a broad ottoman, while the young Scotch girl went to the door, tried it, and even peered out.

All was still.

"It is quite safe, my lady," she said, returning.

"Good," said Lady Dalrymple; "and now, dear Alice, *do* begin."

"Quite safe?"

She had on many occasions heard strange things said of Dalrymple House.

Rumours of terrible deeds had floated about for years.

Memories of past horrors had been kept alive by strange and mysterious events in the present.

She knew not, therefore, how many secret doors were in that old mansion, or how many methods of entrance her husband and his myrmidons had both to the house itself and its various chambers.

There *was* danger, though they knew it not.

The same pair of gleaming eyes which had glared at them as they ascended the stairs now glanced at them from behind the tapestry, where a panel had noiselessly slided upon well-greased grooves and admitted a dark figure.

However, as I have said, they knew nothing of this.

"Well," said Lady Dalrymple, "tell me all you have heard."

Lady Clanberris took her friend's hand and pressed it.

"My dear Margaret," she said, "I have heard from abroad—from my brother. You guessed this."

A crimson flush overspread the features of Lady Dalrymple.

"Yes, yes," she said, in a tremulous voice; "yes, yes; I guessed it. And is he well?"

"Yes, well, and coming home."

"Coming home!"

The flush was succeeded by a deadly pallor as she repeated these words, and her bosom heaved violently.

"Yes; are you sorry?" asked Lady Clanberris, smiling.

"What would you have me do; what would you have me say?" returned Lady Dalrymple, in a low voice. "How *can* I welcome him; how *can* I be glad to hear of his return? True, I was forced into a marriage with this man whom I hate; true, I was compelled to quit Henry without a word; but I *am* the wife of Sir Hugh Dalrymple, and, as such, I understand how to conduct myself. Not a shadow of suspicion must fall on my good name."

Tears stood in her eyes as she spoke, and Lady Clanberris pressed her hand warmly.

"Cheer up, my dear Margaret," she said; "who knows what the future may have in store for you? Henry Clanberris, be it remembered, is not one who would run even the slightest risk of compromising one whom he loved. He would wish to see you once and that is all."

Lady Dalrymple withdrew her hand, and pressed it convulsively over her eyes, as if striving to collect her thoughts, or at least to gain courage.

Then she withdrew them with a sudden start.

"Alice," she said, "this *must* not be—I cannot see him. I *will* not. It would be wrong!"

Lady Clanberris smiled.

"And yet," she said, "yet you were so eager to hear of him."

"Oh, Alice!" returned Lady Dalrymple, passionately. "You know not how I loved him, or you would understand that I know not what I *do* wish sometimes. But I can explain all. I wish to hear of him; I wish to know that he is happy; I wish to know that he is well and fortunate, but that is all."

"Good," returned Lady Clanberris, "he *is* well, he *is* fortunate, wealth has been showered upon him. Whatever he has touched has seemed to turn to gold. I tell you all this—but you say you wish also to know whether he is happy—shall I tell you that he will bring home with him a wife?"

A deadly pallor overspread the features of Lady Dalrymple.

These words seemed to chill her very heart.

She bowed her head, and half averted her face.

"You are cruel," she murmured, "and yet scarcely know what you say. Is it so?"

"No," murmured Lady Clanberris, "it is *not* so. He is *not* wed. He loved you too well to permit another to take the place he destined for you. He wishes to see you to tell you that his heart is still yours."

"Ellen, I *cannot* see him—I cannot see him," said Lady Dalrymple; "tell him what you know of me when he *does* come—tell him how I have cherished his memory, but say that duty forbids my seeing him again. Never—never must we meet again."

Lady Clanberris rose sadly.

"Well," she said, "*I* have no right to dictate other feelings to you. It would be wrong, I know. But I dread to see Henry."

"Let his cousin, your husband, then, tell him for you. He might break it better to him than *you* can. I cannot—will not see him."

Lady Clanberris rose.

She was evidently somewhat disconcerted.

"Well, well," she said, "perhaps you are right—It might lead to no good results. Good-bye, dear; I will try to do the best for you. And now I will go while we are safe."

They indulged then in a loving kiss, and Lady Clanberris was led out of the room by Mary Macpherson, and down the stairs.

"You need not return to my chamber to-night, Mary," said Lady Dalrymple, as she closed the door. "I would rather be alone."

Then, when Mary and Lady Clanberris had gone, she flung herself down upon the ottoman and burst into a flood of tears.

For some quarter of an hour she remained thus.

When she roused herself, she saw sitting opposite to her, with the back of the chair in front of him, a coarse, ill-looking fellow, who was dressed like an Alsatian bully.

CHAPTER IV.

THE TRAITOR.

THE man laughed coarsely as he saw the alarm so plainly depicted on the face of Lady Dalrymple.

"You didn't expect to see me here, did you?" he said.

Lady Dalrymple sprang from her seat, and rushed to the bell-rope.

But something peculiar in the manner of the man restrained her.

"Hold a moment," he said, "before you destroy yourself."

"Destroy myself!"

"Aye, destroy is the word," said the man, "destroy is the word."

"And why? What right have you here? Do you suppose I am going to permit you to remain?"

"Of that I am not aware," answered the man; "but it will be against your interest to expel me. I am come, not to do you any harm, but to inform you of something which is to your interest."

"It cannot be. I will not listen," returned Lady Dalrymple; "leave my chamber at once or I will alarm the house."

The man rose at once

"Very well," he said, "very well. I'll go. But to-morrow, when Sir Hugh returns, and taxes you with your strange feelings towards an old lover, you will wish you had permitted me to warn you."

With these words he turned to quit the chamber.

Very slowly, however.

He knew well that he had touched the right chord.

"Stay!" cried Lady Dalrymple, "if you have anything to communicate speak, and speak quickly."

The man laughed a short, dry laugh, and reseated himself.

"My name's Barton," he said; "I'm one of Sir Hugh's men. You might have seen me if you had taken the trouble, for I've been in and about Dalrymple House a long while. Well, I've amused myself, when Sir Hugh has not required me, by finding out what I could about the house. It's a queer old place, as I've found out, and I've found among other things a private door to this room."

"Well, is this all?"

"No, no. You are impatient," returned the fellow. "I have been here some time, and I have heard all that has passed."

She had almost expected this, yet the announcement came to her, notwithstanding, with terrible force.

Though she paled slightly, however, and her bosom trembled with the sudden leaping of her heart, she did not delay her reply.

"Well," she answered, "if you have heard all, you know also that I have acted in such a way that I care for no one."

"So you think, madam," returned the man, "but you are wrong. Suppose I repeat the conversation differently."

"Villain, I have witnesses," cried Lady Dalrymple indignantly.

"Witnesses!" repeated the fellow, sneeringly, "a bosom friend and a confidential servant. I have myself—the jealousy of Sir Hugh, and the fact that your lover is positively on his way to England, aye, may be here now for aught I know. These things are evidences; but in addition there is the knowledge in your own heart that if he *does* return you *will* see him, in spite of all you have said!"

A crimson flush of shame and anger overspread the features of Lady Dalrymple as he spoke.

"Wretch!" she cried, "how dare you insult me thus? What is it you want of me, that you use these taunting words?"

"Ah! now you are coming to the point," said he. "I want money."

"How much?—tell me quickly," she answered.

"Oh—I don't want much now," he said; "a little now and a little again will suit me better than having a lump of cash, which I should spend all at once. You can give me ten pounds now, and when I want some more I'll ask."

Lady Dalrymple shuddered at the very thought of the answer she felt obliged to make.

"I will let you have what you require, and if I do you swear to be silent?"

"I swear," replied the man, with a chuckle.

Foolish woman!

If she had boldly told her husband the truth, she could have saved herself from calumny, though she might have endangered the freedom of her position.

Now, by placing herself in this fellow's power, she was destroying her last chance of liberty!

This view of the case, however, never occurred to her.

All she thought of was her husband's violent temper, and the danger there was of a hostile meeting between him and Henry Clanberris, her old lover.

So she rose, approached her secretaire, and took from it the gold which was to buy the fellow's silence.

With a shudder she placed it in his coarse hand.

"There," she said, "I have fulfilled my promise; see that you fulfil yours. Circumstances have not as yet drawn me into stern action; but I know that if you betray me I am capable of taking a terrible vengeance."

For an instant, as she glanced at him, the ruffian quailed before her.

There was a strange gleaming in her eyes, which meant more than in her own heart she felt herself capable of.

"Be assured," he said, "I will keep my word; and now I will depart."

"When does Sir Hugh return?" she asked, as his hand was placed upon the panel to slide it into its place.

"By midnight to-morrow he will be here," said the man.

The next moment he had gone, while Lady Dalrymple sank upon her knees, and burst into a passionate fit of weeping.

CHAPTER V.

IN THE LION'S DEN.

As may be supposed, Allan of the Glen waited with the utmost impatience the arrival of the hour which was appointed for his meeting with Mary Macpherson, whom he had naturally supposed lost to him for ever at the time of the dispersion of the Hidden People.

The night, fortunately, was a somewhat dark one, and when he reached the old tree, therefore, which she had pointed out to him, he was enabled to conceal his horse behind some heavily-growing bushes.

Mary Macpherson was punctual to her appointment.

As the clock of the old house tolled out the hour, she tripped lightly up from the postern and met him.

I will not describe their joy as they met.

Those of my readers who know what it is to be separated any length of time from one dearly loved can imagine to themselves the scene.

I must hurry on, therefore, to the development of my story.

"And now, dear Mary," he said, after awhile, "I have a favour to ask."

"And what is that?"

"I want to enter Dalrymple House secretly."

"Oh, you cannot—you cannot," she said; "it would be death to you."

Allan smiled.

"I must chance that," he said. "I have lived a strange life, one in which I have had to dare many dangers worse than this. I must see him in private. Will you not manage this for me?"

Mary thought awhile.

"Does he know you?" she asked.

"No, but he has seen me once before," replied Allan; "but that would not matter. I wish to see him on business."

Mary smiled up into his face.

"You are deceiving me somewhat," she said; "I am sure you are. You do *not* know him, and you have some mysterious reason for desiring to see him now."

"Mary," said Allan, reproachfully, "have you not sufficient trust in me to believe that I am on no bad errand. You know your master to be a bad man."

"Yes; but I am his trusted servant," said Mary.

"Or rather the trusted servant of his wife," returned Allan. "But never fear; I will not compromise you. I will return to London, and seek out one who knows him, if that is necessary to my introduction to him. However, for our love's sake, Mary, I had thought you would aid me in this."

"Do you know any of his friends, then?" said the young girl.

"I do not. Name one or two."

The Scotch maiden thought a moment.

"THE GLEAMING EYES WERE ON THE WATCH."

"There is Sir Oscar Penraven, for one," she said. "Do you know know him?"

The question staggered Allan of the Glen for a moment.

Oscar Penraven one of Sir Hugh Dalrymple's friends! How everything seemed working in a circle of crime.

"I do," he said. "I know him well. He is an assassin, a murderer, a poisoner; a villain who has oft and oft attempted the life of my greatest benefactor—the one who saved me from ruin and death when I first reached London. Believe me, Mary, you will do right in admitting me. Your master is a murderer and an associate of murderers. Come now, dear one, after our long separation grant me this favour."

Then, without awaiting for her reply, he told her, under pledge of secrecy, the whole story; the mysteries which surrounded Rupert Dreadnought's life, and the hideous crime which had given to Sir Hugh Dalrymple his wealth and his power.

Whatever scruples Mary Macpherson might have entertained in regard to permitting Allan of the Glen to enter Dalrymple House were now entirely overcome.

Her love for him prevented her from criticising too closely the motives which made him anxious to enter secretly; and so it was arranged that, on the following night, he should be admitted.

Then, with a tender embrace, the two parted.

It may be imagined that Allan of the Glen awaited with intense impatience the arrival of the following night, which would find him face to face with the man whom Rupert Dreadnought was sworn to destroy, but whose destruction he had resolved to accomplish for himself.

At length, though not soon enough for his anxious spirit, the time arrived, and as darkness spread itself over the scene, the fair form of Mary Macpherson quitted Dalrymple House and approached him.

"You have come at last then," cried the ardent lover, as he clasped her to his breast. "Is Sir Hugh at home?"

"Yes, he is; in his study," replied the young girl; "and if you enter at once, you will be able to enter unperceived."

Even love was forgotten at this speech.

"Let us lose no time, hen," he said. "I am ager to see him."

"Come, then, Allan," aid the maiden; "though I fear that in going you run a risk which you will not confess to me."

"Fear not," he said, as he kissed her once more. "He will greet me far differently to what you expect."

In a few minutes the postern had been reached, and they were ascending the dark stairs where, a few evenings before, Lady Clanberris had been seen by the spy.

"Shall I knock at his door and announce you?" asked Mary, as they reached the door of Sir Hugh's apartment.

"No; I will enter alone. Fear not, my love," he added, seeing the frightened look upon her face; "I mean no harm to him, and he shall do no harm to me."

He kissed her fondly again, and then made his way quickly towards the door which led into the chamber of Sir Hugh Dalrymple.

Turning the handle quietly, he entered noiselessly, and advanced towards the table without being perceived by the master of the house, who sat by a table with his head buried in his hands, engaged evidently in deep thought.

Had Allan of the Glen been of the assassin type, how ready to his hand now was his victim.

One raising of the knife, one strong blow, and Rupert Dreadnought's second mission would be over.

But such a consummation would not have suited the noble heart that beat within the bosom of the Scotch boy.

Yet he paused a moment.

He had truly succeeded in entering the presence of the man whom he desired to punish, yet even now how could it be done?

Was he not absolutely in the lion's den?

What excuse could he give for his presence?

He saw plainly now that his youthful enthusiasm had led him into an error; but he was gone too far to recede, and, indeed, the idea of doing so never occurred to him.

Drawing a pistol from his belt, he suddenly placed his hand upon Sir Hugh Dalrymple's shoulder.

The latter was instantly roused from his reverie, and started back in his chair with undisguised wonder, not unmingled with alarm.

His features, however, when he carefully scanned Allan's form and face, were far more expressive of astonishment than fear.

He rose.

"Pray, young sir, and who may you be, and how dare you thus intrude yourself upon my presence unannounced?"

"I have dared," answered Allan, playing with his pistol, "because I know I can defend myself. I have desired the interview in order to explain certain matters to you, and after the explanation to kill you?"

"Well, Master Scot," replied Sir Hugh, with a smile, "you must be either a madman or a robber, and an insolent one too. But, since you hold in your hand so conclusive an argument, I must e'en listen to you. Tell me, what it is that you desire to explain?"

"Simply this," returned Allan. "I will be brief, since delay is useless to either. You had a brother, Edwin. He is dead. *You* murdered him!"

Sir Hugh's features assumed a ghastly pallor, and his hand naturally was placed upon the hilt of his sword.

"Insolent madman!" he said, "you shall suffer for this."

"Stay," returned Allan, coolly, "when I have told you all, I will place my pistol in my belt and fight you fairly. If, however, you attempt to attack me before I have time to give an explanation, or if you alarm the house, I shall fire!"

The determined manner in which the youth uttered these words was enough to prove to Sir Hugh Dalrymple that he was not to be trifled with, and inwardly he could not avoid feeling a kind of respect and reverence for the bold young Scotchman who thus dared him on his own hearth.

"Good. Speak on then," returned Sir Hugh Dalrymple, "and quickly, for I have much to settle to-night."

"You have," said Allan of the Glen, significantly. "Well, as I said before, your brother Edwin is dead, and you are his murderer. You killed him in the vaults of St. Andrew's church, Chichester, that you might inherit his fortune. A friend of his has sworn to avenge him; but *I* take the duty off his hands. Do you not know my face?"

Sir Hugh Dalrymple scanned keenly the bold features of the handsome Scotch boy.

But he really failed to recognise him.

"No," he said, "I know you not."

"Not long ago, when you were in London," replied Allan, "you came out of the 'Golden Sun' in Eastchepe with other roysterers, who rudely pushed the crowd hither and thither. Among that crowd was I, and when I resisted your intemperate haste you called me insolent Scot and struck me in the face. I drew my sword to avenge the insult, when the crowd carried me away and we were separated. Since then I have been burning to avenge the insult, and the opportunity has at length arrived. My friend's vengeance devolves on me, and here am I to take it."

"Foolish boy!" cried Sir Hugh, contemptuously, "why, if I chose, I could call my servants and have you cast forth into the road, or thrown into a dungeon. I like you for your courage. Go while you are in safety."

The eyes of Allan of the Glen flashed fire.

It was insult to his mind to be addressed thus.

"I defy you," he cried, "I defy you to execute your threat. While I hold in my hand this pistol you dare not do as you say. Let us talk no longer—let us fight."

"Good," returned Sir Hugh, with a malignant smile, "good—then since you *will*, I suppose that I must consent. Let me first lock the door, however, that I may be sure that we shall not be interrupted. I would not have my servants see me bearded in my own house by such a boy!"

So saying, he drew his sword, as if to convince Allan that he really intended fighting, and then walked slowly towards the door.

Then occurred what seemed like a miracle.

Sir Hugh stood still for a moment, and then stamped on the floor.

In an instant a panelling shot away and hid him from view.

Allan sprang forward, sword in hand.

But all was in vain.

He was completely hemmed in.

"A prisoner! by Heavens!" he cried; "he has duped me after all."

He had scarcely uttered the words when the panelling slid back into its place.

The door was open now, and within it stood several armed men.

"Seize him!" cried the stern voice of Sir Hugh Dalrymple, "seize him, and bear him to the dungeons."

In an instant the place was invaded by about seven or eight armed men.

They were all dark-looking, rough-featured fellows, evidently not the ordinary servants of the house, but men whom he could hire upon any occasion to perform deeds of robbery or bloodshed.

As all my readers are aware, Allan of the Glen was a brave and resolute character.

Young though he was, he had gone through so many scenes of peril that even in this extremity he felt no sinking of the heart.

But for the moment he was taken so aback that, though standing in the middle of the room, with his sword drawn, he made no effort to defend himself.

But in another instant he recovered his presence of mind.

He glanced around him quickly.

Behind was an open window.

An idea of escape at once occurred to him.

Driven to bay as he was, there was not the slightest use in attempting the execution of his original plan.

He saw now the folly of his attempting the enterprise alone.

But what could he do?

There was no use in trying to defend himself.

He must fly.

Turning suddenly, therefore, he made a rush towards the window.

But it was of no avail.

Below him was a terrible depth.

The darkness, also, was so intense that it was impossible to see where he would fall.

There was not a single shrub or tree within reach.

He felt he was indeed trapped.

He turned round savagely.

To his bold young heart there was something astounding—impossible, as it were—in the thought that he could be thus caged against his will.

His blood boiled within him, and forgetful of the fact that he was in the nest of enemies, he rushed madly at the crowd of murderous villains, whose numbers he did not pause to count.

Had he done so, perhaps he would have seen the madness of what he attempted.

There were at least ten ruffians in the room, each one of whom regarded murder as a matter of business.

But the Scotch youth thought not of this.

Whirling his sword round his head; he sprang into the midst of them just as they were about to close round him, and ere he knew what he had done, one of his enemies had fallen, bathed in blood, upon the floor.

Full of fire and energy now, he swung his weapon round his head, and brought it down with terrible force upon another of his foes, who fell pierced through the shoulder, while *he* remained unscathed.

For a minute the foe seemed paralysed.

The fiery young Scotch boy, standing before them with gleaming eyes and panting frame, caused them for a moment to fall back.

But only for a moment.

In another moment their energies returned, and they dashed upon him in a body with revengeful features and fierce shouts.

The sight of their comrades—one dead, one dying—on the ground might well have inflamed their worst passions.

But, demons as they were, they were compelled to restrain their feelings.

They were not to kill.

Such were the instructions of Sir Hugh Dalrymple.

So, although they assaulted with determined energy, they sought only to wound him so far that he might be easily overcome.

This was easily effected.

Treachery did what fair and open fight would not.

One of the men, clubbing his pistol, rushed in upon him from behind and struck him violently on the head.

He staggered forward.

His sword described a wild circuit in the air and then he fell prone upon his face.

"Good," said one of the men; "he is nigh a dead 'un now. Take him up and bear him to the dungeon. He'll rot there for all I'll do for him. See, poor Lomax there, he's dead; and Bill Locksby don't look much as if he'd ever recover."

While the fellow was thus grumbling, they raised the inanimate form of Allan of the Glen in their arms in by no means a tender manner and bore him from the room.

Passing along the dark corridor, they approached the stairs where Allan had ascended, and, passing through the little secret door where the head of the treacherous fellow had protruded on the night of Lady Clanberris's visit, descended another flight, where the cold, chill atmosphere betrayed the fact that they were going beneath the earth.

The cold and chill air increased in its chillness and coldness as they descended, and a suffocating moisture, like that of a charnel house, invaded their nostrils.

To Allan, had he been in possession of his senses, it would truly have seemed as if he were entering his last home—as if he were being placed in a living tomb; but, of course, senseless as he was, he knew nothing.

Pausing when they had descended some depth, they entered a dark dungeon, where now, at night, not a ray of light was visible, and which in the daytime was only illumined by a few feeble beams struggling through the bars of a diminutive window, high up in the murky wall.

Entering here, they placed Allan against the wall, and fastened him by an iron chain to it.

Then one of them fetched some dry straw, and placed him upon it.

After this one of them administered to the stunned man some liquid, which seemed to revive him, and when the first signs of reanimation were observable, they left him to himself.

The door clanged to with a woeful sound, and Allan was alone and a prisoner!

CHAPTER VI.

ANOTHER TRAITOR.

SIR HUGH DALRYMPLE sat in his room, waiting nervously for the arrival of the news of Allan's discomfiture and capture.

He desired not his death.

To kill him would be to destroy for ever his chance of obtaining from him the secret of his mysterious visit, and his more mysterious knowledge of his history.

Sir Hugh felt greatly disturbed in spirit.

The secret of his cowardly murder of his brother

had been buried so many years that it seemed strange, indeed, that it should now be revived.

The Phantom of his Crime truly had ever stalked at his side, save when his brain was clouded with drink.

It had stood by the altar; it had stood in his nuptial chamber; it had followed the tracks of his prosperity.

But it had appeared only to his own vision.

To others he had imagined his evil deed to be dead and forgotten!

By his side now, as he sat near a blazing fire, shivering with an inward cold, stood a youth of some nineteen summers.

He was dressed in the costume of a page, and stood before his master in an attitude of respect.

But though he stood thus, his features expressed anything but a meek and gentle disposition.

There was that in his eye and in the lines of his mouth which was expressive of stern determination and a cold resolve to make his own way in the world irrespective of the wishes or the good of others.

"They are a long time, Colin," said Sir Hugh, addressing the page; "a very long time."

The page smiled.

"Your wishes speed quicker, maybe, than their swords, Sir Hugh," he said; "but from all you have told me of this youth, he is most brave, and mayhap may give them some trouble."

"True; but no one man, however brave, can stand against such odds as those that have surrounded *him*. Hark! they come!"

Sir Hugh turned eagerly towards the door, through which in another moment one of the ruffians entered.

"Well," he asked impatiently, "is all right?"

"Yes; he is in the dungeon," returned the man; "but he gave us immense trouble. Lomax is dead, and Locksby is nearly so."

"Curses on him! but he is safe now. And is he wounded?"

"Yes, slightly. He has a shoulder scratch and has been stunned by a severe blow on the head."

"Ah, well, I will see that he is well taken care of," said Sir Hugh Dalrymple. "You can leave me now. See to Locksby, and then go down into the hall; you will find there something to cheer you after the battle. Your reward will be bestowed to-morrow."

The man bowed and left the room, and Sir Hugh turned to his page.

"Colin," he said, "proceed to the dungeon where this upstart Scotch youth is confined, and see to his wounds. I know you are dexterous at such things, since you saved my life at Worcester."

"Why wish to save his life, Sir Hugh?" returned the youth. "He came here to beard you in your own house, and I cannot tell why he should not lie where he is and rot."

The eager way in which the page said this appeared somewhat to surprise his master.

He turned and glanced at him fixedly for a moment.

"Ah," he said, "you understand not what you say. He has a secret of mine which I had imagined none else knew, and I must know how far his knowledge extends and whence he derived his information. I have more foes somewhere than I knew of, and I desire to discover them."

The page bowed.

He had guessed as much.

"Very good, master," he said; "I will see that your commands are obeyed."

Then he turned and quitted the room.

"A strange but faithful youth," said Sir Hugh, as he went.

He would have thought differently had he looked into Colin's heart.

"I must find out this secret for myself," was the thought of the "faithful" servant.

He had not proceeded far along the corridor when a figure glided out from behind a statue, which cast its shadow heavily across the passage.

It was Mary Macpherson.

Her face was ghastly pale; her bosom heaved violently, and her whole person, in fact, was tremulous with emotion.

"Colin," she said, "a word with you."

The youth smiled and tapped her under the chin, with a kind of insolent familiarity.

"Yes, pretty one, a dozen if you please," he answered; "what can I serve you in, my sweetheart?"

"Oh! this is no time for love-making," she said, in a voice expressive of intense irritation; "I wish to speak of the prisoner."

The page's smiles vanished at once at this.

"What of him?" he asked quickly.

"He is a countryman of mine, and in danger," she answered, hurriedly.

"And how know you he is here, and in danger?" he asked. "Are you the traitor, then, who admitted him to the house?"

Mary trembled.

But her love for Allan of the Glen kept her from much display of emotion.

"You speak riddles to me," she said; "I heard from the men who are drinking and carousing below that a Scotch youth who has been here to see Sir Hugh has offended him—has killed one of his retainers, and is now confined in a dungeon. They say he is wounded and in need of help. Suffer me to go to him in your stead."

"Impossible," returned Colin; "you would be watched, and they would know well that Sir Hugh would not send a woman down to succour one of his prisoners."

"I know it," replied Mary, "and in my own mind I have provided against that. You must lend me your clothes. I will tend him, and in return for your kindness——"

"You will give me what I am dying for," said Colin; "your promise to be mine?"

"THE SHRIEKING CROWD FOLLOWED HIM MADLY!"

"No; in return for your kindness I will go with you next Thursday to Calswell Fair," returned Mary.

"Good," returned Colin, wh) saw in this a nearer app oach to what he wished, the hand of Mary Macpherson, "good; I will agree. Wait here a few moments, and I will bring you what you desire."

"I will await you at the door of my room," returned the young girl, whose heart was now bounding eagerly in her bosom.

Within ten minutes Colin had changed his clothes, and handed them to Mary, who was soon indued into them, her rounded and supple limbs and elastic figure showing to good advantage within them.

Colin glanced at her with undisguised admiration as she once more emerged from her chamber.

"You look so well in them," he cried, "that you ought never to leave them off."

"There, don't keep me," she said, blushing; remember, the poor prisoner is now waiting for me. Give me the key and whatever you intended to take him."

The page handed to her a flask of spirits, some soft linen to bind up Allan's wounds, and a lantern, and then the young girl hurried away.

The door of the dungeon was soon reached, and Mary entered.

In the dim light of the cell she could scarcely at first see anything, but, as soon as the mask of the lantern was removed, she saw Allan seated on his wretched heap of straw, and his head bowed down upon his breast.

He was apparently asleep.

Carefully closing the door behind her, Mary Macpherson approached her unconscious lover, and discovered then that he was insensible.

The pain of his wounded shoulder had evidently caused him to faint.

Taking his head tenderly, and drawing it down upon her bosom, she poured some brandy down his throat, and bathed his brow, too, with some of the liquid.

In a few moments he opened his eyes, and seeing someone kneeling by him in the costume of a page, he drew back in surprise and some alarm.

But the voice of the one he loved soon reassured him.

"Allan dear, it is I," she said. "I am here in disguise."

He took one glance at her face as she raised the lantern so that the light might fall upon her face, and in another instant the two lovers were clasped in each other's arms.

"Dear Allan," said Mary, sobbing, "did I not tell you that you were throwing yourself into the midst of danger? Why did you persist in periling your life?"

"It was my duty," answered Allan, "and that I never shirk. But is there any chance of escape hence?"

"Not this night," said Mary. "But come, while I am here let me bind up your wounds. As I am doing so, try and explain to me whether I can go to seek your friends, and bring them to your assistance."

As clearly as he could, Allan of the Glen explained to her the position of Rupert Dreadnought's house.

"Do you think you can safely find your way alone," he asked, "or have you anyone that you can trust?"

Mary shook her head.

"No," she said, "there's no one I can trust here. I'll go myself. In this dress no one will know me."

Allan glanced at her, and smiled, as he thought how little her round and pretty limbs were disguised by her male attire.

"You had better wear a long cloak and a sword," he said, "although if it comes to hard knocks I doubt if your use of a sword would not betray you more than anything else. I should know you to be a woman anywhere."

Mary blushed, as her lover's eyes scanned her pretty figure.

"I shall go on horseback," she said, "and wear a cloak as you say. But as for the use of a sword, I am not so ignorant of it as you fancy. I have practised in jest, and when the Hidden People were discovered I defended myself with a claymore against two Lowlanders. But I must go now, or I shall be suspected."

"And when do you start for London?"

"This night."

"So that you will see Rupert Dreadnought by morning. 'Tis well—ere to-morrow's sun declines in the west, Sir Hugh Dalrymple perhaps may regret the steps he has taken."

Then there followed another loving embrace, and leaving the brandy flask by Allan's side, Mary Macpherson moved away, and passing through the door, closed it after her as quietly as possible, and crept up the stairs.

Colin, of course, expected that as soon as she returned from her visit to the prisoner she would divest herself of her male clothing and return it to him.

But she had no such intention, as we have seen, and this was evident enough to him as she came up.

So he resolved to watch.

He was mad with jealousy.

He had made up his mind, in spite of entire absence of encouragement, that she should be his wife; and now a suspicion had entered his mind that the stranger whom he had in the heat of the moment permitted her to see was, perhaps, after all, some favoured lover.

He had followed her to the door of the cell, and had listened.

But all in vain.

Not a sound could be heard through its thick platings of iron.

So he had retired thence discomfited.

Now, however, he resolved to watch, as I have said.

Mary Macpherson entered her room, and remained there a few moments.

Then she came forth, still wearing her male costume, and proceeded towards Colin's door.

Here she knocked twice.

"This is curious," thought the page. "I will keep my eye on her proceedings here too."

But what followed surprised him more.

When she came out again she wore his plumed hat and cloak.

He ground his teeth with rage.

"She is deceiving me," he muttered. "Never mind; I will not betray myself, but watch."

She glanced round her rapidly, but, seeing no

one, made off as swiftly as possible towards the public staircase.

This she descended at a run, and was soon outside the house.

Her make-up was now so exactly like that of Colin, that she was unchallenged until she arrived at the stables, where she admitted herself, and procured a fine horse.

With a joyous smile now she leaped into the saddle, and was soon careering along the high road to London.

She knew not that, at no great distance, a horseman was following her.

This was Colin!

CHAPTER VII.

THE FIGHT AT THE INN.

WATCHED, but not knowing what was impending over her, happy in the idea that she was about to save her lover, Mary Macpherson rode on, and by dint of many inquiries, found little difficulty in finding the house of Rupert Dreadnought.

Rupert had not risen when she arrived, but in a few minutes he had dressed himself, and was standing before her in surprise.

He had certainly remarked upon the unaccountable absence of Allan of the Glen, but he had never dreamed that anything was wrong; and now that he saw before him the handsome form of the disguised page, he could in no way understand the meaning of the first words that were uttered.

He could plainly see from the rounded contour of the person before him that it was a woman in disguise.

"You come from Allan of the Glen?" he said, in surprise.

"Yes, he is in danger—in peril," said the young girl, feeling no degree of bashfulness in the presence of the noble-hearted young hero. "I come to you, as his only friend, to save him."

"Be quick, then," said Rupert Dreadnought, "and explain all, that we may go to his rescue."

It was in a few words that Mary Macpherson explained the position of her lover.

"So you, then, are his mountain love?" said Rupert Dreadnought. "Strange, indeed, that you should meet him thus. And what say you is the name of his enemy?"

"Sir Hugh Dalrymple."

I have before described the effect that was made upon Allan of the Glen when he first heard these words.

Upon Rupert Dreadnought the effect was still greater.

His frame quivered, his lips trembled, his eyes were ablaze with excitement.

"Sir Hugh Dalrymple!" he repeated; "by heavens, my mortal enemy!"

Then he paused for awhile, overcome by the intensity of his emotion.

Mary Macpherson did not disturb him.

She saw the fulfilment of the mystery at which her lover had hinted, and she was anxious to see the result.

After a few moments Rupert Dreadnought recovered his presence of mind.

"We must start at once," he said; "but it will not be well to attempt anything before nightfall. How far reckon you it from London?"

"Eight miles."

"Good; then there is no hurry. An adventure such as this would be destroyed in its effect by being prosecuted in the daylight. I will send my men on before me, and you and I will follow."

"I will do just as you please," replied Mary Macpherson. "I know you are Allan's friend and will act for the best."

In the space of two hours Tom the waterman had been summoned, and together with the retainers of the house, had started for their destination.

They were told to dispose themselves in the wood near at hand and watch the place, and if Allan of the Glen was removed from his prison they were to capture him if they were strong enough, or follow and see where he went, if the other party were too strong.

Towards dusk Rupert started with Mary Macpherson.

They had no sooner left the door on horseback when a figure emerged from its hiding-place opposite.

This was Colin.

He came from his hiding-place so stealthily, however, that neither of those he followed perceived him, and they accordingly proceeded on without suspicion.

His purpose, however, was not to follow them.

He knew well which road they would take, and what places they would have to pass, and he therefore turned his horse's head another way, and proceeded at full speed across country.

Arriving at the half-way inn, he tied up his horse to an old tree, and called for refreshment.

The half-way inn was the last tavern on the road before you reached Dalrymple House, and as the next house of entertainment lay at some considerable distance, it was generally crowded with visitors of all grades.

The public room was at this moment full of men and women eating and drinking, and Colin, as he elbowed his way through them, assumed an air of great gravity.

"You look serious, young sir," said a jovial-looking farmer, as the youth took his position near the fire.

This was just what the page wanted.

He would now put in practice his cowardly scheme.

"You would look serious too did you know what villany is afloat," returned Colin.

"Of what do you speak?" asked the sturdy farmer.

"Of highwaymen."

"Highwaymen!" echoed several voices, "have we any hereabouts, then?"

"You will have shortly," said Colin, "and, unless there be those among you who will aid me in arresting them, the mail coach will be robbed this night, and murder will be done!"

The landlord had heard a few words of the conversation, and he now pressed forward.

"What does all this mean?" he cried. "Speak less in enigmas, boy, and tell us all about it."

Thus pressed, Colin at once commenced his story, a tissue, of course, of most atrocious falsehoods.

"I was in London not long since," he said, "and on my way to Dalrymple House, when I chanced to overhear a few words that proved some villany was afloat.

"An attack, in fact, is meditated upon the mail coach, which will pass here in an hour.

"The villains who are to assist in the attack have gone on before.

"But their leader is on his way now."

"Is he alone?" asked the sturdy farmer.

"No; but his only companion is his mistress—a young girl of some eighteen years, who is disguised as a page."

"They must be secured," said the farmer, valiantly, now that he knew that there was only one man and a girl to contend with. "We must organise an attack."

Colin smiled.

"There'll not be much trouble, I should imagine," he answered, "in effecting their capture with all those who are here; but there will not be much time for organisation; if what I heard was correct they will be here in an hour's time."

"And will he pull up here for refreshment?" asked Boniface.

"Yes, such is my belief."

"And how shall we know him? Is he a villanous-looking fellow?"

"Oh, I shall be able to point him out," replied Colin; "but he is by no means what you would suppose him. He is a young and handsome man, and she who accompanies him is fair and graceful. I will go now to the door and watch, that they may not elude us. A goodly reward will, no doubt, be ours if we seize them."

So saying, the young traitor moved towards the entry, and took his station at a point where he could command the high road, leaving the yokels within to wonder and make many boasts as to their intentions.

It was not long before he saw approaching along the highway two figures on horseback.

His heart beat high within his bosom as he beheld them.

His cowardly vengeance was now about to commence.

Rushing back into the room, he announced to the anxious crowd that the daring highwayman was approaching, and bade them conceal themselves in a yard at the side of the inn, where they could rush out upon him unawares.

They accordingly passed out by a side door and waited.

Rupert, of course, had no idea of danger, and reining up at the door of the inn, called for some ale.

"Egad!" murmured the landlord, when he had observed him, and his eyes had taken in all the details of the form of the pretty girl at his side, "egad! if that's a highwayman and his mistress, I can only say that he's a fine fellow, and *she* seems a lady. However, there's a deal of deception about, and there's no use in going by appearances."

So he brought out the ale and received the money, for he was a prudent man, and Rupert, having drank it, prepared to go.

Then it was that it seemed as if a very Babel had been let loose.

The door of the yard was flung open, and a crowd of men and women rushed forth, armed with every imaginable kind of weapon.

Clubs, sticks, swords, pitchforks, were flourished just as it had been at the old house where Rupert had been led by Redlock in search of Helen.

For an instant Rupert was paralysed with surprise.

What did it mean?

What treacherous villain had betrayed him?

He soon saw, however, that there was no time for reflection.

If surrounded by this yelling crew, what could he say if taken to the constabulary?

"You had better fly, Mary," he said, addressing the girl who was with him; "fly and make your way into Dalrymple House."

"But you! what will you do?" she answered.

She already felt a deep interest in the handsome fellow at her side.

"I will cut my way through," he answered; "fear not for me—fly to Allan, and tell him I am coming to his rescue."

The young girl glanced round her.

Not an instant was to be lost.

They were even now prancing and careering in the middle of the crowd.

So, putting her spurs into her horse's flanks, and pressing her legs against his sides, so as to secure herself in the saddle, she suddenly wheeled him round and darted away, overturning Colin as she did so, and inflicting a severe gash upon his forehead.

She did not observe him, however.

It was the last thing in her thoughts that he would make his appearance in such a scene.

Though she knew him to be her lover, she did not suspect him of treachery.

So, thinking merely that she had overturned one of the rustics, she darted on, and was soon plunging away swiftly across the open country towards Dalrymple House.

She must not for this be accused of cowardice, or of leaving her best friend in the hour of need.

It must be remembered that her own betrothed was in danger.

It must be remembered also that Rupert Dreadnought had sent on before him a number of fellows to aid him in the rescue of Allan of the Glen, and it occurred to her at once that perhaps she would be able to meet with these, and send them back to aid Rupert.

So away, as I have said, she went at full speed, while the yelling crowd, having now only one to deal with, became more courageous and determined.

They struck the horse, tore at the rider, endeavoured to drag the bridle from his hand, and were cast down to the ground every moment by the kicking out of the terrified animal, and the blows which Rupert freely gave with the flat of his sword.

Then suddenly Rupert drew his right rein violently, caused his horse to perform a complete pirouette, and then suddenly, as the yelling throng fell and stumbled back, he dashed away.

The shrieking crowd followed him madly, some

with sticks, and others with pitchforks, the women crying at the top of their voices—

"Stop the highwayman!"

"Seize the robber!"

"Kill him—kill him!"

But, seeing that he had not attempted to shed any blood, there was no one in the crowd courageous enough to fire, although the landlord had supplied several of them with pistols.

So, with a loud shout of defiance, Rupert Dreadnought dashed away, and the discomfited throng could only gaze and wonder at his energy, and their own folly in permitting him to escape.

CHAPTER VIII.

A STRANGE MODE OF LOVE-MAKING.

Having started across country, instead of taking the direct route along the high road, Mary Macpherson had to proceed a far greater distance than Rupert, or anyone going by the ordinary way.

When, therefore, Colin recovered from the blow which her horse's foot had given him, he darted away eagerly along the highway.

His face was, of course, entirely unknown to Rupert Dreadnought, and he therefore regarded him simply as one of the crowd flying from the scene through cowardice.

He was bent on quite another errand, however.

He was longing for vengeance.

ALONE IN A LIVING TOMB.

True, he loved Mary.

But she had duped him.

He now saw how thoroughly he had been deceived.

The stranger who was languishing in the dungeon was evidently a dearly-loved friend, and the young girl had risked all to save him.

The demon of jealousy and hate had now possession of Colin's heart.

He would revenge himself terribly.

He would cause his death, and she should witness the disaster. So he dashed eagerly on.

It was now getting on towards night, but he could, nevertheless, see for some time the graceful figure of Mary Macpherson bending over the horse as he advanced at full speed over hill and dale.

But though she rode so rapidly, he gained on her, for the road he took was not half the distance, and all even ground.

As he passed along, running at full speed, he encountered a number of men who were, as it seemed, lying in ambush by the roadside.

They knew nothing of him, however, and they took, therefore, no notice of him, and away he ran towards the old house.

As he reached the postern, the thick twilight had deepened, and he could not see anyone approaching.

It enabled, however, the traitor to conceal himself and wait.

He had not to do so long.

In a very few minutes the sound of a horse's hoofs was heard, and then the figure of Mary Macpherson was seen approaching.

She leaped off her horse, and was about to lead him to the stable, when she was seized suddenly in Colin's arms.

She uttered a cry of alarm, but upon seeing who it was her fear subsided.

She had no idea of his treachery.

"Ah, Colin," she cried, "this is no time for love-making. Let me go. I have something most important to do."

She tried to disengage herself gently from his embrace, but she could not.

Then she saw with wonder the fierce glitter in his eye. His words, however, soon explained his meaning.

"Love-making!" he cried. "Is it not for that I detain you. Did you not see me in the crowd at the inn when your horse kicked me, and inflicted this gash upon my face?"

"*You* in the crowd Colin?" she said. "I saw you not. What did you there?"

"I know all," said Colin; "how you have duped me for another, how you disguised yourself with my cloak, and took my sword, and rode my horse to London; I know how you have brought a friend with you to rescue Allan of the Glen, as he is called, and now you will see how I intend to spoil all your plans."

Then suddenly, before she knew what he was going to do, he tied a thick handkerchief over her mouth; then he secured her wrists, and forcibly tied her legs together.

"Now," he cried, as he lifted her in his arms and bore her towards the little gate, "now you will see how I will foil you. You are my prisoner, and nothing but your promise to be my wife will obtain your release."

What emotions were in the young girl's heart as she heard these words, and felt herself being borne away in the arms of the man she disliked, and who had now discovered himself to be a dupe, I shall not now pause to describe.

In vain she struggled.

Her limbs were so strongly confined that all her efforts were useless, and, as they entered the dark passage of the old house, she subsided into a faint yielding.

In a very short space of time, therefore—less time, in fact, than it takes to describe it, she found herself occupying a chamber, or rather a dungeon, not far from that in which Allan of the Glen was confined.

Here he hurriedly unfastened, or rather loosened, her bonds, and darted from the room.

He had no fear now.

Scream as she might no one would hear her.

So, closing the door of communication between the cells and the house itself, he hurried up again to the postern.

He had a good plan in his mind now.

He was dressed in clothes almost identical with those of Mary Macpherson.

In the dark Rupert Dreadnought would not know him.

He would deceive him, therefore, and lead him into an ambush.

He was just in time.

Rupert rode up upon his panting horse just as Colin emerged into the dim light that the rising moon shed over the precincts of the postern.

"Are you there, Mary?" said Rupert.

"Yes," answered Colin, in a feigned whisper, "yes. Where are your friends?"

"Among yonder trees."

"Be quick, then," continued the traitor, still in the disguised whisper. "Call your men and enter quickly."

"How shall I know when all is ready?"

"You will hear the shrill cry of an owl," replied Colin; "then enter one by one, and I will lead them to their places."

He said this at random.

He knew not, of course, what arrangements had been made by Rupert and Mary.

"Do you remember my instructions?" said Rupert.

"Yes; I know their import," replied Colin, "but you may as well repeat them. You wish, of course, to see Sir Hugh Dalrymple secretly."

"I do," replied Rupert Dreadnought; "we must seize upon him, and then, at the sword's point, force him to yield his prisoner to us. Now, then, I will go and fetch my men. No time must be lost."

He then turned his horse's head and rode away, while Colin rushed eagerly into the dark passage.

Now was the time for action.

He knew the nearest cut towards what might truly be called the guard-room, where he could always make sure of finding a number of rough fellows.

In a minute he had made his way in, and found himself in the midst of a rough, rollicking set of drinkers, who burst into a loud laugh as he made his appearance.

"Have you seen a ghost, Colin," said one, "that you look so eager and scared?"

"No, no; but I have work for you," he said.

"What work—is it work that will pay?" cried one brawny ruffian.

"Yes, yes; only listen," replied Colin; "there is no time to lose. There is a plan to surprise the house, to seize Sir Hugh, and release the prisoner. You must follow me, and before Sir Hugh knows anything of the matter we shall have trapped and secured them. You know well the secret gate on the stairs?"

"Yes."

"Well, then, that must be opened, and they must be allowed to enter there and descend towards the dungeons. Then the gate must be closed and Sir Hugh must be apprised of the capture."

"But whom will they trust who will admit them?"

"I shall. They believe me to be someone else—they believe me to be helping them. The man who leads them is Sir Hugh Dalrymple's greatest enemy, and a rich reward will be ours if we capture him. Come."

The men rose, as if by a natural instinct, and buckled on their swords.

"I can't see why Sir Hugh should not be told of this," said the leader, as he proceeded to the door.

"There is no time; delay would spoil all," returned Colin; "besides, when the deed is done, his pleasure and our reward will be all the greater."

The young traitor had an aptitude, apparently, for command, and, turning as he spoke, as if the matter was settled, he led the way down the staircase.

Arrived close to the secret gate, he pointed out to his followers the positions they were to occupy, and having seen that they were so placed as to be entirely screened from observation, he hurried to the entrance, and uttered the shrill cry which had been agreed upon as the signal.

Within a minute, Rupert and his men, leaving their horses in the shadow of the trees, under the care of one of their number, had approached Dalrymple House, and advanced to the edge of the moat.

"Now, then," said Colin, in a low and somewhat tremulous voice, "now, then, enter quickly one by one. Follow me, and I will show you the secret door which leads to the cells in one of which Allan of the Glen is confined."

Rupert Dreadnought was thoroughly trapped.

How *could* he suspect that this page, who was dressed like Mary Macpherson, and spoke, too, like her, was a traitor, and that the pretty companion of his ride was a prisoner?

Advancing boldly, therefore, he reached the secret gate.

"Descend," whispered Colin; "your men must enter one by one."

Within five minutes Rupert and his companions were safely within the passage.

Then the door clanged to, and they found themselves in utter darkness.

Colin had trapped them without having need of his friends.

They were caged without the shedding of a single drop of blood.

For a few moments complete silence reigned.

Then finding that no one spoke, and that there was a sound of whispering outside the door, he said—

"Mary, where are you?"

"Here I am," said a voice which sounded strangely through the closed door.

"Are we to remain here in the dark, then?" asked Dreadnought.

"Yes; but only for a time; keep still while I go up and procure the keys of the dungeon."

So Rupert and his men waited while the cunning traitor darted up the stairs, and proceeded towards the room of Sir Hugh Dalrymple.

Sir Hugh was surprised to see him enter.

In fact, there was a strange look of sternness on his face.

"Where have you been?" he asked.

"On your business, Sir Hugh," he said.

And then as briefly as possible he told his story, omitting the capture of Mary Macpherson and her confinement in one of the dungeons.

"This is some of Lady Dalrymple's treachery," muttered Sir Hugh, when Colin had told all; "Mary Macpherson is her companion. Where is this treacherous maiden?"

"I know not," said Colin; "she fled from the attack at the inn, and I have seen nothing of her since. In fact, I saw not which way she went, for the blow her horse's hoof gave me nearly deprived me of consciousness."

"And you say now that you have caged his friends?"

"I have; they are now in the dark subterranean passage, over which, as you know, runs the open gallery."

"Good; and what is the name of the leader of these fellows?"

"Rupert Dreadnought."

Sir Hugh Dalrymple staggered back in surprise.

Had a thunderbolt crashed through the ceiling and dashed through the flooring, he could not have been more utterly overwhelmed for the moment.

"Dreadnought!" he said; "well do I remember that name—the name of my old enemy—my brother's friend. I can see now the network that is being woven round me. He must die, and his friends too. Good fortune has delivered them into my hands. Colin, where are the men?"

"They have returned to the guard-room," replied the page, "and are awaiting your orders."

"You must go and lead them to the secret gallery, then," said Sir Hugh, excitedly. "Let each be provided with a flambeau, so that at a given signal the whole corridor may be lit up. Then we can fire down upon them without their being able to make any resistance."

Colin's heart leaped with a savage joy as he heard these words.

Such a massacre would indeed be a terrible excitement.

And then, also, could he not include in it his rival?

"And this Scotch boy," he said. "Shall I let him out of his dungeon, so that we can destroy him as well?"

Sir Hugh pondered a moment.

"Well," he said, "I kept him only that he might reveal to me secrets which would now be of no use to me. Yes, let him join his friends. But have a care, they might suspect you."

"Not they," said the cunning young traitor. "I can deceive them. I will just explain to the men their orders, then I will proceed down the stairs, and release Allan, after which I will rejoin you."

He hurried towards the door, but there he halted a moment.

"And I suppose you will grant me a reward for this?" he said.

"What do you ask?"

"Liberty to marry Mary Macpherson, and a present such as you think proper."

"Liberty to marry Mary Macpherson, the traitress who has brought about all this misery—who has nearly cost me my life! Why, are you mad, boy?"

"I can explain all," said Colin. "Still what I ask we will not discuss now; there is no time. I will at once away, and see to our caged birds."

And then, with an exulting smile—a smile of diabolical triumph and zest, he turned from his master's presence.

"A thorough-paced young villain," said his master, musingly, as he quitted. "Had I been—ah! well, memories will not now avail. I must to work. Ghastly work it is truly, but it must be done."

He turned to a cupboard near, drew out a bottle, and drank off a large glassful of raw spirits.

Then he took from a drawer a pair of long and finely-chased pistols, and placing them in his belt awaited Colin's return.

CHAPTER IX.

THE MASSACRE.

The young traitor at once proceeded, according to his instructions and his own eager wishes, towards the guard-room, and gave to the men Sir Hugh Dalrymple's orders.

Though grumbling at being thus disturbed as it seemed for nothing, they drank off the tankards of foaming ale before them, and having seen to their muskets, prepared to follow their leader, for such, indeed, Colin seemed for the time to have constituted himself.

The place to which they were led was a strange one, in truth, if we consider the age in which the events occurred.

The passage in which Rupert and his men were waiting was, as my readers are aware, a subterranean one, much below the level of the house itself.

Round it, at a distance of some twelve feet from the ground, ran a gallery which thoroughly commanded it, and yet was quite inaccessible to anyone below.

Into this gallery, therefore, it was that the men were to be led, so that leaning over the balustrades of the gallery they could fire down upon the helpless prisoners beneath.

Rupert Dreadnought and those with him could not of course imagine what a hideous tragedy was contemplated.

It certainly seemed odd that they should be left thus to wait in the darkness; but, when the door was once more opened and Colin appeared, even the slightest suspicion that might have arisen in the minds of any was banished.

"Here," said the young traitor, in a low voice, "here is the key which opens your friend's dungeon. Quickly release him. See where yonder light glimmers; that is his place of confinement. I will be with you directly, and perhaps without any bloodshed you may be enabled to carry him away with you."

"But why do you hurry away?" asked Rupert Dreadnought.

"I shall be missed—besides, I do not wish to be seen in this attire," replied the assumed maiden; "I will return in a few moments, when I have seen my mistress, and let you once more out."

"But why need you lock this door?" asked Tom the waterman, in a tone of suspicion.

"I will not lock it, then," returned Colin; "but if you take my advice you will make no attempt to go out until I return; you do not know your way sufficiently, and may fall into a trap. However, I am but a poor weak girl, I cannot pretend to know so well as you, so you must judge for yourselves."

There was something in the words and the manner in which they were said which might have struck Rupert on another occasion as extremely unlike those of a young girl.

But if it had struck him, he had but little time for thought.

The youthful betrayer darted away at once.

The door was closed, and they were once more alone—locked in, too, for the key had been turned noiselessly.

The faint glimmer of light which had been pointed out by Colin came from a grating opposite the little window where the moonlight struggled through into Allan's cell.

Towards this they now made their way, and in a few moments reached it.

Eagerly they inserted a key in the lock, and turned it.

Then a pitiful sight met their eyes.

Allan, chained and helpless, lay upon his bed of loose straw.

"Who is there?" he cried, as one of the men drew from his pocket a dark lantern, and cast its light upon him.

"Rupert Dreadnought and Tom the waterman," said the one who carried the lantern. "We have come to save you. Be still, and we will soon release you."

Mary Macpherson had informed them that her lover was chained to the wall, and they had, therefore, brought with them the implements necessary to release him, and in a few minutes they had succeeded in filing through his fetters.

A few words sufficed to explain to the Scotch boy the state of affairs, and they at once hurried out into the open space.

As they did so, a plaintive cry struck their ears.

It seemed like the groaning of one in deep distress and pain.

They stood still and listened.

Again the cry.

This time they were enabled to tell that it issued from some chamber at the far end of the corridor, and thither, forgetful of their own danger, they at once rushed.

They guessed that someone else was in confinement and peril, and, whoever it might be, they resolved to release him.

On arriving at the end of the passage, it was a matter of no difficulty to discover whence the sounds proceeded, and they found, to their great joy, that the key given them by Colin fitted the lock.

In another moment the door was flung open, and the light of the lantern revealed to them the form of the real Mary Macpherson, lying on the ground with a pile of fallen bricks upon one of her legs.

Allan rushed forward distractedly, crying, as he pressed his lips to her cheek—

"She is cold—quite cold! She is dead—lost to me for ever!"

"And we," cried Rupert, "are trapped and betrayed!"

The fact of Mary Macpherson being found lying in such a place proved that someone in disguise had been misleading them.

Who it was no one was able to say.

Colin was not known to any.

His voice had seemed that of a woman.

At any rate, they *had* been deceived, and all recognised the necessity of immediate action.

The first thing to be done, however, was to extricate Mary Macpherson from her perilous position beneath the fallen masonry.

The ready hands of all were soon at work, and, before many minutes, the bricks had been removed.

Then a little brandy was poured down her throat.

Presently her sweet eyes opened.

She gazed in wonder around, and then recognising her lover flung herself into his arms.

The injury she had received was, after all, only a terrible series of bruises on her limbs, and after few minutes she was enabled to stand.

Then occurred what caused them to stand still with astonishment.

The place was inundated with roseate light.

Into the gallery filed eight men, bearing torches.

These they stuck in the walls, so as to illuminate the whole place.

Then they raised their guns and waited.

This was the preparation for the massacre.

"What can this mean?" said Rupert Dreadnought breathlessly.

Allan shook his head.

"I know not," he said, "but it seems like the commencement of some hideous treachery. Let us stand to our arms, and be ready to act instantly!"

RUPERT DREADNOUGHT.

"IN VAIN RUPERT WAVED HIS HAT."

It was quite evident that some horrid scheme of treachery was on foot, though it might reasonably be considered a difficult task to guess at its extent.

They were not left long in doubt.

The men in the gallery, acting on an order given by their leader in an undertone, raised their guns and fired.

Whether it was the peculiarly cowardly mode of warfare which displeased them or made them nervous, or whether the glare of light was too much near them, and the darkness below too intense, I cannot say.

At any rate this first volley took no effect.

The balls rattled against the stone walls, but no one was injured.

In an instant there came a response.

The pistols of the little party, cooped up as they were in the narrow passage, were raised as in one body, and the reports were followed by groans of agony.

This rendered Sir Hugh furious.

"Take better aim, and fire coolly," he cried. "Now, altogether."

At this moment, however, a figure sprang from the side of the gallery, and flung itself before the guns of the retainers.

It was Colin.

"Hold! hold!" he cried, "see there!"

And he pointed wildly to a form which stood within range of one of the muskets.

He had recognised, even in the semi-darkness, the form of the disguised Mary Macpherson.

"What means this folly?" cried Sir Hugh Dalrymple, angrily. "Out of the way, mad boy, and let the men do their duty."

"No, no, Sir Hugh," exclaimed Colin; "that page yonder is the one of whom I spoke. Spare her, if not the others."

"She is the traitress; let her then die!" returned Dalrymple.

The young traitor was for an instant dumbfounded by the words of the elder traitor, who was his master.

Then he recovered his senses suddenly.

Dashing up the levelled guns, he suddenly sprang over the balustrade, and, regardless of the depth, dropped into the darkness below.

He was saved from any injury, however, by those below, who caught him in their arms.

"This way," exclaimed he, as he landed safely on *terra firma*; "for *her* sake I will save you all; follow me."

With these words he led the way to a corner of the passage, opposite that where they had entered, and hastily touching a spring, disclosed a small doorway.

Through this the men dashed furiously, and succeeded in passing through just as a discharge of musketry rang through the subterranean corridors.

Not a shot, however, took effect, for they were far beyond the reach of any, and as the little gate closed they could hear a shout of disappointed vengeance.

"Now," said Rupert, as they halted in utter darkness, knowing not, of course, how to proceed, "now where are we?"

"We are at the bottom of a flight of stairs, which winds round and round until it reaches a high and isolated terrace at the summit of the castle. When you arrive there you will be able to enter a chamber, where you must remain for a time."

"But this man will discover and destroy us by some treacherous means," returned Allan. "Is there no method of reaching the free, fresh air?"

"Not yet—the wing of the castle in which I am leading you is isolated from the rest of the building, and there is but one door of communication, which is the one by which we have just entered. You and your friends could defend the stairs against a host of foes. But you will not be called upon to do so. Master though he is of this place, Sir Hugh Dalrymple knows not of this door; he will fancy that you have escaped by the other gate, and will not even seek you here. Follow me."

There was no choice.

Colin had shown himself to be a thorough traitor, and there might even now be a doubt as to his sincerity.

But there was just a hope that the manner in which Sir Hugh had proposed to destroy the one he loved would lead him to act really in this as he had promised.

So, without full faith—keeping, that is to say, a thorough look-out—Rupert and his friends decided to follow their strange guide.

"Lead on," said Dreadnought, "and we will proceed after you. But how can we see in this utter darkness?"

"You have a lantern, have you not?"

"Yes; but is it safe to use it?"

"Quite," replied Colin; "through this door no ray of light can be seen. Come."

Tom the waterman at once turned on the light of his lantern, and it was then easy to see that they were at the bottom of a well staircase, leading up so far that they could see nothing of its summit.

Colin at once singled out the form of the one he loved.

"Follow me, Mary," he said.

Allan made a gesture as if to start forward.

But Mary Macpherson restrained him by a whisper.

"Keep back," she said; "arouse not his jealousy, or he might betray us all."

Then, with the speed and grace of a fawn, she sprang forward, and followed her would-be lover.

CHAPTER X.

THE ASCENT—THE ISOLATED TERRACE—THE MYSTERIOUS SUITE OF APARTMENTS—COLIN'S RETURN—THE IMPROMPTU BANQUET.

A LONG and wearisome ascent brought them to a small doorway, which yielded readily to a gentle push from Colin, and admitted a fresh and welcome current of air.

Then they stepped out upon a wide terrace overlooking the country for miles round.

"This way," said Colin.

Crossing the terrace, he proceeded through a French window into a large and richly furnished apartment.

Gorgeous as it might be, however, there was that in it which sent a chill to the heart.

It had a close, musty smell about it, as if it had been long disused.

A damp, unhealthy atmosphere pervaded it, as if it were but a gilded sepulchre.

However, for the time, it was a place of safety, and the tired band were glad to avail themselves of it.

They could see but little of its details, for their

only light was that given by the lantern which Tom the waterman had produced.

"I will bring a lamp and some provisions before morning dawns," said Colin, "so I will leave you now."

"But are you not afraid of being discovered and seized?" asked Rupert, doubtingly.

"Not I; I know too well the secrets of this old place," returned the page. "I will bring what I promise ere dawn."

"And," whispered Mary Macpherson, "bring me my own clothes. I have no wish to preserve longer this masquerading attire."

"Which you only assumed to dupe me," replied Colin, in an undertone. "However, I have now risked my life for you and your friends, and I hope you will be grateful."

Then he hurried away, and disappeared once more through the little doorway.

"Let us explore this new place," said Rupert to Tom the waterman; "you other had best remain where you are to watch and also to guard this lady."

So saying he took the lantern, and sword in hand he passed through a little door at the further end of the chamber.

He now found himself in a bedroom, which seemed, by its atmosphere and its appearance, to have been more recently used than the other they had just left.

This, again, led into a third, and there the suite of rooms stopped on this side.

On the other side there were two rooms also, and no more.

"This is, indeed, a strange place," said Rupert, as they returned to the centre one, where the men were sitting round dozing on the chairs, while Allan of the Glen and Mary Macpherson were talking sweet nothings in a corner.

"Yes, it is strange," replied Tom the waterman, "but it is just the thing for us."

"How so?"

"We can remain here until we have a chance of descending and punishing our treacherous enemy."

"Yes," replied Rupert, "if Colin remains true to us. Upon that everything depends, and that is but a poor thing to trust to. A man who has once betrayed you can never be believed in."

The night wore away but slowly.

Everything without the castle was very still and solemn, while within the conversation soon flagged, and, save those whose duty it was to keep watch, all dozed off into a sleep more or less sound.

Just as the first golden streaks of light began to shoot up from the eastern horizon, the little door on the terrace opened, and Colin made his appearance, bearing a large bundle and a basket of provisions.

These he carried in triumph into the room.

"Here," he said, "are enough provisions to last you the day. To-night I will bring more, and a lamp as well."

"To-night!" exclaimed Rupert, in astonishment; "why then I hope we can leave this place for good. I must meet Dalrymple face to face ere I quit the castle."

Colin gazed at him in amazement.

"What," he said, "thrust yourself once more into the lion's den?"

"Yes; for what else did I come here?" said Dreadnought. "Did I not come to avenge a friend, to punish an assassin?"

"Yes, and were caught instantly in your own trap. Of what use was it my saving you, if you are going to return to his power?"

"I am bound by an oath," said Rupert Dreadnought, "and from that oath I cannot depart However, if this night will not be convenient to your plans, we will stop for the next, but see him I must ere I go."

"To-morrow night he quits this castle," replied Colin, "and to-night he has a large concourse of people—a ball to all the neighbouring gentry—on neither, therefore, can you see him. At dawn, however, when all the guests have departed, I will lead you to him; but you will surely not compromise the safety of all for the sake of carrying out a whim."

"It is no whim, but a sacred duty," replied Rupert Dreadnought. "However, since it is more suitable to you, I will await your coming. Do you remain here?"

"No, I will return this evening," replied Colin; "meanwhile, keep as quiet as possible, and do not show yourself on the terrace."

He then departed.

Mary Macpherson lost no time now in taking off her male attire and donning her own.

She came into the room looking so pretty and so different to what she had seemed in the disordered and unaccustomed dress of the page Colin, that she excited the admiration of all.

She was like a sunbeam among them, and soon had made a difference in the appearance of the room.

The meal was spread on the centre table, and there, in the very lion's den, the men whom Sir Hugh Dalrymple had designed to murder sat down to feast upon his good things.

CHAPTER XI.

SIR HUGH DALRYMPLE'S RAGE—THE UNEXPECTED MEETING—AN OLD SORROW, AND AN OLD LOVE—THE BALL—THE MOONLIT TERRACE—THE DECLARATION OF A MAD PASSION—THE FIRE!

WHEN the page had leaped, as I described, from the balustrade of the subterranean gallery, and rushed in among the ranks of the very men he had betrayed, Sir Hugh Dalrymple had been for the moment struck dumb with amazement.

Then, in a fit of fury, he had ordered his men to fire.

This proving useless, he had dashed down to the little door by the winding staircase, and searched everywhere for the second little gate.

But in vain.

Not knowing anything of the secret spring by which Colin had admitted himself and his companions, he merely spent his time uselessly, and retired, breathing vengeance upon the youth who had so quickly destroyed all his plans of revenge.

The retainers were nothing loth to avoid the massacre, which, savage ruffians as they were, was quite against their usual manner of business.

The whole night having passed without any sign

whatever of those who had mysteriously disappeared, Sir Hugh concluded on the following day that they had really made good their escape, and cast the matter for the time from his mind.

The next evening he proceeded to his wife's boudoir, and found her there dressing for the ball.

"You have not forgotten what to-night is then," he said. "I wish you to look your best. I have a friend coming—in fact, I believe he is here already—to whom I desire to introduce you; he has just returned from abroad. His is quite a romantic story, I believe, and he worships fair women."

Lady Dalrymple smiled languidly.

She was so weary. It all mattered so little.

So, with a little shiver, she proceeded with her toilet, and, soon after her husband's departure, she was ready to descend to the reception room.

As she entered it a young man, who had been standing near the window, advanced to meet her.

He was tall, fair, and pale, and as he gazed upon the beautiful vision that confronted him, he grew yet more ghastly.

They stood looking at one another.

No sound came from either.

Could it be possible that her husband had brought *him* there?

Was she going mad, or was it Henry Clanberris that stood before her?

"Oh! Henry—Henry!"

The voice, hoarse and broken, came forth in gasps from the parched lips.

"Oh! Margaret, my darling—my Maggie!"

And then she was clasped in his arms, his hot breath upon her cheek, his passionate kisses on her brow!

Was this trembling, sobbing woman the cold, calm Lady Dalrymple?

All was forgotten in that first embrace—all the past long years, the pain, the weariness, her husband, honour, all.

There was a step in the corridor at this moment, and Sir Hugh entered.

The pair had left each other now. Lady Dalrymple was seated on the ottoman, and Henry Clanberris was standing once more by the fire-place, more deadly pale than ever.

"Why, Rolliston, you look more ill than I've seen you before," cried Sir Hugh. "Come with me and taste my wine. That will revive you, I'll warrant me!"

This was enough.

Sir Hugh Dalrymple had addressed him as Rolliston.

He had come there purposely, therefore, under an assumed name.

The assassin's punishment was truly commencing in earnest!

* * * * *

Lights gleamed that night on smiling faces and graceful forms; on rainbow-hued silks and foam-like lace; on wreathing flowers and gleaming jewels.

Fairest among the fair, peerless among the beautiful, reigned Margaret Dalrymple.

Her beauty had only required animation to make it perfect.

To-night those eyes, which had usually been so hard in their cold brilliancy, beamed with the softening light of intense happiness.

A deep flush crimsoned the pale cheek.

The delicate features had lost their stony expression.

The marble statue had become a living woman!

All eyes followed her.

By her side, gloomy, pale, abstracted, stood Henry Clanberris.

His very soul was bitter within him.

More selfish than she—as men are ever more selfish than women—he had loved her as deeply as his nature would permit; but never with the purity that distinguished her affection.

He had been left for dead upon a battle-field, but had only been wounded.

During years of captivity that followed, the memory of the fair English face had haunted him.

The tones of the clear rich voice rang in his ears day and night.

Had his love followed on tranquilly, perhaps he might have forgotten her, or only remembered his love for her as a pleasant episode in his life.

But with thoughts of her fresh in his mind trouble had come upon him.

With nothing to distract his attention, he had dreamed of her continually.

Now he returned to find her the wife of another; and that other one who had been forced upon her by friends, and who bore a character by no means loveable or even upright.

And as he gazed upon her perfect loveliness, he swore in his heart that she should be his.

The rich strains of music were now sinking into a sobbing sigh, now swelling into a burst of wild exultant melody, as Henry Clanberris led her from the heated room out upon the moonlit terrace.

It was a calm and lovely night, and the silver moon had shed its brightest mantle over the hushing country.

For a few moments they stood in silence.

Never school-girl with her first love blushed and trembled more than did the haughty Lady Dalrymple.

Henry gazed in unrestrained admiration upon the delicate profile, half turned from him; the exquisitely graceful fall of her snowy velvet draperies; great coils of hair of living gold wreathing the small head; even the diamonds sparkling amid her tresses, and the blood-red rubies nestling on her white bosom.

Then he spoke.

"Maggie," he said, "it was on such a night as this I left you. Do you remember the moonlight in the long avenue at the Grange? But no; you have forgotten all now. Many and many a time, when weary and sick at heart, I have thought of you. But for the memory of your love I could not have lived those long years of captivity. I might have expected to find you changed, but *not* another man's wife."

The great violet eyes filled with tears, but she never spoke.

So he went on.

"Tell me you have not quite forgotten me, Maggie. I once thought that time, absence, nay, even death itself, would not kill our love. Oh! darling, I have loved you so dearly—how could you cast me off? I would sooner have believed that the sun would fall from heaven, than that you would be faithless to me. You never loved me—tell me that you never loved me, and I will leave you, and never look upon your face again."

"Oh, spare me, Henry!" she cried, "spare me—have pity. I have suffered so terribly."

"Suffered!" he cried, "and have I not *too* suffered? Do I not suffer? You are as cold as stone—a true woman, fickle as the wind. Oh! love, forgive me, I know not what I say. My beautiful Margaret, say you once loved me—only tell me that."

"I never loved anyone in the world but you," she murmured.

And Henry Clanberris, with triumph beaming in his dark eyes, bent over her, whispering—

"Nothing will then persuade me that we shall be parted for ever. I shall wait, and——"

Then he drew her once more towards him, and imprinted a long and fervent kiss upon her lips.

She drew herself gently away.

"Enough," she said; "this is wrong—very wrong, Henry. We will wait, and hope if we will; but such meetings like this must not take place."

Henry did not attempt to detain her.

Gladly would he have whispered of flight—of instant departure from the power of one she did not love.

SIR HUGH DALRYMPLE.

But he saw how she would receive it—loved her the more for her purity, and resolved in his heart of hearts that if ever the chance occurred she should be his wife.

He might, truly, have years to wait, but meanwhile no other woman should claim one moment of his thoughts!

Again his arm encircled her elastic waist in the dance; again the voluptuous music filled the air, when suddenly some affrighted servants sprang into the ball-room, while at the same moment a cloud of hot smoke came whirling in at the open door.

"The castle is on fire!" cried the domestics, in frantic accents.

Sir Hugh Dalrymple stood for an instant as if paralysed, while all his guests gathered round him in a huddled group, as if they could find security near him.

Eyes which, a moment before, had been gazing tenderly into those of loving partners, now glanced in horror and dismay at the master of the castle.

There were no means near for extinguishing the fire.

In those days fires were attacked by means of a little parish engine, which it would have been an absurdity to have used against a huge building such as that which was the home of the Dalrymples.

So the only thing to think of was escape.

"This way, my friends," cried Sir Hugh, pointing to the great doorway, and leading the way, at the same time taking his wife's arm, and running rapidly towards the great hall.

But there he found that he had miscalculated distances.

They were met by a wall of fire!

CHAPTER XII.

THE CONFLAGRATION REACHES THE PRISONERS—MARY'S TERROR—THE FRIGHTENED VILLAGERS—COLIN'S SCHEME OF SAFETY—THE DESCENT FROM THE WINDOW—THE MYSTERIOUS SPIES—ALLAN'S DESCENT—THE PUNISHMENT OF THE TRAITOR.

MEANWHILE, before pausing to describe how they fared in this unexpected and fearful emergency, we must return to the prisoners who were cooped up as it were at the top of the burning castle.

The smoke, rolling over the top of the building, was the first intimation to them that the conflagration had commenced, and then Colin rushed up frantically.

"Be still," he said; "do not give way to fear; I shall soon be able to release you. Do you remain here, Master Dreadnought, and watch the open space yonder, while your men assist me. Mayhap the villagers may flock to the rescue with their ladders. If not, in ten minutes we shall have broken through into another part of the castle, whence we can descend easily by a rope."

So saying, he rushed excitedly away.

Rupert Dreadnought remained standing on the terrace.

He was not, however, left long alone, for he had not been standing more than about a few minutes before Mary Macpherson rushed out of the chamber, dressed in a long white robe.

Her eyes were ablaze with terror, and she ran towards Rupert, crying—

"Oh, save me! save me!"

She had awoke to find her room filled with dense

curling smoke, and, despite the assurances of Allan, whom she met at her door, she could not believe that escape was possible.

"Keep up your courage," said Rupert, as the terrified girl clung to him. "See yonder, they are coming to our assistance."

As he spoke, he pointed to the open space before the castle, where a crowd of excited villagers were gazing up at the blazing edifice.

In vain, however, Rupert waved his hat; in vain Mary Macpherson frantically fluttered her handkerchief in the breeze.

"Oh! they come not; we are lost!" she cried.

"Nay, then," said Rupert Dreadnought, as he passed his arm comfortingly round her waist, while he still raised his hat on high, "this is but one mode of safety. Colin will save us."

But though he spoke thus bravely, his heart somewhat misgave him.

The fire was evidently gaining ground upon them.

The smoke curled above them in huge wreaths.

The flames roared and flickered near, and their heat could be felt distinctly now.

Even the tips of the tongues of fire now and then glinted out through the crevices of the little doorway.

If Colin failed to find the passage he sought, how *could* they escape, cooped up as they were?

However, as the terrified girl clung to him and waved her hand to the villagers alternately, he whispered words of comfort.

"You have here brave and willing hearts to aid you," he said; "do not give way to fear; that will aid in destroying our chances of escape."

Mary Macpherson looked up inquiringly, fixedly, at the face of the strong man by her side.

"Do you fear, or, rather, have you any hope?" she asked, eagerly.

"Yes," he said, firmly; "I believe we shall be saved from this."

"Then," she answered, standing up as determinedly as she could, "I will hope too."

She had scarcely uttered these words, when the voice of Colin was heard calling them.

In another instant he burst through the French windows, and appeared before them full of excitement.

"This way, this way!" he shouted, eagerly; "lose no time!"

Then, without leaving Rupert Dreadnought the chance, he seized Mary Macpherson in his arms, and hurried away with her into the large room.

Passing from this into the sleeping chamber, where she had rested, he entered the small anteroom beyond, where, to Rupert's astonishment, he found his friends standing near a large hole in the wall, which they had battered through.

Smoke was to be seen issuing slightly from the other portion of the building, which was thus laid bare, but only as if it were oozing from some fissure.

"Where are we?" cried Rupert. "Are you about to lead me to Sir Hugh Dalrymple?"

"By this time," replied Colin, "he has doubtless escaped, and taken refuge in one of the neighbours' houses. No, this would not be the way to find him. Quick! let us lose no time in talking. Follow me."

He had now released Mary Macpherson, who by her struggles plainly told him that his assistance was not only not required, but was disagreeable; and so, with a growing hate at his heart, which made him invent another treachery, he led the way towards a room, where a narrow window overlooked a wooded garden, which emerged gradually into the large wood beyond.

"Here," he said, "is a stout rope, which, if doubly twisted, will bear the weight of two. Mary here cannot descend unassisted. Will you, Master Dreadnought, bear her down while we assist you? We can follow."

There was no time to deliberate.

Leaping on the sill of the window, therefore Rupert securely seized the rope, and Mary Macpherson, who was now trembling with intense agitation and alarm, was raised against her own will into his arms.

It was a terrible and perilous descent.

The rope, truly, was a stout one, but it had never been intended to bear two persons, and, moreover, the distance from the window to the ground was full thirty feet.

However, those above adopted the best plan to prevent an excessive strain.

All those in the room held the rope, and let it run down as swiftly as was consistent with the safety of those descending.

Allan of the Glen was the one who had handed Mary Macpherson to Rupert Dreadnought, and he therefore remained at the window, and eagerly and without the slightest tinge of jealousy watched Rupert as he held the young Scotch girl in his strong arms.

To *him* he was grateful.

In the case of Colin he would have felt a bitter burning at the heart.

As Allan watched them descending, his eye suddenly caught a sight which was lost upon Rupert, engaged as he was with his fair and precious burden.

Two men in masks, and with swords drawn, were standing beneath the shadow of the trees.

They were evidently on the watch for Rupert and his charge.

There was no mode, however, by which Allan of the Glen could apprise him of the danger, as he was now near the ground.

The only possible way to aid him was to rush down the rope immediately that his master and Mary Macpherson reached *terra firma.*

This spoiled entirely the plans which Colin had framed for himself.

He had hoped that when Allan descended he would be able by some manœuvre to cause his fall upon the hard ground below.

But in this he was foiled.

Directly that Rupert and his fair burden had reached *terra firma*, the young Scotch boy cried aloud to his companions—

"Hold fast, my friends."

Then, without giving them further intimation of what he was going to do, he seized the rope and ran down it with the nimble steps of a wild animal.

The men who had been watching below saw his movement.

They understood that he had seen them, and that for the present their plans, whatever they might be, were foiled.

So, ere the active young Scot had sprung to earth, they had disappeared.

Where, it was impossible to say.

There seemed truly no place where they could have concealed themselves.

Yet that they had done so was evident.

They had not had time to clear out of the grounds, and yet when Allan reached the ground they were nowhere to be seen.

"You have saved what I hold dearer than life itself," cried Allan to Rupert, as they met. "How can I ever repay you?"

Rupert smiled.

"You forget," he said, "your own services to me. But come, let us not neglect our friends. See, they are even now waiting our aid."

They accordingly seized the end of the rope and steadied it.

Then one by one the men came rushing downwards.

Colin came last.

He was thoroughly disappointed.

He had seen in this perilous descent the means of killing Allan of the Glen, and to hide his anger he now remained behind all the others.

The result was disastrous.

He had tied the double rope to the heavy furniture in the room ere the last three descended, and it had by this time been grated continually and heavily against the sharp stones.

When, therefore, he began his descent, he rushed down now as quickly as the others.

For two reasons he did this.

In the first place, the flames were beginning to belch out from the casement immediately below the one from which he had to emerge.

In the second place, he desired to take Mary Macpherson from the hands of his fortunate but hated rival.

Dashing down, therefore, as he did, he paid no attention to the fact that the rope had been so frequently and roughly used before, and in a very few moments he found it was visibly giving way.

There was no help for it now, however.

To ascend was to risk as much danger as to descend, and he kept on, therefore, quickly though cautiously.

After a few moments of deadly suspense, the crisis came.

It was unexpected below, and those who witnessed it were far more surprised than the horror-stricken victim.

Suddenly, without any previous notice, the rope snapped asunder, and Colin, clutching wildly at the air, was flung headlong down upon the rough stones beneath.

CHAPTER XIII.

THE BALL-ROOM AGAIN—WILD THOUGHTS OF LOVE —THE ESCAPE—THE DESTRUCTION OF THE CASTLE.

We left the dancers in the ball-room of the castle, huddling together in dismay when the affrighted domestics entered with the news that the place was on fire.

No sooner had they passed out—it will be remembered, Sir Hugh Dalrymple leading the way with his wife—than they were met by a wall of fire, and in the confusion and delay that ensued, Henry Clanberris rushed to her side.

"Can I do anything to aid you?" he cried, nervously, yet bravely, thinking only of the safety of the one he loved—ignoring the presence of her husband—ignoring the flames that lapped up near them—only hoping, wishing that he could do something *for her*.

Up to this moment Sir Hugh Dalrymple had been entirely unsuspicious.

He saw now in his manner nothing but earnest friendship to himself.

"Yes," he cried, "you can. Take care of my wife while I rouse the servants to their duties. I know of but one chance of egress from this place, and that will have to be forced open."

So saying he placed the arm of Lady Dalrymple in that of Henry.

She clung to him now in terror, overwhelmed in fact by a multiplicity of feelings.

What a terrible meeting this was!

The first for so many years.

And now they were facing death together.

"Oh, Henry!" she murmured, as the huddling crowd thronged round her, "is this to be the end of all?"

He pressed her arm warmly.

"No, no," he whispered, "no, no. You will be saved—saved by me. Wait and hope; remember our motto. You will be saved for the future. Fear not; the past is but a trial."

She trembled as he spoke.

Not with fear.

Death was before—behind—around them—everywhere.

Yet no dread invaded her heart.

She trembled at the words and the voice of the one whom fortune had compelled her to discard.

She then knew how much she loved him.

She then brought to mind the words of the treacherous villain who had overheard the conversation she had had with Lady Clanberris, and who had threatened to betray her.

Was he not right?

He had prophesied her feelings towards her absent lover.

Were not her feelings just as he had predicted?

In the midst of this danger, a perilous idea suggested itself to Henry Clanberris.

Perilous to her peace of mind—perilous also to his own.

Could they not escape together in this hour of terrible danger?

Could she not be his now?

Could she not allow it to be supposed that she had perished in the conflagration, and thus forsake her husband for ever?

His love for her was so pure that, under other circumstances, the idea would never have suggested itself.

But, looking down upon her lovely form, and seeing the devouring flames surrounding her, contemplating her utter loss, he began to regard things recklessly, and be ready for any desperate action.

"Oh! Margaret," he whispered, "in the face of this awful peril, tell me, do you love me still?"

The soft arm of the unfortunate wife trembled in his.

"Oh! Henry," she said, "do not ask me again. I have already said too much to you."

He was about to say more—to beg of her to fly with him—to speak words which would have caused him to curse himself on the morrow, when Sir Hugh Dalrymple returned excitedly to the terrified group.

"This way, my friends, this way," he cried, and, flinging open wide the door by which he had entered, he showed the entrance to a broad staircase leading to a subterranean corridor.

Down this dark and unwholesome-smelling place the terrified guests were hurried. Just in time.

They had, as I have said, been met by a wall of fire, which, for the time, had confined itself to one spot; but now the lurid tongues of fire began to spring in spiral columns, and lick the ceilings, and thrust themselves along the floors.

One spark flung out from among them, and falling amid the lightly-dressed throng, would have set the whole place in a blaze—the whole crowd on fire—and death to everyone would have been the result.

So it may be imagined that the throng of merry pleasure-seekers dashed madly after the master of the castle, and Lady Dalrymple, as if conscious that in her own heart she was wronging him, was the first to leap to his side.

She knew nothing of his desperate villany.

She knew not that he was the assassin of his brother.

She knew not that he had projected the cool and deliberate massacre of innocent men, and had only been prevented by an accident.

Otherwise, wrong as it now appeared to her, she would have still shrunk from him and clung to her lover.

As it was, thinking him only a tyrant—looking upon him unlovingly only as the one who had been forced upon her by her friends, she took his arm, and with him headed the escaping throng.

Thanks to their good luck Sir Hugh Dalrymple was soon in the open air.

Here he, and all his guests and servants, were in safety at least.

But this was all that could be said.

The castle, that had been his pride, its grand pictures and its wondrous secrets, were now all things of the past.

Nothing on earth could save them.

A neighbour's house, as Colin had surmised, sheltered him for the night—the morning dawned to find him once more on the track of revenge!

CHAPTER XIV.

THE TRAITOR ONCE MORE—THE SCENE IN THE FOREST—THE CONSULTATION—THE TWO WATCHERS—MARY MACPHERSON AT THE INN—THE VILLAINS EFFECT AN ENTRANCE—THE ABDUCTION.

MANY persons who had suffered as much as Rupert Dreadnought and his friends in the pursuit of Sir Hugh Dalrymple, would have certainly felt inclined to abandon the affair altogether.

But our hero was not to be so deterred.

He had sworn to carry out the mission entrusted to him by his father, and he resolved therefore to remain in the vicinity of the castle until an opportunity occurred once more to come face to face with his foe.

Towards his punishment he had resolved now that Colin should be made to assist.

The unfortunate youth, victim of his own treacherous hatred, had not been killed instantaneously by his fall from the window.

He had broken both his legs and otherwise desperately maimed himself, but he was still breathing when the men raised him from the ground, and bore him away among the trees to the spot where Rupert had led Mary Macpherson.

The wretched creature opened his eyes and gazed painfully and wildly round him, and as his eyes fell upon the lovely form of the Scotch girl bending over him, it seemed to soothe his agony.

When restoratives had been applied to him by Rupert, who knew nothing, of course, of the hateful feelings he entertained towards Allan of the Glen, a litter was hastily made, and in accordance with his own wishes he was borne away to the house of the village surgeon.

When the men returned, a consultation was hastily held, and it was decided that Mary Macpherson, under the care of Allan of the Glen, should proceed to London, and be placed in charge of Helen Penraven.

Allan was then to return with two more of Rupert Dreadnought's retainers, and two friends of Tom the waterman.

After taking leave of her preservers, therefore, Mary Macpherson leaped up before her lover, and they dashed rapidly away.

Not unnoticed, however.

The two men who had watched the night escape from the old castle saw their departure, and followed in their track.

There being not sufficient hurry to warrant Allan in risking the health of Mary Macpherson by a fierce and desperate ride to London when she had neither sleep nor rest, he resolved to stay for a few hours at the first inn he came to, and give her refreshment and an opportunity for sleep.

Dressed as she was, moreover, it would have attracted some little attention had he borne her along in the daylight in the streets of London; and he wished if possible, therefore, to procure for her some more suitable habiliments.

Not far from Dalrymple House, it will be remembered, stood the inn where the attack had been made upon Rupert a night or so before.

To this, therefore, he at once made his way.

Arriving there he found, as he expected, that the people had all turned out to see the fire, whose lurid flames were still leaping up towards the sky, and illumining the country for miles around.

"RUPERT'S SWORD PINNED HIS ARM TO THE TREE!"

It was nothing strange, therefore, for him to ride up in hot haste with a lady half dressed in his arms.

The crowd at the inn door, who had been so anxious to seize and drag to justice the supposed highwaymen, now made way at once for the lady in distress, and Allan found it a matter of no difficulty to reach the door, and assist Mary Macpherson into the inn.

"This lady has been just saved from the fire at Dalrymple House," he said to the landlady, who came bustling out; "I want her to have a bed and refreshment, and by to-morrow afternoon some clothes, for which I will pay you well."

"Certainly, certainly," cried the worthy woman, whose good nature was brightened by the promise of good money; "come this way, my dear. I will see that you have everything you wish. And you, master, you will require a bed and some refreshment also?"

"Yes; and the sooner the latter is brought, the better."

And so saying he walked into the room.

Presently the landlady returned, bringing with her the materials for a substantial meal, as well as Mary Macpherson, dressed in some of her daughter's clothes, which, scarcely a good fit, were at any rate more fit for travelling than the undress she had been compelled to quit the castle in.

The meal was not long in being dispatched, and then, after an affectionate embrace, the lovers parted and went to their respective chambers.

During all this time they had not been un watched.

The two mysterious men who had, as I have said, seen the escape, had followed them, and had during the whole period of their supper been near them, though unnoticed either by Allan of the Glen or his mistress.

In fact, so many persons went in and out during the progress of their meal, that they did not observe anyone in particular.

Had Mary Macpherson done so, she would have noticed the faces of two of Sir Hugh Dalrymple's retainers.

They were cunning rascals.

They had no desire to risk an open rupture even with one man, and, whatever their errand was, they appeared bent upon performing it by stratagem.

They had their ale, listened to Allan's arrangements, and then quitted the inn.

They had, in fact, heard enough.

The young girl and her lover were to sleep there, and, whatever their design was, they knew the time in which they had to perform it.

The sky was still rosy with the tremendous conflagration, and they soon beheld the room in which the young girl had retired to rest.

Having satisfied themselves of this fact, they concealed themselves among the bushes and quietly waited.

It was not more than an hour before the throng quietly dispersed, tired of looking at the same monotonous flames, the inn was once more closed, and the inmates retired to catch a few hours of repose before being compelled to open again.

When everything was quiet, the two mysterious watchers left their covert and looked around them.

It was evident now what they were after.

They halted below Mary Macpherson's window, and then one of them, raising himself upon the shoulders of his companion, drove, as noiselessly as possible, a long nail in the wall.

When this was firmly embedded, he raised himself up by it, and, steadying himself upon it, grasped the window-sill.

After this he drew from his pocket what seemed to be a coil of strong though slender rope, but which, when shaken out, proved to be a rope-ladder.

At the end of this, which the man held in his hand, was a spring of iron, so formed as to close on the window-sill, and sustain itself the more firmly the greater the weight imposed upon it.

Having fixed this, he stepped upon it, and commenced the work of opening the window, which he found no difficult task.

Having opened it, he passed into the room, and called to his companion, who, having fixed in the earth the long spikes which were at the other end of the ladder, at once climbed up.

"Look," said the one who had first entered; "we're in luck. She's never undressed herself."

He was right.

Mary Macpherson was lying fast asleep upon the bed fully dressed.

The men approached the lovely sleeper with cautious steps.

Then suddenly one of them drew a handkerchief from his pocket, and pressed it to her face.

A slight quiver passed through her limbs; there was a slight clenching of the hands, and the sleeper slept on.

It was the sleep now, however, of insensibility.

They lost no time.

One of them raised the senseless girl in his arms, while the other hurried back to the window, and getting out, stood on the ladder ready to receive her form.

To bear her to the ground was a matter of no difficulty.

Rupert Dreadnought had done so with the aid only of a single rope, while they had a rope ladder.

They were soon on *terra firma* once more, the window closed, the rope ladder removed, and everything left as it had been.

The kidnappers' horses were close at hand in the wood, and in a few minutes they were dashing back towards Dalrymple House.

When she awoke, she found herself in the bed-chamber, and supported in the arms of Lady Dalrymple.

"Oh! madam," she said, "why have you done this?"

"Alas! my child," said Lady Dalrymple, in tears, "I, too, am a prisoner."

CHAPTER XV.

ALLAN'S MAD SORROW—HE RETURNS TO THE FOREST—THE STRANGER—THE QUARREL—THE DUEL, AND THE STRANGE DISCLOSURE THAT RESULTED.

THE rage and terror of Allan of the Glen can well be imagined when the landlady, pale with affright, informed him of the disappearance of Mary Macpherson.

It was indeed a terrible disappointment to him.

He had so suddenly and unexpectedly met her after so long and weary an absence; and now, after going through unheard-of perils to save her, she was lost to him again.

At first he felt inclined to blame the people of the house.

Certainly it *did* seem strange.

The bed had not been slept in.

The impression of her person was on it certainly, but that was all.

The window was closed, but the door, being locked on the *inside*, precluded at last any notion of attaching blame to the landlady or landlord.

How she had gone was a mystery.

But not a moment did he doubt her love for him.

Not a moment did he imagine that she had fled of her own free will.

The tender words whispered to him when her soft warm arms were round his neck in the room at Dalrymple House were quite enough to prove this.

Discarding all foolish feelings of jealousy, he also discarded any notion of proceeding to London upon Rupert Dreadnought's business before returning to the neighbourhood of Dalrymple House, and informing his master of the misfortune which had occurred to him.

So, leaping on the horse he had ridden there on the night preceding, he paid the landlady for her kindness and trouble, and rode away towards the wood which abutted on the old house.

Here he had not much difficulty in finding Rupert and his friends.

During his absence they had made themselves as comfortable as they could in a little inn which abutted on the forest; and now, as the dawn overspread the land, they had once more taken up their station at a point where they could overlook the approaches to the castle.

It was with the utmost surprise that Rupert beheld Allan approaching.

"What ails you, Allan?" he cried, seeing his wild and disordered looks; "have you been to London and back in this time?"

"No, I have not attempted to go," replied Allan, almost impatiently. "I am distracted—mad! I have been robbed of her I love best in life. Think not I am neglectful of your interests, for I desire as eagerly as you do to avenge myself on Sir Hugh Dalrymple, but I could not rest till I had told you all and asked you to aid me in recovering the one I prize so dearly."

Hurriedly he told his story.

Rupert Dreadnought listened attentively, and at once a light broke in upon his mind.

"Allan," he said, "this is the work of Sir Hugh Dalrymple."

"Why so? What spite *can* he have against her?"

"It is easily to be seen," returned Rupert, "why he should have an enmity against her, and what use he hopes to make of her."

"In what way?"

"In the first place that arch traitor, Colin, consented to our death. Was it not so?"

"It was."

"Well, had it not been for his love for Mary Macpherson, we should have all been sacrificed. It was the sight of her among those to be massacred that made Colin leap from the balustrade of that subterranean gallery, and form our escape. There is not the slightest doubt that Sir Hugh Dalrymple has inveigled her away in some manner, and expects to learn from her our numbers, our purpose, and our whereabouts."

Allan's countenance fell at this.

In the power of Sir Hugh Dalrymple.

If Colin recovered then he would be able easily to communicate with her.

"You will, I hope, keep a good watch on Colin," he said; "*he* will be the one who will be best informed of her whereabouts."

Rupert thought a moment.

"You had better remain, Allan," he said; "I fancy, now that we have no ladies in the company, we can do with the force we have."

It was on the next morning that, while Allan and Tom the waterman were keeping watch at the entrance of the wood, they saw approaching them a tall gentleman dressed in semi-military costume, with a beard and moustache which reminded him of Sir Hugh Dalrymple.

He at once acquainted Tom the waterman with his surmise.

"What are we to do?" asked Tom.

"Follow him," said Allan, "and when we have him far away from the high road accuse him."

"And if we make an error?" asked Tom.

"We must chance that," said Allan. "I feel sure it is he. If not, it is some one whom I have seen in his house. Come, be not afraid. I am not," he added with a smile; "I am not going to ask you to assist in murdering him."

Tom at once followed Allan, and they hurried after the stranger into the forest.

As luck would have it, whatever errand he was on led him towards the spot where Rupert and his men had located themselves; and as he entered the glade where they were seated, a shrill whistle from Allan apprised them of the approach of a stranger.

In an instant they all sprang up.

"Who are you?" demanded Rupert, who guessed, from Allan's warning, that his enemy was at hand.

The new comer started back haughtily.

"What have we here?" he cried. "Have I found myself in the lair of a new Robin Hood? What want you?"

"Your name," replied Rupert.

"I refuse it, then," returned the stranger. "You have no right to ask."

Rupert's eyes flashed fire, and he drew his sword from its scabbard.

"Your words assure me that I *have* a right," he cried. "You are Sir Hugh Dalrymple."

The stranger laughed derisively.

"I see now that you are thieves and robbers," he answered, "who want a specious pretence for your villany. Tell me what money you require and let me pass."

"Not so," replied Rupert. "I refuse. Tell me, who are you?"

"I refuse again," said the haughty stranger.

"Then with my sword will I compel you to speak!" cried Rupert Dreadnought. "If you are a man draw and fight."

"You are assassins as well as thieves, I see," exclaimed the stranger. "Nevertheless, since you compel it I suppose I must fight."

"We are neither assassins nor thieves," answered Rupert; "but since you disbelieve us we will adjourn hence. I will appoint one of these two to be your second. Yonder Scotch youth shall be mine. Fear not, you shall have fair play."

To this proposition the new comer, who imagined these proceedings to be only the prelude to some deed of villany, felt himself compelled to assent; and, passing into a woodland glade near at hand, they prepared for action.

Before swords were crossed, Rupert Dreadnought once more gave his antagonist a chance of avoiding the contest.

"If you tell me your name, and prove it to be correct," he said, "I will no longer delay you, unless, indeed, you be the Sir Hugh Dalrymple I seek."

"I again tell you I am not he," returned the stranger; "but I shall, nevertheless, refuse to disclose my name. I have reasons for keeping it secret; and how do I know you may not be in league with the very men from which most I would keep the knowledge?"

There was no further parley.

Rupert Dreadnought was determined that the stranger should speak.

Both he and Allan suspected that it was, indeed, Sir Hugh Dalrymple that stood before them.

The only way, therefore, to force the secret from him was at the sword's point.

CHAPTER XVI.

AT THE SWORD'S POINT.

The manner in which the two strangely-matched opponents stood was enough to show that they both knew well the use of the sword.

Their eyes gleamed brightly, but with far different feelings.

The one with resolution, the other with anger at being thus forced into a contest.

The duel waxed warm.

Several times Tom the waterman, who had been appointed the stranger's second, expected to see him pierced through, while, on the other hand, Allan felt his master to be in constant danger from the brilliant swordsmanship of his adversary.

As they fought they grew eager and more eager.

They became less careful in their passes, and their hot breath steamed in the chill air.

They forgot what they were fighting for, in fact, and finding before him an enemy who was nearly his match, Rupert Dreadnought felt as if it were indeed his enemy that confronted him.

Presently the stranger, becoming inflamed with anger, made a desperate lunge, and Rupert, parrying his stroke just as he backed against a tree, passed his sword right through his arm, and pinned him to the trunk.

The sword fell from the stranger's hand, and involuntarily he uttered a cry of pain.

He was completely at the mercy of Rupert Dreadnought.

But the latter had no wish to take an unfair advantage of his position.

"Now, then," he cried, "I have you in my power completely. Tell me who you are. I seek Sir Hugh Dalrymple, a dastardly ruffian and assassin; a villain whom I am hunting down for the murder of his own brother. If you are he expect no mercy at my hands. If you are *not* he, prove to me that you are not his friend, and you shall go free."

The manner in which Rupert Dreadnought said these words was enough to prove his sincerity, and a most wonderful change came over the face of the stranger as he spoke.

"Had I known what you said before to be true," he cried, "I should not have refused to reply to your inquiry. As it is, the pain of my wound is great. Release me, and, while my second here binds it up, I will explain who I am. In the first place, however, I am not Sir Hugh Dalrymple, but Henry Clanberris."

The name had in it a familiar ring for Rupert.

Allan of the Glen had heard from Mary Macpherson many particulars in regard to the love of Lady Dalrymple for an absent one, and now, eagerly withdrawing his sword, he offered him a drink of brandy and bade Tom at once bind up his wound.

Briefly then Henry Clanberris told him his story.

He said very little of Lady Dalrymple; not a word in regard to her love for him.

He spoke bitterly, however, of the forced marriage and his own blighted hopes; expressed his belief in the unhappiness of Lady Dalrymple, and honestly declared that if Sir Hugh Dalrymple *was* the villain that Rupert represented him to be, he would gladly aid in his destruction.

Rupert saw at once that he had to do with no impostor.

He therefore briefly recapitulated the reasons for his invasion of the Dalrymple mansion; the cause of Sir Hugh's not daring to call in the assistance of the authorities; and wound up by explaining his own name and station.

"Well," said Clanberris, "I am here also in a position of difficulty. Time has changed me. Sir Hugh Dalrymple does not see in me the hated Henry Clanberris of old; he only knows me by the name of Rolliston. Despairing of being able otherwise to see Lady Dalrymple, the love of my youth, I assumed this name, obtained an introduction to him, and was received at his house. The result you know. It remains now to seize upon this man, drag him to the place where the murder was committed, and where you have sworn to punish him, and there force from his lips a confession of his crime."

"Such is our course. But where am I to find him?" said Rupert.

"*I* will see to that," replied Clanberris, who, mingled with his sense of justice, could not help recollecting that the destruction of Sir Hugh Dalrymple would mean happiness for himself and Lady Dalrymple. "I am now proceeding to see my sister. When I return this evening I will arrange with you as to how this villain is to be secured."

Having arranged matters thus far, and settled the time of meeting, he then quitted them, and in spite of his wound passed on with alacrity towards Clanberris House.

The wound, in fact, had far more pleasure than pain in it.

It was a token that he was on the road to success.

It was a sure sign by which he might remember how the happiness he had so longed for might be obtained.

Visions of bliss floated through his mind.

He should now ere long be enabled to possess the one for whom he had so long waited.

How glad was he now that his half-framed words had never left his lips; how glad that the terrible fire had not resulted in his asking her what she would have refused, perhaps in tears, perhaps in anger!

Rupert Dreadnought had made no stipulation with him as regarded informing Lady Clanberris of what had happened.

He told her all, therefore.

She had, as we have seen, pleaded his cause to Lady Dalrymple on a former occasion, and she was happy enough, therefore, to see a chance of his being able at least to make her happy.

"Say nothing of all this to Margaret."

Such was her advice.

"I will not even see her," replied Henry. "It would be wrong to do so."

He was resolute now.

He would not give himself the chance of giving way.

At the appointed hour in the evening he met Rupert in the wood once more.

The latter was awaiting him with anxiety.

"You have come then," he cried. "I am all eagerness to commence and bring to a successful conclusion my work."

"Well," returned Henry Clanberris, "I have been thinking over the matter, and I come to this conclusion. I have entered Sir Hugh Dalrymple's house by stealth and under a false name, and I will not so far continue my treachery as to betray him into the hands of those whose bounden *duty* is to kill him."

Rupert started.

The angry blood flew to his cheek.

"You wish to back out of your bargain now, then, I presume?" he said, with a frown.

"No, no," he said; "what I meant I, perhaps, did not express very clearly. I mean this; I will proceed to his house, I will enter, and at a certain hour I will place a light in a window. When you see this, you will understand that a certain little gate, which I shall show to you, is open. You will enter there, and ascend to the top of the staircase, where you will find me, most probably with sword drawn against Sir Hugh."

MARY MACPHERSON.

"Why so?"

"Because, as I have said, I will no longer sail under false colours," replied Henry Clanberris; "I will tell him all and leave you to do the rest. But stay; I have not yet explained myself. I told you I would not betray him to men whose duty it was to kill him."

"Well."

"You must, if I place him in your hands, consent to permit him to fight fairly for his life."

"It shall be so."

"And when and where he likes."

Rupert shook his head.

"No," he said, "I cannot concede that."

"Why not?"

"You forget my vow," replied Dreadnought; "I have sworn that when I have captured him, I shall bear him to the old church—place him in the vault—kill him, and bury him in the same stone coffin as contains the bones of the brother he murdered."

"True, true, I had forgotten," replied Henry Clanberris; "nevertheless you can give him his sword, and I, if you like, will be his second in that dismal fight."

"Agreed," said Rupert; "in such a cause I shall feel my arm doubly nerved for the fight, though in very truth I am sorely tired of blood. But come—let us go. You wish me to accompany you, I believe, as far as the house?"

"Yes; but we must be cautious," said Henry Clanberris; "if we are watched I must explain to you from afar the locality of the little door; come, let us hasten."

Bidding Allan and his other friends await him in the wood, at the same spot, and be ready to rush after him at a given signal, Rupert Dreadnought then passed away with Henry Clanberris, and they were not long before they reached the corner of the wood, which abutted, as it were, upon the house where Sir Hugh Dalrymple had taken temporary refuge.

"Yonder," said Henry, as they paused here, "yonder is the house in question. At the side you observe a willow tree, whose branches hang almost to the ground. Behind that natural screen you will find the little door of which I speak. As soon as you see the light hurry in with your men, for it may chance that I am in danger, and in need of your aid."

Having settled those preliminaries, they parted,

and Henry Clanberris knocked boldly at the door of his enemy's house.

"Is Sir Hugh alone?" he asked of the man who admitted him.

"Yes," he said. "Shall I tell him you desire to see him?"

"No," replied Henry, "I will go up to his study; I know my way."

The man made no objection.

He knew him as a friend of his master's, and could have no suspicion of his mysterious errand.

Henry Clanberris, therefore, quickly ascended the stairs.

On arriving near the door of the study, where Sir Hugh Dalrymple was sitting, he halted a moment, and then, instead of proceeding straight on, turned sharply to the right.

This led him at once to the top landing of a narrow staircase, which conducted to the small postern to which he had alluded in speaking to Rupert Dreadnought.

Noiselessly he descended.

Then he cautiously withdrew the bolts and left the door open to the extent of an inch.

Then as noiselessly he ascended the staircase, and knocked lightly at the door of the study.

"Come in," said Sir Hugh, languidly.

Henry drew a long breath, and, making his way in, locked the door behind him.

Sir Hugh gazed at him in surprise.

"Ah, Rolliston," he said, "you have something very private to tell me, I expect, since you close the door so carefully."

Henry eyed him sternly.

"I have," he said, "something most private. It was not until to-night that I discovered that I was in the house of an assassin and a parricide."

For an instant this sudden blow paralysed the efforts of Sir Hugh Dalrymple.

A greenish pallor overspread his features, and he gazed at the speaker in wonder.

Then he sprang to his feet.

"Madman!" he said, "do you come to beard me here since you dared not in my own house?"

"This house is yours for the time," returned Henry, coolly, "therefore you're master as much here as at Dalrymple House."

"At any rate I will not suffer this insolence," cried Sir Hugh, furiously; "quit my presence at once."

"I refuse," replied Henry, "for two reasons. In the first place——"

"I will not listen," cried Sir Hugh, drawing his sword. "Leave this apartment, or I will call my servants to eject you."

"I have prepared myself for that," said Henry Clanberris.

And drawing a pistol from his breast, he levelled it at Sir Hugh.

"Coward!" cried Sir Hugh, as he sank back in his chair. "Say on, say quickly what you have to say, and quit my presence."

"In the first place, then," said his strange guest, "my name is not Rolliston; it is Clanberris."

"Clanberris!" exclaimed Dalrymple, his face blanching again.

"Aye, the one whose fair name you aspersed—the one whose bride you stole. But never mind that. I would not put you to the shame of this knowledge before. Now that I know you for what you are, I care not—I glory in it. But speak not. Listen. You are, as I have said, an assassin and a parricide. I am about to deliver you into the hands of those who have sworn to punish you."

"Traitor!" cried Sir Hugh Dalrymple, quivering with rage.

"Not so," replied Henry Clanberris, "not so. When I first came into your house, I imagined you certainly to be a slanderer and a deceiver, but I knew not that you were a murderer. Had I done so I would have proclaimed it aloud before your guests. At any rate, I consider myself to be acting conscientiously. No matter what I do, therefore, beware of calling out, or I shall fire and take upon myself the responsibility of judging you."

A cold sweat now invaded the limbs of the parricide.

He saw before him the quick approach of his punishment.

"You are in a hurry, indeed, to commit your dastardly crime," he said, with a ghastly effort at being satirical. "Might it not occur to you that I may have things to arrange before I am dragged away to certain death by assassination?"

"Your words are but a ruse," he said, "you cannot deceive me. If you have made a will, well and good. If you have not, your next heir will receive all."

"And leave my wife destitute," said Sir Hugh, catching at this as a drowning man catches at a straw.

Henry's eyes gleamed with a strange meaning.

"Fear not for your wife," he said, "*she* will want for nothing."

"Curse you!" muttered Sir Hugh Dalrymple, "if I escape from this enemy's trap your punishment shall be such as shall make you shudder to contemplate it."

"You will not escape," said Henry Clanberris, solemnly, and taking the lamp from the table in his left hand, he moved with it towards the window, still keeping the pistol ready in his right.

Having placed it on the window, he approached the door, still proceeding carefully backwards, and, unlocking it, left it a little ajar.

He listened awhile.

But no sound came.

In fact, he was a little before his time.

He had forgotten to give Rupert Dreadnought sufficient time to go back to the forest glade and return with his men.

He sat down therefore and waited.

It was now growing dark, and Rupert Dreadnought therefore could not be long.

Black clouds began to roll along the sky, and the wind began to rise and howl around the house, and shake the few walls which still remained of the burnt castle.

The two men sat silently watching one another.

Presently there was the tramp of approaching feet.

"They come," said Henry Clanberris.

A tremor invaded the heart of Sir Hugh Dalrymple, in spite of all his daring courage.

He was absolutely surrounded by unavoidable peril.

The tramp of feet came nearer, and then the lower door was cast violently open.

A violent gust of wind roared up the staircase, and flung open the door of the room.

In an instant the lamp that stood in the open window was dashed out into the road, and the room was left in total darkness.

The report of a pistol followed instantly.

Determined that the parricide should not escape if he could by any means prevent it, Henry Clanberris had fired the shot, and then rushed eagerly forward.

But it was of no avail.

In the darkness it was impossible to tell with precision where the person was whom he wished to attack, and the ball took no effect.

As Henry Clanberris rushed upon his adversary, therefore, he received a violent wound with a sword and fell backwards heavily to the ground.

In another instant Sir Hugh Dalrymple had dashed out of the window and was gone, just has Rupert Dreadnought and his men burst into the room.

CHAPTER XVII.

THE ESCAPE—THE INNOCENT WIFE AND THE REMORSELESS HUSBAND—THE QUARREL—THE SUPPOSED ILLNESS—THE RIDE TO CHICHESTER—THE FOLLOWING PHANTOMS—ALONE WITH THE MURDERED DEAD!

SIR HUGH DALRYMPLE knew well that, with such a host of enemies on his track, it would be utterly useless to attempt any real escape from the vicinity that night.

All his pride was gone now.

All he thought of was dear life.

He saw himself helplessly in the toils.

What he must do now was to remove all evidences of his crime, and if he could not then brave it out fly to the Continent.

But first he must see his wife.

She was near, in a friend's house—her residence known only to himself and the two willing ruffians who had abducted Mary Macpherson.

At her place, therefore, he would find the best safety.

And, more than this, he would have the demoniacal triumph of punishing her for her fault—a fault not her own!

How could she avoid being loved by one who had been her childhood's friend, and who had been her heart's desire until Sir HughDalrymple had appeared like an evil genius upon the scene?

Dropping from the window, at the peril of life and limb, he rushed towards the house where Lady Dalrymple was, so to speak, confined.

She had told Mary Macpherson she was a prisoner.

This was literally true.

A few vague words dropped by a guest had set his mind in a flame, and he had rigorously concealed her.

Now he felt more than ever the justice of what he had done.

And yet there was no necessity!

The clock was warning the ninth hour, she was just preparing to go to her lonely couch, and with a weary heart she rose to leave her room.

Softly she had opened the door and glided down the dimly-lighted corridor, thinking of the past—of her present almost forlorn condition, and—of Henry Clanberris.

No wonder, thinking of him, that she started back.

Who stands before her with set, haggard face and blazing eyes?

No words escaped his pallid lips as he passed his arm round her shivering form, and carried her through the dressing room into the bedchamber beyond.

As she sank trembling upon the couch, her heart quailed with deadly terror as she looked upon the face of the husband whom she hated.

"Where were you going, Margaret?" he asked, in a stern voice.

"To bed. Where else, since all here is drear and lonely?" she replied, almost angrily.

"Are you sure you were not trying to leave the house by stealth?"

She clenched her hands tightly and gazed at him boldly.

"Why should you think so?" she said. "Why should you dream of such a thing? Do you know that I am justified in desiring to escape your tyranny, that you speak thus?"

Sir Hugh Dalrymple saw he had gone too far.

He assumed, therefore, a sanctimonious air, if we may so express it, and said, in low, hoarse tones—

"I know all, Margaret; you wish to leave me, but *I* can prevent that. You will live to thank me for saving you from being the vilest thing on God's earth. You need not fear. I shall not harm you, and I shall not expose you. *Your* honour is *mine*. But never again shall you occupy the place of wife. You shall be as dead to the world as though you slept in the grave. Never shall you have the opportunity of disgracing me. My mother, thank Heaven, was a good woman; and one who has sinned, even in thought, shall never take her place!"

He thought that all this would be very terrible to her.

It was not so.

She merely smiled.

"I fear you not," she said; "neither do I pay heed to your menaces or your insults. I am your faithful wife, and I have ever behaved as such; treat me as you will, you can never drag from me a confession of anything that is wrong. *You* know that you stole me from one who loved me; that I was forced into a marriage with you when I hated the idea. But in the face of all this you know how I have behaved; how devoted I have been; how I have striven to conquer my aversion. But there; I will not attempt to defend myself when I am guilty of nothing. Read your own heart, wretched man, and if it accuses me, say so."

He had no time to reply.

Before he could utter a syllable, there was a loud and impatient knocking at the door.

Sir Hugh turned ghastly pale.

He was not only foiled again, but these might be enemies.

If they were, he stood the chance of losing his wife also.

"Margaret," he said, solemnly, "will you swear to me that you are not in league with the men who this night have made a dastardly attack upon me?"

"I know nothing of it," replied Margaret earnestly, "to this I swear. I know not even what you mean."

"Good; then understand me," said her husband, "this knocking at the door portends danger to us both. Take this pistol; go into that inner room and lock the door. If anyone threatens to molest you, fire!"

Gazing at his beautiful wife—seeing his own danger—knowing that her old lover, Henry Clanberris, was the leader of his enemies, he was determined that she should not fall into their hands.

In giving her the pistol he had a deep design.

He hoped that Henry Clanberris would force his way into the room in the darkness, and that her own hand would take her lover's life.

She took the pistol, and he gently led her into the adjoining chamber.

The door of this she locked, and then, drawing his sword, Sir Hugh Dalrymple advanced to open the door.

There had been a repetition of loud and impatient knocking during the short conversation which had ensued between Sir Hugh Dalrymple and his wife.

But it was not as he had anticipated.

The person who had given the summons at the door was not an enemy, but one of the servants.

He looked pale and scared.

"What ails you?" cried Sir Hugh. "Quick! speak!"

"I know not what it means," replied the man, "but there is some devilment about."

Sir Hugh frowned.

"Explain yourself," he said. "This is no time for folly. Quick, say—what is it you mean?"

"Well, Sir Hugh," said the man, who still trembled violently, "I was leaning out of one of the back windows, when I saw a crowd of men approaching from the direction of the house which had been given up for your reception. They stopped in the highway opposite this, and one of them, who was dressed in a Scotch dress, advanced and pointed out this place."

"Well?" said Sir Hugh, impatiently.

"Well, Sir Hugh, they then proceeded in different directions, and I thought I had seen the last of them for the time—but no?"

"Are they there now, then?" asked Sir Hugh.

"No, Sir Hugh. I will tell you. I kept looking still out of the window, when I thought I saw one of the bushes move.

"It was not fancy.

"They were now in the gardens.

"I could see their forms moving about, and ——"

"Where are they now?"

"Here," cried a voice, and, as it spoke, Rupert Dreadnought and Henry Clanberris, followed by their men, burst into he room.

Too late now Sir Hugh Dalrymple saw the truth.

He had been betrayed by one of his own retainers.

The conversation which the man had held with him had been only a pretext for delay.

"Cowards!" cried the parricide, now really at bay. "Cowards! is it thus you attack one man?"

Rupert Dreadnought advanced towards him.

"We came not here to attack you," he said.

"Why thus in arms, then?" cried the other.

"Because we come to arrest you and are prepared for resistance," replied Rupert. "I come in conformity with the vow which I have made, and the particulars of which have been given you by Henry Clanberris, who stands beside me. I come not to assassinate you as *you* assassinated your brother. I come to take you to the spot where that foul murder was committed, and there, with my own arm and my own sword, to punish you for that deed or perish. You will have fair play, doubt not."

A sneering smile passed over the lips of Sir Hugh Dalrymple.

He pointed to his drawn sword.

"I am armed," he said, "and ready. Why not fight now?"

"Because," returned Rupert Dreadnought, "that is not according to my vow. It is of no avail to keep it unless I keep it thoroughly. Come, sir, sheathe your sword and go quietly. Resistance is utterly useless."

Sir Hugh did as he was bidden.

"Providence," he said, with an affectation of solemnity, "will watch over me. You are either murderers or madmen. But stay," he added, as a sudden thought occurred to him, "may I take leave of my wife?"

It was a simple request.

They knew not its deep meaning.

Rupert, of course, could not refuse him such a thing as this, and, under guard, he was allowed to enter.

He had thought he could have a chance of escape but he was wrong.

Within half an hour he was mounted on a horse and on his way to St. Andrew's, Chichester.

This was the place where his terrible retribution was to take place.

RUPERT DREADNOUGHT.

"THE BULLET, SENT WITH A TRUER AIM, SOON LAID HIS ADVERSARY IN THE DUST."

After a short journey Sir Hugh Dalrymple was removed from horseback and placed within a close carriage.

This expedient was adopted in order to preclude the possibility of his crying out and attracting the notice of passers by.

It was none of Rupert Dreadnought's plans to follow the carriage which contained the prisoner.

He knew well that so large a concourse of persons guarding a prisoner would excite suspicion.

So he placed the party in the hands of Tom the waterman.

"Be careful," he said, "to guard him, but do not let him be seen more than is absolutely requisite."

"I will not let him leave the carriage. We will travel post. He cannot cry out bound and gagged as he is, and there is, therefore, no fear of detection. And where, tell me, is the place of rendezvous?"

Rupert thought a moment.

"At the 'Chequers,' near Chichester. Opposite that inn there is a dense wood; in that you can place the carriage and its prisoner, and await my arrival."

"Good," said Tom; "but will these men obey me?"

Rupert turned to the men who were on guard round the carriage.

"Remember," he said, "Tom Braxley is going upon a mission which involves a subject very dear to my heart, so obey him as you would me, and doubt not that I will amply reward you."

A murmur of approbation and consent passed through all as he turned towards the spot where his horse was standing.

CHAPTER XVIII.

PERILS BY LAND.

"ADIEU then, my comrades! Bear in mind the instructions I have given you, and all will be well."

So said Rupert, as he vaulted to the back of his gallant steed, and waved his hat to his companions.

"Now, away! away!" he continued, patting the noble animal's neck, and slightly touching his flanks with his glittering spurs.

How wonderful is the attachment which sometimes exists between the noblest types of human and brute creation. The noble horse knew his master's voice, and, obeying the word of command, started off at a rapid pace.

The numerous steeples and turrets dotting the smoky horizon grew larger and larger in his vision, as he neared the great city.

Rupert would have avoided London had he not been pressed for time.

It was necessary that his journey should be performed quickly as well as secretly; so, as he rode on, he held mental debate with himself.

Unless he reached his destination within a given time, his journey would be, to a certain extent, useless.

So he resolved to brave the chances of recognition in the streets of London, rather than journey by a roundabout route.

Still, as he rode through the streets of London, he glanced cautiously about him to be certain that he was not watched.

At length he saw before him the frowning gateway of old London Bridge, and he cast a shuddering glance at the ghastly relics of mortality which grinned above the gateway.

"Pray Heaven mine may never be there," ejaculated Rupert. "Yet how many a noble life has been sacrificed to gratify the malice of treachery!"

The bridge was passed.

Rupert felt more at ease, for he fancied that now his greatest dangers had been encountered.

Little did he dream that the quiet, shady lanes in which he soon found himself contained far more perils than the busy haunts of men.

A few miles more and the perspiration reeking from the sides of his gallant horse told him that it was time to rest.

He looked about him somewhat anxiously for a glimpse of a human habitation.

Some little distance ahead was a clump of trees, from which arose a column of blue smoke.

A nearer view revealed to him a small wayside inn.

"The very place for me," thought Rupert. "Here, at all events, I can rest awhile without fear of being disturbed."

He rode up to the door.

"Ho, there, landlord!" he shouted.

For some moments there was no response.

He shouted again, and a voice was heard replying.

"Coming, good sir," it cried; "curb your impatience for a few minutes."

Rupert dismounted.

"A strange-looking place this," he said to himself; "but one in which I shall not be likely to meet any acquaintance."

The landlord appeared at the door.

He was a stalwart man, in the prime of life; and Rupert noticed, as he stood uncovered by the side of his horse, that his head was bald, and bore the traces of a deep wound.

"What is it you want, sir?" he asked, gazing in the face of the traveller.

"Food and drink for myself and horse," replied Rupert.

The landlord answered by leading the steed to the stable, pointing at the same time to the doorway.

Rupert strolled up the sanded passage, and entered a little room on the right.

In a few moments the landlord joined him.

"I have attended to your beast," said the man; "now what shall I have the honour of serving you with?"

"A bottle of your best wine, and any food that you can place on the table within the space of five minutes."

The host of the roadside tavern gave the necessary instructions to his buxom spouse, and in a very short space of time, Rupert was seated before a flask of Burgundy, a loaf of brown bread, and a substantial joint of roast beef.

"This is the best I can give you," said the landlady, as she dropped a curtsey, and lingered in the room a few moments to see whether the handsome young stranger had any commands.

But Rupert's modest wants were satisfied, and he politely intimated that he could dispense with the good woman's presence.

As soon as his simple meal was ended, Rupert strolled up to the window and looked forth.

"Would that I could end my days in such a scene

as this," thought he, as he gazed at the green fields and the waving cornfields, from which came no sounds save the hum of insects and the song of birds.

All seemed peace, yet near him was fearful danger.

Behind the hedgerow which skirted the road lurked a man.

That man had seen Rupert enter the inn, and was now waiting anxiously for his re-appearance.

"The bill, mine host," cried Rupert.

The young traveller threw a piece of gold upon the table, and ordered his horse to be brought to the door.

"One glass with me, good sir," said the host, when Rupert was once more fairly in his saddle; "it is not usual for my guests to refuse the stirrup cup at parting."

A glass was brought, and Rupert raised it to his lips.

"A pleasant journey to you, good sir," said the host.

"Amen!" returned Rupert.

"Ha! ha! ha!" laughed a hoarse, discordant voice.

Rupert glanced round.

A man's face had for a moment appeared among the bushes near.

But he was now gone.

No one was in sight save the host, and thinking that his ears had deceived him, he resumed his journey.

But his ears had not deceived him.

The man who had laughed rushed away into the wooded country near, and in a few moments was dashing after him on a splendid horse.

CHAPTER XIX.

THE APPARITION.

It was some minutes before Rupert knew that he was pursued.

At length he heard the sound of other hoofs besides those of his own horse.

He turned to see who was coming.

He did not recognise the face of the stranger, and at first thought that he was some peaceful traveller on the king's highway.

But as time passed on, and the unknown still persistently dogged his path, he began to think that it was time to enquire his business.

He turned his horse's head and halted.

The stranger did the same, and the two men remained facing each other.

"Who are you, and why do you follow me?" demanded Rupert, sternly.

The stranger at first made no reply.

Rupert repeated the question, giving his words additional emphasis by laying his hand on the hilt of his sword.

"It matters not who I am," replied the stranger, "but my business is with you."

"With me?"

"Aye."

"What do you desire to know?"

"Whither you go and your object in going."

"You are insolent, sir," responded Rupert. "Begone, rascal, nor dare annoy me again."

The stranger suddenly drew a pistol from his belt, and levelled it at Rupert's head.

"Ha, traitor!" thundered Rupert, as he imitated the example of his adversary.

The pistol held by the unknown stranger exploded with a loud report; but Rupert was quicker, and his bullet, sent with truer aim, laid his adversary in the dust.

In an instant our hero dismounted, and gazed well into the features of his fallen foe.

"Why did he foil me thus?" he mentally remarked.

There was no solution to this question.

Our hero searched the pockets of the dead man, but there was no document of any kind to prove his identity or give a reason for his strange conduct.

He pondered for a few minutes.

"I must give information," he thought, "or some poor fellow who chances to pass by this way will be arrested for murder."

So he reluctantly rode back towards the inn.

But ere he had traversed half the distance, a strange, unaccountable feeling came upon him, filling his mind with vague doubts and gloomy presentiment of coming evil.

His head felt heavy, his eyes became dim.

He reeled in the saddle, and with great difficulty reached a little brook that crossed the road, dismounted, thinking that a draught of the cold water would refresh him.

But he was mistaken, for, as he knelt down to drink, he fell senseless.

* * * * *

An hour afterwards two peasants returning home from their labours saw a dark object lying on the moonlit road by the side of the brook.

It was Rupert.

His faithful steed was bending over him, endeavouring to call back life to the senseless form of his beloved master, rubbing his nose against his face, and caressing him in a hundred different ways.

The peasants were startled.

They feared that a murder had been committed, and trembled lest they themselves might be accused of the crime.

After a short consultation they decided upon a plan.

Rupert was laid across the back of his horse, and so conveyed to the inn.

A sleeping apartment was hastily got ready for him, and a surgeon who had just arrived volunteered his services.

"He will soon recover," said the medical man. "Aid me in pouring this effervescing draught down his throat and the unnatural slumber will quickly terminate."

These orders were obeyed, and the patient was then left to himself.

It was nearly midnight when Rupert awoke.

He felt confused, and for some time was unable to clearly account for his presence in a strange place.

At length, when he could clearly recollect all that

had taken place up till the time he became unconscious, he endeavoured to rise.

But bodily weakness had succeeded mental oblivion.

His limbs refused to fulfil their office, and much as he wished to rise and continue his journey, he was compelled to remain recumbent till his strength had returned.

The moon's light shining through the lattice window enabled him to see pretty clearly the various objects in the room.

On the table by his bedside was a bottle.

Rupert seized it, and tasted its contents, which he found to be good wine.

A moment after a rustling sound in the room attracted his attention.

"Who is there?" he asked. "Is it you, mine host?"

There was no response.

The draught of wine had reinvigorated Rupert's frame.

He sat up on the bed, and glancing towards the window, saw a strange sight.

There was a tall ghost-like figure, clad in garments of the orthodox spiritual hue, being draped n a long white cloak or mantle.

Rupert grasped his sword, which had been left by his bedside, and sprang up.

The figure in white saw the movement and disappeared through the open window.

Rupert followed; but ere he reached the ground the unknown was lost to sight behind the stables by the side of the inn.

A thought struck Rupert's mind as he followed in pursuit.

He had caught a glimpse of the face of his ghostly visitor, and he felt certain that the features were those of the man whom he had left for dead on the road three hours before.

"Then I did not kill him," thought he; and at that moment, as if to strengthen his conviction that the man still lived, he heard sounds resembling the galloping of a horse over the adjacent meadows.

Our hero was now thoroughly roused.

He hastened back to the stables, opened the door, and saddled his steed.

Two courses were before him, either to follow the strange intruder or continue his journey towards Chichester. He decided on the latter.

First carefully loading his pistols and seeing that his sword was loose in its sheath, he led his horse out of the stables and mounted.

He cared not now for any danger he might encounter, for he was prepared.

The night was very dark, and objects were not plainly visible.

Yet, now and then, it seemed to Rupert that some one was following him.

That he should be followed thus was, of course, no matter of wonder.

The mission he had in hand was one of stupendous importance, and of a nature unsanctioned absolutely by law.

It was not to be wondered at, therefore, if many persons connected intimately with the man whom he was forcing to his doom should attempt to destroy him.

However, he thought little of it.

He was engaged upon a good errand.

Providence had hitherto watched over him with care.

Why should he doubt now that it would cease its protection?

So on he rode.

On the road the mysterious apparition never once made his appearance, and he arrived at the appointed place with no further interruptions.

CHAPTER XX.

IN WHICH SIR HUGH DALRYMPLE ACTS A NEW PART.

WE must now follow for a while the fortunes of the one whom Rupert's friends were carrying to his just doom.

When Rupert arrived at the inn, he found that his friends truly were there, but the prisoner was gone!

Here was a mystery.

But he *had* gone!

They had never once ceased to watch him, but he had slipped away during the journey.

There was, in fact, a traitor among them.

He had pretended to be the most zealous of the party, and during the slow passage of the carriage along a rough portion of the road, he had opened the carriage door and let him escape.

Sir Hugh, who knew well the destination to which he was going, was more mad than sane as he rushed away, and conceived the idea of destroying the church where lay his murdered brother and papers which implicated him.

So he proceeded to the house of the old sexton, who knew him well, and who was somewhat startled by his haggard appearance.

"Go, old Thomas," he said, "and fetch me your friend Langton. I have work to do this night."

There was the glitter of madness in Sir Hugh's eyes.

The old sexton feared him.

But he had been a friend to him in times gone by.

So he resolved to obey him.

"Good," he said, as he slipped on his heavy cloak. "Be careful with the place."

A presentiment that he was being deceived made him speak thus, but Sir Hugh only nodded, and, as he passed out, sat down moodily.

For some time after the departure of old Thomas, Sir Hugh Dalrymple sat very still, gazing at the flames.

Then the fire grew dead, and he became cold, and rising, searched the cottage for fuel.

In this search he discovered certain objects which made his eyes gleam and his heart leap in his breast.

Once before he had sought for them when his mind was still strong and healthy within him.

Now, amid the ruin of his health, both bodily and mental, they suggested to him a wild and terrible idea.

And what were they?

The keys of St. Andrew's church.

He took them down from the nail behind the door, and eyed them curiously.

Had he been quite sane the idea might have suggested itself to him that he had acted foolishly in hiding documents in a coffin, and that it would be well for him to destroy them even now.

But he was cold, and the idea of a fire suggested itself naturally to him.

A grim smile stole over his lips.

A demoniacal smile it was, as if he appreciated and enjoyed beforehand the huge and terrible conflagration which would hide among it, ashes relics of family mysteries, and registers of births, marriages, and deaths—registers upon which depended the hopes and fortunes of many a house.

He walked to the door, and looked out.

The sky had been very dark, and threatening snow.

Now the mist, which had spread itself over the country, was dispelled, however, and here and there the heavens were visible.

Not a mouse stirred.

All was hushed, as if in expectancy of something.

Sir Hugh cautiously closed the door behind him, and walked calmly towards the church, quickly, boldly, in the dim light, as if he were afraid of no man.

He passed into the church, shut the heavy door behind him with a slam, and made his way to the vestry.

As luck or ill luck would have it, two men were returning about this time form a friendly gathering at an inn a little above the church, and as they passed they noticed an unusual light in the building.

There was a flicker on the windows, a dull glare among the pilasters of the belfry, and then a pane of glass cracked.

After standing in wonder a moment, they rushed to the "Chequers," and gave the news.

Rupert and his friends at once hurried out, and rushing to the spot pulled the bell of the churchyard.

Receiving no answer, they leaped the low paling, and knocked at the cottage door.

There being no reply here, they pushed the door open, and looked in.

The room was empty, and the fire was nearly out.

"We'd best go up to the church," said one of them, "and see for ourselves."

They went up.

There was a strange smell—a crackling and a snapping noise.

The door was hot.

The vestry was on fire.

They thought, too, they heard a moaning wailing cry, within, but of this they were not sure

"Master Dreadnought," cried Tom, "I will run to the village, and tell the people to come up. You stop here; you may, perhaps, see something."

Without waiting to explain his meaning, he ran off and left Rupert alone.

What he saw then, no one believed, when he told them, until he had solemnly assured them of the truth of his words.

"A MAN'S HEAD APPEARED AMONG THE BUSHES."

He drew himself up by his hands to the sill of a window, and then gradually stood up, and forcing in the ventilator, gazed in.

The church was alight in a dozen places.

The altar, the pulpit, the pews, the vestry, and everything inflammable, in fact, were slowly burning.

And here and there in every part of the church, now in the black of the choking smoke, now in the red of the fearful glare, he saw flitting to and fro the form of a man.

Who he was he knew not.

He had never seen, to his recollection, his face before, and could not see it now plainly.

As far as he could make out the features, they were set in a face of a wild and unearthly mould, a pale, ghastly, spectre-like face, such as few have seen and few would care to see again.

In vain Rupert endeavoured to force his way into the edifice.

The framework of the windows was of stone, and the part where the glass was was too narrow to allow of his squeezing his body through.

And so, without being able to raise his hand to help, he gazed hard at the form of the madman now at the road where he expected help was to, arrive.

There was a strange smoke ascending from a door near the altar, and the horrible conviction forced itself into the watcher's mind that the bodies and their coffins were burning below.

He shouted to Sir Hugh Dalrymple, whom, in the fearful light, he did not recognise.

But amid the roaring of the flames, and the crackling of the wood, and the splitting of the glass, the madman heard him not.

The heat was now becoming so excessive that Rupert Dreadnought could bear it no longer, and leaping over he looked eagerly towards the village to see if help was coming.

The fire could now be seen for miles around.

The hugh lurid flames shot up in horrid tongues towards the heavens, through window and roof and skylight, and vacant places, where huge beams had been, were soon filled by a red-hot glare.

Up from the town streamed the crowding population.

Round the church they gathered, standing awe-struck amid the tenements of the quiet dead, wondering how the place could be saved, yet not one suggesting the means.

Then, while they were considering, a huge piece of blazing timber fell from the belfry, and dashed down upon the ground.

A myriad fiery particles floated through the air like flakes of red snow, and whirling in through the open door of the cottage, set that also in a blaze.

It was now that a whisper ran through the crowd that there was a man in the burning edifice.

No one could see him, for the place was all aglow, and in the white heat no objects could be distinguished.

But Rupert had told them what he had seen, and they had heard a moaning cry ever and anon ascending through the crackling of the timbers and the roaring of the flames.

So they began to break open the door.

Again and again they attacked it with pickaxes and spades and strong shoulders, and at length the hinges, yielding from the burning wood, gave way, and a heavy body wavered and fell in among them.

It's was a man's form.

He uttered a hollow groan, as they seized him in their arms, and, placing him on a shutter, bore him away towards the village.

As they did so, he uttered a few disjointed sentences about the cold and "Sir Hugh Dalrymple."

Rupert heard the name and sprang forward.

"A moment!" he cried. "What name was that he spoke?"

The bearers stopped at once, and Rupert ran to the man's side.

"Lower him a little," he said, and the suffering man was at once lowered.

"What name was that you spoke?" asked Rupert.

"Sir Hugh Dalrymple," whispered the man, in tremulous accents of great pain. "The sexton is a friend of his; don't trust him."

At the very moment he was speaking, Sir Hugh Dalrymple, who had escaped from the church by a side door, had hurriedly crept up to where the sexton was standing watching eagerly the attempts made to save his cottage; attempts, be it said, which turned out to be successful.

"Say not a word," whispered the villain, "say not a word. The vault is unharmed. See that it is locked and that no one touches it. Here are the keys. I will return to-morrow night at ten and meet you at the 'Chequers Inn;' a good reward shall be yours."

Then he turned and fled away into the night.

It is not necessary to speak of how the cottage was saved sufficiently to enable the old sexton to resume his dwelling in it, or how St. Andrew's church was almost levelled to the earth.

Suffice it to say that the whole population of the suburb of St. Andrew's, Chichester, was unable to fight against the huge conflagration, and that it was almost morning before they returned to their homes.

CHAPTER XXI.

THE OLD SEXTON MAKES AN ERROR.

On the following night old Thomas, who generally spent his whole time at the "Chequers," remained at home in spite of the admonition of Sir Hugh Dalrymple.

Over his glass, and with his welcome pipe, he sat by his wood fire, which blazed and crackled merrily up the chimney.

He was thinking of the strange events of the night before.

The quiet around was deathlike.

But Thomas was used to this.

His cottage was near the large gate, with its quaint awning, and its bell to ring in the dead.

And yet he lived, amid a cluster of tombstones.

The early inhabitants of St. Andrew had not reckoned that posterity would die as well as they, and the burying ground was so small that it was necessary to encroach upon what had been a kind of ornamental ground, around the sexton's dwelling.

Old Thomas had made no objection.

As long as he could remember he had been accustomed to death.

Death had been his companion, his employer, and it had no terror for him.

Yet a little sound from some object without startled him.

A deeper shade on the wall—a rustle as of gliding footsteps on a marble floor, and it was gone.

He was unused to the slightest noise in that lone spot, except a chance vehicle along the road; and now he had not noticed even a footfall.

Had any one approached, he felt sure he must have heard his coming, for the night was frosty, the ground hard, and in that deathly silence a pin-fall might have been detected.

He rose and looked out.

All was still.

The moon was high in a blue, clear sky, studded with stars.

The tombs looked white, weird, unearthly.

There a plain, stone slab; here an iron-nailed block of wood; here a tall pilaster standing in bold relief against the cold sky; here a mound of turf-covered earth, to show how the head that rested there was humble while it lived, to show, too, how man strives to keep up after death the hollow distinctions of life.

Clear away the headstones, break up your marble monuments, dig down two feet below, and level the ground.

Who, then, in searching shall distinguish noble from peasant, king from subject?

What are these headstones but tributes to regret—monuments to our own littleness.

Do we not place them there in sorrow because our life is so brief?

Do we not place them in fear lest the world should pass by in its wanderings and forget us for ever?

So old Thomas stood at his door and looked out.

But he could see nothing—hear nothing.

"Ah!" he said, "I must have made a mistake. However, I'll leave the door ajar, and listen."

He half closed it, and then, returning to his seat by the fire, resumed his pipe.

Whether it was the soothing effect of the fragrant tobacco, or the cool night air, I cannot say, but certainly the old man closed his eyes and dozed.

From this he was aroused by the rustle of feet once more, and, as he started, he caught sight of the shadow of a man's form in the doorway—deep, clear, unmistakable, as it fell between it and the moonlight.

Alarmed, and full of superstitious awe, Thomas sprang up, and rushed out into the night.

There was nothing to be seen.

All was again still, hushed as usual.

The sexton trembled.

"This is very dreadful," he murmured, as he wiped the cold drops of perspiration from his brow. "Me, an old man, too, and all alone. I don't half like it, and I wish I had gone to the inn."

He looked fearfully around him.

"Yet I don't know," he went on, "as anybody would harm me. There ain't no good to be got by it. An old man here like me, what has nothing to be robbed of, and has done no harm to no one. Put on your hat, Thomas, and go and see what it is, that's what I say."

So talking and murmuring to keep his courage up, the old man re-entered the cottage, took his hat and a stout stick, and walked out along the broad path towards the church, never dreaming that danger was before him.

Meanwhile, Sir Hugh Dalrymple, who had no idea of trusting the sexton at all, had approached the cottage at the very hour which he had appointed to meet Thomas at the "Chequers Inn."

Clambering over the churchyard railings, he went to the sexton's door.

Here he listened.

Old Thomas was talking to himself, and through the keyhole Sir Hugh Dalrymple saw him rise and approach the entrance.

Sir Hugh drew back, and hid himself among the tombstones.

"Hang the old fool," he muttered; "at this moment I made certain that he was at the 'Chequers Inn.'"

When the sexton, therefore, left the door open, and started at the sound of rustling feet, it was Sir Hugh who had entered and purloined from behind the door the heavy keys admitting to the vaults of the destroyed church.

Making his way, then, swiftly towards the ruins, he found the staircase leading to the vault of the Dalrymples.

This he descended quickly, and was soon in a stone chamber, with ledges round it, upon which were stowed away the ancestors of the family in stone coffins.

Placing his dark lantern on a ledge, he took from his pocket a short piece of iron, and prepared to force open the lid of one of the coffins.

It was that marked—

"Horace Dalrymple."

CHAPTER XXII.

THE FIGHT IN THE DEATH VAULT.

Any one less bold, or rather, any one less under the influence of semi-madness than Sir Hugh Dalrymple, would have trembled at the task he had set himself.

His idea, however, was to destroy the papers he had foolishly concealed in the coffin of his murdered brother, and to destroy also the skeleton upon whose fractured skull still rested the evidence of guilt.

So he resolutely worked away, driving back the feelings which every now and then sent a tremulous fear to his heart.

The coffin had originally had a key by which to open it.

This key, however, was now in the possession of Rupert Dreadnought, and nothing could, therefore, be done but wrench it open.

Sir Hugh Dalrymple was so intent upon his terrible work that he noticed nothing else.

With all his force he wrenched away at the stone-work, which presently yielded with a crash and split in several places.

For a moment Sir Hugh stood still, his chest heaving with intense agitation.

Then he placed down the piece of iron, and with an almost superhuman effort raised the lid.

Then he stood petrified.

The skin of the murdered corpse was still upon the face, while the head of the grinning skull was bare, and showed the fracture.

He gazed at this sight in horror, and his thoughts were just wandering back to the fearful night when he had committed the terrible deed, when a loud voice exclaimed—

"Sir Hugh Dalrymple, you have come to your own judgment."

Had a thunderbolt suddenly crashed through the ruins of the old church and riven the ground at his feet, it could not have taken a greater effect upon Sir Hugh than did these words.

He started back and clasped his hands.

A greenish pallor overspread his face.

His whole person trembled with emotion, and he raised his eyes slowly towards the spot where the sound proceeded.

What he saw proclaimed to him his doom.

There, standing on the stone steps, was Rupert Dreadnought.

With him were Allan of the Glen, Tom the waterman, and Henry Clanberris.

In an instant, his madness appeared to leave him, It fell from him like a film from his eyes.

Resolutely he spoke.

"What want you here, gentlemen?"

"You need no information on that score," replied Rupert Dreadnought. "This gentleman, Henry Clanberris, whose life you attempted, told you long since the reason of your appearance here. You are now about to be punished for the murder of your brother. If you wish to make your peace with Heaven, make it now."

A bitter smile crossed the lips of the man thus brought to bay.

He turned to Henry Clanberris.

"It is as I said," he cried; "it is no fair fight. It is assassination."

Clanberris would have answered, but Rupert interrupted him.

"You have been told that you are to have the free use of your sword to combat me," he cried. "Nevertheless, I feel my arm nerved to the combat—strengthened by justice; and though Henry Clanberris is to be your second, I see before you no chance of avoiding the just punishment of your sins. Come, gentlemen, close the door, and let us at once to work."

Sir Hugh Dalrymple saw death staring him in the face.

But he was resolved that the papers he desired to destroy or save from others should never fall into the hands of his foes.

With a sudden dash, therefore, he seized the documents which were lying near the dead man's side, and rushing to the flame of the open lantern thrust them in.

To attempt to save them was useless.

Brittle and dry with age, they flashed up into a flame at once, and evaporated in fire and smoke long before any one could reach out his hands to prevent the catastrophe.

"What papers are those you have just burned?" cried Rupert, angrily.

"Papers which I desired should not fall into your hands," replied Sir Hugh Dalrymple. "What they are will never be known either to you or your friends. Secrets whose knowledge would be useful to those who hate me I will never betray. Come, I am ready for this ordeal."

He said these words with considerable courage.

He had recognised the uselessness of resistance, and had strung up his nerves to meet his fate, or, if possible, to gain the combat.

Some men would have given up the case as useless, and have begged and implored for mercy.

But Sir Hugh Dalrymple, though regarding Rupert as an inplacable foe, still recognised in him one who would keep his word.

If he could kill Rupert, therefore, he was free.

So the two antagonists placed themselves into position.

Tom the waterman sat on the staircase to prevent escape or to warn of the approach of any one.

Allan of the Glen ranged himself on the side of Rupert, while Henry Clanberris, according to his promise, took his position as the second of Sir Hugh Dalrymple.

"Now then, my friends," said Rupert, ere the swords crossed, "listen to me. I am not carrying out any quarrel of my own, I am but fulfilling a mission which by a vow I have taken upon myself to perform. So let there be no interference. Let me alone take the brunt of this affair. If I fail, I must die."

Then he turned towards his antagonist.

"Now then," he said, "now then I am ready."

The contest was but similar to all those through which our hero had passed, but it was rendered somewhat different by the peculiar surroundings of the place.

The gloomy vault, the coffins, the stone sarcophagus holding the bones of the murdered man, all were illumined only by the weird light of the torch which Tom the waterman held in his hand, and the feeble rays emitted by the lantern which Sir Hugh Dalrymple had brought with him.

It was a most unpleasant place to choose for a combat of any kind.

The smell of the recent conflagration was not yet gone; the heat had not quite dried up the darkness of the place, but had settled it in steam upon the walls and the ceiling.

There was an unpleasant smell, consequently; a kind of misty atmosphere, which penetrated the nostrils and raised a kind of dimness before the vision.

Nevertheless, despite all difficulties, they fought on; both very calmly and deliberately, without any false moves, looking in each other's eyes to avoid any unskilful movements.

Such a conflict became at length only a question of endurance.

He who first felt his wrist becoming weakened was the one who must first succumb.

In stature Rupert Dreadnought was quite a match for his antagonist.

But not in bodily build.

Sir Hugh Dalrymple, both from his age and the wild adventurous life he had led, was a stouter and heavier man.

But he was unable to keep his temper as well.

The thought that he was there alone with three men, all of whom desired his death, no matter how honest and straightforward might be their actions, seemed to enrage him.

He consequently rapidly lost command over himself, and made frequent and angry dashes at his adversary.

Rupert Dreadnought received all these coolly.

He did not care for delay.

There was no immediate necessity for hurry.

He took no notice of his adversary's lunges than was required to parry them, and to watch for a favourable opportunity to drive his sword home.

At length the opportunity presented itself.

A false step brought Sir Hugh Dalrymple within such an easy distance of Rupert's sword that it entered the fleshy part of his arm.

This enraged the fratricide, and, with a yell, he sprang forward—forgetting all principles of fencing—and whirling his sword round his head to deal a savage downward blow.

This Rupert Dreadnought, however, easily parried, and had just the chance he required.

Rushing in, ere Sir Hugh could recover himself, he dashed in rapidly, and his keen blade flashed through the yielding flesh.

"SEE—SEE! HE COMES!" CRIED MARY MACPHERSON.

There was a cry of horror and pain from the stricken man.

Then his sword fell from his grasp, he staggered backwards a few paces, and fell heavily to the ground.

He was not quite dead when he fell.

But his game was over.

It was easy to see that.

His hands clutched at the yielding earth beneath him.

His glazing eyes rolled hither and thither as if for aid, and, when his second approached, he leaned his head heavily on his knee.

"It is all over with me," he murmured. "Heaven have mercy on me."

This was all he said.

The power of speech was gone.

One glassy stare more!

One shiver of the convulsed limbs!

Then all was over.

"Now," said Rupert, pointing to the stone coffin, "now, my friends, we must raise this skeleton, and place the parricide at the bottom of the coffin. So will my vow be fulfilled."

Taking out as gently as they could the bones of the murdered dead, they deposited them on the ground.

Then they raised the still warm but lifeless body of Sir Hugh Dalrymple, and placed him within the stone coffin.

After this the bones were replaced, and the coffin lid let down.

Upon the lid was then carved, in rude but easily distinguishable characters, the words—

"MURDERER AND MURDERED LIE SIDE BY SIDE. SEE THE RETRIBUTION OF HEAVEN!"

Rupert was much moved.

"Come, my friends," he said, in a hoarse voice. "Come, let us leave this place. The air of it now oppresses me. There is an atmosphere of blood within it which, in spite of my eagerness to carry out my vow, is far from agreeable to me."

Without further words, he began the ascent of the staircase, and passed through the door which Tom the waterman had opened for him.

The air was very cool, the sky dark, and Rupert, overwhelmed with sad thoughts, walked slowly and solemnly among the tombs.

"My friends," he said, when they had reached the high road, "my friends, you have seen that I have fulfilled my mission, and for your assistance in it I thank and shall reward you. But now I would be alone. This constant bloodshed weighs upon my mind."

"Whither go you, then?" asked Allan of the Glen.

"To London."

"And I?"

"Can go whither you please. It will be some weeks before I open the THIRD COMPARTMENT OF THE IRON CHEST, for I fear lest some deadly vengeance may not be again exacted at my hands."

"I shall gladly, then, take advantage of your leave," said Allan of the Glen, "to find my mistress."

"In that case," said Rupert, "you had better all travel by separate routes. I go to London."

"And I to Finchley by London."

"Our roads are the same, our destination the same, then," said Henry Clanberris. "We could have gone together, but Master Dreadnought's wishes shall be obeyed."

It was not long before, after a warm leave-taking, the leaders and retainers started *en route*.

We must follow now the fortunes of Allan of the Glen.

CHAPTER XXIII.

IN WHICH ALLAN OF THE GLEN PROCEEDS IN SEARCH OF MARY MACPHERSON.

ALLAN OF THE GLEN was nothing loth to have such a leave of absence as that now granted him by Rupert Dreadnought.

For his master he felt the utmost friendship and gratitude.

He had been the first to offer him a helping hand.

Ever since he had treated him like a friend, when he might have treated him like a master.

However, even the gentle rein held by Rupert had prevented him from carrying out any object of his own, and he felt now a sensation of release.

The horse which he procured at the nearest inn was the gallant steed which had brought him to the town of Chichester.

He was fresh now from his temporary release from work, and as soon as he felt his master on his back he went prancing away at a splendid rate on the road to London.

On his road he passed a horseman riding very slowly.

He seemed absorbed in his own thoughts, and did not even observe Allan of the Glen as he passed.

But Allan knew him.

It was Rupert Dreadnought.

Knowing well that the latter had no desire to be disturbed, and in fact might be angered by his joining company with him after his decided prohibition, Allan rode swiftly by without even a word or a bow of recognition.

The country near Chichester was very lonely, and as soon as practicable, therefore, Allan of the Glen put up at an inn.

It was not many miles from the spot where he had passed Rupert, and ere he retired to rest he gazed from his window and saw the muffled form of his friend and master riding slowly by.

His journey to London would be very uninteresting.

We must hurry him across Old London Bridge, therefore, and introduce him again to our readers when we find him riding once more into the wood near the house where Lady Clanberris was waiting impatiently news of her husband's death or safety.

It was early morning.

The dew was just drying beneath the warmth of the morning sun.

It was, of course, too early to commence anything like a search, or to ask any question in the neighbourhood.

So he resolved to rest awhile.

First he fastened to a tree his faithful steed.

It had borne him many miles that night, and was as fatigued as himself.

Then he took off his plaid, spread it on the ground, and laid himself down beneath the shadow of a tree.

He was used to this.

In his life he had roughed it greatly.

A sleep in the wild woods, therefore, was far more to his taste than a slumber between the sheets of a civilised bed.

So in a few moments he was fast asleep.

It was now that something happened which proved that he had not been very observant on the journey.

No sooner was it absolutely certain that he *was* fast locked in slumber than some stealthy forms emerged from among the trees.

Slowly they approached him.

One of them was a man who belonged evidently to the higher class. This one was masked.

The others were burly ruffians of the lowest stamp, who had no compunction in showing their brutal features to the bright light of day.

They approached their victim with rapid steps.

But they were noiseless on the soft, dewy grass.

The leader stood somewhat aloof, while one approached to see if the sleeper were really so far locked in slumber as they imagined.

This man bent over him, saw by his hard breathing that he was quite unconscious of all things around, and, pointing to his recumbent body, beckoned his companions to approach.

This they did in a body.

Suddenly surrounding him, they seized him before he had time to put his hand to his sword, and in a few moments he was a helpless prisoner.

The leader then approached, and kneeling down by the side of the captive, bent over him and slightly removed his mask.

Allan knew the features at once.

They were those of Oscar Penraven.

"The vengeance is about to begin," said Oscar; "you have escaped us long, but now we shall crush you beneath our feet. Where is your master?"

"Do you mean Rupert Dreadnought?"

"Yes."

"I know not."

"And where is Sir Hugh Dalrymple?"

"That villain, then, is a friend of yours?" exclaimed Allan of the Glen.

Oscar frowned.

"I am not here to be questioned," he said; "I am here to ask questions. Where is Sir Hugh Dalrymple? I repeat."

"And I can say nothing but that I believe him to be dead."

"By whose hand, then, did he fall?" said Oscar Penraven.

"That," said Allan of the Glen, "is a secret, and shall remain so. I know by whose hand he died, but I shall keep the knowledge for ever to myself."

Oscar Penraven might have proceeded with his questioning, but the stern resolution visible on Allan's face proved how little use it would be.

He sprang to his feet.

"Off with him, my men," he said; "you understand the spot. When night falls he can easily and safely be removed."

The men at once raised him in their arms and bore him away, one of their number having first gagged him, lest his cries for help might rouse the few passers-by.

They did not go far.

They simply bore him to a denser part of the forest, and into a kind of alcove formed by interwoven bushes.

Here, after a time, food was brought to him, and here he remained until evening.

As soon as it grew dark, Oscar Penraven once more made his appearance.

He made some mysterious communication to his men.

Then Allan of the Glen was once more gagged, seized, and borne away.

The appearance of the place to which he was carried when they reached the high road appeared to him strangely familiar.

It seemed, in fact, just similar to the house where Sir Hugh Dalrymple had been seized, and where Rupert had allowed him a last interview with his wife.

Here, then, a kind of hope entered the bosom of the young Scotch boy.

Even if he had been ungagged, however, he would have made no remark, but waited on events.

CHAPTER XXIV.

MARY MACPHERSON TO THE RESCUE.

Arrived at the gate of the house where Lady Dalrymple resided for the time, Allan was passed in by the postern, and led into a room at the summit of the house—a room with a window strengthened by iron bars.

Here his chains were removed, and his gag removed.

"You will have to remain here until the council has decided what to do with you," replied one of the men to a question put to him by the Scotch boy.

"What council?" demanded Allan in surprise.

"The dread tribunal which you so often have had cause to fear, which pursues to this moment your master, Rupert Dreadnought, and whose vengeance will fall upon all who aid him," returned the man, solemnly.

Allan smiled jeeringly.

"You allude to the Poisoners, I presume," he said, "the infamous crew who have so long been a scourge to London. I fear them not."

"Have a care of insolence," returned the man. "You are in their power."

"I defy them."

"They could order you now to be put to death."

"Nevertheless I say again I defy them. Providence will deliver me out of their hands," returned Allan of the Glen, resolutely; "but, since it is the desire of the council that I should be kept a certain time waiting for their decision, perhaps you will be kind enough to send me food and wine, for I am hungry."

"One of the attendants shall at once bring you in some refreshment," said the man pompously; and so saying, he made a sign to his men, and they all filed out of the room.

As soon as they had departed, Allan had time to look about him.

The room he was in was not *very* small, but it was one in which no degree of comfort was apparent.

The window, in the first place, was barred, as I have said.

The view below showed that the chamber was high up from the ground.

The walls were of plaster, and cracked and dirty.

A plain wooden table, a plain wooden chair, and a bench completed the furniture, with the exception of *one* thing.

This was a picture.

A terrible picture for a prisoner to continually gaze at!

It represented a scaffold.

Upon the block a victim had laid his head, and above it was uplifted the gleaming axe of the headsman.

In this cheerful abode Allan had not remained long when the door opened, and a female form made its appearance.

The room was illumined only by the feeble rays of a grimy lamp suspended in one corner.

But Allan of the Glen recognised at once the face and figure.

They were the face and figure of Mary Macpherson.

She placed her finger on her lips as she approached.

"Speak not," she said; "to speak would be dangerous until I have been in a second time. Wait and hope till morning."

In spite of this warning, Allan of the Glen could not resist pressing her warm, rich lips as she bent down to place the comestibles on the table.

Mary blushed and smiled, and lovingly returned the pressure, whispering—

"Dear Allan, fear nothing; you will be saved."

Then she tripped away, and left him once more alone.

But he was not devoid of hope now.

He knew Lady Dalrymple to be the friend of Mary, and she would therefore, of necessity, be a friend to him.

After partaking of the good and substantial meal set before him, without paying any attention to the fact that the viands might be poisoned, Allan accordingly stretched himself fearlessly on the wooden bench and, soldier-like, was soon asleep.

When morning dawned, he anxiously awaited the arrival of Mary Macpherson.

Time seemed to pass by on leaden wings, but at length the tramp of feet was heard, and the key was once more turned in the lock.

He glanced eagerly towards it, grasping his sword, which, with unaccountable negligence, they had left to him.

But he had no cause of fear.

The new comer was Mary Macpherson.

She closed the door gently behind her, and approached her lover.

Allan drew her down upon his knee, and kissed her fondly.

"Prison is no prison where *you* are," he said, tenderly.

"Ah! but of what use is love in such a place as this?" she answered. "*I* pine for freedom, *I* who am no captive. I long for my native hills—my free mountain air. How must *you* feel who fancy yourself in a prison?"

Allan smiled.

"Fancy!" he said; "I fear it is no fancy."

"Yes; it *is* but fancy after all," returned Mary Macpherson, in a whisper.

"How *can* it be so?" asked Allan in amazement.

"Oscar Penraven," continued Mary, whose whispers were drowned almost to others from the fact that she was so closely nestling on her lover's breast. "Oscar Penraven has no conception that Sir Hugh Dalrymple is unloved by his wife. He fancies that she would gladly join in punishing those who have destroyed him. He knows nothing, moreover, of the fact that I am your betrothed wife."

"Well."

"He has explained his plan fully to Lady Dalrymple, and she advised him at once to place you in safe custody here."

"And does he suspect anything?"

"Nothing."

"Why then can I not escape at once?" asked Allan.

"Simply because at the present moment there are several of his men in the house," said Mary Macpherson. "We heard him give them instructions; all save one to quit the place in three hours upon some expedition, of what nature I know not. At any rate, there will be but one person in the house to guard you."

"And then I can escape, and you will fly with me to London," said Allan, eagerly.

He pressed her still more warmly to his heart as he spoke.

Mary blushed deeply.

"Yes, yes," she said; "both I and Lady Dalrymple will fly to London. She is very kind to me, and I wish to remain with her. In a few minutes I expect Henry Clanberris to arrive."

"He is her lover!"

"Yes, long and devotedly he has loved. Hark! what is that?"

She sprang from his knee, and gazed out of window.

"See, see," she cried, pointing through the casement towards a horseman who was dashing along at full speed. "See, here he comes."

Allan had risen, and now stood beside her, leaning on his sword.

As they stood thus, they observed not a slight noise near them. But so it was.

The door opened gently, *almost* noiselessly behind them.

Then a face peered in.

They still stood unobservant.

"Ah!" thought the new comer, "I will enter and listen."

The one who now entered was a young girl of some seventeen years, tall and finely formed.

But her face spoilt her.

It was the face of a traitress.

Small eyes, a sharp, thin nose, sharp, thin lips, cadaverous-coloured skin.

Such was the picture.

She had always hated Mary Macpherson.

Her beauty and her goodness raised spite and malice in her evil heart.

Now there seemed a chance of taking her revenge.

He had been deprived of her by a man whom she hated.

He had seen *her* sorrow and *his* crime, and knew well, too, how she loved him.

He regarded her husband solely as a hateful obstacle, which Heaven's justice had removed.

So on he sped on the wings of love, and though arriving many hours after Allan of the Glen, he had yet hardly rested on his way.

Rupert had especially enjoined upon them that they were all to proceed by different routes, and they had obeyed his instructions.

Henry Clanberris, therefore, had come by a longer route, and, having arrived so soon after Allan, he was tired and travel-stained.

But who shall restrain the impatience of love?

Casting his rein to the man who came to the door, he was about to dash upstairs, when the latter said—

"Master Clanberris, have a care."

"Of what?"

"Of your enemies."

"There are none here."

The man approached near.

"You know one Oscar Penraven?"

"I know him well. But what of him? He knows not that I am here—he knows not, or if he *does* know, he is an enemy of Lady Dalrymple."

"He *is*," whispered the man; "but he is not aware of the fact that she knows him to be a foe. He knows only that Sir Hugh Dalrymple was a friend, and he fancies that his widow would desire to avenge him. Now, does this man know you by sight?"

"He does not."

"Then take my advice; disguise yourself as one of the retainers, and let the tide of events roll on."

Henry Clanberris stared.

This was, indeed, a strange kind of servant.

He spoke as one far above him in station.

Yet, disguised or not, he looked like an ordinary retainer.

"You *are* not what you seem," said Henry Clanberris. "You may, for aught I know, be a traitor. Stay! take no offence. Even now you were warning me against treachery. Why should I not suspect you?"

The man smiled.

It was an honest smile—the smile of a true man!

"You speak truly," he said; "why should you not suspect me? I can give *no* answer, except to say that I must leave all to you. I know that I am acting for the good of you and yours, and if you connot trust me I cannot blame you."

Henry Clanberris took his hand.

"I believe you to be honest," he said; "I read it in your eyes; but tell me, you *are* disguised—you are *no* servant."

"There you are right," said the man; "I am an old friend of Henry Clanberris; I need say no more. So now come in with me, and we will choose a disguise."

They entered together, and the man at once led Henry Clanberris into a side room, where there were a number of clothes and strange costumes of all sorts.

Some of them were the last relics of the fire,

Saved from old store-rooms promiscuously, and hurried to friends' houses.

"Now," said the mysterious man, the strange friend of Henry Clanberris, "now, if you will but follow my advice, you are safe."

Henry Clanberris would have taken any advice so that he was enabled quickly to see the one he loved.

"What *is* your advice, then?" he said.

"You see yonder costume?"

"Yes."

"It is that of the retainers of Sir Hugh Dalrymple."

"Well?"

"You are not too proud to take the character for a while."

"I am not. Quick. Say, what do you desire me to do?"

"Dress yourself in that costume as rapidly as you can, then await the time of Oscar Penraven's departure, and then——"

"Well, then?"

"You are at liberty to act as you please," returned the man.

"Good," replied Henry Clanberris, "I will do as you wish, although I like not anything which keeps me so long from her."

"Never mind," returned the other, as he busied himself in preparing the clothes for Henry Clanberris's wearing, "never mind. It is better to see her safely than to rush precipitately into danger. When Oscar Penraven is gone, you can fly at once."

Henry Clanberris, eager as he was to clasp to his heart the form of the one he adored, saw of course the reasonableness of this argument, and quickly moved himself into the clothes.

Then he quitted the room and followed his mysterious friend into another, where he sat down by a fire with a book he pretended to read.

Time went slowly by.

People flittered in and out of the room.

But no one observed him.

If they spoke he shammed sleep.

It was but two hours' delay which he had to endure.

It seemed a week.

At length a familiar voice spoke.

"Now, then, Master Clanberris, are you ready?"

It was the voice of his mysterious friend that uttered these words.

He started up eagerly.

"Yes," he said, "I am ready."

"Follow me, then."

"Is Oscar Penraven gone?"

"Yes; he has just left with all but one retainer. Come."

Eagerly Henry Clanberris ascended the stairs, and entered the room where Lady Dalrymple was sitting.

For an instant she did not recognise him in his disguise.

Then she rose with a strange smile, saying—

"I am glad you have come, Henry."

The words were said oddly and slowly, as if she knew the position to be an awkward one.

Henry Clanberris fondly clasped the hand extended to him, and raised it to his lips.

"Yes, dearest Margaret," he said; "I am here to save you. You are now a widow, and to the widow of such a man I need not mind speaking, even so soon after her husband's death. I come to save you, as I have said, but I came also because I love you."

Lady Dalrymple blushed.

"Oh, speak not now of that," she said.

"And why?"

"Because my brain is in a whirl; I know not what I am doing; you can forgive me for it, I know; but when all is over, when my mind is in a state of quiescence, I may then find courage to say, 'I love you too, dear Henry.'"

He took no notice of her words, but advancing towards her, clasped her in his arms, and imprinted a passionate kiss upon her lips.

Her resolution now gave way, and she sank impassive into his arms.

"You love me?" he whispered, as he pressed her still closer to his breast.

"Yes, yes," she said, "I do; I confess it. But ask me no more now. Tell me, what are your plans?"

"I wish to go to London at once. You are not safe here."

"Yes, I will go," she said; "that is our best place. I have those here who will watch me because they deem me unable to guard myself against the world; in other words, because they imagine me to have been instrumental in my husband's death. God knows I am innocent of that, and can even regret that he died so suddenly and so unprepared."

"Is it true," said Henry Clanberris, who desired to change the subject, "is it true that Allan of the Glen is here?"

"Yes, he is below."

She rose from the sofa to which he had drawn her, and rang the bell.

In a moment the mysterious friend made his appearance.

"What is your ladyship's wish?" he asked, with all humility.

"Is Oscar Penraven completely out of the way?" asked Lady Dalrymple, eagerly.

"Yes; his form passed over the hills long since. I watched him and his men from our topmost window, and, unless they fly, they cannot return under half an hour."

"And his retainer?"

"He is below in the room."

"Does he suspect anything?"

"Nothing."

"Well, then, we must to work at once. Mary Macpherson has the key of his cell; *she* will release him."

At this moment there was a gentle tap at the door.

"Come in," said Lady Dalrymple.

Her voice trembled.

She feared lest even now some unknown danger might be threatening her.

The door now opened and Mary Macpherson entered.

Her face was very pale, and her bosom heaved with intense agitation.

"There is danger afloat," she said.

"Where?"

"In this very house," replied the girl. "Rose Alford, my enemy, is concocting a scheme of villany between herself and Colin, who is the worst enemy that Allan of the Glen has in the world."

"How know you this?" asked Lady Dalrymple.

"I overheard their villanous conversation," returned the agitated girl.

"And is their plan to betray us?"

"No, it is to poison Allan and myself, and for this treacherous act Rose Alford has the promise of being made Colin's wife."

Lady Dalrymple smiled.

"We can foil their plans then easily," she said. "Do you," she added to the mysterious friend of Henry Clanberris, "proceed directly with Master Clanberris, and gag and bind the retainer which Oscar Penraven has left here on the watch."

"But Colin?" urged Mary Macpherson.

"You will then proceed to the cell of Allan of the Glen and release him. Then we will quit this house together, and leave Rose Alford and Colin alone."

"But in regard to their pursuit of us. They can release the retainer from his bonds, and put him on our track."

"True, both of them had best be bound also," said Henry Clanberris. "We will leave word (when we have two miles start) at the inn on the roadside that there are prisoners in the house. They will then be released when it is far too late to pursue us."

This scheme was at once put into execution.

Henry Clanberris at once descended with his mysterious assistant, and gently entered the room where Oscar Penraven's man was waiting.

He was nodding in his chair.

Never, therefore, observing their entrance, he started both in surprise and anger when he found his arms seized.

His hand flew naturally to his sword.

But it was of no avail.

Henry Clanberris was binding his arms, while the other was pressing the cold barrel of a pistol to his forehead.

"Who are you, and what want you?" he cried.

He had never seen either of them before.

"We are no enemies of yours, and desire to save you trouble," said Henry Clanberris. "You are the retainer of Oscar Penraven, who is our greatest enemy. We shall not harm you so that you do not resist."

The man saw that they meant him no harm.

Besides, he saw the impossibility of resistance.

RUPERT DREADNOUGHT.

"THE STRANGER FELL HEADLONG TO THE FLOOR."

So he remained quite still while they gagged and bound him.

Then they secured him in a chair, so that it was quite impossible for him to move, and proceeded to dispose of those who were more easily managed.

They imagined, of course, that they would find Colin in his room of sickness with the traitress Rose

Afford by his side. In this, however, they were disappointed.

When they entered the apartment where they expected to find the conspirators they were not there.

A chill invaded their hearts.

Perhaps they were even now too late.

The wretches might already be carrying out their nefarious design.

Rushing down towards Allan's place of confinement they quickly opened the door and entered.

As they did so they beheld a sight which quite carried out the suspicions of Mary Macpherson, but at the same time assured them that there was no immediate fear.

Rose Afford was engaged in laying out upon the table a tempting repast, while Colin, even then hovering at death's door, was endeavouring to prove to Allan of the Glen the sincerity of his friendship.

The words, however, which he had heard fall from the lips of Mary Macpherson, when Rose Afford had entered the room on a former occasion, were sufficient to prove to him how little faith he could place in their professions, let them be ever so plausible.

Colin was just pouring out a glass of wine for Allan, when Henry Clanberris and his mysterious friend entered the cell.

Clanberris rushed forward.

"Hold, Allan!" he cried, "there is death in the cup, drink not!"

The guilty pair turned towards the speaker in as much astonishment as fear and anger.

It seemed truly astounding that their secret plans should thus publicly be known to their enemies.

Allan sprang up.

He was about to dash the wine in Colin's face, when Henry Clanberris restrained him.

"Stay," he said, as he quietly locked the door on the inside, and advanced towards the table, "stay, I have a better way of disposing of that wine than the one *you* propose. Colin—I know you by no other name—and you, Rose Afford, is it true that, failing to destroy Allan of the Glen here by any other means, you formed the project of poisoning him?"

Rose raised her hand aloft in token of her surprise and horror.

Colin concealed *his* emotion under the semblance of extreme and sudden pain from his recent wounds.

"Poison!" cried the girl, with well-assumed disgust and abhorrence. "We never dreamed of such a thing. I don't know the gentleman, and why then should I wish to kill him?"

"You love Colin here?"

"Yes."

"*He* hates Allan of the Glen?"

"I don't know. That's got nothing to do with me."

"It has. You are speaking falsely. We know, from good authority, your infamous compact. You have consented to aid Colin here in the destruction of Allan of the Glen, on the condition that as soon as he is well he will marry you."

"It is false—a base, treacherous lie!" cried the girl, wringing her hands.

Her courage was now beginning gradually but surely to desert her.

She saw that she was discovered.

She had, in fact, seen this from the very beginning of the scene.

She now saw more.

The stern implacable faces of Henry Clanberris and his companion told her what mercy she and her base lover could expect.

"Good," returned Clanberris, "you deny it all."

"We do, we do," said the girl and Colin, as with one breath.

Clanberris turned to his companions with a strange smile.

"We may be wrong," he said, "but it is easy of proof, and I should be very sorry to punish persons unjustly. Since the wine and the food you have brought here is not poisoned, pledge the health of the prisoner whom we are about to release. Here, Colin, is the wine which you intended for Allan. Drink."

The traitor had expected that something of this kind would be demanded of him.

Yet the order came upon him with a crushing weight.

A ghastly pallor overspread his blood-stained and haggard features.

"I drink no wine," he said; "in my wounded state such drinks are suicidal. I will eat, but not drink."

A stern, terrible determination was visible on the face of Henry Clanberris.

"Colin," he said, "I am for the moment your judge. If I left you here when I fled from the place, I should leave you free to escape within a few hours. No one would know the fearful and cowardly crime you intended, and you would escape for ever the retribution due to your crime. Now, however, as both you and your companion here have been discovered in a base attempt to destroy a friend of mine, I constitute myself your judge. If this wine is not poisoned you can suffer no harm; if it *be* poisoned, a just death is yours. Time presses; drink."

Colin glanced round him.

There was no hope.

He and Rose Afford, his treacherous accomplice, were in the hands of three strong and resolute men.

What could he do?

He took the glass.

Rose knew it would be her turn next, and fell upon her knees.

"I drink to your Eternal Destruction. Curses on you here and hereafter," cried the traitor.

Then he hesitated.

"Give me a sword," he said, "and let me fight for my life."

"No," replied Clanberris; "your refusal to drink condemns you as poisoners. Into your own trap you have fallen. Die, then, by the potion you prepared for the innocent. Drink!"

There was now no further use in delay.

Perfect silence reigned everywhere.

Oscar Penraven had gone to London, was now many miles distant, and had no intention of returning for two days.

There was nothing for it but to yield.

Death in its cruellest form had overtaken the traitor.

Better death then at his own hands, than death forced upon him by his enemies.

"The curses of a dying man light upon you then," he cried, as he raised his glass to his lips. "Courage, Rose; it is but an instant and all is over."

Then casting a look of intense hatred at his self-appointed judges, the wretched poisoner drained the glass to the dregs.

Having done this, he replaced the glass on the table and sat down.

The deadly liquid was not long in taking its effect.

The eyes quickly became glassy—the lips turned of a blueish tint—the hue of death overspread the whole features, and then with a gasp and a gurgle the traitor gave up the ghost.

His hands clenched, his limbs quivered, and his head fell forward upon the table.

"Our task is half ended," said Henry Clanberris, solemnly. "Now, Rose Afford, you have seen the fate of your companion in guilt. Prepare to share it at once."

The girl, still on her knees, threw her head back, clasped her hands, and glanced at her judges in wild entreaty.

"Oh, mercy, mercy!" she cried; "as you hope for mercy grant it."

"There is *no* mercy for murderers," answered Henry Clanberris. "Drink."

And he profferred her a glass of the rich red wine, so bright and so deceptive.

"No, no! I cannot—I will not!" she shrieked, wildly. "Oh! mercy!—no, no!—will no one help me? I cannot—I will not drink!"

And she grovelled upon the ground in a shapeless heap.

Henry Clanberris made a sign to his friends.

In a moment they stooped down, and, despite her struggles, raised her from the ground, and placed her in a chair, where her head sank upon her breast.

"Rose Afford," said Henry Clanberris, "were we to leave you to be dealt with by the laws of your country, you would escape punishment, because, for certain reasons, we should not wish to come forward to denounce you. We know your crime—we know you to be guilty, and we are resolved that you shall die by the poison you intended for another. One more strong-willed than you has been compelled to yield. See, he sits dead beside you! Drink!"

The girl was now roused to madness by the utter impossibility of escape.

Seeing the bottle of poisoned wine before her, she dashed it wildly to the ground in the hope of destroying it, and thus effectually preventing the enforcement of Henry Clanberris's threat. But this was useless.

The glass of wine—enough to harrow up her vitals—was already poured out, and was in the hand of Henry Clanberris.

"Curses on you, villains—cowards!" she shrieked. "Heaven will punish you for this!"

"Drink," said Clanberris.

He suffered her not to touch the glass.

He guessed at once what would be the result if he did so.

While the mysterious friend who accompanied him, therefore, kept down her hands, Henry Clanberris held her head and pressed the glass to her lips.

With bubbling curses the wretched creature then swallowed the draught, and when she had done so fell back in hysterics on the floor.

From these she never recovered.

Justice was soon appeased, for swiftly the bright, deceitful eyes closed, the red lips whitened, the pretty limbs stiffened, and Rose Afford had passed from this world to join the traitor who had planned with her the dastardly attack on Allan's life!

"A sad scene," said Allan, as he raised the body of the wretched woman, and placed it on a chair by the side of Colin. "Would that we could have been more tender-hearted."

A sneer passed over the lips of Henry Clanberris.

"Tenderness of heart towards criminals is an incitement to crime," he said. "No, no; the world is well rid of such wretches, no matter what sternness is required to accomplish it. Come, let us leave them here, and quit as soon as possible this scene of infamy and horror."

Nothing loth, Allan and the other left the chamber with Clanberris, and hurried up to the apartment where Lady Dalrymple and Mary Macpherson were awaiting them with all anxiety.

"Ah! my young preserver," cried Lady Dalrymple, as Allan approached her, "you are, then, safe?"

"Yes, madam, though my friends came but just in time to save me. Another moment and they would have been too late."

A brief explanation, which sent a thrill of horror through the breasts both of Lady Dalrymple and Mary Macpherson, was then given, and then all haste was made to the stables.

Here they procured four horses, and within ten minutes they were galloping away at full speed along the high road to London.

Here Lady Dalrymple and Mary Macpherson took refuge in the house of a friend, and the two couples parted in greater happiness than had been theirs for many a long day.

END OF BOOK III.

BOOK IV.

THE THIRD COMPARTMENT OF THE IRON CHEST.

CHAPTER I.

IN WHICH AN OLD FRIEND IS INTRODUCED, AND SEES A PHANTOM, WHICH TURNS OUT TO BE TOO SUBSTANTIAL AFTER ALL.

I HAVE no doubt that there are few of my readers who have not recognised, in the pale, ghastly-looking man who on several occasions befriended Rupert Dreadnought, Gascoigne, the police spy, whose death had been apparently consummated by Oscar Penraven, at the command of the Chief of the Poisoners.

It was he who had so materially assisted on the night when, at the old house near the river, Rupert Dreadnought had rescued Helen Penraven from the hands of her villanous cousin.

He had escaped the attack made upon him by Oscar Penraven in a most miraculous manner.

The wound inflicted was, of course, a most deadly one, and he had fainted from the effects of it.

But he was not dead.

When the Chief of the Poisoners and the others entered, therefore, and, opening the trap-door, flung him from the room down a seemingly fathomless abyss, the plunge into the cold water revived him, and, with the strong instinct of self-preservation, he struck out.

The water in the usual course of events was very deep in the pit that yawned for the victims of the hideous crew.

But on this occasion there had been a very low tide, and consequently the part where the waters of the river entered was almost exposed to view.

When the body of Gascoigne fell, therefore, it lived far down and ascended outside among the rushing waters of the River Thames.

Here a few feeble strokes brought him to some floating pieces of timber.

Upon these he crawled.

His strength sufficed him so far and no farther, and, clinging on with the grim grasp of a dying man, he lost consciousness.

He awoke to find himself in bed and well cared for, and, when fully restored to health, he swore a terrible oath to be avenged upon the Society.

He would drop his identity and fight them as they fought the world—in the dark.

In the recent adventures in which Rupert Dreadnought had been engaged, Gascoigne had not figured.

He had, in fact, been engaged in a twofold manner.

He had been gathering health in the first place.

In the second place he had been steadily and secretly on the watch.

He had discovered many things during this interval of quiet.

He had found out the new retreat of the Poisoners, a pleasant country spot in Essex, on the banks of the river, as before described.

He had seen them going to and fro, and among those most frequent in their visits were Rosalie St. Aubyn, the man with the red gleaming eyes who had claimed to be Allan's father, and Oscar Penraven.

Gascoigne knew well from Alford (or Richard Penraven, as we might properly call him) the whole of her infamous career, and, somehow or another, he connected the assault on him by Oscar Penraven with the influence of this beautiful demon.

We have not seen anything of her since, through the instrumentality of Redlock, Alford and Lesbia escaped from her house.

She had now quite recovered from the wound inflicted upon her by Lesbia Howard, and had, as I have said, resumed actively her connection with the Poisoners.

What Gascoigne noticed as being so peculiar was that on her return from the house of the Poisoners she was always accompanied by a gentleman—never the same one.

These persons went with her to her house, but they never returned.

He watched once for days, but all he saw was that the victims (for such he believed them to be) entered and never departed.

He resolved, therefore, at the peril of his life, to enter the house and discover its hideous secrets.

He waited one evening until the shades had fallen, and he had seen the fair demon take her way from the house.

Then he crept over into the grounds, and made his way to a point where he had particularly observed an open window.

It was always open up to a certain hour, as if to serve as a signal for some one.

Near it grew a poplar, whose lithe trunk swayed almost into it.

Up this tree the active man clambered until he came opposite the casement.

Then he took from his pocket a rope with a noose at the end of it, like a lasso.

This he adroitly threw over the post of a bedstead within, and then, dropping himself, came with a bump against the wall.

Undismayed by danger, and the bruises he had

received, he clambered up once more and was soon within the room.

The chamber in which he now found himself was very small.

It was, in fact, nothing but a servant's bedroom.

But the door was open, and Gascoigne knew well how to proceed.

He was just about to pass out into the corridor, when he heard footsteps approaching, and he had hardly time to conceal himself beneath the bed when a young female domestic entered, and going up to the window closed it.

"Just in time," thought Gascoigne; "another moment and I should have been too late."

The girl did not remain long, and after a few minutes of suspense Gascoigne was once more alone.

He waited until her footsteps died away in the distance, and then he quitted the room and passed down the corridor to a staircase which seemed to lead to the grand apartments.

Here he boldly entered one of the chambers and ensconced himself in a recess behind some deep folds of heavy tapestry.

It might be supposed that being thus in the house of an enemy—in the very den of a crue- and bloodthirsty murl deress—he would have experienced a tremulous feeling at the heart, and would have watched eagerly hour after hour.

It was not so.

Drawing his cloak tightly round him, he drank some of the brandy he had brought with him, and leaning back against the recess of the window he suffered himself to fall into a sound slumber.

He knew well that, under ordinary circumstances, Rosalie St. Aubyn would not return from the Retreat of the Poisoners until nearly midnight.

His sleep, he reckoned, would be over by that time at any rate.

He was wrong.

He was visited by hideous nightmares, by awful visions, by phantoms that pursued him with spectral and bloodstained hands.

Yet they did not wake him.

They seemed, indeed, to chain him all the more tightly in his slumber, and he slept on for hours, till he awoke at last to hear the sound of voices near him.

He listened intently, and then found the sounds came from beyond the room.

He crossed the saloon with a hasty step, and went out of the door which opened on a corridor communicating with the staircase of the right wing.

The wax light in his hand burned dimly, and flickered as the draught from the closing door caught it.

The light showed Gascoigne he was not alone.

From the far end of the corridor, to the centre of which he had emerged, something came towards him.

Something which chilled his blood and made his heart stand still.

Something in human shape, which yet seemed not human.

"ROSE FELL UPON HER KNEES."

It seemed the form of a beautiful woman, yet not a woman.

An awful phantom with a shadowy face as of a woman with brown, bright eyes, and rich brown hair heaped up from the broad brow, and falling on bare, polished shoulders, majestic, yet terrible, for the form seemed to have no earthly substance.

The phantom came towards him, walking with an onward sweep of the limbs unlike anything he fancied himself to have seen before.

It was clothed in garments of rich trailing brown satin; the robe was held aside with one little hand, showing a small but pretty foot, which glided almost noiselessly along, gleaming with diamond buckles.

In one hand was a pistol.

This showed at once to him who watched that what he had taken for a phantom was, after all, no vision, but a reality.

He stood up as near to the wall as he could while she passed.

But it was evident from the manner of the person, whom he now in passing recognised as Rosalie St. Aubyn, that she was too much occupied by her own thoughts to observe him.

She was evidently upon the eve of some great trial.

The way she swept by, noiselessly gliding, with set features and pistol firmly clenched, proved this.

"Whither can she be going?" thought Gascoigne.

The sounds of merriment he had heard accorded ill with the firmly clenched pistol.

But this was soon remembered by Rosalie St. Aubyn.

When she reached the door, she appeared to rouse herself suddenly from a reverie.

Thrusting the pistol into her bosom with a start, she changed the expression of her face swiftly.

A smile crossed her features.

A sweet smile.

Yet how deceptive!

When she quitted the corridor, she looked sweet and loveable as an angel.

"I will follow her," thought Gascoigne.

At the peril of his life, he resolved to do this, for he knew well that if he discovered no immediate mystery which would be of benefit to him, he would, at least, be enabled to see the meaning of these constant visits to her house of gentlemen who never returned.

CHAPTER II.

THE NOISELESS MURDER.

At the extreme end of the corridor Rosalie St. Aubyn turned to the left, and pushing aside a heavy curtain, disappeared.

As she did this, a flood of light inundated the gallery.

But as the curtain dropped, all was again veiled in semi-darkness.

Gascoigne crept on.

In a few moments he was safely ensconced behind the folds of the heavy tapestry, where he could see and hear all.

In the centre of an elegantly furnished room was a large table, on which were spread delicious viands, fruits, and wines.

At this table sat a man not over thirty years of age.

He was handsome, noble-looking, and had features which were perfectly strange to Gascoigne.

This was, in fact, part of the mystery.

All he had seen with her had been utter strangers, and he began now naturally to suspect that, like Margaret of Burgundy, she was engaged in some foul conspiracy to decoy persons to her house and then destroy them.

The young stranger turned upon Rosalie St. Aubyn as she entered a look of intense admiration.

It was the look of one who was under the influence of a fatal fascination.

"Ah! sweet one, you have returned," he said, as he took her hand, and drew her down beside him on the couch where he was sitting.

"Yes; have I been so long, then?" she said, gliding her arm round his neck.

"It has seemed an age, dearest," he said; "but now you can stop."

"Oh, yes, I will remain now, and take some refreshment. I feel faint and weary."

In a few moments the fair demon and her companion were engaged in disposing of some of the delicate viands.

Scarcely any conversation passed during this time.

Ardent looks and kisses, and sweet whispers, were exchanged, and that was all.

When the viands and the fruit were disposed of, however, and they lapsed into drinking wine, the conversation began afresh.

"Now, then, pretty one," said the handsome stranger, "you must tell me what it is you wish me to do."

"Yes, certainly," replied Rosalie. "You see I am somewhat of a politician."

"Yes."

"I am one in a tremendous conspiracy, which is formed for the purpose of bringing back to the throne the Pretender—Charles Edward!"

The stranger started.

"Restore the Stuarts!" he cried.

"Yes. Are you their foe?"

"Foe! No. It is and has been always my dearest dream to see the restoration of that dynasty," cried the young stranger. "But you astonish me."

These words were said with no spirit.

Gascoigne saw he was acting.

So also did Rosalie St. Aubyn.

"In that case," she said, as her warm arms still treacherously encircled his neck, "you will not refuse to aid the cause?"

"In what way? by my sword?" asked her companion, nervously.

"No, no, not by your sword," said Rosalie; "you shall not waste your precious blood; you can aid by money. Money buys soldiers."

As she spoke, she drew him fondly to her, and imprinted a kiss upon his lips, looking full into his wondering eyes with her ardent ones.

"What want you?" he asked. "If I can aid in money I will; but I must not—cannot have my name mentioned in the matter."

"You are rich," said the temptress; "five thousand pounds will not harm you. I will get you pen and ink—you can afford me that."

Five thousand pounds!

To aid in a cause he secretly abhorred to win a smile from this fair demon!

But he was in the toils.

She rose, brought the pen, and ink, and paper, and kissed him lovingly again.

Then she placed the paper before him, and put the pen in his hand.

The stranger hesitated but a moment.

One look at the fair being by his side, and he heaved a sigh and wrote quickly.

The fair demon allowed not her face to be seen by the stranger while the order was being written.

But Gascoigne saw it.

There was on it a look of triumphant malignity which sickened him as he gazed.

When the victim had completed his task, Rosalie St. Aubyn took up the paper and placed it in her bosom.

It was now expected by Gascoigne that the unfortunate man whom the temptress had got so completely entangled in her tails, would fall into a slumber, and die off from the effects of some deadly narcotic.

But it was not so.

For some reason or another Rosalie had no recourse to poison.

"Now," she said, when she had placed the order in her breast, "now if you will take that lamp and light me on my way I will retire to my boudoir; I am tired and ill to-night."

The flush upon her cheek and the gleam in her

eye spoke rather of madness than illness, or of some fell purpose just about to be fulfilled.

Her companion saw in her brilliant orbs, her heaving bosom, and flushed face, only the natural results of the wine, and rising from his chair he took the lamp, as she had desired him, and preceded her towards the corridor.

Gascoigne at once concealed himself still further back among the shadows.

As the stranger passed by him how he wished that he were able to warn him!

But he knew it to be vain to do so.

If he showed himself he would, of course, put off the execution of her fell design, and claim the protection of her guest.

So he was compelled to see him walking to his death.

Why, he knew not.

But he felt sure murder was at hand.

He seemed to feel a chill of dread as he had felt before when he had looked on her as a phantom.

She seemed to be walking along in an atmosphere of horror, and as the two entered the gallery, the stranger in front, he involuntarily held his breath.

The fair demon permitted her victim to precede her some yards, and then, quickly presenting her pistol, she fired.

There was a flash, and the stranger fell headlong to the floor.

But there was no report.

The ammunition, whatever it was, was thoroughly noiseless, and not a single trace remained of the fatal deed but the motionless body on the floor and the shattered candelabra by its side.

The beautiful devil moved the victim with her foot.

"Quite dead!" she murmured, and clutching her pistol she moved away.

The natural impulse in the mind of Gascoigne was to rush forward and seize the murderess.

But he restrained himself.

To have acted thus would have been to destroy all chance of discovering the secret he longed to know.

To avenge *one* man's death he might fail in finding a clue to the disappearance of hundreds of others.

So he waited until she had disappeared.

Then he hurried forward.

Kneeling down, he leaned over the prostrate form of the guest.

There was no doubting the truth.

He was stone dead.

The only mercy in his death was that it must have been instantaneous.

Hardly had he ascertained this fact, when a rustle of approaching feet was heard, and he had hardly time to conceal himself when Rosalie St. Aubyn and four attendants entered.

"There he lies," she said, in a somewhat hoarse tone; "carry him to the vaults, and place him with the others. Follow me."

"*With the others!*" thought Gascoigne. "I, too, will accompany her. Now is my time for discovering the extent of her hideous villany."

CHAPTER III.

LOVE AND HATE.

BEFORE describing how Gascoigne succeeded in his efforts to discover the secret of the death vaults of Rosalie St. Aubyn's house, I must return for awhile to Helen Penraven and Rupert Dreadnought.

The latter had resolved, as I have said, to give himself a short cessation from the labours which his father had so rigorously inposed upon him.

There was no specified time in which he was forced to accomplish his vow.

The only thing from which he was debarred by his vow was his marriage with Helen Penraven.

Even this, however, scarcely offered sufficient inducement to him to throw himself at once into another terrible conflict—to embrue his hands in fresh blood.

He had already sickened of the task.

Although he had trodden in the strict path of stern justice, he often wished that his stern old father had never exacted from him such a terrific task.

The only time when he felt free from his sterner life was when he was in the companionship of Helen Penraven, and to her now he flew in his grief.

She had, as my readers will remember, taken refuge in the house of Tom the waterman, and with Mrs. Braxley and Agnes Mayland, she had passed a very happy time.

The disguise she had assumed, as one on an equality in position with those with whom she lived had not been penetrated.

Introduced to friends as the daughter of a relation in the country, she was spoken of as possessing most distinguished manners.

But that was all.

Her beauty was nothing.

Loveliness exists as much in the lower classes as in the higher.

For this then she was not noticed, except that people said when she walked out with Agnes Mayland—

"What a pretty pair!"

It was a novel life for her, and its very novelty succeeded in preventing the regret which would have come sooner or later, regret for the grand old house and the society of polished people.

She was glad enough to see the face of Rupert Dreadnought appear one morning at the door, and in the fervent embrace that followed there seemed to be concentrated a lifetime of bliss.

He speedily told her his plans.

After the stirring adventures through which he had passed, he desired a short time of rest before embarking in the accomplishment of the third task imposed upon him by his father.

Under these circumstances, he wished her to proceed to the house which Lady Dalrymple had taken for herself a short distance from London.

He was going to remain there with her a short time, and there was no danger, therefore, of any attempts on the part of Oscar Penraven.

At least so he thought.

No steps had been taken as yet in regard to the marriage into which Helen Penraven had been forced.

Oscar knew well the impossibility of enforcing the contract.

Rupert knew well, on the other hand, that it was absolutely invalid.

Neither, therefore, cared for the present to take any active steps in the matter.

The matter of the visit was soon arranged, and taking leave of those who had been so kind to her, she quitted Tom the waterman's house, and proceeded westward with Rupert Dreadnought to the charming retreat which the widow of the parricide had selected for her home.

I will not pause to describe it, for I must hurry on to stirring scenes.

There is one part of it, however, which I *must* mention, because it was there that occurred an event which tended materially to urge our hero on to the quick accomplishment of his mission.

This was a terrace, wide, and overhung with trees, which overlooked a beautiful tract of country, for, in the days of which I write, bricks and mortar had not entirely destroyed the picturesqueness of the suburbs of London.

Close up to this terrace were thick bushes and plants, too, which clambered over the parapet, thus completely obscuring the view of that part of the garden immediately beneath.

It was here, on the third evening after their arrival, that Helen Penraven and Rupert Dreadnought strolled out just as the sun was shedding its last golden rays over the landscape.

It was a lovely evening, cool but not chilly—a genial warmth pervading the atmosphere—a light zephyr stirring the leaves.

Another set of lovers were in the verandah of the house.

These were Henry Clanberris and Lady Dalrymple.

They had now yielded to the force of love, and made a mutual confession of thei passion, and their marriage was to take place in a few weeks.

Helen Penraven and Rupert Dreadnought sat down side by side on the broad marble bench which stood on the terrace.

"Dearest Helen," said the young lover, as he passed his arm round her waist, and in that sweet seclusion fearlessly kissed her ruby lips, "does it not seem hard that my father's will keeps me from making you my wife?"

The young girl smiled and kissed him in return, while a rosy hue overspread her pretty cheeks.

There was no shrinking away, no false modesty with her now.

She was his betrothed wife; she knew well that he loved her and that she loved him, and she clung to him in innocent purity.

"Yes, it *is* hard, Rupert," she said; "I feel it hard myself. I seem lost now, with no protector, no one who has the right to guard me."

So they went on in sweet converse, saying the sweet nothings that lovers will say

They little knew who was near them.

They little knew what danger was near.

A deadly peril, however, was at hand.

When they first emerged from the house, a man concealed among the bushes had beheld them.

A chuckle had escaped him as he saw them sit down, and observed how closely they were engaged in conversation.

When they had been seated some moments, he glided out from behind the bushes.

When the light of the dying sun fell upon his face it was easy to recognise him.

He was one of the bullies who had aided Oscar Penraven when Rupert had made his attack upon the old house on the Surrey side of the Thames to save Helen.

Slowly he glided on towards the happy couple, knife in hand.

A demoniacal smile overspread his face.

For two reasons.

He liked the reward which he had been promised by his employer.

In the second place, he liked the shedding of blood for its own sake.

His object was to stab Rupert in the back, and then make his escape ere Helen could succeed in alarming the house.

His features expressed a deadly triumph.

His face and Helen's presented, in fact, a perfect picture of Love and Hate.

On, on, stealthily he came.

But he was not destined to fulfil his hideous mission.

Just as he rose—just as his gleaming knife was raised on high, there was the report of a pistol, and Rupert sprang up to see the villain sink, knife in hand, weltering in his blood.

Helen clung to him in horror.

"What does this mean?" she murmured in accents tremulous with fear.

"I cannot tell," said Rupert; "it is a mystery. This fellow, who lies there still grasping his knife, was apparently on some murderous errand. But whence came the shot that stopped his hand?"

As if for answer there was a crashing among the bushes which separated the garden from the high road, and a man, booted and spurred, stood before them.

It was easy to recognise him.

He was no other, in fact, than Stanley Sherrington.

He advanced towards Rupert Dreadnought with a cheery smile, and grasped his hand.

"It was you then who shot this fellow," cried Rupert. "You arrived just in time."

"No. That shot," replied Stanley Sherrington, "was the result of much deliberation. I arrived just at the moment when the villain was crawling out from behind the bushes. I guessed at once he was on no good errand, and I resolved to watch. I did so, and saw then two things which decided me. He had that knife in his hand, and he was gliding towards you stealthily. I knew then that he was on no good errand, and, as he raised his hand to strike, I fired. Ah! he's moving; he must be questioned."

"THEN THE FAIR DEMON GLIDED MAJESTICALLY AWAY."

As he spoke he leaned down, and raised the head of the would-be assassin, who was bleeding from a deep wound in his chest.

The man slowly opened his eyes, and uttered a groan of pain. As his lance fell upon Stanley Sherrington, a scowl of hate overspread his features.

He seemed to reccognise in him the one who had stayed his murderous hand.

"Who are you?" asked Stanley Sherrington, "and who sent you hither?"

The man muttered something between his teeth which sounded like an oath.

Then he said—

"I am dying, I feel it. My secret shall go with me. To betray my master would be to take from me my only chance of revenge. You shall never know who sent me."

The exertion required to say these words appeared to paralyse all further efforts.

He gasped for breath; blood now oozed from his mouth, and he sank back exhausted.

Then his eyes glazed, and with a last convulsive shudder he fell dead.

During this scene Helen Penraven had hidden her face on Rupert's shoulder.

She could not bear to look upon so fearful a death.

Stanley Sherrington, as soon as all was over, searched the pockets of the man.

But all was in vain. Not a clue could be found to the person from whom he had come.

While this was going on, however, Henry Clanberris hurried out, and making his way to the group, inquired what was the matter.

One glance at the man's face seemed to settle the question in his mind.

"That," he said, "is one of Oscar Penraven's friends or retainers. I met him and Oscar on the road to London after his visit to Lady Dalrymple."

"You can be certain of that," returned Stanley Sherrington; "it is of him that I come to speak. There is some conspiracy afloat against you in London."

"How know you that?"

"Men have been watching your house day and night," replied Stanley, "and last night as I and some friends were passing we were only in time to prevent three ruffians from entering by a window."

Rupert Dreadnought glanced at him in wonder.

"Where are my retainers?" he said; "surely they ought to be better on the alert than that? Did you knock and inform them of the attempt?"

"We did," replied Stanley Sherrington, "but with no effect."

"They would give no answer?"

"None; we knocked again and again, but with no effect. They seemed deaf to all our demands. No doubt they had been alarmed, and, perhaps, deceived by others who had made similar attempts at entrance, and thought it prudent not to come to the door."

Rupert shook his head.

"I fear you are wrong," he said; "my men could never permit a person to go away without at least challenging them through a window. There has been, in my opinion, foul play somewhere!"

Then he turned to Helen.

"You see, dearest," he said, "it is quite useless for me to attempt to remain with you for any length of time until my enemies have been swept from the face of the land. I must return to London this night. My retainers have been, perhaps, foully murdered. Come, let us enter the house. I must take a hurried farewell of Lady Dalrymple, and start for London at once."

So saying, he gently drew her arm within his, and hastened into the house.

Then, having taken leave of his hostess, and left her in charge of his young and beautiful betrothed, he mounted his horse, and with Henry Clanberris and Stanley Sherrington started at full speed for the metropolis.

His heart was full of care, for he felt that he was about to discover some fresh and h deous crime.

CHAPTER IV.

THE DEAD WATCHER.

They reached London just as night had folded its wings over the city, and without delaying a moment pressed on towards Rupert Dreadnought's house.

It was suggested by Henry Clanberris that, in order to guard against accidents, it would be better to call in the assistance of Tom the waterman or one other of his friends, but Rupert was far too impatient to reach his home.

"We are strong enough at any rate," he said, "to discover what is the matter. If we find the place invaded by our enemies we can then send for our friends."

When they arrived at the door they knocked quickly and imperatively.

But—no answer came.

Not a light was in any window.

It was like an uninhabited house.

Again and again they knocked still more loudly than ever.

Only the same success attended this.

There was no reply.

A sickness invaded Rupert's heart.

"I fear the worst," he said.

"What mean you?" asked Stanley Sherrington.

"I believe," returned Rupert Dreadnought, "that they have been murdered."

"Let us break the door down," said Henry Clanberris; "let us begin at once."

No sooner said than done.

The three young men, each possessed of great strength, drove their shoulders against the woodwork of the door.

Then they forced their knives between the door and the lintel, and one of them rushed at it with all his force.

After several efforts they succeeded in forcing it open.

Not without attracting the notice of the passers-by, who were somewhat numerous, and collected in a wondering crowd round the door.

But Rupert Dreadnought paid no attention.

He simply pushed aside the persons who opposed him—pushed them aside as one who had authority, and entering the passage with his friends placed a heavy chair against the door and descended to the servants' hall.

There they found that Rupert's worst suspicions were not exaggerated.

On the ground lay the bodies of six men, stiff in death.

Their faces were ghastly blue; decomposition had, in fact, already begun.

Their death had evidently been by poison.

Not a sound was to be heard anywhere in the place.

All was as still as the tomb.

"You see," said Rupert Dreadnought, turning sternly to Henry Clanberris, "my words were true. There has been foul murder here."

"Yes," replied Henry Clanberris, "you are right. But are these all the servants you left here?"

"No; there are three more. Let us ascend to the upper chambers and see what other hideous scenes are prepared for us."

With Rupert leading the way they accordingly proceeded upwards until they reached Rupert's chamber.

In this room a man lay on Rupert's bed.

He, too, was stone dead.

In another a faithful retainer was also stretched a corpse.

They then descended once more until they reached the chamber where was the closet containing the IRON CHEST.

Here a strange sight presented itself.

Propped up against the secret panel, with his back firmly set against it, and one hand clutching a a chair near, as if for support, was the last of the retainers.

In his other hand was a pistol, and his eyes were fixed with a glassy stare upon the door.

"He has died doing his duty," said Rupert, with emotion. "This is, indeed, a strange and hideous crime!"

"What do you propose doing now?" asked Stanley Sherrington.

Rupert paced the room a moment.

"I will tell you," he said; "the door below shows only by the lock that it has been forced open."

"True; well?"

"We will fix the door so that there shall be no evidence of our entrance, then we will leave the window slightly open and watch."

"And supposing that they come in large numbers?" said Henry Clanberris.

"We must chance that," said Rupert Dreadnought. "If we found ourselves being overpowered we could easily call in the assistance of our neighbours. But I do not believe that there will be any necessity."

"And why?"

"Because, as they have poisoned all my servants, they will not expect any resistance, and will not come in force."

"You are right, I believe," said Henry Clanberris. "We will at once see to the door, and then we will find hiding places."

The door was soon secured.

Then the three friends returned to the room where the Iron Chest was concealed.

The dead man was left as they had found him, staring with his glassy eyes at the door, and the three watchers hid themselves away behind the tapestry.

It was the Iron Chest itself that Rupert Dreadnought expected to be the object of interest to his enemies.

CHAPTER V.

THE WATCHER—THE DEATH-VAULTS—THE SILENT COHORT—A COURAGEOUS ACT—THE SECRET ENTRANCE—THE GROANS OF THE DYING—SAVED FOR A SECOND DEATH—THE DEPARTURE OF THE WATCHER.

IN order properly to follow the sequence of events and prevent the necessity of retrospection, I must return to the point where Gascoigne was following in the wake of Rosalie St. Aubyn.

The attendants were far too engaged to observe him, and in the semi-darkness he contrived to glide behind tapestries, and from pillar to pillar, until they reached a black and winding staircase.

Here they descended cautiously until they reached a vault, whose ceiling was supported by pillars spreading wide at the top.

It was easy here to glide behind one of these, and Gascoigne, who had now taken the precaution to place upon his face a black mask, passed at once into a position where he was concealed entirely from view.

Rosalie St. Aubyn had, up to this moment, led the way.

She now, however, quitted her position as guide, and halting, pointed to the door, which was of massive oak, and studded with heavy iron nails.

"There," she said, "you know your duty now. Place him with the rest, and leave him."

Then the fair demon glided majestically away.

"Is it possible that Heaven's lightning will spare this woman?" muttered Gascoigne, as he watched her myrmidons bearing the body away.

As soon as the door was open he glided in with the rest.

It was a brave deed.

Brave almost to recklessness.

But he had a good and necessary purpose to serve, and he was resolved not to flinch from his duty.

The men did not observe him.

They were far too much occupied in their fearful work to do so.

So, when he entered the vault, he ensconced himself in a corner behind a pillar and waited.

He watched carefully the spot where they deposited the dead body of the lately murdered man.

Then he thought only of his concealment, and watched no more.

The men were not long in doing their work, and presently the great iron-bound door was clanged to with a sound that resounded through the Vaults of Death.

Gascoigne waited until the echoes of their footsteps had died away.

Then he stepped forth into the open space.

Here he drew from his pocket a dark lantern, and raised it high above his head so as to reconnoitre.

The sight that met his eyes was truly appalling.

On every side were piles of dead bodies.

At least a hundred.

They were not in coffins, but placed each on a plank which served as a shelf.

Their faces truly were veiled from view.

But the knowledge that they were all dead—*all murdered*—imparted a feeling of terrific horror to the mind.

A suffocating atmosphere, moreover, pervaded the place.

Many of those, of course, who lay there in the still majesty of death had been dead a long time, and I need say no more than that scarcely any means of ventilation existed.

With a shudder Gascoigne proceeded to the spot where he had seen the retainers place the body of the newly-murdered man.

He soon found the spot.

The young stranger was placed upon his back on one of the shelves.

His face was very calm, like the face of one in sleep.

But from the wound in his chest welled the blood which told of the murder.

In every pocket Gascoigne searched to see if he could find the slightest clue to his identity.

In his pockets, however, there were no papers of any kind.

In fact, the only thing he found was a portrait.

The portrait of a beautiful, fair-haired girl—a perfect stranger to Gascoigne.

"So far so good," thought Gascoigne.

But now came the question—how was he to make good his escape?

Having discovered this receptacle of wholesale murder, how was he to leave it?

To say that this idea had never occurred to him before would be false.

But he had risked the chance.

Convinced that another murder would be perpetrated on the following night, he was resolved to wait patiently, and quit the place when the retainers brought in another victim.

Sleep, of course, was an utter impossibility.

Even if drowsiness began to overcome him he would not have yielded to it, for how could he have brought himself to lie down with the dead?

Drawing from his pocket a flask of spirits, he drank a good draught, and was about to commence a further exploration of the place when a strange sound startled him.

It sounded like a groan.

Naturally, in such a place, it roused his astonishment.

The man who had just been brought into the vault was most certainly dead.

He had ascertained that ere he quitted the gallery where the deed had been committed.

Who, then, could it be?

He raised his lantern and once more glanced round the huge vault.

But nothing moved.

"I must have been mistaken," he murmured; "nevertheless, I will listen and see if the sound is repeated."

So he stood motionless, listening.

He was not long kept in suspense.

Presently the groan was repeated—louder still than ever.

It seemed to come from behind the ledge where the newly-murdered man had been laid.

He immediately rushed to the spot.

The idea at once occurred to him that the victim of the evening before might not be yet dead, and that he would naturally be found near the victim of that night.

Drawing away the body of the handsome stranger, who had but a few hours before been sitting at supper with his murderess, and clasping her fondly round the neck, and thrilling to the magic of her gleaming eyes, Gascoigne glanced eagerly behind.

He then quickly saw whence the sounds proceeded.

The next body moved slightly.

Reaching out his hands he drew it gently towards him.

As he did so he felt a slight warmth, and a tremour, too, ran through the frame of the still man.

Gascoigne poured a small quantity of spirits down his throat.

Then the eyes of the man opened slowly, and glared round with a glassy stare.

"Where am I?" he said, in a whisper. "Oh, ah, I see. In the tomb—in the tomb!"

The face of the sleeper betokened a man of about thirty years.

The voice was that of a man of sixty.

"No," said Gascoigne, "this is not the tomb. I am a friend. I am here to save you from this dismal vault. Do you know where you are now?"

The man rose slightly, and glanced around him eagerly.

Then he pressed his hand to his brow.

"Yes, yes," he said, faintly; "I fancy I can remember now. Am I not in the house of Rosalie St. Aubyn?"

"You are," said Gascoigne.

The man shuddered.

"Ah!" he said, in a voice which was full of despair; "then *you*, I suppose, are one of her myrmidons? Could you not let me die in peace, or has that monster in human form ordered me fresh tortures?"

"No," returned Gascoigne, "I am no myrmidon of hers. I hate her as strongly as ever *you* can. I was a witness—an unseen witness—of her hideous crimes this night. I saw yonder man fall beneath her weapon, and I followed hither to see the number of her victims, and the place where they were deposited. You must escape with me. The next thing to be done is to discover the means of exit."

The man, who had once more partaken of some spirits, felt somewhat revived now, and could speak far more freely.

"I see now," he cried, as he glanced round at the bodies, "that I am not the only victim."

"The only one!" exclaimed Gascoigne; "not by a hundred. This place is a very den of murder. But come, we will not waste time in talking. I will see if by chance there is any mode of egress. Fear not," he added, as he saw the man's eyes turned wistfully upon him, "fear not. I will return."

So saying, he once more took up his lamp, and passed quickly towards the extreme end of the vault.

Here he found a door, or rather an open archway, leading into another vault, of dimensions quite equal to the other.

There were no dead bodies here, but there were shelves ready to receive them, just as if the murders were intended to be continued wholesale.

From this vault there appeared to be egress by means of a small doorway at one end.

To this Gascoigne made his way eagerly, and pushed hard against it.

It did not yield at once, but it was evident, from the way in which it gave, that to force it would be a matter of no difficulty.

Exerting all his strength, therefore, Gascoigne pushed against it, and presently, to his intense satisfaction, he felt the fastenings giving way.

One more strong push, one more strenuous effort, and away it went, bolts and all, into the darkness beyond.

Gascoigne was thrown to the ground, and was so shaken and bruised by the fall, that he could not rise, nor could he tell where he was.

What he had fallen on was soft earth, but his head had come in contact with some brickwork.

When he had recovered sufficiently to enable him to stand up, however, he soon discovered that he was in some place where he was open to the free winds of heaven.

He could feel the cool air rushing upon his forehead, and having stood still a moment to ascertain in which way the current came, he advanced slowly and carefully towards the welcome spot.

He fancied he was in some subterranean passage of very narrow dimensions, so narrow, indeed, that he could touch both sides with his hands as he walked.

Though sincerely hoping and believing that he had discovered some secret means of egress with the outer world, he was yet very careful lest he might come upon a pitfall.

However, he met with no accidents.

After a tedious journey of only a few minutes—but appearing twice the length—he reached an opening which led through some dense bushes to the high road.

The passage through which he had come was, in point of fact, the one through which Alford and Lesbia had been led by Redlock on the evening when Lesbia and Rosalie had had the encounter.

He gazed around in delight at the free country round him.

"By heavens!" he cried, "I have tracked the murderess to her lair, and more than that, I have found the means of destroying her."

After a few moments' inhaling of the fresh air, which was infinitely delightful after the close and fetid atmosphere of the death vaults, he turned back and made his way more easily and rapidly back.

He was aided, in fact, in his return by the twinkling of a small ray of light from the vault, for he had left the lantern with the resuscitated victim of Rosalie's treachery.

Resuscitated, alas! but for a moment.

When Gascoigne returned he found him lying back stark dead, with the lantern grasped tightly in his death clasp.

The sudden awakening in such a place—and perhaps, the spirits also—had been too much for him; and his spirit had this time fled from misery for ever.

This was, of course, a great loss of evidence against Rosalie St. Aubyn.

But there was no use in despairing.

Moreover, the presence of this vast number of corpses in the vaults of a private house would be enough to bring down the anger of the law upon her.

"A HAND WAS SUDDENLY PLACED ON HIS SHOULDER."

With a sigh, he replaced the body in the place where he had first found it, having unsuccessfully searched every pocket to discover some papers which would throw a light upon the name and vocation of the victim he had hoped to save.

Then, placing the lost victim exactly where he had found him, he proceeded towards the secret passage.

Here he replaced the door as well as he could, shooting the bolts into their places, and filling, with the soft soil of the passage, the holes which he had made by forcing them out.

Then, closing his lantern, he passed out into the night, and made all haste in the direction of the inn where he had left his horse.

He felt truly like one in a dream.

The adventures and horrors he had endured during the past few hours were truly enough for a lifetime.

In all his experience he had never come across so terrible a mystery—never seen a demon invested in so fair a human shape.

However, he lost not much time in thought.

What he desired was to hasten as quickly as possible to London, and see Rupert Dreadnought, whom of all others he regarded as the best able to aid him in his enterprise.

As may be supposed, the night was far advanced, and, in fact, morning was already beginning to break when he started.

But he heeded this not.

In spite of the fatigue both body and mind had gone through, he was resolved not to delay.

Life and revenge were involved in the accomplishment of his enterprise.

CHAPTER VI.

THE FIGHT FOR THE IRON CHEST.

I MUST now return to Rupert Dreadnought and his friends, who, in the still old house, were waiting eagerly the arrival of those who had, in so dastardly a manner, poisoned the domestics.

They waited fully an hour, exchanging only whispered words now and then.

At the expiration of this time they heard a slight jarring noise at the window.

Then it was gently raised, while a man's form showed up darkly against the sky.

When the casement had been opened more widely the man, who was closely masked, entered, and fixed a rope ladder to a heavy piece of furniture within the bed-chamber.

Then he gave a cry like that of a screech-owl, and waited a few moments.

The cry was soon answered from some little distance, and after another short delay four more men entered the room.

Then the window was fastened down, and the masked strangers struck a light and lit the lamp which stood on the centre table.

A loud, coarse laugh escaped the lips of the one who appeared to be the leader, as his eyes fell upon the figure of the domestic sitting propped up against the door with the pistol grasped in his hand.

"Ha, ha, old fellow! your days for fighting are over," cried he. "You look very solemn, but your fidelity has cost you your life."

The cruel insolence of this speech was almost enough to make Rupert spring from his hiding place and rush at the speaker.

But he restrained his anger for the moment for a reason.

He wished to see what was the object of the new-comers, and also how far their knowledge extended.

The voice of the man who had spoken had told him nothing.

It was that of a perfect stranger.

The leader now dragged away the body from before the doorway, and then felt everywhere for the spring by which to open the panel.

"They are at fault there," thought Rupert.

He was right.

Although they knew the existence of the IRON CHEST, and the place where it was stowed away, it was quite evident that they were far from being aware of the secret spring by which they could reach the receptacle of the mysteries of Rupert's life.

"Here, Frank," cried the leader, addressing one of the men, "bring your crowbar here and wrench this panel open."

When he uttered these words, both Henry Clanberris and Stanley Sherrington imagined that Rupert Dreadnought would spring to his feet, and give the word to them to rush on the foe.

But he made no sign, evidently desiring to see how far they would go.

The man whom the masked intruder had addressed as Frank advanced at once to the wall with a long iron bar.

He was a broad-shouldered, tall young fellow, of herculean mould, and a few blows, given with all his force, soon told their tale upon the woodwork, which splintered up, and quickly left a wide opening.

After about five minutes' work, the others, with their hands, tore away the broken panelling, and it was not long before the IRON CHEST stood revealed to the eager eyes of the five men.

"Quick!" said the leader, in a voice full of emotion; "drag it out into the light. We will first see what secrets it contains, and then we will destroy it. There will be an end then to the bloodthirsty mission of Rupert Dreadnought."

Scarcely had the man advanced to lay his hand upon the iron handle of the box, when there was a sharp report, and he fell prone upon his face—dead!

Then Rupert sprang to his feet, and shouted in a loud voice—

"At them, my friends! No quarter for the robbers and assassins!"

My readers can well imagine to themselves the utter astonishment of the intruders when the shot was fired, and the three friends rose from behind the tapestry.

But the latter did not give them much time for thought.

Rushing at them at full speed, with sword in hand, they took them quite by surprise, and had them by the throat ere they had time to draw their weapons.

The leader, however, contrived to seize his knife and stabbed Rupert in the arm, compelling him for an instant to draw back.

Between them, therefore, there was a fierce encounter with swords.

With the others the fight resolved itself into a hand-to-hand struggle, in which they rolled hither and thither in a fierce wrestle for the mastery.

The one whom Rupert attacked was a good master of fence, and, though only armed with a short knife against a long and keen-bladed sword, he contrived for a long time to keep his antagonist at bay.

Then suddenly he performed a feat which placed him on equal terms with Rupert.

Seizing his opportunity, he dashed suddenly into the dark recess where stood the IRON CHEST.

Here in the shadows he was enabled to draw his sword, and in an instant he was on an equality with Rupert Dreadnought.

Our hero was in no way discouraged by this change of tactics on the part of his antagonist.

But he stayed his hand a moment.

"You are a brave man, and can be no personal enemy of mine, since we are utter strangers," he said; "tell me who are you, and why you are here, for I feel certain that you are acting under some misconception."

The other laughed scornfully.

"You fear me now we are on equal terms," he cried. "See, my men hold their own! No matter who I am, you will find that my sword is as keen as yours, and the arm that wields it is as strong."

"You shall see I fear you not," exclaimed Rupert. "When my sword is at your throat, and you are craving for mercy, then you will see that I will force from you the knowledge of who you are."

So saying, he attacked his antagonist with greater fur than ever.

The stranger, whoever he was, was right when he said that his men were holding their own.

Being built on the same herculean mould as the one named Frank, who had fallen a victim to Rupert's pistol shot, they were more that a match for Henry Clanberris and Stanley Sherrington.

Three men are always more than a match for two in a struggle, and they found it as much as they could possibly do to prevent themselves from being wounded in the struggle.

Presently, however, there was a change for the better.

One of the men rolling over, Henry Clanberris contrived to drive his knife home, and left them with but one adversary each.

Meanwhile, Rupert and his adversary attacked one another furiously.

There was no fear of interruption.

The windows were tightly closed.

Heavy curtains obscured the glass, while the doors were tightly closed, and not a sound crossed from the chamber into the street below.

As I have said before, Rupert's antagonist was quite his equal in the art of defence, and it seemed as if in that confined space he had the advantage.

Rupert found himself, in fact, on several occasions driven back, and obliged to drop the offensive and act on the defensive.

To the mind of our hero fear was a thing unknown.

Yet he regarded the doubtful nature of the contest with a feeling of exasperation.

He felt certain that the man with whom he was contending was a stranger to him, and he had also an idea, a conviction, in fact, that he could not shake off, that he was acting throughout under misapprehension, both of his character and the motives which actuated him in the course of his strange and varied adventures.

If, therefore, any accident should occur to him which should delay the fulfilment of his last vow, he would never forgive himself for having delayed its commencement.

Again, as he began to regain his position, he demanded of his adversary—

"Who and what are you?"

He received no reply.

The stranger seemed resolved to preserve his incognito at all hazards.

This seemed to nerve Rupert's arm with fresh strength.

Pausing a moment to gain breath, and acting for the time only on the defensive, he looked his antagonist straight in the eye, and then rushed at him.

It was a sudden rush.

The stranger, taken off his guard, was obliged to fall back, and in parrying Rupert's sword, his own weapon snapped some inches from the point.

Still he refused to give in.

Planting his back against the wall, he seemed still determined to do battle *à l'outrance.*

Meanwhile, Henry Clanberris and Stanley Sherrington were fiercely engaged with their foes.

It was, as I have said, a hand-to-hand struggle, and no one for the time could use his knife or weapons of any kind.

But all men tire, no matter how eager they may be for victory.

After a time, just about the moment when Rupert and his masked adversary paused, the four wrestlers stopped also.

Then, as with one accord, they sprang to their feet and glared at each other.

Savagely they glared like wild beasts.

But even now they had no time to spare in which to draw swords.

Their knives, however, were quickly raised, and for a moment it would have been difficult to say who meditated the attack and who were the aggressors in the fight.

"Hold," cried Henry Clanberris, addressing them, "you are but the servants of yonder man. Why fight you? Let them decide the battle. We have no wish to shed the blood of retainers."

The men laughed scornfully.

They mistook his words, or pretended to mistake them, for evidences of cowardice.

"Retainers or not we fight when our master fights," they cried, as with one voice; "we surrender when he surrenders."

There was something in their manner which seemed scarcely to belong to retainers.

They spoke haughtily, and as people used to good society.

"Your blood be on your own heads, then," cried Stanley Sherrington.

"Or yours on yours, insolent," shouted one of the antagonists, as he made a rush at the speaker.

On all sides the battle now was waged in desperate earnest.

The struggle between Rupert Dreadnought and the masked stranger was fierce enough.

But that between the others looked the most deadly, as the struggle took place with knives.

I will not unnecessarily prolong this scene.

Suffice it to say that the superior skill and resolute courage of Henry Clanberris and Stanley Sherrington at length prevailed.

The two men fell, desperately wounded, to the ground, and thus the two friends were free to assist Rupert.

Rupert saw this.

He determined to take advantage of it at once.

His object was to wound or disable his adversary in some way—not to kill.

To do the latter would be to lose, perhaps, all clue as to the identity of the stranger himself, as well as to the person who had sent him on his errand.

"Help, here!" he cried.

The stranger burst into a loud laugh.

"So, ho! Master Dread-*nought,*" he shouted, "you need help against *one* man."

"I wish to save your life, madman," returned Rupert, angrily. "I want your secret, not your blood! Seize him, my friends."

Both Henry Clanberris and Stanley Sherrington dashed at once forward, and drawing their swords, menaced him on both sides.

But even now he would not yield.

He seemed resolved to die before he dreamed of yielding.

But three were too strong for him.

Just as he made a desperate lunge at Rupert Dreadnought, Henry Clanberris dashed forward and seized him.

This was the end of the fight.

He made a feeble struggle.

But it was of no use.

Stanley Sherrington seized his other arm, and in a few moments the stalwart stranger was helpless on the floor.

"Now, then," said Rupert, as they disarmed him, you see we are not cowards. We sought not your life. Your friends yonder have suffered terrible injury, if not death, through their obstinacy. *You* ran the same risk, but your good luck saved you. Clanberris, get something with which to bind our prisoner. In the room yonder you will, I think, find some rope."

In a few moments Henry Clanberris returned with the required coil of rope.

The stranger spoke not while he was being bound.

He seemed resolved to be obstinate to the very last.

But there was one thing he could not avoid.

That was, a search throughout his pockets.

This was very successful.

In this case there had been no suspicion that Rupert or his friends would return so opportunely.

The stranger consequently did not take the precaution to destroy any documents which he had about his person.

The first paper which Rupert came across was a letter from Oscar Penraven :—

"DEAR FLAXMAN,—Be sure and procure for me the men of whom I spoke. I have reason to believe them to be trustworthy and brave.

"The IRON CHEST is to be found in the chamber adjoining Sir Rupert Dreadnought's bedroom.

"You will find it behind a panel in the wall on the left hand side of the door.

"I cannot tell you where the spring opening it is concealed, but if you have any difficulty break through the panelling, which you will find very light.

"I am supposing, of course, that you have disposed first of the domestics in the manner we arranged.

"As soon as you have taken from the IRON CHEST all its documents, destroy the rest of its contents, and leave the empty chest in the room.

"OSCAR PENRAVEN."

"A somewhat imperative missive," said Rupert Dreadnought, "but one which proves that he knows more than I wish him. We must see to this."

A further search revealed still further secrets.

All except the identity of the stranger.

There were letters and memoranda proving his intimacy with Oscar Penraven.

But that was all.

His name, Flaxman, led to nothing.

When unmasked he presented the features of a handsome, well-looking man of about thirty.

But no one had seen his face before.

"This is enough for our purpose," said Rupert Dreadnought; "as the search has proved his connection with and employment by Oscar Penraven, I have learned enough!"

"You will then suffer him to go?" asked Henry Clanberris.

"Yes; his companions are all dead. See, there they lie. I will send him back to his employer with my last words. Raise him up and unbind him when you have placed all weapons beyond his reach, then place him near the window."

Rupert's orders were soon obeyed.

The stranger stood with folded arms, stern and defiant.

"Master Flaxman," said Rupert, "I know not who or what you are. But I have discovered who it is for whom you risk your life. It is Oscar Penraven."

"Well?"

"He is a poisoner—an assassin. He has misrepresented me to you," continued Rupert. "I am pledged to certain missions by a vow to my father on his death-bed. You call them bloodthirsty. They may appear so to *you*, but each one devoted to destruction is an assassin or a parricide. Go, tell Oscar Penraven I have discovered his schemes. Tell him I fear him not. Say that there is an Evil Genius hovering over him and all the guilty, which will lead them into the snare at last, no matter through what rosy scenes it may conduct him at first. Go now and give him this message. Let me not see you again, for remember, wherever I meet with you, I shall run my sword through your body. Go!"

As he spoke he opened the casement, and pointed to the rope ladder which still depended from it.

The stranger hesitated a moment.

But only for a moment.

To have resisted now have would been utter madness.

With an angry scowl, therefore, he turned impatiently away, and as quickly as possible descended into the street, which was now devoid of all passers.

"Now," said Rupert, "we have a sickening task before us. We must bear the bodies into yonder—or rather, they can remain here, and I will retire to my bedroom. Aid me to place the IRON CHEST back into yonder closet, and then let me beg of you to make my house your own, and choose a bed for the night."

The IRON CHEST was soon replaced.

Then another panel was slid aside, and some choice wines were disposed of by the tired combatants.

They then retired to one of the upper chambers, while Rupert, entering his own, placed a tankard of wine before him, and sank into a deep reverie.

He was deep in thought, when a hand was laid suddenly upon his shoulder.

Glancing up, and half starting from his chair, he saw a masked man standing beside him.

"Who are you?" he cried, drawing his sword, "and how came you here?"

RUPERT DREADNOUGHT.

"LYING ON HER SIDE UPON THE WOODEN CORNER OF THE WELL WAS A FEMALE FORM."

CHAPTER VII.

THE THIRD SECRET.

"FEAR not, I am a friend," said a voice.

Then he threw off his mask and disclosed the features of Gascoigne.

"I meet you in a house of death," he added; "I stumbled over dead bodies enough on my way to this room. Egad! with the piles of corpses I have seen elsewhere this night, I thought I had had enough dealings with the Arch Destroy-r for once."

"You surprised, me, indeed," said Rupert, as, re-sheathing his sword, he sat down once more. "How, in the name of wonder, did you enter?"

"I found the street door open," replied Gascoigne. "the wind had blown it easily in, for the locks and bolts were wrenched off. I secured it as well as I could, and then coming up the stairs I entered your room. I never, as you know, gave over my plan of bearing with me a dark lantern, and this I at once turned on, to find myself once more in the presence of Death by Violence!"

"Once more you say!" exclaimed Rupert. "Pray explain yourself."

"I will," said Gascoigne; "but if you will allow me I will take a draught of that wine. I have suffered much, and ridden long and rapidly."

Having taken a goodly draught Gascoigne told his story.

Rupert listened in wonder.

It seemed to him, as it had seemed to Gascoigne, a mystery that such terrible villany should exist in so lovely a body.

"This is no longer for us to deal with," replied he, when Gascoigne had concluded his narration; "we cannot deal with such wholesale enormity. We must inform the authorities."

"May not that interfere with your fulfilment of your vow to your father?" asked Gascoigne.

Rupert thought a moment.

"Perhaps you are right," he said. "I am afraid I have too long delayed the reading of the third mystery. I am resolved this night to investigate it, and I have been resting after my labours ere I opened the Iron Chest once more."

"But you have not told me yet," said Gascoigne, "what adventure has happened to you this night."

Rupert briefly told him.

Gascoigne listened intently.

"This is certainly becoming too perilous," he said. "Action at once—that must now be your motto. Shall I accompany you into yonder chamber of death?"

Rupert rose.

"No," he said. "I alone must touch that repository of dread secrets. Remain here, and rest awhile while I search for my next dread task."

It was evident to Rupert Dreadnought now that he must lose no time in investigating the further secrets of the Iron Chest.

It was for this reason he had desired his friend to remain where he was.

He wished to be alone.

Much as he had desired to avoid immediate action, it was now plain that neither his own life, nor the lives of those he loved, were safe until his foes were disposed of.

He could not doubt that, among those who now pursued him, there were many who were connected in some way or another with the mysterious bequest of his father, and he resolved now, in the stillness of the night, to unfold the third mystery.

He accordingly passed—not without some heaviness at heart—into the next room, and approached the dark closet where the Iron Chest stood.

With a heavy sigh he placed the key in the lock, turned it, raised the lid, and bent down to search with eager and wondering eyes for the THIRD SECRET.

The instructions which the old earl had left were very brief.

They were written on a piece of parchment, in which was enclosed a Diamond Cross.

The third enemy which Rupert Dreadnought had to clear from his path, was none other than Dr. Henzollern, the chief of the Poisoners!

This name was but an assumed title.

His rea name was Ishmael Hasser; he was, in fact, none other than the gipsy chief mentioned in our first number as the friend of Robert Penraven, and the grandfather of Oscar.

When Ishmael Hasser had aided Robert and his brother to seize Alice, the latter had fallen in love with the gipsy's daughter; and, after first endeavouring to induce her to fly with him, he was forced into a marriage.

The gipsy had been a terrible enemy to the old earl; he had been the instrument used to work out all the dastardly designs of the Penravens; he had dyed his hands in the blood of the earl's best friends.

"Therefore," concluded the writing on the parchment, "either destroy him yourself, or give him over to the authorities. I care not which.

"The fact of his being at the present moment at the head of a great conspiracy (for what purpose formed I know not) will, of course, render it a matter of difficulty for you to approach him.

"When you suspect yourself to be in his presence, however, the diamond cross will reveal to you his identity.

"Say to him—'The Cross and the day.'

"If he then refuses to acknowledge his identity. say—"The Vaults and the 15th January.'"

Then followed an elaborate description of him, chief among the specialities of which was a scar extending across his left cheek.

It needed not the description to enable Rupert Dreadnought to guess who it was that was meant by his father.

The chief of the great conspiracy was, of course, no other than Dr. Henzollern, the leader of the Poisoners!

Gascoigne was the first person whom he consulted. His advice was good.

"The new retreat of the Poisoners is in Essex, on the river's bank," he said. "The best thing to do is to proceed to that neighbourhood, and establish yourself in a house close to it. There you can be on the watch."

"Had we not better at once give notice to the authorities," said Rupert, "and let the runners seize upon him and his villanous crew? You see my father gives me such permission in his instructions."

Gascoigne smiled.

"Take my advice," he said, "and give no such information. I have been a Bow Street runner myself, and know how you will find it if you act as you suggest. Do you suppose for one moment that among a vast conspiracy such as that of the Poisoners there will be no secret agents, avowedly in the pay of the government, but really in the pay of the Terrible Band? If you let the runners know, information will at once be given to your enemies, and all your efforts will be in vain."

Rupert saw plainly the force of this argument.

Gascoigne had too much experience in the workings of the secret spy system to make it advisable to disregard his counsel.

"I will do as you advise," he said. "After we have disposed of the dead bodies of my faithful domestics, and obtained the services of someone who can take charge of this house, we will proceed in the search for a suitable habitation."

"Or, better still," said Gascoigne, "*I* will set out to-morrow, and seek a place for you, while you are making your arrangements in London."

CHAPTER VIII.

ON THE TRAIL.

It did not take long to settle what little matters Rupert Dreadnought had to arrange.

The unfortunate men who had died in defending their master's interests were duly interred, and Mrs. Braxley, Agnes Mayland, and Tom the waterman were installed as guardians of the old house, while Gascoigne gave strict injunctions to the watch to keep a good look-out upon it night and day.

Gascoigne had meanwhile discovered a pleasant rural retreat not half a mile from the house occupied by the Poisoners, and to this, as soon as convenient, our hero removed.

The position of this place was doubly pleasant to him.

It was so close to the retreat of his enemies that he could be constantly watching his foes; and, in the second place, it was at no great distance from Brentwood, where Henry Clanberris had bought a beautiful residence, which he named after himself.

Lady Dalrymple had no reason to pretend any deep feeling of sorrow at the death of Sir Hugh.

She had hated him before marriage, and patiently borne with him after, and now that she was free to marry the love of her heart, she no longer saw cause to hesitate.

When, therefore, he urged on an early marriage, she no longer hesitated, but consented at once; and one bright morning she became his bride.

They had now removed to Clanberris House, and Helen Penraven had gone with them.

He would thus, therefore, be able not only to be on the watch, but to visit constantly the one he loved.

About a week after his arrival at the house which Gascoigne had obtained for him, the latter had proceeded on a voyage of discovery to the house of the Poisoners.

Rupert, being thus left alone, started upon a lonely walk through the wooded grounds which almost entirely surrounded the beautiful retreat.

He was proceeding along leisurely among the dense trees, thinking over the past, when a loud cry aroused him from his reverie.

At first he was doubtful whether it was the cry of some bird, or that of some human being in distress.

So he stopped still.

For a few moments all remained quiet as the tomb.

Then there arose a second cry, more shrill and despairing than the first.

"Help! help!"

There was no mistaking it now.

It was the voice of a woman in distress.

"Help is near," shouted Rupert at the top of his voice, and drawing his sword, he plunged through the brushwood towards the place whence the cries proceeded.

By the aid of the moonlight he found his way to a spot where there was an incline, and where some rough steps descended towards a disused well.

Here he beheld a strange sight.

Lying on her side upon the wooden corner of the well was a female form.

It was that of a beautiful woman about nineteen, dressed in the extreme of fashion.

She was quite insensible now, but no one was near.

Rushing down, Rupert knelt by her side, and raised the beautiful head upon his knee.

He did not recognise the features of anyone he knew, but it was one whose name was well known to him, but whom he had never seen.

It was, in fact, Lesbia Howard.

A goodly draught from his flask of spirits revived the unconscious beauty, who, as her eyes opened, smiled sweetly upon her preserver.

"You arrived just in time," she whispered, faintly. "In another minute I should have been hurled to the bottom of this well."

"By whom—and why?" asked Rupert, eagerly.

"By Dr. Henzollern, the chief of the terrible society whose crimes are decimating London."

This was enough.

Anxiously Rupert inquired her history, and listened with wonder as she recounted her adventures—her love for Alford, and the reasons of her entering the dread society.

She had been denounced at last, as threatened by Rosalie St. Aubyn, and the president himself had received the task of destroying her.

He had inveigled her into the wood by representing that they were being watched, and there, at the well, he had told her how she had been denounced as a traitress, and that the hour of death had at length arrived.

"And where is this villain now?" said Rupert, as he tenderly aided her to quit the dense wood.

"I know not; having failed in obtaining his end, he will not return to the retreat; but I can tell you where you will find him in three days hence."

"And where is that?"

"At Brentwood, among the throngs of gipsies. He has work before him that requires the aid of his old friends and relations, and he goes disguised among them."

For the time being Lesbia Howard resolved to accompany Rupert to the house he had taken, and, arrived there, she heard with surprise and pleasure into whose hands she had fallen.

She gave him full directions in regard to the future movements of Dr. Henzollern, and Rupert determined at once to take advantage of her information, and proceed to Clanberris House.

This accordingly he did, and the next day saw him at their destination.

At the time of my story Brentwood was a quiet and thrifty village.

Since the advent of railroads, it has assumed grander dimensions.

But in the days of which I speak, the only time when there was an air of life and activity about the place was when the country agricultural fairs were held there.

Within the limits of this, there was a race-course, which, at certain seasons of the year, brought together a motley crowd, the major part of which was composed of characters not the most reputable.

As may readily be imagined, there was not that good order preserved, nor were they governed by those wholesome regulations which characterise the race-courses of the present day.

Drinking and gambling booths abounded, cards and dice met you at every turn, and drink flowed freely.

As a matter of course, licence and misrule prevailed almost unchecked.

There was a sprinkling here and there of the better classes, and that was all.

The gathering this time was larger than usual, and Brentwood was crowded with people.

Among them was the usual collection of noisy brawlers, flash gentlemen,and gamblers; but among all, as Rupert Dreadnought and Henry Clanberris strolled through the crowd in search of the one he was so eager to find, there were two who particularly attracted their attention.

They put up at the inn where Rupert had stopped on the previous night.

They were dressed in tawdry finery, and bore a very sinister expression.

One of them, the most talkative, had a slight cast in his eyes, which impressed you at once unfavourably.

He was evidently a shrewd fellow, and knew his way in life too well—the criminal way be it said.

The other had more of the bull-dog in his disposition, and was in every respect a surly brute.

A scar on his left cheek-bone and a nose battered out of shape, did not add to his good looks.

One could see, at a glance, that they were desperate characters—men who would stick at nothing to accomplish their ends.

They seemed to have plenty of money, and spent it freely, but were unusually quiet in their manners.

Rupert noticed that they had no acquaintances among the crowd, or if they had they did not recognise any; and, although attending the race-course, they appeared to take very little interest in the proceedings.

They wandered about apparently without any special purpose.

There was that about them, in fact, which excited the suspicion of both Rupert and Henry Clanberris, and they accordingly watched their movements closely.

From the first moment they saw them, in fact, they seemed to connect the strangers with themselves, as if they meditated a personal injury to one or the other, or to one in whom they were nterested.

If either Rupert or Henry Clanberris had been asked to say why he thus felt, he would have found it impossible to tell.

Neither was more than naturally suspicious, neither was superstitious, yet they both suspected the two men, and had a vague foreboding of impending evil.

We have all of us, I daresay, at some time or another in the course of our lives, been subject to similar impressions—shadowy premonitions of some calamity awaiting us.

We may array reason against them, we may ridicule them; but reason or ridicule as we will, we cannot dislodge them.

There they remain, clinging pertinaciously in spite of all our efforts to loosen their grasp.

It is one of the mysteries of our nature which we have not yet fathomed.

As a general thing, the ladies in those days did not frequent the race-ground.

Sometimes a few would gather in the outskirts away from the vicinity of the crowd.

It was among these Rupert saw that the two men were usually to be found, idly sauntering about without apparent object.

But a close scrutiny would have detected, notwithstanding their nonchalant manner, that they were very busy with their eyes, casting quick, furtive glances among the ladies, which rested, as was natural, on those who were the most attractive.

There was nothing offensive in all this, and yet there was a something in their look which created a feeling of uneasiness for the time.

Henry Clanberris had always been an ardent admirer of horses, and Lady Margaret, too, was a skilful rider, and cherished her favourite pet in the stalls.

On the third day of the race there was to be a trial of some noted horses, and Henry Clanberris, Lady Margaret, and Helen Penraven were on the ground in an open carriage.

Rupert was on horseback by them, and had been holding a brief conversation with them, when he noticed the two strangers standing a little apart, gazing fixedly on Helen.

As he turned towards them, a meaning look was exchanged between them, and drooping their heads, they slowly shuffled their way through the throng.

There was nothing in the look that Rupert would have noticed, had it not been that his curiosity and suspicion had been aroused by his previous observation of the strangers.

As it was, it affected most unpleasantly the mind of my hero.

The beauty of Helen was so prominent that one would not be satisfied with a casual glance at her brilliant features and graceful form, therefore it was not strange that she should attract more than ordinary notice.

But there was a brutal admiration expressed in the stare of the two men that grated on Rupert's feelings.

Helen did not observe it, or after her many adventures she would have feared some terrible consequences.

During the race the same two men hovered in the vicinity of the carriage, and when the sports were over, they contrived to ascertain which direction the carriage took.

All this Rupert observed narrowly.

And why?

What occasion was there for uneasiness?

What reasons had he for suspecting these strangers of evil intentions, and what harm could now befall Helen when under the protection of such friends?

"What folly this is," thought Rupert, "to permit my mind to be distracted from my great purpose by such suspicions!"

Yet though he said this to himself, he fouud himself instinctively forming plans to thwart them.

At last the races were over, the booths were cleared away, and quiet reigned once more.

Rupert had seen nothing of his gipsy foe.

But he still remained in the neighbourhood, making an excuse to stay at the inn to sleep instead of at Clanberris House.

Late the next night, as he sat down in the public room to take a glass of spirits before retiring, he was surprised to see the two strangers enter.

Once more suspicion leapt into his breast.

Why had they remained?

"Very fine country about here," said the one having the cast in his eye, as he sipped his grog.

Rupert nodded assent.

"Some beautiful spots I have observed in my rambles round," pursued the other. "Are you a resident here?"

"No," returned Rupert.

"Still perhaps you can tell me who owns that lovely place a little out of the village to the south."

"His name is Clanberris," said Rupert.

"Indeed! a good name. He is very wealthy, I believe," replied the other.

"He is reputed to be," said Rupert.

"Won't you join us in a glass of something?" added the other.

Rupert declined, and presently they parted company for the night.

"THE TWO MEN SLUNK HASTILY AWAY

CHAPTER IX.

THE ABDUCTION.

THOUGH nothing of any consequence had as yet transpired, it was strange how the feeling haunted Rupert Dreadnought that Helen in some way was in danger.

Try as he would, he could not shake it off, and when morning came he found himself in such a state of excitement, that he was compelled to enter an apothecary's shop to obtain something to allay his nervous irritation.

As he entered he observed that the atmosphere was strongly impregnated with ether, and he remarked upon it.

"Yes," returned the apothecary, "I have just put up a quantity for some customers, and accidentally spilled a part. I sold it to two strange-looking persons who are at the 'Arundel Arms,' I believe."

Rupert started.

"How long since?" he asked, hastily.

"About two hours ago They wanted it, they said, to bathe the limbs of their horses."

Rupert waited to hear no more, but hastily quitted the shop.

A terrible thought had flashed into his mind.

Hastening to the tavern, he inquired for the strangers.

They had been gone about an hour and a half, and had departed in a dark-covered waggon they had brought there that morning.

They had gone directly out of the village, taking the western road.

This was all the information he could glean, and for a moment he was irresolute how to act, that terrible thought brooding—brooding continually—giving him no peace.

Clanberris House was about three-quarters of a mile from Brentwood—that is from the heart of the village—and lay towards the south-east.

A strong impulse led Rupert on to hasten thither and see if Helen was at home.

Ordering his horse, therefore, he put spurs to it, and hurried away, never thinking of any excuse he could offer for making his appearance so suddenly and in such evident alarm if Helen herself were there.

His eager haste soon brought him to his destination, and arriving there he at once rushed in.

Helen was out.

That his first question elicited.

"Good Heaven!" cried Henry Clanberris, as he saw his pale and agitated features, "surely nothing has happened to her?"

There was no room or reason for holding back the truth.

Rupert told him briefly his suspicion, and then, without waiting to ask him to accompany him on the journey, put his horse to his utmost speed down the gravelly road, leaving Henry Clanberris in a state of great alarm.

He felt that the moments were far too precious to be wasted in explanations.

Rupert's brain was in a whirl as he dashed through the village, and out on the western road.

Up and down the inequalities of the road he urged his swift-footed horse, keeping a sharp look-out for Helen.

He had gone a mile or more without a sign of her, when at the bottom of a slight descent, in a hollow, he descried something white fluttering by the road-side.

He reined in his horse, jumped down, and picked it up.

It was a lace handkerchief, and in the corner were the initials "H. P."

He cast a hurried glance around the spot.

There were footprints leading to the side of the road, and others, near the middle, huddled in that confused manner which plainly indicated that a struggle had taken place there.

It needed not these, the handkerchief was enough to confirm his worst suspicions.

Presently he reached a gentle eminence where he could see a turnpike.

Towards this he galloped.

Here there might at last be a clue.

"Have you seen a lady pass by this way?" he asked, as he drew up his steaming horse, and accosted the keeper of the gate.

"Yes; a lady passed through here, and returned again about an hour ago. You ought to have passed her on the road, if you come from Brentwood."

"Has any vehicle passed since?"

"Yes; a dark-covered waggon not long after coming from the village, and driven as if the old boy was after them."

Rupert hardly heard the man out, but putting spurs to his horse, started away at full gallop, leaving the keeper of the gate gazing after him in bewilderment.

His horse flew over the ground with the speed of a bird.

He was a mettlesome animal, and he was now put to his utmost effort.

Not an idea of the existence of danger entered Rupert's mind.

His sole object was to overtake the waggon, when he felt quite equal to cope with both the villains single-handed.

He passed over three or four miles without slackening his speed.

Not a single person did he meet on the way.

Here a dilemma threatened to upset everything.

He noticed that, not a great distance ahead of him, the road forked, one branch running off to the north-east, the other to the west.

Which should he take?

It was as puzzling as it was all-important.

He thought that, perhaps, the wheel-tracks might guide him, for all along the road he had observed them.

But even this guide was quickly lost, for suddenly they disappeared.

While cogitating upon this matter, he came upon a small farm-house standing a little back from the highway, just beyond which was a barn, with its doors wide open.

A casual glance revealed a dark-covered waggon inside.

Turning at once into the little lane that ran up to the house, Rupert accosted a man who stood near.

"Is that your waggon?" he asked, as he drew rein.

"Yes, master."

"Has it been out to-day?"

Yes; he had lent it that morning to two men to go to Brentwood.

"When did they return it?"

"Well," said the man, "what I'm going to say may seem strange, but they didn't return it at all. The horse came back of his own accord, and pretty well done-up he was, too—all smothered in foam. It was a cruel shame to serve the dumb creature so."

The horse, it seemed, had returned about three-quarters of an hour before Rupert's arrival.

At some distance from the farm, and over some rising ground, was an old, disused road leading into the highway to London, and close by the junction was a large inn, where post-horses could be obtained.

Rupert could see the place at a glance.

They would carry the insensible girl to the place say she was ill, and hire post-horses to take her to her "friends" in London.

It did not take long for Rupert to reach the tavern alluded to.

It had happened just as he had anticipated; she had been carried there as an invalid, and they had engaged a post-chaise to carry her to London in safety.

Borrowing a fresh horse, and leaving his own, Rupert once more dashed away.

Burning as he was with desire to save his mistress, and to avenge the outrage which had been put upon her, he yet saw the necessity of caution.

He must be cool and calculating.

One rash move might defeat all his purpose.

He this time was in reality unaware who his enemies were.

The idea of Helen, the pure, angel-hearted girl, being in the power of these two ruffians, in a large city, surrounded by their creatures, helpless and hopeless, would intrude upon his mind.

The question—"Was it for money, or for a fouler purpose that she had been carried off?" would also come up in spite of all his efforts.

Such thoughts as these made him shudder, and he strove to throw them off—to close his mind against them, for they made him almost frantic.

After a time he mastered his feelings, and recovered in a measure his equanimity.

As he galloped on, the fresh air cleared his bra-

and all his thoughts were bent on the means to be employed to rescue Helen.

In those days the telegraph, that nimble thief-catcher, was not known, or it would have been a far easier affair to catch the scoundrels.

Click, click, click ! and all the detectives of London would have been on the alert.

It would be needless waste of time to speak of the torture he endured on his passage towards the city.

All the love that was in his heart was quickened into immediate action for the imperilled girl; every fine feeling was on the throb.

She had been dear enough before; she was still dearer now.

CHAPTER X.

A DETECTIVE OF THE OLDEN TIME.

IT was late in the evening when Rupert arrived in London.

Rupert had obtained some little information as to a posting house, which might possibly be the one where the postboy would stop, and here he found that a carriage *had* stopped there.

It contained two men, and a woman, who appeared to be a great invalid, as she had to be lifted from *one* carriage to the other.

Rupert was thus absolutely defeated.

The people of the inn had entertained no suspicions, and, of course, therefore, had not followed the party.

He himself had merely the vaguest suspicion as to the person who had given directions for the outrage, and it was utterly useless, therefore, to act upon his own ideas, or without the assistance of the law.

With this, therefore, he resolved at once to proceed to the house of Robert Lavarette, a "*runner*," or detective, as we call them now, of the most acknowledged ability.

It was not long before he stood in the office of that worthy, who eyed him with a keen and scrutinising glance.

"Take a seat, Master——" he said, hesitating at the name.

"Lord Rupert Dreadnought," replied our hero, "though for reasons of my own I desire rather to be called plain Master Dreadnought."

The name seemed to take an electrical effect upon the wiry, parchmenty individual who had so great a reputation as a thief-taker.

Without much preface, Rupert detailed all the circumstances connected with the two men, from his first meeting them to his arrival in London.

He heard Rupert in silence.

When he concluded, he said—

"I hope you were not too particular in your inquiries at the inn in regard to the carriage, and the way it took?"

"No; I thought you could manage that best," answered Rupert.

"A very judicious conclusion, my lord," returned the other. "It might have occasioned remark. Now please repeat the description of the men."

He did so as accurately as he could.

"Did you hear any names mentioned?"

"Yes; in the room where they were drinking their grog I heard one call the other 'Cozens.'"

"Ah!" said the detective, eagerly. "Cozens was the one with the broken nose and scarred face."

"You know him, then?"

"Yes, I fancy I do," replied the detective, "as one of the most desperate characters in London. His companion is as bad, if not worse. We shall have to go about this matter cautiously."

"They must be employed by my private enemies, or I cannot see their object," said Rupert.

"Oh, money; that's their object. The lady is wealthy and *you* are wealthy, and they may hope for a great reward. But they may yet have another object.

"You say the lady is young and beautiful. Beauty commands a high price in London, especially when combined with youth and freshness. You shrink at my remark, my lord, but you must know it is the truth, and we may as well face truth first as last."

He rang the bell as he concluded, and the summons was answered by a young man.

"Philip," he said, "send in Nos. 8 and 9."

The young man left, and presently two men entered whose appearance somewhat astonished our hero.

You could have sworn at a glance that they had lived all their lives in the precincts of Alsatia—rough, brutal-looking fellows in tawdry finery.

Very few words passed.

"Have you seen Red Brampton and Bully Cozens lately?" he asked.

"No; they have been missing four days," said No. 9.

"Well, they returned to London this evening in a post-chaise," said the detective. "I want you to get upon their track. It is an important case, understand—a very important case. They have abducted a young lady in the country under the influence of ether, seemingly an invalid. These are the main points. Be off immediately, and report whatever you discover as soon as possible."

"Aye, aye, master," was the brief rejoinder, and the men started on their mission.

When they had gone, the detective rubbed his hands genially, and said—

"My lord, what kind of job does this promise to be?"

Rupert was pleased with the man's candour.

"Rest assured that you will be well rewarded," he said. "The lady is more to me than life itself."

"Well, that is enough. I will take your word, my lord. Where are you stopping?"

"Oh, now I am in London, I shall remain at my own house," said Rupert Dreadnought; "but cannot something be done to-night?"

"Believe me, my lord," replied the detective, in a kindly tone, "I fully appreciate your feelings; rest assured there shall be no delay on my part. I have already put two of my best men on the scent, and I shall set others to work immediately. I promise you that all that can be done shall be done. It is a very complicated machine that I have to take charge of, but I will not fail. Good-night, and keep up your spirits."

Upon this hint Rupert left.

There was nothing now, in fact, but to wait the issue of events.

He was satisfied, by the prompt action of the

detective, that the matter was in good hands, and he returned home to pass the night as best he could.

It may well be imagined that it was a restless one.

He did not court sleep by seeking his bed even.

Racked as his mind was with thoughts of Helen, Rupert knew it to be useless.

In vain he endeavoured to banish his dread.

Her terrible position haunted him continually; alone, exposed to insult—to a fate compared to which death was a blessed boon.

In such torture he passed the night, counting wearily the hours as they were pealed away heavily from a neighbouring clock tower.

In all his life he had never passed such a night.

He thought it would never come to an end.

But the morning came at last.

About the middle of the forenoon Lavarette made his appearance.

Rupert almost feared to ask him a question.

He could read nothing in his face, encouraging or discouraging, as he entered the room.

"Well, I am here at last," he said, "somewhat later than I intended, but the fact is I did not get to bed defore daylight. But I see you are impatient for news. Everything is working favourably. I have picked up a thread or two which may help us to unravel the scheme. No. 9 has got Red Brampton in hand. The latter is a sly dog, and close as an oyster when sober; but he has a weakness for spirits, which is pretty sure to loosen his tongue. Enough has already been gleaned to assure us that no personal violence has yet been offered the lady."

"Thank Heaven," murmured Rupert, "you have lifted a weight from my heart."

"As I remarked at our first interview," proceeded the detective, "money is undoubtedly their object."

"Then, in Heaven's name," exclaimed Rupert "get at their terms at once. Let them name the amount, and it is ready for them."

"Not so fast, my lord," said the cool detective; "if money is to be freely dispensed, I am for its falling into honest hands. Besides, I desire to dispense justice as well as golden coins. Now, I will let you into a little secret. In our business, you know, we have to work with all sorts of tools. No. 9 and Red Brampton are old friends, and have robbed together, and may do so now for all I can tell to the contrary. Yet I have the utmost faith in the man. But, to make sure of him, a little money is necessary."

"Name the amount," cried Rupert, eagerly.

"Well, say a hundred pounds."

"You can have the money at once," said Rupert.

"Very good. I will not mind telling you why I want it. No. 9 has made a bet with Red Brampton that he is only romancing about kidnapping the girl, and will not be convinced of the fact until he has ocular demonstration. When he has seen her he will forfeit the stakes, and not before. So it is arranged for him to see her this afternoon. Once made acquainted with her place of concealment, I will take good care that she is not spirited away."

"Cannot your man contrive to convey a note to the lady?"

"Perhaps so. What is it you wish to write?"

Rupert at once took pen and ink, and wrote—

"DEAREST HELEN,—Keep up a good heart. I am at work to rescue you. "R."

The detective took Rupert's slip of paper, and, having received the money, and made an appointment for the afternoon, he departed.

Rupert now felt like a new man.

A great stone had been rolled away from his heart.

That calamity which he had shuddered to contemplate had not befallen Helen.

It was true she was yet in peril, that as yet her deliverance was not sure, but as they were really on the right track there was now every cause to hope. Late in the afternoon Rupert proceeded to the house of the detective, according to agreement.

He had not long been there, when No. 9 entered.

"Well," said his employer, addressing him, "how are matters progressing at Exborough Street?"

The man gave a start of surprise.

"You have been dogging me?" he said, in a tone and with a look of reproach.

"No; upon my honour, I have not," returned Robert Lavarette. "I received my information from quite another quarter this morning. But then, you know, she might have been removed. It seems she has not been, and I must rely upon you for a description of the interior and the room she occupies. Did you give her the note?"

"Yes; and it seemed to have a wonderful effect upon her. I am glad," he continued, "that you learned about the house from other parties, for I hated the idea of peaching upon Red Brampton. Has the gentleman agreed to your arrangement?"

"My man and Red Brampton, a great many years ago, my lord," said the detective, with a look which Rupert understood, "were great friends, and for old acquaintance sake he does not like to be the means of bringing him to harm. The arrangements he speaks of is, that we shall not arrest Brampton, or if we do, we will let him slip through our fingers. Bully Cozens, in fact, has been the prime mover in the business, and Brampton a mere tool. Now Cozens, I have got in a tight place, where conviction is sure, and I am bound he shall not escape me. As to Brampton, he is of no account and always accessible. Do you consent to the arrangement?"

"One word first, excuse me," said the man, whose confused appearance attracted Rupert's attention; "that story of my betting with Brampton was all a sham."

"So I supposed," said the chief; "the pretended stake was, in fact, a bribe."

"That's it," said the man, brightening up. "I said to Brampton—Bully Cozens is only using you as a cat's-paw; if a reward is offered for the girl, he will take the lion's share and put you off with scarcely anything. So I took the liberty of offering him the hundred pounds, and he's done it. I don't care a rush what becomes of the other fellow, but you'll give Red Brampton the go-by?"

"HELEN CLUNG TO HER LOVER FOR PROTECTION."

"If his lordship is willing."

"Oh, I am willing!" exclaimed Rupert.

"Then you can consider that matter settled," said the detective, addressing his man.

No. 9 then left the room.

Shortly after, it having been agreed that Lavarette should be at Rupert's residence between eight and nine o'clock that evening, our hero returned home.

Between eight and nine o'clock in the evening, the detective came.

According to agreement, Rupert had a carriage waiting at the door, and they at once entered, and drove to Exborough Street.

There, a short distance from the house, they found No. 9 waiting.

"All right," he said, in a low tone. "You had better hurry. Remember, it's the third door on the right, at the head of the second flight. I and Brampton will remain at the outer door; you two can manage him."

Rupert and the detective were cautiously admitted into the hall.

He could hardly curb his impatience.

Hurrying on, they reached the head of the second flight, when he heard the noise of a struggle going on in the third room, followed by a piercing shriek of—

"Help! help!"

Darting forward, he reached the door, and dashed in.

Pale and terror stricken, Helen was on her knees, senseless, in the ruffian clutch of Bully Cozens.

Rupert sprang forward, and grasped him by the throat.

He was a powerful man, but he was a child in the hands of our hero, who held him until he grew black in the face, and then shook him off as he would a viper.

Helen stared and gazed in bewilderment, for a moment, and then springing forward, clung to her lover for protection.

But turning his head, he saw that the scoundrel had regained his feet, and was in the act of springing on him. He drew from his breast-pocket a pistol.

"One step forward, and you are a dead man," he said, in a calm, determined voice, as he covered him with his weapon.

"Two can play at that game," scowled the ruffian, and a formidable pistol was levelled directly at Dreadnought's head.

Before he could press the trigger, his arm was stricken down, and a slight scuffle followed, and the man was a helpless, handcuffed prisoner, in the hands of the detective.

Rupert had to support Helen downstairs, for she was nerveless in every limb.

They at once drove off towards Rupert's house, and Helen was for the time again in safety.

Rupert made the best of his way to the house of the detective.

Here they had taken Bully Cozens, who, bound and gagged, remained seated in the detective's room, until Rupert made his appearance.

He was then permitted to speak.

"Curse you!" he said. "Who are you, and where am I? If I am not before my judges, why am I a prisoner?"

"You will be a prisoner no longer, if you confess the truth," said Rupert. "Now, in the first place, where is Dr. Henzollern to be found?"

The man hesitated.

"Speak," said Rupert; "your life depends upon your answer."

The man saw he was in the hands of resolute men.

But even now he did not know how far he would have to proceed in his tale.

"Do you know the retreat of the society to which Dr. Henzollern and Oscar Penraven belong?" he asked.

"We do," responded Rupert.

"He is there," said the man; "I can tell you no more."

"You can," replied Rupert, "and that, too, something far more *àpropos*; that is the sign and countersign, and the password."

The ruffian at these words turned deadly pale.

"I know the password," he said; "but that I dare not tell."

"You must and shall," replied Rupert.

"If you refuse to speak, your life will be forfeited. Speak, or die."

The cold rim of a pistol applied to the head of the man, was a convincing proof that he was with those who did not intend half measures.

"Well," he said; "since you insist upon my telling you, I must.

"You must knock three times at the door, faintly.

"Then, when the man who opens the door appears, you must say before he speaks—

"Companions of the fourth order.'

"'By what signal?'

"'The silver cross.'

"You must go masked, and dressed in black velvet.

"You are not required to unmask, unles they suspect traitors to be present, and then all would have to show their faces."

"Why should they suspect, if you have told the truth?" said the detective.

"I know not; they have spies everywhere," returned the man.

"There are only a certain number of persons admitted to the meeting, which takes place every Thursday evening—one hundred. If one hundred and two are counted at the door, they will know two strangers are present."

"We will risk that," said Rupert, "and take strong measures for our safety. This is Wednesday; to-morrow, then is the day."

CHAPTER XI.

THE preparations which Rupert made for the following evening were somewhat elaborate.

He was resolved to penetrate the dark secrets of the order, and in the destruction of the chief to involve the entire society.

To make themselves in any way a match for the hundred men of whom the man had spoken, he would certainly have had to call in the aid of the Government and surround the place with an army of watchmen or soldiers, but Gascoigne had advised him that perhaps among those very watchmen and soldiers there might be present spies, if not positive members of the society.

So it behoved them to be cautious.

Rupert therefore decided that his own friends and their connections should be the only ones to know of the scheme.

It was arranged consequently that Tom the Waterman, Allan of the Glen, Stanley Sherrington,

Henry Clanberris, and the retainers of the two latter should be posted in a spot near at hand, ready to create a diversion at a given signal, and that Rupert and the detective shauld enter the den of infamy over which Dr. Henzollern presided.

When the little army of friends mustered in the grounds, Stanley Sherrington was found to have brought four men, Henry Clanberris five, the detective three, so that altogether they mustered eighteen persons.

At nine o'clock they saw the members of the dread society coming up one by one to the place of meeting, and entering after the usual challenge.

The time had now arrived for action.

The men were accordingly placed beneath a high and wide window which was evidently that of the place of meeting.

Arrived there, they approached boldly and tapped lightly at the door.

It was opened, and a tall, masked man stood before them.

"Companion of the fourth order," said Rupert, in a disguised voice.

The detective uttered the same words.

"By what sign?"

"By the sign of the silver cross," said Rupert.

"Good," said the man, "enter."

On entering the council chamber, Rupert and the detective seated themselves at the table, and helped themselves to some of the wine which stood there.

Presently the door opened, and a tall man entered.

Cheers greeted him, and with a bow, he passed to the head of the table.

"Brethren," he said, "I told you on a former occasion I was about to quit you for a time.

"I am going to Scotland, and thence proceed to Germany.

"I shall be gone two months, and during that time you must have a chief.

"And now, since it is my province, I beg to suggest for this post Oscar Penraven."

There were loud cheers at the mention of his name.

"I see," said Dr. Henzollern, "you approve of my choice, and now I will add that our society is progressing well.

"Sister Rosalie St. Aubyn has brought to the society in two months, forty thousand pounds, *and every victim is dead*, but, I regret to say, she is dead also; through an accidental administration of poison.

"Sir Denis Prothero died yesterday, and his nurse too, which brings us a hundred thousand pounds.

"Lady Letitia Barfoot, whose death will bring twenty thousand more, will die to-night.

"Let me hope that when I return matters will have progressed equally well.

"But now," he added, as he raised his hand to enforce silence, "now I must turn to a less pleasant duty.

"We have traitors among us.

"Lesbia Howard, Alford, and Lionel Armer have all of them been discovered to be conspiring with our enemies, and have been denounced.

"You know well, therefore, how to act.

"Whenever and wherever you meet them, the knife or poison must do its work.

"Lesbia Howard I myself undertook to destroy, but she escaped me.

"To you therefore I commend this trio; let them not escape."

"We swear," cried the members in a horrible chorus.

"We must quit this place with the others," said Rupert in a low whisper.

"Oscar Penraven and Ishmael Hasser must perish first before we proceed with this great enterprise."

So when the assemblage broke up, our friends passed out with the rest, and without any suspicion, departed towards their own homes.

"To-morrow night we will meet again," said our hero.

CHAPTER XII.

THE PURSUIT—THE FIGHT—THE DEATH—THE DISPERSION OF THE POISONERS.

KNOWING now the route which Dr. Henzollern was going to take, Rupert and his friends were quite satisfied as to the spot where they would be most likely to meet him.

This was at a bridge on the North road, called Talbot bridge, from the name of the inn near at hand.

In those days what was called the North road was the one invariably used by travellers to Scotland, and all that was necessary, consequently, was to push on to this first inn, and there await the coming of the enemy,

So early in the evening of the day on which Dr. Henzollern was to make a start the four friends stationed themselves under the shadow of some trees on the side of the bridge furthest from the Talbot Inn.

There was a bend in the road here, and a delve as it were, so that even on horseback as they were they could conceal themselves from those who were passing on the road.

It must not be supposed that Rupert Dreadnought had brought three friends with him to assist him against one man.

The truth was that he knew not how many of the wretched gang might accompany him, and on the other hand, though scorning any aid in such a quarrel, he was determined that Dr. Henzollern should not escape.

They had not long to wait.

Presently they heard the sound of the approaching horse's feet, and then on the rise of the bridge they saw the form of the doctor looming up against the sky, on the back of a tall horse.

"Now," said Rupert Dreadnought, "I will await him; do you stay here. Hurrah! see there—Oscar Penraven is with him. Stanley Sherrington, aid me."

Stanley at once advanced, and the two stood in the middle of the road.

"Ishmael Hasser," exclaimed Rupert, "hold; I wish to have a word with you."

"Who are you?" cried the chief of the poisoners, in astonishment.

"I am Rupert, now Earl of Dreadnought," said our hero, "and your destruction is a legacy left me by my father."

Ishmael was quiet for a moment.

A dread was at his heart.

A thrill, as of something warning him of a dread future, passed through his body.

"Speak," said Rupert, as he drew his sword, "or I shall think you add cowardice to your other bad qualities."

"I am no coward," returned Henzollern (or Ishmael, as we may call him now), "and though you come upon me like a highwayman on the road, I will fight you."

"Good," cried Rupert exultingly, "and you, Oscar Penraven, I leave to my friend."

There was little of science at first in the combat that ensued.

The four horsemen dashed at one another, sword in hand, and for a few moments nothing was heard but a wild clash of swords.

They were so confused, in a medley of horses and men and glancing weapons, that it was impossible to tell one from the other, and Henry Clanberris and Allan of the Glen, as they watched, were utterly unable to tell friend from foe.

But unscientific as the fight was, there were desperate thrusts exchanged, and it was not long before Oscar Penraven had fallen beneath the terrific blows of Stanley Sherrington.

Ishmael Hasser and Rupert Dreadnought were now left to fight out their quarrel alone.

The fight was not of long duration.

Both were desperate in their determination, and at length, taking advantage of an intemperate thrust from Rupert, Ishmael wounded him in the left arm.

This ended the battle as it were, for as the poisoner withdrew his sword, Rupert thrust his weapon clean through his heart.

In an instant he sheathed his weapon.

"Let us hope this is the last time it will be used," he murmured.

He little knew what adventures he was yet to go through.

On the third night, Rupert and his friends once more made their way to the abode of the poisoners.

They already knew of the death of their two chiefs, and for the moment they had elected one of their number to take Oscar Penraven's place.

"Now," said the new chief, when all were assembled, "now we must resort to extreme measures; our rule is that no one be asked to unmask, but we have had traitors among us, and may have them now. Cancel this rule then, and let every man here who is not a traitor show at once his features."

"One moment," cried a voice, and a man advanced towards the table, "at our last meeting, Lesbia Howard, Alford, and Lionel Armer, the trio of traitors, were commended to us for death; I have killed them all."

A murmur of approbation ran through the assembly.

"Alford," continued the man was the most difficult to catch. He posted off to the coast, but I followed him, and caught him as he reached the edge of the cliff, to descend upon the beach.

"Here we struggled, and as he grasped me by the throat, and the bough of a tree to which I clung was just giving way, he fell—crash—down the rocks, and was dashed to atoms."

It will be remembered that on the former occasion a pistol shot had been arranged as the signal for the attack.

It was the same now.

When, therefore, the new chief cried once more, "let all unmask," Rupert Dreadnought fired at the lamp, which shivered in a hundred fragments and left the room in utter darkness.

In an instant, as if by magic, Rupert's friends and the soldiers that had accompanied them rushed in, and all was confusion.

The numbers of the attackers were not so great as those attacked.

But they were conscious of a good cause, and had the best of it inasmuch as they had surrounded their enemies.

They fired murderous volleys indiscriminately among the poisoners, until at last the latter surrendered.

Within an hour they were all in gaol, awaiting their justly merited fate, and the band of poisoners, the curse of London, were dispersed for ever.

"Now," thought our hero, "my task is coming to a conclusion; I must hesitate no longer."

CHAPTER XIII.

THE FOURTH AND FIFTH SECRETS.

WITH an eager heart Rupert Dreadnought made his way once more to the vaults, where the Iron Chest lay.

Sincerely in his heart did he hope that the last secrets had no reference to any deed of violence such as he had hitherto been made a party to.

So once more he knelt down by the side of the receptacle of his father's secrets.

The fourth document was soon lying before him.

It was very short and ran as follows—

"There is but one more duty you have to perform; and the fifth secret will constitute your reward.

"There is in the neighbourhood of Ellerston, in Shropshire, a family of the name of Hawley. The father Richard Hawley, is another deadly enemy, one who kidnapped a dear friend of mine, and placed him in a lunatic asylum.

"He did this for the sake of his wealth, and had I been able to have lived after receiving proofs of his treachery and villany, I would have met him face to face myself.

"But it was not to be.

"Death has claimed me for its own, before it was possible to perform this act of justice. Therefore I leave it to you.

"Go down to the vicinity of Ellerston, you will find there an inn known as the 'Ellerston Arms.'

"There you will discover a little man known as Joey the ostler.

"He knows all about the Hawley family, and will give you such information as will aid you in taking your revenge upon this man and his family, all of whom are as bad as himself

"Take with you the last document in the chest, and when you have reached the 'Ellerston Arms' and seen Joey, you can read it and act upon it simultaneously with the other. And now, my son, accept my blessing before you start upon this, the most dangerous of all your missions.

"May Heaven protect you in it, and may you live to be happy with your Helen!

"R. Earl of Dreadnought."

Rupert, in spite of the promised danger, heaved a sigh of relief.

He had at least a chance of accomplishing the whole of his father's behests, and clasping to his heart as his bride the loved one he so longed to claim.

He lost no time in making his way to Ellerston.

Of course it is needless to say that he did not go alone.

He was, in fact, accompanied by Stanley Sherrington, Henry Clanberris, and Allan of the Glen.

On reaching the "Arms" he soon found Joey, freed him, and discovered more about the Hawleys than he hoped to discover in a month.

When Richard Hawley had expended in waste the money he had pilfered from Earl Dreadnought's friend, he and his family became an absolute terror to the very neighbourhood.

Murders and crimes of every kind were laid to their charge, and in some cases, although it was absolutely proved that they had been guilty of murders, the constables had, through fear, pretended that they were unable to find them.

He learned, too, that among them they were keeping against his will, a young fellow of the name of Ralph Egerton, who would do anything against them if it lay in his power to perform it.

Several times Rupert was enabled to communicate with this young man.

But suddenly all such communication ceased.

One night after Rupert had retired to his room, he heard a strange scratching noise just outside his casement.

He listened to it.

The night was very dark, but he could see that a man was on the ledge outside.

That was all.

What kind of person it was, he could not distinguish.

Presently a voice spoke, a whispering voice—

"Let me in."

"Who are you?"

"I am Joey, the ostler."

"Very well, wait a moment," said Rupert Dreadnought.

Then returning to the table he lit the lamp and carried it to the window.

Sure enough it was Joey.

In another moment the casement was thrown open, and little Joey rolled in.

He was shivering with cold.

"What on earth possessed you to avoid the door and come in by the window?" said Rupert.

"Well, my lord," said Joey, "you see what I've got to tell is particular private, and I wasn't even to let the landlord see me a-speaking to you."

"Another mystery," thought our hero.

"Well, my man," he said, aloud, "what is it? Speak freely."

"You see, my lord," said Joey, "I was a-closing the yard gates about half an hour ago, when I felt someone's hand a-gripping hold of my neck and was dragged out into the road.

"I never had the ghost of a chance of hollerin out, for I felt a cold pistol pressed up agin my forehead, and the man says—

"'If yer cry out, I'll blow out yer brains.'

"So in course I keeps still.

"'What's all this for?' I says, in a low voice.

"'Tell me,' says he, in a stern kind of voice, 'are those fellows from London gone away yet?'

"I hadn't no idee he was alluding to your lordship.

"'We ain't got no fellows from London here,' says I.

"He swore an awful oath, then said—

"'I've been a-watching them.'

"'Oh, if you means the gentlemen as are lodging here, they're all fast asleep.'

"'And the landlord?'

"'He's in bed.'

"'Very good,' he says; 'I've got some horses up here as wants a feed and a drink, so just bring us some hay and water.'

"It wasn't no use saying no.

"He came with me.

"Well, I took the hay and the water out, and while he was busy putting the feed into the nosebags, one of the chaps on horseback slips a piece of paper into my hand.

"Of course, I knew at once it was a secret, so I says nothing and slips it into my waistcoat pocket.

"I was standing near the yard door again when the fellow who had spoken came up to me.

"'You're the chap as set the constables on to us,' he says.

"And then he began fumbling in his pocket.

"I saw a kind of nasty glitter in his eyes as he was a-speaking and I guessed I was in danger.

"So I flings my empty pail right clean into his face and slams to the yard door.

"'Be off, Jonas, or I'll have the whole inn about yer.'

"In a few minutes I hears them galloping off.

"Then I comes in and I looks at the paper.

"Here it is."

Rupert took it eagerly.

Outside was written—

"To be given to Lord Rupert Dreadnought in strict secresy."

Breaking it open, he read as follows—

"I am a prisoner in the hands of the Hawleys, and cannot say much. If you want any further information about the Hawleys, go to the cottage of Luke Waldron on the other side of the wood. He will tell you a great deal I can't write about to you now.

"Ralph Egerton."

"Well, this is most strange," said Rupert.

Then turning to Joey, he said—

"You are lucky you did not fall into their hands. They were the Hawleys."

Joey stared.

"You'd never have had the letter then, my lord, if I'd known that," he said; "I'd have run and took my chance. Why, they'd have right down murdered me, if I hadn't cut away as I did."

"Well, it seems likely. But here are five guineas for yourself," said Rupert. "Say nothing of this to anyone."

In a few moments, after many bowings and scrapings, Joey had passed out of the window once more and dropped into the yard.

Then Rupert closed the casement and retired at once to bed.

CHAPTER XIV.

THE FOUR ADVENTURERS VISIT LUKE WALDRON—THE CONFERENCE—THE ESCAPE OF RALPH EGERTON—A TERRIBLE VENGEANCE.

WHEN, on the next day, Rupert told his friends, they were for instant action.

"Fear not," said he; "I will let no grass grow under my feet."

"But who is this Luke Waldron?"

"I know not. But, at any rate, Joey can give us the information we require."

"Undoubtedly," said Sherrington, "and we may also discover such news in regard to the treasure that further pursuit of these Hawleys will be unnecessary."

Rupert shook his head.

"You forget," he said, "I have to meet this Richard Hawley and punish him."

"When then shall we start?"

"At once."

It was not long after this that the four adventurers mounted on their splendid steeds, and were dashing off on an expedition which was by no means without hazard.

I must here explain that the document which Rupert was to open at the "Ellerston Arms" described a treasure of great extent which was believed to have been amassed by the Haw leys, and which the old earl desired his son to take possession of in compensation for old injuries.

They had, of course, obtained from Joey the exact particulars of the position and appearance of old Luke Waldron's cottage, and after a by-no-means long ride they came in view of the little, lonely cabin.

They rode up hastily, and Rupert, with a loud voice, shouted—

"House!"

Luke came out grumbling, for he happened to be in the middle of his dinner.

"I've got a few questions to ask you, my man," said he, as the cottager came out. "I don't come to waste your time though, so here's a gold piece for you."

Old Luke grinned.

He was a thin, parchmenty, grey-headed old fellow, and his grin expressed about as much merriment as you would expect from a death's head.

"It be something important you want to know, I'm thinking," he said.

"It is," said Rupert. "I have come to put a few questions about the Hawleys."

Luke's countenance fell.

"The Hawleys be dangerous people to meddle with," he said. "I'd rather have nothing to do with them."

"You need fear nothing from them any more," said Rupert; "they've got the hue and cry after them, and if they save their own skins it will be as much as they can do, without interfering with other people."

As Rupert spoke, there was a slight movement in the bushes near.

But all were too busy to notice it.

"Oh, so they're being pursued, eh?" asked the old man.

With a look of anything but displeasure this was said.

"Aye, right and left," said Rupert; "but it is of no use beating about the bush like this. I want a service from you. I want to know where the Hawleys are now."

"Ye want me to turn informer, eh?"

"Yes, if you choose to call it so," said Rupert; "and now you are out of Richard Hawley's power, it cannot be a matter of anger to you."

"How out of his power?" cried Luke.

"Simply this, that he will never be able to show his face in this neighbourhood again. But come, I have no time to lose; is this a bargain or not?"

"What is the exact thing ye require?"

"Where will they be to-night? Here are two guineas for you."

He seized it greedily.

"Do you know Carter's mill?" he said.

"No."

"Then ask Joey the ostler; he'll tell ye."

"When will they be there?"

"At ten to-night. They'll be there to consult about the treasure they have buried in the ruins."

"Good, and now farewell," cried Rupert. "If we find your information correct, you shall have twenty guineas more."

Then, as he and his friends rode away, the old man hobbled into his cottage.

As he did so, two men rose from the undergrowth and hurried in after him.

Some little time after, Ralph Egerton, the youth whom the Hawleys—who were smugglers, thieves and murderers—had imprisoned, and who had succeeded in escaping from their place during their absence, neared the cottage of the old man.

All was still about it.

He knew not why, but he felt very uneasy.

It seemed to him that all was not right here.

He had hoped to meet the old man at his stable or in the yard, and so avoid going in by the part where there ought to be visitors he would not want to see.

He could see nothing of him.

"Hullo, there!" he cried.

"No answer."

"They've gone to bed, both Luke and his wife," thought Ralph. "I'll go round the front of the place, after all."

In front of the cottage was a porch, and Ralph saw standing under it before the door, perfectly motionless, in the gloom of the early evening, the form of a man.

He stood like a statue, his arms behind him, his head on one side, in an attitude of most profound meditation.

He had on a strange thing in place of a hat, and seemed very tall.

"Good evening, sir," said Ralph.

No answer, no motion.

Ralph's hair seemed to thrill to its roots.

What fearful mystery was here?

At the instant, Ralph saw near the motionless figure an old woman with a wound on the temple, and her grey hair clotted with blood, lying on the porch floor.

He looked up at the man again now, and saw that his hands were tied, and that he was hanging by the neck, by a rope attached to a rafter of the porch.

That was what made him look so tall.

Such was the vengeance of the Hawleys.

With a shudder, Ralph turned away, and hurried off in the direction of the "Ellerston Arms."

CHAPTER XV.

THE "EAGLE'S TOWER"—THE SMUGGLERS—THE TREASURE—THE END.

THERE stood on the rocks, up at Ellerston, high above the sea, an inn which seemed to have been built up out of numberless stray pieces of wood, any odds and ends picked up by the way.

Everything at the "Eagle's Tower" was good, and especially the spirits, but how the landlord, Tom Truman, obtained them was always very questionable.

The real customers were a rough lot—fishermen, smugglers, and men who picked up on the coast a strange living.

To these, the best of everything was given, while to strangers the most vile concoctions were presented for the very purpose of keeping them away.

The Hawleys were well known to Tom Truman, the landlord.

They had been rare smugglers in their time, and often aided in a run, but their business was of a very different class—aiding in transporting goods, and concealing them also when any danger was afloat.

For this purpose, the old ruins of an abbey had always afforded a splendid receptacle.

But now it was all over with them, on this part of the coast, so away they resolved to go to another part of England.

No one could help them better in this than the landlord of the "Eagle's Tower."

The swift-sailing cutter of which he was the owner was just the craft to carry them safely away from the dangerous shore.

So it was to the "Eagle's Tower" they made their way.

It was very late when they reached it, but the sound of songs and merry jest rolled slowly over the cliff-side.

Every man within flew to his sword, while the landlord opened the door.

He burst into a loud laugh as he recognised them.

"It is Richard Hawley and his cubs, by all that's holy," cried he; "enter, and welcome."

"Just in time to aid us in a run," said one of the guests.

"What, to-night?" asked Hawley.

"No, to-morrow night. We expect the 'Caroline' round the point at midnight," said Tom Truman; "and we're short of hands. I know you too well to think you'd shirk aiding us."

Old Hawley chuckled.

This was just what suited him.

If he gave help, he could obtain help in return.

Taking the landlord aside a moment, he told him what he required.

At the mention of the box of treasure, the smuggler's eyes glistened.

"All right," he said; "you aid me, and I'll aid you."

And so the bargain was struck.

The next night came.

Twelve o'clock, the time for the grand run, was fast approaching.

For hours men had been hurrying along the dark and pebbly beach towards Sandy Point.

Richard Hawley's sons had not made their appearance since they had gone out early in the evening.

For they were lying stark and dead on the rocks beneath the crags, where they had rushed to avoid some officers of the law.

"A rare night for work," said Hawley, as he looked up at the dark, starless sky.

"Aye, if the 'Caroline' is not behind time," said the landlord.

"Never fear," said Hawley, as with their companions, they reached Sandy Point. "See, here she is."

And so it was.

She loomed nearer and nearer out of the gloom and presently glided gracefully into the still basin of the little bay.

All was now bustle and eagerness, each was set to his work, and in utter silence the little craft was unloaded.

Just as this was concluded, and they were about to return to the "Eagle's Tower," where Hawley resolved to await the coming of his sons, there was a rush of men, who sprang from the darkness like shadows starting into life.

With a rush the coastguard and twelve soldiers, under the command of Ensign Mornington, with Rupert Dreadnought, Allan of the Glen, Stanley Sherrington, and Henry Clanberris, dashed upon them.

Surrender was called for, and mercy offered to all.

In vain.

The daring smugglers, who had no belief in the clemency of the law, refused to yield, and a terrific combat ensued.

But the smugglers were overpowered.

One by one they were beaten down, and a bullet from the pistol of Rupert brought Richard Hawley to the ground just as he had raised his cutlass to cut down Allan of the Glen.

Soon after this the smugglers were all either cut down or taken prisoners.

After this, there was nothing for Rupert Dreadnought to do but to find the treasure and transport it to London.

This he found in the vaults of the ruins, as he

had been told, and on opening it he discovered that most of the treasure was there.

We have little more to tell now.

Our hero, glad enough, so gave up the roving life to which his father's wishes had condemned him, hurried to London, and sought Helen.

Who shall describe the rapture of those hearts when Rupert clasped her to his breast and whispered—

"Now, Helen, at last you can be mine; now I can claim you for my bride?"

No false modesty prevented her from smiling her happiness up into his face.

"Dear Rupert," she said, ' I cannot express my joy to you. I had almost feared that from this last expedition you would never return. It has been such a long, dreary time, this waiting and waiting."

"It shall be ended now, dear," said Rupert, kissing her again; "to-morrow we will be wed."

And so it was.

On the next morning, the lovely Helen Penraven became the bride of her handsome lover, and for many, many years, surrounded by their old friends, they lived in happiness together.

The old sword rusted in its scabbard where it hung, for the necessity for its use seemed to have passed away with the early youth of its master, the galla t Rupert Dreadnought.

THE END.

www.ingramcontent.com/pod-product-compliance
Lightning Source LLC
Chambersburg PA
CBHW080830280626
47161CB00018B/3124
* 9 7 8 1 5 3 5 8 1 0 6 8 5 *